One?

Jennifer L Cahill

Clink
Street

London | New York

Published by Clink Street Publishing 2018

Copyright © Jennifer L Cahill 2018

First edition.

Jennifer L Cahill asserts the moral right under the Copyright, Designs and Patents Act 1988 to be identified as the author of this work.

ISBN:
978-1-912562-15-2 - paperback
978-1-912562-16-9 - ebook

We are living in extraordinary times, and roles and relationships are changing as fast as technology will allow. I wrote this for each and every one of you who have loved, lost, sought, fought for or are still looking for the one, in one of the most innovative periods in living history.

JLC
xo

Chapter 1

Circa '79

With a sigh, Miss Miller adjusted her horn-rimmed spectacles to survey her classroom of five-year-olds. The heat was really getting to her, mixed up with the sporadic hot flashes, it was becoming unbearable. A small bead of perspiration made its way slowly down the middle of her back. Her polyester, pointed collar shirt was growing clammy from the heat. Miss Miller stood up and gazed down at the children who were fidgeting and terribly restless. Her hands were clammy, and suddenly, without warning, she dropped her wooden blackboard duster onto the desk. The loud thud broke the silence, and a little cloud of chalk dust puffed up from where it had landed. The sunshine was streaming in through the windows, and the children watched... mesmerised, as the chalk dust particles danced on the sunbeam. They were convinced that the fairies were busy at work in their classroom that sunny June afternoon. This was quite enough to unsettle the class of five-year-olds especially so near to going home time. The children started giggling and wriggling around in their seats. Miss Miller gave them a stern look and settled herself behind her desk on the oak rostrum. She decided that it was Alyx's turn to share his homework with the class. 'Alyx,' she said, as she peered over her glasses.

Alyx didn't flinch; he was far, far away… gazing at the fairies on the sunbeam…

'Alyx! Alyx! Wake up! Come along now, we are waiting…' Miss Miller snapped. Alyx nearly jumped out of his little skin! He began to stammer.

'What? Em, ok,' Alyx stuttered as he struggled to his feet from behind his tiny little desk. '… when I grow up, I wish I were, no, I wish I would be a Beatle!' Alyx breathed a small sigh of relief, he was happy that he had remembered the words in *English*.

Miss Miller went puce, as the whole class started laughing. Alyx stood there defiantly. Alyx hated talking in front of the whole class; he was used to speaking *French* in school….not *English*! He would only be in this school for a few weeks while his mother was on location for a film in London, he didn't understand these English people at all! He was constantly in trouble!

Miss Miller was livid! All she needed was the most minor disruption to set the class of five-year-olds off, today of all days. It was easily 30C outside and there was no escaping the heat. Miss Miller struggled to regain composure.

'Don't be silly Alyx, you can't be a beetle, you are a little boy… why would you want to be an insect?!' Miss Miller snapped.

'No, Miss, not an insect… I want to be like one of the Beatles!' Alyx went bright red, and started staring down at his feet, while he shuffled from one tiny little foot to the other.

'The rock group?! Alyx really! Everyone else in the class has prepared their homework, sit down and come and speak to me at the end of class!' Miss Miller was still puce as she said this, she took a deep breath to regain composure. She had no time for these ungrounded "celebrity" fantasies…

Meanwhile the whole class had erupted into fits of giggles. Alyx slumped back into his tiny little chair, feeling very sorry for himself indeed. Life is tough when you are five and grownups keep trying to break your dreams.

Miss Miller looked down at her list again, completely exasperated. Who should she ask next, who would be a "safe bet"?

'Next? Who is next?' Miss Miller spoke sternly to silence the laughing five-year-olds. 'Yes, Penelope?'

'Miss? Miss? May I go next?' Penelope's little hand shot straight up the minute Miss Miller had said 'Next?' She was dying to tell the teacher her ambition.

'Well, yes dear, if you really want to, I don't see why not....' Miss Miller sighed as she sat back in her chair.

Penelope stood up in front of her desk, her little hands clasped tightly behind her back.

'When I grow up, I want to be a beautiful princess, and I want to live in a castle...' Penelope beamed at Miss Miller, waiting for the praise that she was so used to. The teacher usually said things like 'Excellent, Penelope' and 'Good girl' to her. Sadly Penelope did not expect the reaction that was heading her way.

Miss Miller started to go puce again; she simply could not cope with another minute of this carry on.

'Really Penelope?!' she exploded. 'I have heard quite enough of this nonsense today, sit down and come and speak to me at the end of the class...' Miss Miller gasped; her patience had run out, she was completely exasperated at this point!

'But Miss?' Penelope answered back, in shock.

'That's quite enough out of you, now...' Miss Miller warned her.

Tears welled up in Penelope's eyes, it was the first time her teacher had ever been *cross* with her, and she did not like it one little bit.

'...who is next? Tommy? Tommy, please go next.' Miss Miller took another deep breath to regain composure. Tommy stood up.

'Miss, when I grow up I would like to be a fireman...' Tommy began describing the kind of things a fireman does.

'Now that is more like it.' Miss Miller thought to herself, the children had finally stopped fidgeting and giggling, as they all listened to Tommy.

At going home time, Miss Miller sat behind her desk with the two five-year-olds standing side by side in front of it. Both

3

of the children were wearing their most angelic expressions, Penelope looked up from beneath her mop of fine blonde curls, and Alyx batted his extra-long dark eyelashes. Alyx looked bewildered, the poor little guy was used to going to school in France, and he was not used to the English ways at all. Penelope looked worried, she had never been in *trouble* before, and she didn't quite know what to do with herself.

'Now children I specifically asked you to prepare a future job that you would like to have when you are grownups, and Alyx... a Beatle, and Penelope... a princess, well they are not real jobs. Why didn't you ask your mummy and daddy for help?' Miss Miller's tone was much softer now, but she tried to look as stern as possible hiding her urge to smile. The two children looked so serious... Alyx was shifting from one tiny little foot to the other, and Penelope was afraid to even look at him. Her nose was wrinkled up, and the teacher knew that Penelope was looking for just the right words to say... Penelope decided to get in there first.

'But Miss, I *did* ask my mummy and she told me to ask daddy, and when I asked him... he told me to ask mummy, so I just did my homework myself.' Penelope wrinkled her nose again, she just couldn't understand what she had done wrong, but one thing she did know... Alyx was in *so* much trouble! She was afraid to even look at him in case it rubbed off on her!

'Alyx, did you ask your mummy and daddy for help?' The teacher turned to Alyx who was still shifting from one little foot to the other, looking very much like he needed to go to the toilet.

'Yes, and my Dad told me the story of The Beatles... so I want to be like that when I grow up!' Alyx could not understand why his teacher was so angry with him, and with Penelope too, she just wanted to live in a castle when she grows up... just like his granddad does.

'Really! Children! What am I going to do with the two of you!?' Miss Miller snapped, and then she paused for effect... 'Alright, I have heard enough now, seeing as you both did prepare your homework you are not in trouble anymore… even if the results were a little… unrealistic..' Miss Miller sighed.

'Thank you teacher!' the two of them chanted in unison.

Penelope was completely relieved; she couldn't believe that she was going to be in *trouble* ! Her mummy would be sooooo angry.

Alyx turned to Penelope and said, 'Pen-lopeee… my granddad lives in a castle, and sometimes I go there.' Alyx was still shifting from one little foot to another, he was struggling to pronounce Penelope… it was a very big word for such a small person… He thought Penelope was so beautiful with her golden hair and her huge blue eyes; she always wore pink dresses to school.

Penelope decided, now that they were not in trouble anymore, it was safe to speak to Alyx… 'Is your granddad the King?' Penelope enquired matter-of-factly.

'I dunno, maybe he is, I will ask him.' Alyx shrugged his little shoulders, he had never considered the fact that his granddad could be the King!

'Well… is your granny the Queen?' Penelope stood there with her hands on her hips, speaking to Alyx as if he was a complete idiot! Secretly she was really interested now!

Alyx considered this for a moment and said 'She's not the real *Queen,* the one that lives in London… but maybe she is a queen…' Alyx considered the possibility that his granny was a queen.

'Well that's what I want to be when I grow up… a beautiful princess and I want to live in a castle.' Penelope was holding onto her dream, she didn't care what any grownup said…

Chapter 2

72a Abbeville Road

Mrs Evans took her job very seriously, after all… first impressions really count, and in her day women dressed like women, there was none of this *denim jeans at work* carry on. She made sure that she wore a suit to viewings, tweed of course, she was not going to be intimidated by these young estate agents whizzing around in their Mini Coopers. Mrs Evans had been in this business longer than they had been alive! She fussed around in her little brown crocodile handbag, which had stood the test of time, until she found the right key…

She turned the key in the lock fifteen minutes before her next appointment. As always she did a quick run through the house, opening a window here and there and checking for anything off-putting.

At 1.55 pm Charlie and Penelope hovered outside The Abbeville pub.

'It couldn't possibly be here?' Penelope looked at the Google Map that she had printed off in work again. 'This is a pub, there must be some mistake.'

Charlie shrugged. 'Let me take a look.' She offered him the map. 'Well this is where you have marked on the map, so it must be right.' Charlie flashed her a winning grin, in his experience charm always worked to alleviate stress and he could sense her getting a bit uptight.

'Hmmm,' Penelope agreed with him stifling a laugh. 'We are a little early, so let's hang around and see if the estate agent shows up… if not… I finally give up on finding somewhere, and resign myself to living with my mother forever.' Penelope sighed. Charlie grimaced at her at the mere mention of this.

'There you are.' Mrs Evans appeared as if by magic, through a brown inconspicuous door right in the centre of the front of The Abbeville pub.

'Good lord, you startled me there, hello, I'm Penelope and this is Charlie,' they exchanged introductions.

'We actually thought we had got the wrong location, all we could see is the pub. This door is very inconspicuous.' Penelope wasn't sure how she felt about living above a busy pub, no matter how lovely it was.

'Ah yes, very inconspicuous.' Mrs Evans beamed at them, keen to change the subject, and veer away from the fact that it was above a pub.

'I'll just let you in so that you can have a look around. This is a communal front door for 72a and b, we are straight ahead.'

The three of them crowded into the tiny dusty hallway, and Mrs Evans motioned to the door to 72a. She went ahead of them and opened the door to reveal a steep staircase leading up to the property.

'The deposit is one and a half month's rent in advance, and of course the first month's rent needs to be paid in advance also… there are four bedrooms…' Mrs Evans started her monologue, she spoke rapidly, it was clear that she had done this before.

'What do you think?' Charlie leaned over to ask Penelope, hoping that she would finally like this one!

'It looks ok so far… a bit dusty though' Penelope gave a half smile; she was not impressed so far. Penelope liked her home to be clean and orderly, and not like some kind of student squat.

'You might notice that it's a bit dusty in here… hatchoooo!… the landlady has had builders in for the past four weeks renovating the kitchen. She intends to get the place professionally cleaned before the new tenants move in...' Mrs Evans droned on in the background as Charlie and Penelope looked around.

'That explains that then... it's nice and bright, wow! The kitchen is amazing, perfect for a bachelor pad,' Charlie was delighted with what he had seen so far. He was sold on the area; Clapham in South West London, was full of aspiring musicians, young professionals and cute twenty-something blondes... apart from that Charlie couldn't care less what the actual house was like!

'Bachelor pad? Bachelor pad! Do I look like a bachelor to you?' Penelope roared with laughter, she was having none of it! Now that she had seen the brand new kitchen, the place was starting to seem more acceptable.

'No... but you know what I meant.' Charlie shrugged and grinned at her.

'You needn't think that you are turning this place into a groupie den. Let's get that clear from the start.' Penelope shrieked playfully, just out of earshot of Mrs Evans.

'Ok! Relax! I was just saying that I liked it.' Charlie grinned at her, tucking a strand of hair that had come loose behind his ear. He plonked himself down on the stairs as Penelope inspected the kitchen.

'All of the appliances are brand new as you can see... The bathroom is quite large, and there is also a small en suite bathroom attached to the double room at the front of the house on the top floor...' Mrs Evans droned on and on...

'Do you think we can afford it?' Penelope whispered to Charlie behind Mrs Evans' back; she thought that the rent was a bit steep for just the two of them.

'I'm not sure... we'll definitely have to get two more in.' Charlie saw no major issue with living with strangers, it was all part of the adventure of life...

'I thought we agreed just one *unknown*.' Penelope really liked her home comforts... she worked such long hours that she didn't have time to get to know new people so that they could all live happily together.

'I know but it's turning out to be much more expensive than we thought with the council tax and all of the bills thrown in, and you didn't like the other three that we looked at today.' Charlie had already made up his mind, and he knew he was going to get his way… he always did after all.

'Yes, and I really do need to make a decision today, this house hunting is taking up way too much of my time.' Penelope was working really long hours in an investment bank in the City, and taking half days every other day was not a clever move so near to bonus time! On top of everything else, living back at home was no fun at all… her mother was driving her mad! Asking her about her "day" and if "she met anyone nice", and following her around the house… what a nightmare!!

'I'll just show you into the living room, as you can see it is quite airy. The previous tenants decorated it in these colours… but the landlady is flexible if you would like to paint it…' Mrs Evans was constantly blabbering on about the house, she barely paused to draw a breath.

'Oh my god! Did a coven of witches live here or something?' Penelope mumbled to Charlie as they walked into the living room to find that it was painted deep purple with pagan-looking black spiral shapes.

'What was that dear?' Mrs Evans couldn't hear a word they were saying, she was so busy talking herself.

'Oh, I was just saying to Charlie what a lovely view there is out of this window.' Penelope said the first thing that came to mind.

'Yes it is lovely isn't it. There is nothing nicer than watching the world go by in the Abbeville Village.' Mrs Evans paused for a moment, with a far-off look in her eyes, 'Now about this *purple*, and I'm not a hundred percent sure what these shapes are? Spirals…? Would you say…? As I said, the landlady is open to the idea of painting it a new colour, and this can be organised before new tenants move in of course… on the first floor we have one double and one single bedroom…' Mrs

Evans marched up the stairs and Charlie and Penelope dutifully followed her.

'But seriously... purple... I mean... I didn't think they even made that colour purple after the seventies!' And then it suddenly dawned on her... 'Oh no, Charlie, you don't think that it hasn't been painted since then do you!?' Penelope was horrified at the thought! The living room was so dingy, it was such a stark contrast to the newly decorated kitchen and bathroom.

'Shhh! She'll hear you... and this place is starting to grow on me,' Charlie hissed at Penelope, he had made up his mind and nothing was getting in the way of this.

'Mrs Evans, has there been a lot of interest in the house?' Penelope put on her most innocent expression, she didn't want to seem too keen.

'Oh, yes dear, I have had to traipse up and down these stairs at least ten times a day for the past two days, we are expecting it to be taken quite soon.' *'Now that's it,'* Mrs Evans thought to herself, *'I have them now, what's a little white lie in business, and anyway I should not be climbing all of these stairs with my angina.'* Mrs Evans waited for Penelope's reaction.

'I see.' Penelope started to get nervous, this house was growing on her and up until this point she thought that they had been the only ones to see it, but she knew how fast a rented house could go in London, sometimes... in a matter of minutes. That was the reason they went to view houses midweek, the weekend house hunting circus is a complete nightmare in London!

'Yeah, if you believe that, you'll believe anything!' Charlie whispered to Penelope, he didn't believe her at all.

'I don't know... it's kind of growing on me... let's see what the two bedrooms on the top floor are like...' Penelope whispered back.

'Oh I have to catch my breath! Those stairs get me every time... I have to be so careful with my angina.... now, here are the final two bedrooms, these are not identical to the two on the second floor, the double room here is bigger and the single room is slightly smaller than the one downstairs…' Mrs Evans droned on and on.

'The big room is lovely. There's going to be a fight over this one if we decide on this house,' Penelope stated, she loved the room, she could actually see herself fitting all… well nearly all… of her shoes into the built-in wardrobes.. The big original sash windows were lovely and because it was on the top floor there was an amazing view. It was also so high up that street noise wouldn't be a problem.

'Mrs Evans, is the landlady open to the idea of the bedrooms being painted also?' Penelope had her fingers crossed behind her back.

'I'm not too sure dear, I will have to check… now where did I leave my glasses. I know I left them here somewhere… I'll leave you two lovebirds up here while I have a look for them…' Mrs Evans straightened the jacket of her tweed suit, while she clipped the clasp of her handbag open to look for her glasses.

'Does she think we are married?! That's hysterical!' Penelope exploded with laughter as soon as Mrs Evans was out of earshot.

'What's so funny about it? Do you not think that I would make a good husband?' Charlie looked offended, trying his best to keep a straight face.

'Em… no!… potential rock stars make the worst boyfriends, let alone husbands!' Penelope shrieked with laughter.

'You shouldn't be so narrow-minded! Musicians are not all the same, I'm quite hurt by that actually,' Charlie sniffed 'We have feelings too you know… and for your information Penelope, we do make nice boyfriends…. isn't that why we have all of these girls fighting over us?' Charlie sighed… as if it was such a burden. 'There we are trying to concentrate on the music and we have all of these hysterical women throwing G-strings at us… it's a tough life.' Charlie sat down on the stairs for extra emphasis, with his palms facing Penelope, as he shrugged his shoulders. Charlie loved all of the attention, he loved every single second that he spent on stage, and he was constantly living for his next gig.

'I don't believe a word of it!' Penelope couldn't stop laughing, Charlie was staring intently at her, with his mock-serious tone trying to convince her that all of the attention was a burden… what a joke!

'And I'm not a potential *rock star*! I'm a serious musician thank you very much!' Charlie retorted as he stood up proudly.

'Here they are!… I found them in the kitchen… eventually… Have you two made a decision yet?' Mrs Evans' glasses had been on her head the whole time that she had been looking for them… but nobody mentioned this…

'We do really like it, but we are going to have to go away and think about it, if that's alright with you?' *'Never let them see how keen you are'*, Penelope thought to herself, *'that's a major rule in negotiations…always be willing to walk away… well at least make them think that!'*

'That's quite alright…' *'I will be very surprised if these two don't take this place, very surprised indeed,'* Mrs Evans thought to herself. Penelope and Mrs Evans eyeballed each other in the hall, each knowing what the other was thinking. Charlie tried his best not to laugh, and spoil the moment.

'One of us will give you a call tomorrow, either way.' Penelope broke the silence, and then the two of them made their way down to the front door.

'I will look forward to it… now… where did I leave those keys…?' Mrs Evans rummaged around in her little handbag for the keys.

'We'll see ourselves out. Thank you Mrs Evans.' Penelope smiled sweetly.

'Alright, Goodbye, dear,' Mrs Evans called after them.

'Thanks, bye.' Charlie couldn't wait to move his stuff in.

Charlie and Penelope took one of the tables outside the nearest café on Abbeville Road. It was strange being around in the middle of the day during the week, but they were grateful to get a seat outside in the sunshine.

'Well, what do you think?' Penelope asked as she sipped her oversized cappuccino. Penelope was really keen, and now that she was far enough away from the flat she was happy to let her emotions show.

'I thought it was cool, I could totally get all of my amps and stuff in the end of the living room, and that shed in the garden could be really handy for the band's stuff.' As far as Charlie was concerned they were moving in.

'I suppose that is one selling point for you… but I was hoping to just have to get one other person in, and not two… the less strangers we live with the better.' Penelope sounded tense… life in London is hectic, and Penelope knew she didn't have time to get to know strangers… let alone to put in all the effort to find housemates.

'Would you relax… it'll be cool… we are hardly going to move an axe-murderer in!' Charlie could not see the problem, he couldn't understand why girls got so worried about everything.

'Well… you never know..' Penelope had heard some real horror stories about living with strangers.

'It's in a pretty cool area too… did you see all of the bars… I wouldn't have to stagger far to get home.' Charlie thought it was time to change the subject, and to focus on the advantages..

'That's a major bonus for both of us.' *Hmm, he has a point, after all we do go out around here all the time, it would be so great to just wander home and not have to fight for a taxi.'* Penelope considered this, it did make sense.

'And we go out around here all the time, so it'll just make everything more *convenient*.' Charlie was convinced now, that this was the end of the house-hunt.

'That's a good point.' Penelope knew he was right, her free time was scarce enough, and anything to make life a bit more convenient was very welcome.

'And I really think it's the best place that we have seen so far, and I think we could get away with sharing with one other person if we set the rent at the right level.' Charlie knew that they could both agree on that, some of the other places had been pretty grim.

'I definitely agree with that! Ok… even though I'm not a huge fan of sharing with people we don't know… let's do it!' Penelope hugged Charlie.

It was as if a great weight had been lifted off their shoulders, they had been looking with no luck for two whole weeks, and finally the search had come to an end. Two weeks may not seem like a long time, but in a city full of young professionals, all looking for a place to rent, two weeks is like a lifetime. Finding the right flat in the right location, is an essential make or break step towards happiness or complete misery in London. It's important to live near, if not with, some friends, and of course the all-important transport links. Clapham South was perfect for Charlie and Penelope on both accounts.

'I'll call Mrs Evans first thing to let her know.' Charlie was relieved, he couldn't face the prospect of another afternoon of rejecting what he thought were perfectly good houses!

'Provided that we can change the Wicca HQ!' Penelope was so excited about their new place, she was mentally packing and organising all of her clothes and shoes and picking out the right space for them in her new built-in wardrobes.

'What the hell is that?' Charlie laughed nervously.

'You know… the purple living room!' *Sometimes you just had to spell it out for guys'…* Penelope thought to herself.

'Oh yeah, right, I'll make sure we can repaint it.' *'What a relief! I thought she was talking about something serious there…'*

'Great.' Penelope was really excited now. She was dying to live with Charlie. She had only lived with other bankers since leaving University, and she had the feeling that living with Charlie would be a whole new experience..

Chapter 3

The First Day of the Rest of Our Lives...

It's funny how these things happen sometimes. It doesn't really seem that significant at the time, but when you look back you realise that one chance encounter can potentially change the whole direction of the rest of your life. Penelope hadn't seen Charlie since the beginning of University. They both went to University in London, but he dropped out after a year to focus on his music. They hadn't kept in touch so much since then, as their lives had taken very different paths. Penelope followed the more traditional route, business degree, a masters in economics and a job in banking in 'The City'. Charlie was happy enough living off his Trust Fund and fuelling the song-writing process with lots of *life experience*... well that was one way of putting it... Charlie was constantly teetering on the edge of 'getting signed' or 'getting a deal' or 'writing a number one'. If you speak to any of the thousands of aspiring musicians in London, this is the kind of chatter that you will hear, so nobody really took him seriously as a musician. On the other hand, he was very good looking, with his 6ft4 frame, his shoulder-length brown hair, hazel coloured eyes and lightly tanned skin. He always used this to his advantage of course. Countless young blondes fell under his spell, and he left a trail of them dazed and confused the length and breadth of the country.

Penelope was every parent's dream. She came in the top ten in her class in University. On the surface she was successful and glamorous and she had no end of city bankers running after her. Her mother was expecting her to march any one of them down the aisle any day now… this was the last thing on Penelope's mind however, but she didn't let her mother know that. It was expected of her that she should 'marry well', 'after all they had done for her' and sometimes it felt like everyone was watching and waiting, and dusting off their best hats for the big day. There was also the constant reminder that her parents had already been married for some time at her age. At 28, Penelope was positively ancient as far as her mother was concerned. The dreaded 3-0 was looming and it would be game over for her mother if she wasn't 'settled down' by then. She didn't want to let her parents down, so she would keep the charade going for as long as she could get away with it. Even at *this age* she definitely wasn't ready to settle down, after all… surely she hadn't even met *the one*. She was confident that she would know the minute that that happened. *You just know…* that's what everyone said. Being an only child really had its drawbacks sometimes, the pressure was on and Penelope had become something of an expert at deflecting it. Living with Charlie was exactly what she needed at this point in her life.

It was no wonder that Charlie and Penelope had fallen out of touch. She could be found regularly in places like Le Pont de la Tour, The Oxo Tower and The Criterion "on expenses". He was more likely to be found in the Barfly in Camden, or the Boogaloo, with the other "struggling" artists "on stage". Of course he wasn't exactly struggling himself, but that was hardly the point… it was all about the music. It's amazing how for years you can have so much in common and then it seems like all of a sudden you are twenty-something and everything has changed, some people are grownups and some people are fighting the urge to be!

Then one day, quite out of the blue, Charlie and Penelope's paths crossed again. It was a grim, grey day in London, it had been lashing rain all day, and the streets were really badly flooded. These days are not too uncommon in London… but this day the rain was particularly heavy. It felt like the city itself had a heavy heart as the commuters battled with each others' umbrellas, leaped across puddles and struggled to go about their business. Charlie was on his way to Euston, to catch a train to Manchester. His band, The Stone Rats, were supporting a new up and coming band up there for three nights. He was meeting the guys there at 2 pm, he was… as always… a little late.

By the time he had arrived at the platform it looked like the guys were on the train already, so he headed on… not a care in the world, he would definitely find them on board. Penelope was also on this train. As the train began moving away from the platform Charlie fished out his mobile phone to call the others but the battery was dead. They had only been going about two minutes when the train lurched to a halt, and then… silence. Everyone sat there waiting for the driver's announcement, and within seconds there was some garbled announcement about an electrical fault… muffle… muffle… fault… muffle… muffle… delay… muffle… muffle… heavy rain… There was a collective grumble on the train, and then silence again. The silence was broken by the shrill sound of a mobile ringing, which was promptly answered with a curt 'Penelope Chesterfield'. Charlie couldn't believe it… no it couldn't be… but it certainly sounded like Pen. He had a good look around and couldn't see her, then he saw the woman on the mobile phone, he had to have a really good look at her before he decided that it was in fact his mate from Uni. She looked nothing like the girl that he had known back then, she used to be slightly bohemian and she had a real free spirit. He was quite shocked at what he saw, she was dressed like somebody's mother, in her cream suit and tailored trench coat, everything matching! She had cut her long blonde hair into a neat bob. But when he took a good look at her face she still looked quite young… it could be her… yes it definitely… could… was it her? He took a good five minutes before he decided to go over to say hello. When he did, the stern face he saw when she had been barking into her phone, melted into the warmest smile that he had ever seen. Thanks to the rail company they had a good two hours to catch up, and they swapped numbers, promising to meet up soon.

Charlie lost Penelope's number.

Pen saved his into her mobile, and for some reason the chance meeting played on her mind. She really had left that life behind her, the wild parties in Uni, dating artists, actors, and crazy scientist guys… Why was it all so serious now? Had someone waved a magic wand, and all of a sudden she had to take life so seriously. No, that's ridiculous, she made her own destiny… and this was the way that she wanted her life to be. She was successful and you could be fooled into thinking that that was all that mattered in a city like London. She wanted to see him again soon, he was such a breath of fresh air, an antidote to all of the stuffy people she had to put up with in work. She made a firm decision to call him, after all, it sounded like his band needed all the moral support they could get… and that's how their friendship started up again.

Chapter 4

The Big Move

'How many runs are you going to have to do to bring all of your things over?' Penelope was keen to plan the day, so that she could bring her stuff over while he was collecting his next load, it was the most logical way of organising it!

'Just one,' Charlie muttered.

'One! But you are moving house?' Penelope looked horrified, she assumed he was joking!

'Unlike you Pen, I don't need a pair of shoes for every day of the year.' Charlie couldn't help teasing her, she had so many boxes of things!

'I don't have over 300 pairs!' Penelope retorted. '*Do I? Oh my god...do I? That's scary!*' Penelope panicked at the possibility that she did, indeed, own more than 300 pairs of shoes.

'What's in all of those boxes then?' Charlie challenged her, he knew he was right...

'Oh, they are not all full of shoes' Penelope stammered, '*Quick! Change the subject, I'm crap at lying!*' 'They are full of things for work...' '*brilliant he'll never question that!*' She began to relax a bit, she knew that he would not question work things, after all her work was highly confidential.

'Well why do the boxes have "SHOES" written on the side of them?' Charlie smirked at her and pretended to be ready to open one of the boxes.

'Erm… good question… and the reason is… the reason is… that we bought the boxes, in work, from a shoe factory, to put the files in,' Penelope shot back at him. *This is getting easier by the second,'* she thought to herself.

'Let's have a look then!' Charlie knew Penelope couldn't lie to save her life, but he was certainly enjoying seeing her squirm!

'No!' She shrieked, 'I mean, I don't think that would be a good idea, those are C-O-N-F-I-D-E-N-T-I-A-L work papers… and I could get fired!' Penelope was really panicking now, she couldn't be known as the girl with a pair of shoes for every day of the year, she just couldn't.

'Ok, fair enough, but why you would have work papers here is beyond me.' Charlie decided he had had enough fun for one day, and conceded defeat.

'*Great he bought it, now I will have to distract him while I move them upstairs. Maybe I could hide some of the pairs under the bed.'* Penelope was trying to develop a covert operation to get the shoes past Charlie.

'Have you got the keys?' Charlie asked, looking at Penelope with his most innocent expression – he had her in a total tizz now, with the shoe comments, and he knew this would wind her up…

'I thought you had them!' '*Oh my god… if he has lost the keys I will kill him!'* Penelope went pale.

'Just kidding! I do.' '*This is too easy!'* Charlie was delighted with himself.

'Here we are, home sweet home…' Penelope was delighted, it really did feel like home… she leaned against the front door so relieved to be actually on the inside of it, and stood there for a moment to compose herself. Just as she had finally regained composure and she was halfway up the stairs, there was a loud bang upstairs.

'What the hell was that?' Penelope turned to Charlie, she looked terrified.

'I don't know, but I don't think we should hang around to find out!' Charlie wasn't taking any chances… he turned to head back down the stairs.

'I'm scared.' Penelope looked *terrified*, she couldn't move, she was rooted to the spot.

'Hello, is that you Mrs Evans?' A female voice floated down from upstairs.

Charlie and Penelope hesitated for a moment on the stairs, staring at each other, and then Charlie said, 'Eh… Noooo… we are the new tenants, hold on we are coming up.' Charlie was completely fine now that he knew it was a woman… he was something of an expert on those…

'What do you mean you are the new tenants? I thought this place was empty. I dealt directly with the landlady and I moved in yesterday.' The young woman's voice was trembling now, no doubt she was feeling the same way they had been feeling two minutes earlier.

'We dealt with the letting agent, you know… Mrs Evans.' Penelope sounded frantic, this was a lot to take in, in such a short space of time. Penelope found herself face to face with a young woman on the landing.

'Oh… I see well, Dorothy told me that Mrs Evans hadn't filled the place so she was dealing with it herself, Mrs Evans is a bit dotty so maybe she forgot… she tends to do that sometimes.' The young woman's voice calmed down when she realised that there was a woman with this guy, even if both of them looked like they had just stepped out of a magazine.

'I see.' Penelope was not backing down, not for one second.

'Well, we've paid our share of the deposit.' Charlie sighed, trying to be practical, he had now joined the two of them on the landing.

'So have I,' the young woman retorted, they could see now that she was only a girl, early twenties at most.

The two girls stood there glaring at each other. Neither moved an inch.

'*Oh my god, what do I do now? Neither girl is budging. Are they even breathing?*' Charlie thought to himself, it was like watching a bullfight. Charlie knew that he had to do something… fast!

'Ladies, ladies… this is not a huge deal, let's call the landlady and we can sort this out.' Charlie gave them his most winning smile, and waited for them to calm down a little… or at the very least to start breathing again.

'Ok, I'll call her.' Penelope decided to call her to make herself useful. She didn't like the fact that moving day had been ruined by someone being in *their* house!

The time that passed felt like an eternity. It seemed like their whole future depended on whatever the landlady decided. Penelope was not too impressed! Everything she owned in the world was stacked, neatly, and labelled of course, outside The Abbeville pub, and it was only a matter of time before the customers started occupying the tables outside the pub. She had had to pay a fortune to get the movers in, and there was no way she was going through all of that again. It was bad enough packing up and getting her things here.

'Ok, she said she is coming over to sort this out.' Penelope started to feel slightly relieved now that she had spoken to the landlady, and that she was going to come straight over to sort it out.

'When will she be here?' the young woman enquired, she was still completely on edge. Her voice sounded tense. Her cat-like green eyes were nearly black her pupils were so dilated from the shock, and she stood there in a loose sweatshirt and tracksuit bottoms, one rubber glove on, and the other one in her left hand. Her long straight brown hair was scraped back into a messy bun, and she felt like a five-year-old as these two towered over her 5ft2 frame.

'About an hour, she's coming down from North London, and you know what the traffic can be like?' Penelope softened her tone a bit, the poor girl looked terrified.

'What is your name, by the way? I am Charlie and this is my friend Penelope.' Charlie decided to lighten the mood a bit, the poor girl still looked petrified.

'Penelope, Penelope! What kind of a name is that?!' she thought to herself.

'Nice to meet you, I'm Zara, Zara Stephens.' Zara removed the rubber glove, and shook hands with the two of them, they were both way taller than she was, she felt like a small child in trouble! This was not a good start to her new life in London.

'Well, I suppose we should just put the kettle on… that is if we even have one.' Penelope thought it was best to be practical, maybe a cup of tea would calm them all down a bit. Tea was always the ultimate cure, particularly for awkwardness.

'Good idea.' Zara looked slightly relieved, she was dying for a cup of tea, in fact that is where she was headed when these two arrived into her life without warning.

The thoughts were whirring around in Zara's head like a tornado… *'How on earth did this happen, who the hell are these two!? Just when I was settling into my new house, and they show up, I can't believe this. What do I have to do to get a bit of peace and quiet! They nearly gave me a heart attack when they came in. I wonder what Dorothy is going to say, I mean, there are two of them, so that's double the money into her account already. She is a friend of Mum's though, so that should work in my favour,'* Zara reflected.

'Oh my god! The doorbell nearly gave me a heart attack!' Penelope jumped slightly when the doorbell went. They were all still on edge despite the tea and pleasantries.

'I'll go get it.' Charlie was dying to work his magic on the landlady… there was no way he was giving up this place!

'Hello I'm Dorothy, the landlady… I believe we have had a bit of a misunderstanding.' Dorothy surveyed the scene, you could cut the atmosphere with a knife, and poor little Zara looked terrified.

'Yes, well actually it turns out that Mrs Evans told us that we could move in, not knowing that you had told Sara.' Penelope offered an explanation..

'Zara!' Zara shrieked a little more emphatically than she really should have, she didn't normally overreact, but the atmosphere was highly charged!

'Sorry… Zara… that she could move in.' '*Oh my god I have pissed her off already, that's not a good start!*' Penelope thought to herself.

'Oh dear, I'm sure I told Gladys that I was going to look for a new tenant myself, she is a little forgetful, maybe she just simply forgot. Would either you Zara, or you two, be willing to give up the house?' Dorothy was trying to sort this out as soon as possible, she was double-parked outside.

'No.' Penelope was firm.

'Not particularly.' Charlie echoed.

'No.' Zara was not giving up that easily. This was the first time she had even lived away from home, and she couldn't even imagine how to begin to find a place to rent in London, it was so big and scary!

'You see the thing is, Zara has moved all of her stuff in already and my stuff is… well quite literally… on the doorstep, and Charlie's is outside in the car.' Penelope was trying to paint the picture a bit clearer for everyone.

'Ok, well would you be willing to share the house, I usually rent the house out to groups of four people, and I'm sure you weren't planning on paying all of the rent on your own.' This was the only solution as far as Dorothy was concerned.

'Well we were actually planning on advertising for one or two new housemates.' Penelope liked the idea, the thought of any more house-hunting was far from ideal.

'I was going to look for three.' Zara started to relax a bit, she had no idea how to look for housemates… she had only been in London for 24 hours so far, and was only coming to terms with not living at home anymore!

'So if you all decided to move in together, you would only need to find one new housemate between the three of you.' Dorothy was convinced that this was the right thing to do.

'Well… I suppose that does take the pressure off a bit.' Penelope liked the idea, first impressions aside, Zara seemed like a nice girl, and as she seemed to know the landlady… that would make maintenance of the house much easier if anything went wrong.

'I think I would be ok with that, I mean you two don't look like axe murders or anything...' Zara smiled for the first time since they had all met, the others warmed to her immediately.

'Quite the opposite actually, she looks more like Grace Kelly and he looks like a typical trustafarian. Such an unlikely couple! I wonder if there is anything going on between the two of them... interesting...' Zara thought to herself, as she finally looked at them from the point of view of being housemates and not intruders.

'And we were going to have to look for housemates anyway...' Charlie was loving this, no need to worry about these things. The two girls had got so worked up over nothing!

'That's settled then, you three can sort it out amongst yourselves... I have received the money into my account, and I will send you a copy of the lease so that you can all sign it. Zara tell your mother that I was asking after her.' Dorothy was very relieved, she liked the look of the two Londoners, and she already knew Zara.

'Ok, thanks.' Penelope showed Dorothy out. A sense of calm descended on the house, just in time for Charlie and Penelope to move the rest of their stuff in before the Abbevillagers started occupying the tables outside The Abbeville pub to make the most of the sunshine.

Chapter 5

The Battle of the Bedrooms

Now that they had all decided to live together… there was only one question remaining… who got the big bedroom with the en suite bathroom? This was going to be tricky.

'Zara, which room did you move into?' Penelope tried not to sound *too* interested.

'The smaller one on the second floor, the rent is slightly lower on that one, so I went for it… I thought the two doubles would be easier to find housemates for…' Zara had weighed up all of her options very carefully before she moved in, and her room at home was actually smaller than the one she had move into, so she was happy with it.

'Good point,' *Great one down, one to go!* Penelope thought to herself.

'So now it's down to the two of us.' Penelope walked into the kitchen where Charlie was rummaging in the more or less empty cupboards.

'What is?' Charlie muttered, he barely even looked up… he was starving!

'The big bedroom on the top floor?' Penelope wanted *that* room, Penelope needed *that* room… Penelope had to have *that* room!

'It's more rent… the decision is easy, you can have it if you like… after all you have so many shoes… eh I mean "work papers" to store.' Charlie winked at her and went back to scavenging in the kitchen.

'Ah I didn't realise that, well, I don't mind paying a bit more for it.' Penelope was already half way up the stairs with the polish and the vacuum cleaner when she said this to him.

'Ok, that's settled then, I'll take the double room below it.' Charlie turned around and realised he had been talking to himself.

'Zara, did you hear that? Charlie is going to take the smaller double, that just leaves the tiny room upstairs... what way do you want to do it... do you know anyone who might be interested?' Penelope dropped into Zara's room on her way up to hers.

'There is one guy I know, he might be moving to London too, I'll text him to see if he's interested in the little room'. Zara was finally happy with the way things were working out, if her friend took the room that would be great.

'Great!, why don't we get unpacked, and then we can all head out for a drink when we are settled in... Charlie have you got plans tonight?' Penelope shouted down to Charlie.

'Nah, was just going to hang around here...' Charlie shouted back up from the kitchen.

'Zara? What about you? Do you have plans?' Penelope asked Zara..

'No, not at all, I have literally just moved to London, I don't really know anyone here yet, a drink would be good, do you know anywhere good around here?' The mere mention of alcohol perked Zara up immediately, even though she found London very... *very* scary... she was dying to see what the bars and clubs were like.

'Lots of places, there are more bars around here than people.' Penelope was relieved that Zara had said yes, things were off to a good start. She continued her journey up another flight of stairs to her new bedroom.

Zara was really looking forward to going out, but she felt so dowdy compared to them. Somehow her clothes were all *wrong* for living in *London*. This had never even occurred to her before she met these two. Of course she had been to London before, but living in SW4 with pretty much everyone being in their twenties and thirties was a whole different experience. Everyone she had seen so far had been so trendy or so cool, and she had to make a good impression on her new housemates. She found Penelope quite intimidating, she was beautiful, and she was still in her suit from work so she looked extremely elegant, everything matching! Zara had only ever seen people like that on TV.

'Oh no! What to wear!? I know it's only a casual drink, but I'm sure Miss Perfect will be all dressed up to the nines. I bet her shoes cost more than my entire wardrobe. I can't wait to start working and to finally have money! I feel like such a student still! I will go shopping when I get paid at the end of the month... I can't wait. I'm dying for a drink actually, my nerves are in tatters after all of that stuff this afternoon, with the two of them arriving in and the landlady. At one point I did think they were going to get the house and I was going to have to find somewhere else. I can't believe it's my first day at my new job on Monday, I hope the people are nice, and I must try and figure out how to use the bloody Tube... I'm so scared of it, the Tube map looks like the most confusing thing I have ever seen... apparently the colours are supposed to make it easier!? What a joke. They make it look like vomit! I hope I'll get used to it eventually. I couldn't believe that she had so many boxes to move in, they could not have all contained shoes. It said SHOES on the side, but there's no way, unless each shoe was wrapped in bubble wrap or something. Even if they were in boxes in the big boxes, there would be too many. I'm dying to see her collection if they are all shoes. I can't wait to buy new shoes myself actually... that's the first thing that I'll buy when I get paid. That Charlie guy seems so laid back, the two of them are so different, I'm surprised they are friends. Ok, let's see... I think I'll go for jeans and a black sparkly top, I don't want to look like I have overdone it. Ok, that works... now, what shoes? Oh my god! I have barely any shoes down here with me, I left most of them at home. It will have to be these pointy ones. They are ok I suppose, quite dressy. I'll go down to see if they are ready.'

Once Zara had chosen her outfit, she calmed down a little, she had a lot on her mind, as her whole life had just changed in the past 24 hours, and she hoped it was for the better… a new job, a new house, new friends?… a new life!

'Oh, I didn't realise you were waiting for me.' Zara was a bit embarrassed when she came downstairs and the two of them were waiting in the hallway.

'Don't worry… we wanted to let you settle in… I only unpacked a few things, otherwise I would be here all night!' Penelope laughed, Zara still looked so anxious… but it was nothing a few drinks wouldn't sort out!

'Where are we going?' Zara asked.

'Let's go and have a look, there are so many bars around here, my favourite one is called Sand bar, but it might be really packed tonight, there are always queues at the weekends. There are a few others, let's wander down the road and go into the first one we fancy… Charlie, any preferences?' Penelope was dying to go to Sand bar, but they had left it kind of late, and there was no way that she was going to queue. Sand bar was inconspicuously tucked in among the residential areas of Clapham on the border of Brixton. It was the perfect mixture of a beautiful space, beautiful drinks and amazing R&B music. It was a favourite among some celebrities who knew they could visit without being bothered. There was a down-to-earthedness in Clapham that you simply didn't get in nearby Chelsea. It was glamorous without being pretentious.

'Nah, that's cool, whatever… as long as there's beer.' Charlie was so easy to please.

Zara surveyed Penelope's outfit… *'She's not that dressed up really, I was expecting Gucci-looking clothes… she actually seems more down to earth when she is not in her power suit! She looks more suited to be going out with Charlie dressed in Jeans and a trendy t-shirt… the trendy casual look. I bet the jeans cost a fortune, but they are made to look old and worn. I wonder if she gets those eyebrows done or if she does them herself?'* Zara was getting caught up in her scrutiny, she couldn't help herself. It was a lot to take in and process.

'Here we are… ah… the magic words… "Happy Hour".' Penelope saw no queues, great… she could murder a Strawberry Daiquiri.

'Looks good.' Zara smiled at Penelope, nodding like a lemming. *Thank god for Happy Hour I'm so broke until I get paid!* Happy Hour was one concept that Zara was very familiar with! It was starting to feel a tiny bit more like home now.

'Does it include beer?' That's all Charlie cared about.

'I don't know, let's check… yep it's by the bottle though…' Penelope reported back.

'That's cool.' Charlie settled into the leather couch, and patted the seat beside him for Zara to sit down. Zara reluctantly joined him, he was so confident and gorgeous… he made her nervous.

'First round is on me.' Penelope trotted off to the bar.

This was a lot for Zara to take in… apart from the Happy Hour bit this place was nothing like home, everyone seemed so gorgeous and confident! And they all seemed to be in their twenties. Every single one of them?! *This is actually really fun, this place is cool,* she thought to herself. *These two must come here the whole time, the bar staff seem to know them really well. This place is amazing, , and there's a real student, but not student crowd… it's like… yeah… .the first jobbers, that's what it is… I couldn't put my finger on it for a sec there. Still acting like students, but with jobs… excellent! I'm going to fit in here. Penelope is gorgeous! I'm dying to know if the two of them are together! I don't know what to talk to her about! With Charlie it's easy… he just likes talking about himself all the time… and "the music". It's pretty interesting actually, the music that is. At first I thought he was just some rich kid, but he does seem to know what he is talking about. I hope I get to meet the rest of the band. I don't seem to have anything in common with her though. I asked her what her job was and she may have been speaking Chinese for all I understood. Something to do with banking I think. She keeps talking about "the City", I don't know whether that just means London, or somewhere else… she talks about it like it's a different planet. I hope she didn't realise that I hadn't a clue what she was talking about! Having said that, I don't have a clue what I'm going to be doing on Monday. A job in marketing, in an organic food company. At least it's very central. I hope I get to make some new friends down here, it's pretty weird being here and not knowing anyone. Hopefully Simon will want to move in, and at least that's one mate, but he's not too sure whether they are going to offer him the job or not. I really, really like this area here… well what I've seen of it so far. Everyone seems to be twenty-something… even when I popped down to the supermarket there seemed to be no kids running around or haggard housewives like back home… it's pretty cool. Plenty of good looking guys too, much better looking than the guys from Uni, and they dress so well. I suppose I am in London now, a fashion capital… I will really have to brush up my image if I want to fit in here.'* Zara sucked on the dregs of her first Strawberry Daiquiri , and swapped the empty martini glass for the full one sitting in front of her, as she thought about her new life in London. For the first time since she had arrived, she felt as if… everything was going to be ok…

***

The next morning, Zara woke up with a thumping headache.

'Oh no… I feel weak, Happy Hour always kills me, two cocktails for the price of one, the thought of them makes me feel sick now. I really should have taken it easy, I don't really know my new housemates too well yet, maybe that's why I drank so much. I feel like I'm going to die. I hope nobody else is up, I'll wander down to get some water.' Zara summoned all of her strength, and threw her feet onto the floor, the rest of her body remained firmly under the duvet. *'One step at a time… c'mon Zara, you can do it,'* she thought to herself. She pulled herself upright, v-e-r-y s-l-o-w-l-y… and made her way downstairs.

'Oh, hello!' Zara was surprised to see an unfamiliar face in the kitchen… was this the way it was going to be in this house, strangers popping up all the time!?

'Hi, I'm Mandy… I was just looking for a glass of water, where are the glasses?' The girl kept opening and banging all of the cupboard doors in search of the glasses.

'Oh, right, glasses, em, they are over here. Did I meet you last night? Sorry I was really drunk and my memory is a bit hazy.' Zara stammered, she was so embarrassed, they had been speaking to quite a few people last night, friends of Charlie and Penelope's, was this one of them?

'Were you at the party with Charlie?' Mandy enquired, one eyebrow arched.

'Oh that's right, he went off to some party, it's slowly coming back to me now, so this must be his girlfriend…' Gradually Zara started to piece things together.

'No, I think I came home straight after the pub, I'm Zara I have just moved in with Charlie and Penelope.' Zara struggled with the conversation, her headache was getting worse.

'Who is Penelope, oh no! Is she Charlie's girlfriend, does he have a girlfriend?' Mandy shrieked at Zara! Her questions were like machine gun fire, too many crowding Zara's head, *'Can't concentrate, stop talking, stop talking… she's obviously not his girlfriend then, but looks like she wants to be…'* Zara thought to herself. 'No, she is just a close friend of his. Did you just meet Charlie last night?' Zara had never really seen anything like this before, in real life that is.. Zara had gone to her local University, so she had never had housemates before, and this would certainly never happen in her mum's kitchen at home.

'Yep, ok, I'm going to head back upstairs, thanks for the water and nice to meet you…' Mandy was gone.

'Ditto…'

'Hilarious! So that's Charlie's thing. I wonder if he is a bit of a ladies' man… only time will tell. Oh god… my poor little head.' Zara hauled herself onto one of the kitchen chairs, and sat at the table with her head in her hands.

'Morning Zara, oh dear you look a bit pale.' Penelope arrived into the kitchen, she was already dressed.

'I'm dying, I drank way too much last night.' Zara raised her head, she felt like death.

'I'm feeling pretty much the same. You'll be ok once you eat something, I was like you about an hour ago, but I made myself eat some toast and I'm feeling much better…' Penelope felt so sorry for Zara, she obviously couldn't hold her drink as well as she and Charlie could, that was something that would change after a few months living in London.

'Food is the last thing I feel like…' Zara couldn't even think of eating.

'I know, but it'll help,' Penelope assured her.

'You are right, I'll try to eat a piece of toast or something.' Zara knew that Penelope was right.

'We have loads to sort out today, we need to talk about getting a fourth housemate.' Penelope knew that they had no time to waste, after all none of them wanted to have to share the cost of the extra room.

'Oh yeah, my friend Simon might be moving down, so is it ok if I offer it to him first?' Zara started to feel slightly better.

'Absolutely! I have asked around everyone, and there is nobody I know looking for a room, and it's the same with Charlie. If you actually know someone who wants to move in that would be great… otherwise we'll have to advertise for someone.' Penelope was pleased that Zara might know someone looking for a room, it would make life so much easier.

'Oh, I thought that the landlady might get someone else?' Zara couldn't understand why they had to get housemates themselves.

'Oh no, it's entirely up to us, it's better that we choose the person though… because we have to live with them, if you know what I mean,' Penelope tried to convince Zara.

'I see what you mean.' Zara pretended she knew what she was talking about. *'Oh no! How on earth do we find someone? I really hope Simon can move in,'* Zara shuddered, she felt like every time she was starting to feel comfortable with her new surroundings, she was presented with something else that made her feel like some kind of country bumpkin.

'So you let us know as soon as your friend lets you know, and if he can't move in we'll put an ad in Loot.' Penelope was very reassuring.

'Ok, he should find out about his job on Monday, and he will call me then. By the way, what do you think of the living room?' Zara tried to change the subject.

'Oh my god, it's dreadful... we reckon a coven of witches lived here before us... those weird shapes on the wall... and that purple!' Penelope laughed as she pointed at the spirals.

'I think it looks grim!' Zara had been really freaked out by the living room when she first moved in and had barely set foot in it.

'We asked if we could paint it and Mrs Evans said that we could.' Penelope was thinking about colour schemes.

'Cool!' Zara was relieved.

'We were so keen to move in that there wasn't time to get it done before we did. That can be our first house project. Now, we will need to write to the gas, electricity and phone companies to put all of our names on the bills, we can put the new person on the bills when they move in.' Penelope had done the house share thing so many times before, it was second nature to her.

'That's a good idea.' Zara could barely believe all that she had been hearing, but she was a bit relieved that someone knew what they were doing. She was actually glad that she had moved in with the others now, she wouldn't have a clue about all of this stuff on her own.

***

Later that day, Zara returned after her first hungover adventure to the local supermarket... exhausted!

It has taken about five hours but I finally feel a bit more human again... I even struggled my way down to the supermarket. I can't believe I am living in London, I don't think the big change has really hit me yet. I keep expecting mum to walk in asking me what I want for tea. I have only been here for two days now, I suppose, that once I start work it will hit me. I haven't even been on the dreaded Tube yet. I wonder what to do tonight? If I was at home I'd be deciding what to wear now, getting ready for a night out with

the girls. God… I actually really miss them already, and I have only been gone two days. I might give them a ring in a little while…'
Zara put her groceries away, and sat down at the kitchen table. She picked up her mobile phone and dialled the last number.

'Hi, it's me.' Zara was so glad she didn't get the voicemail.

'Zara! So you haven't forgotten us already then?!' Sophie shrieked.

'Don't be ridiculous, and anyway I have only been gone for two days.' Zara giggled.

'Is that all?!… it feels like *ages!*' Sophie was so dramatic, she could not believe that one of her friends lived in *London* now, it was soooooooo glamorous.

'I have a bit of a hangover, I was out last night…' Zara sounded sheepish.

'Oh, where did you go?, somewhere dead glam? And what's the house like? And did you meet any nice boys? It must be sooooo glamorous,' Sophie shrieked.

'I went out for drinks with the people that I live with.' Zara knew that more questions were coming and she hadn't really prepared her answers yet in her hungover state!

'What people!?' Sophie couldn't believe this… she had new friends already?

'Charlie and Penelope,' Zara admitted sheepishly, already regretting the words that had already fallen out of her mouth.

'They sound posh, are they posh?!' Sophie was full of questions!

'A bit, but they are really nice.' Zara started to feel a bit uncomfortable, all of this was quite hard to explain to Sophie. So much had happened since she had left home.

'Well that's the main thing. I better go, Karen is on her way over, we are getting ready here tonight. Zara it won't be the same without you, have a fab night tonight whatever you end up doing, bye.' Sophie was already distracted by the outfit laid out on the bed for tonight.

'Bye, speak to you soon.' And with that Zara hung up, as she burst into tears…

'*Oh my god, what is wrong with me? Maybe it's the hangover, or PMS or maybe, just maybe I don't want to be here... ... I really miss my friends. It looks like I'm staying in tonight, I don't think I have ever stayed in on a Saturday night before in my entire life. There is nothing I can do, I don't know anyone in London yet. This is awful. Oh no!, I think I hear Penelope, better not let her see me like this, I'll run up and wash my face.*' Zara was startled by the sound of someone coming and she darted up the stairs.

'Zara, hi it's only me.' Penelope flounced into the kitchen, and flicked the kettle on.

'Hi, I'm upstairs.' '*Quick hide the tissues,*' Zara thought to herself.

'Come down and I'll show you my new shoes, they are amazing,' Penelope sang up to Zara, she wasn't expecting to see Zara looking so upset. 'Oh, are you ok?' she changed her tone completely.

'Fine thanks, I'm just still feeling a bit off from last night's overindulgence.' They both knew that this was a lie!

'Bloody hell, that's the longest lasting hangover ever.' Penelope tried to laugh it off.

'I know, I really do suffer with them.' Zara's nose was all blocked up now, and her eyes were all red and puffy.

'Ah, you mixed your drinks didn't you?' Penelope tried to offer a practical solution.

'If I could remember that I would be doing well.' Zara was fighting back the tears.

'Oh dear!' Penelope arched one eyebrow.

'Indeed, what are you up to tonight?' Zara asked Penelope trying to change the subject.

'Eugh! I'm going on a date.' Penelope did not look happy when she said this.

'Oh, anyone nice?' Zara didn't understand her tone, she would love to be taken out on a date.

'Well, yes, *nice* being the key word there, he's another guy from the City, very nice, but they are usually very dull, it's like going to dinner with a waxwork.' Penelope began to wonder why she had agreed to go at all.

'Why do you go then?' Zara asked. *'There she goes mentioning "the City" again… I wonder if I'm ever going to find out what she is talking about… maybe that's the name of the company that she works for?'* Zara was still baffled by all of this.

'That's a good question, and it's one that I ask myself repeatedly as I get ready, and on my way home if it was boring, but the thing is you just never know… sometimes the ones who you think are going to be so dull are great fun, and then sometimes you are dead right about them. I have been single now for ages, so I suppose I should make an effort. But sometimes it really just feels like a waste of makeup.' Penelope sighed. 'I'm really getting to the point of giving up on the whole thing! But I always think that if I'm going to meet *him*, I'm definitely going to meet him in London. It's one of the most exciting cities in the world after all.' Penelope gave a weak smile.

'Oh god! Is that what I am going to have to do now that I live in London. I have never been on a date in my entire life. I wouldn't know how to do it. It was so easy back home, we know all the guys that live nearby, and there is none of this dating thing, there is just so much to learn!' The colour drained from Zara's face as she contemplated having to go on dates with dull bankers from "the City".

'I know what you mean, Penelope, I hate dating myself, I try to avoid it if possible.' Zara tried to sound convincing, she constantly felt like such an idiot since she had arrived in London, she felt so clueless.

'Oh god, call me Pen, my mother is the only one outside of work who calls me Penelope, it makes me feel like I'm in trouble… or in work,' Penelope laughed.

'Ok, I'll try to remember that.' Zara was relieved, this might make Penelope seem a little less intimidating!

'It's the only way to meet men in London though, it's such a big city, unless you manage to get together with one of your neighbours! That's how George met her man.' Penelope was like a font of knowledge for Zara.

'Seriously?' Zara was now dying to find out who lived next door to them!

'Yep, they kept running into each other in the hallway or something ridiculous like that. Speaking of neighbours, have you noticed anyone coming or going next door? I think it might be empty,' Penelope asked... she was doing a great job of keeping Zara distracted from whatever had been upsetting her.

'I haven't actually seen anyone. Maybe an old granny lives there with her cat.' Zara grinned, she thought that would be hilarious!

'Oh, no! Don't say that, no parties for us then.' Penelope did not look happy at this prospect.

'It's probably empty.' Zara didn't want to upset Penelope, they had been getting on so well.

'Well we'll soon find out if the post starts piling up.' Penelope nodded at her.

'That's a good point. Pen.' Zara was trying to get used to the shorter name, she was struggling a little with it.

'Right, well, I would love to stay and chat but I must go and pretty myself up... after all he could be the o–' Penelope stopped herself just in time..

'Don't say it!' Zara shrieked, it was an unwritten rule that if you think he might be "the one", you never ever said it... to avoid tempting fate!

'Well you know what I mean...' Penelope winked at her.

'Totally!' Zara was delighted with herself, thank goodness they were on the same page for this at least!

'I have some painkillers in my room if you need some, for the hangover.' Penelope felt so sorry for Zara, she looked awful.

'Thanks, but I have taken some, I should be fine in a while.' Zara choked back the tears, hoping that Penelope couldn't detect the wobble in her voice.

Zara settled back onto the sofa, and tried to take her mind off the dating thing... there were so many other lessons to learn before she started that!

Thank god she's gone... the tears were welling up there, I was struggling to hold them back. I feel so depressed. I think I might have a bath, and see what's on TV. Thank god I have a TV in my room, so I can have a good cry if I need to. I might go and get some junk food, and see if there are any films on tonight. Oh no, my life is so sad, I'm living in the big city, or should that be "the City", and I am sitting in with the TV on a Saturday night! Saturday night!… That kind of thing is ok on a weekday night, but not Saturday! Oh no, here come the tears again. I'd love to ring mum, but they were so proud of me getting a job in London, she told everyone in the town practically, it would break her heart if she thought I wasn't happy here. I might go back up as soon as I get paid to collect some more stuff, and go out with the girls. That's better, something to look forward to.' The prospect of going home for the weekend helped to stop the torrent of tears for the time being.

In W1, Penelope's night out had just begun…

'Penelope, you look lovely my dear.' Gordon took her coat, he sounded like a granddad! He kind of looked a bit like one too, with his receding hairline!

'Thanks Gordon, lovely restaurant. They all seem to know you here, do you eat here a lot?' Penelope was struggling to make conversation, there was definitely no spark here and she hated small talk.

'We take clients here a lot actually, usually during the week of course. So what area of finance are you in exactly?' Gordon could not believe that she had agreed to go on a date with him, he could see all eyes in the room on the two of them.

'I specialise in Capital Markets.' The conversation was dragging on..

'Excellent, so do I, at least now we have something to talk about.' Gordon was thrilled to have some kind of common ground to talk about!

'Oh my god, is this guy for real, talking shop on a Saturday night, there must be a hidden camera in here somewhere, this must be a joke, I must be on TV.' Penelope tried to hide her disappointment.

'Indeed,' she said through gritted teeth.

'I want to go home, I want to go home, I want to go home … now! But we haven't even ordered yet. Why did I agree to this,

what was I thinking?! I'd much rather be at home alone than be here. I might go to the loo and text George to call me and rescue me, brilliant idea… ok I'll wait and order first, I don't want it to look too obvious.' Penelope hatched a plan to escape this rather unfortunate situation.

'How is your personal portfolio looking these days, we all took such a hammering with the tech stocks, none of us saw the dotcom bubble bursting. I mean personally I am risk averse, so I didn't invest too much but many of the others lost a lot of money in that market…' Gordon droned on and on, and on… about the aftermath of the dotcom implosion. It seemed to have been the most exciting thing that had ever happened to him.

'Right that's it! I'm out of here… I can't believe he's still talking about the dotcom implosion, oh my god!' Penelope had had enough. She didn't have a portfolio of tech stocks, much happier to invest in shoes and expensive handbags.

'Excuse me, I'll be back in a moment.' Penelope smiled sweetly as she said this, and she slid out of her chair and headed towards the bathroom.

'Of course.' Gordon stood up as he said this.

'Ok George, I'm counting on you now…' Penelope thought as she started frantically texting her best friend George.

Hi Doll, date from
hell, need help, pls
call with emergency in
5 mins, if not never
spking 2 u again, P xx

'Read Receipt! Yes she's got it… .now, back to face the music.' A sense of calm descended on Penelope as she was sure that George would bail her out.

'Sorry about that.' Penelope's smile was genuine, because she knew that this ordeal was not going to last too much longer.

'Not at all, dear, not at all. I took the liberty of ordering you a glass of champagne.' Gordon was delighted with himself, he felt like James Bond, for the first time in his life. He beamed at Penelope as he said this.

'Oh thank you very much, have you decided what you are going to eat?' Penelope relaxed a bit now, because she knew that she had an escape route.

'Oh, I always go for the same thing.' Gordon smiled smugly.

'*Oh what a surprise!*' Penelope was not one bit surprised, this was the kind of guy who ironed his socks and ate peas one by one… Penelope was counting the seconds!

'Really? I think I will go for the monkfish, no starter for me… oh, hold on a moment, I'm getting a call through and I had better take it. Excuse me again.' Penelope tried to act surprised that she was getting a call..

'Penelope Chesterfield,' she barked into the phone.

'Hi, it's me… so what's the story, is he hideous?' George was in hysterics at the other end of the phone, she was picturing Penelope sitting at the table with a bald version of the Incredible Hulk sitting opposite her!

'Aunt Agatha, is everything alright, you sound manic?!' Penelope adopted a very concerned tone.

'Oh my god, he is that bad then?! I'm sorry I just can't stop laughing…' George could barely get the words out she was laughing so much.

'Stop crying now, I can't make out a word you are saying.' Penelope improvised, just in case Gordon could hear any of the conversation.

'Pen stop it! That mock serious voice is nearly convincing me that there is something wrong with me!' George tried to compose herself, she could barely breathe because she was laughing so much.

'I see, I see, calm down, I am actually with someone at the moment, but I'm sure he will not mind if I slip away a bit early.' Penelope knew that she was out of there within minutes!

'Do you want to drop over on your way home?' George had managed to stop laughing now, and was planning their girly night in. She scraped her long brown mass of curls into a messy bun, and debated whether to change out of her track suit and put on a bit of make-up.

'Yes. Have you phoned the police?' Penelope was managing the two conversations at the same time… getting the message across to George, while still seeming to be speaking to her elderly aunt.

'And you'll bring some wine?' George enquired.

'Yes, yes of course. Alright I will be there as soon as I can.' *'Wine! Of course… good idea.'* Penelope thought to herself, and was already planning where the cab should stop on the way to George's.

'I am terribly sorry about this Gordon, but my aunt is quite old and her house was broken into earlier. She tried to phone my parents of course, but I think they are at the theatre tonight, and the police still haven't arrived even though she called them an hour ago. She is terrified. I'm afraid I am going to have to go, I'm so terribly sorry. I hope both of our hectic schedules leave us some window where we can meet up again.' Penelope feigned regret.

'Yes, of course, you must go. Do you need me to give you a lift?' Gordon jumped out of his seat.

'No!!' Penelope answered a bit too quickly, 'I mean, that is very kind of you, but that won't be necessary, I will get a taxi from outside, there is a long queue of them. I'll just run and grab my coat. Goodbye now, and thanks again.' And without a backward glance… she was gone.

Gordon sat back down, and picked up his glass of pinot noir. *'I knew it was too good to be true,'* He thought to himself, as he relished the last few drops of his wine.

Penelope dialled George's number as soon as she was safely installed in her cab.

'George, hi it's me, thanks you are an angel, I have finally escaped! He wasn't ugly, it was just that he was so boring! All he could talk about was work, what a nightmare! George! Will you stop laughing for two seconds!' Penelope chatted animatedly on the phone to George, she was elated to have not wasted the whole evening.

'I can't help it, you were so funny, you should have been an actress, I had visions of you sitting there in pearls and a Jackie

O suit on an old fashioned telephone that they had brought to you on a silver tray, with your handbag on your lap and a hankie and smelling salts in one hand... just in case... I presume he believed you, I bloody well did!' George couldn't believe all of this drama, she had written off any kind of fun in exchange for a night in front of the TV. This was quite a turn of events.

'Yes he did, I feel a bit bad, but there was no point in wasting both of our nights... and his money, we had nothing in common. I would much rather have been at home having a nice bath.' Penelope tried to rationalise the whole experience.

'Bloody hell, that bad?' George couldn't believe it!

'A total waste of makeup! How come you are in anyway?' Penelope was so relieved that George was at home tonight, otherwise she would have been stuck with Gordon for the entire evening!

'My love is at a stag night tonight, so I decided to stay in in front of the TV,' George sighed longingly.

'Thank god you did! I'll be there in fifteen.' Penelope sped towards George's flat in a cab.

'See you soon babes.' George couldn't wait to hear the full story about the date from hell...

***

In SW4 Zara was still struggling with her first Saturday night in London. She was not used to being so isolated, she was used to having all of her friends living within walking distance from her house. Every Saturday night without fail, boyfriend, or no boyfriend, all of Zara's friends would meet up in one of their houses, to either get ready to go out or to have a girlie night in. The lack of company was killing Zara, it was a cocktail of emotions in terms of the euphoria of living in London, and the frustration of not having anyone to enjoy it with. At this point Zara had no way of telling that this feeling would not be with her for too long. Zara paced up and down in her bedroom...

'This is the longest night of my entire life. I had my bath, and only used up twenty minutes. I tidied my room, again! There is practically nothing in it, so that didn't use up much time either. There is nothing on TV, and I don't even know where the nearest video shop is… I must go and try to find it tomorrow, I'm not about to start wandering around looking for it in the dark. At least I had the Chinese takeaway menus, not great for the figure though. I think I will go to bed and read a bit of my book, I feel like a middle-aged housewife, I just want to go home. I would give anything to be out with the girls at home now, I hate London!' Zara lay down on her bed and cried until she couldn't cry anymore..

The next morning, Zara woke up very early, as the sun streamed in through the gap between the curtains in her bedroom. For a moment she had no idea where on earth she was. For a moment of innocent bliss, she felt like she was still living her old life, but gradually she realised that she was in her new home in London…

'8 am! Bloody brilliant, I'm wide awake now, I don't think I have ever been up this early on a Sunday since I was a little girl. Now I have the whole bloody day ahead of me, with nothing to do. I wonder if the other two are going to be in at all today. Probably not, Sunday is a real family dinner day… oh god, this is grim. I was so bored last night I thought I was going to die of boredom, a full day and night ahead of me, I don't know how I'm going to cope. Thank god for Sunday morning hangover tv, just another hour or so to wait! I'll eat my breakfast v-e-r-y s-l-o-w-l-y.' Zara tried to cope with being up so early. She padded down to the kitchen and made her breakfast very slowly. It seemed like her first Sunday in London was going to be the longest day of her entire life. There wasn't a single sound outside on Abbeville Road, such a stark contrast to the night before. No doubt all of the other urbanites were sound asleep nursing the mild repercussions of the fun that a typical Saturday night in SW4 entails.

Chapter 6

Spaghetti Junction

The only good thing about having woken up so early on Sunday morning was the fact that Zara was nice and tired and ready for bed by 10 pm that Sunday evening, and she knew she had a very early start on Monday morning. She was so nervous about her first day at work. It was her first real, full-time job. She left the house extra early to make sure that she made it in on time... she wasn't too sure how to get there from Clapham.

Nothing could have prepared her for what lay ahead. Zara thought that an hour was more than enough time to get to work, she had no idea that thousands of other Clapham-ites would be thinking exactly the same thing. Zara got the bus from the end of Abbeville Road to Clapham Junction train station. Zara could cope with buses and trains, but the Tube... she did not like the idea of that so much. As Zara sat on the bus taking everything in, the schoolkids, the young professionals, everything so vibrant and colourful... she began worrying about getting to work.

'I knew I should have come in yesterday... on a practice run. At least I have made it to the train station... I was too scared to get the Tube, and I don't really know where the nearest Tube station is to the house!' Zara arrived at Clapham Junction, and she was beginning to wish that she had got the dreaded Tube... *'Oh*

my god! Which platform is my train going from? There are about a million people here and they are all on a mission to get to work. They all seem to know exactly where they are going too, and they are all walking so fast... I wish I was in that position. If one more person pushes me I'm going to start crying! At least I'm nice and early... I would hate to be late on my first day... how embarrassing. This looks like the right one now, I'll hop onto this train. It says it goes to Charing Cross and I can walk from there, this A to Z is like my lifeline, it was one of the best going away presents I got... I'm only realising that now. I laughed when Sally gave it to me, and I didn't believe that it would become one of my most valuable possessions in London. I have no idea how long this train is going to take, I just hopped on and hoped for the best. It's so packed, I don't think I have ever been this close to this many people, it's weird... it doesn't really seem to bother anyone. I'll just have to pretend that it doesn't really bother me either. I'm glad I brought my book with me, that'll take my mind off it.'

Zara settled into her seat on the train, she was so relieved to be out of the warpath of all of the commuters rushing around, she was not used to walking so fast, and she had to keep jumping out of people's way. Just when she thought she was well on her way, the inevitable happened. The train suddenly lurched to a standstill, and the driver made a muffled announcement to the commuters. *'Oh no! Why are we stopping? That's not good!... What is he saying I can't make it out at all, something about a delay? Great this is exactly what I need. I hope it's not for too long, I really don't want to be late.'*

Zara felt a pit of panic grow in her stomach, she could not believe that this was happening. She could not understand why none of the other passengers seemed too concerned, surely this couldn't be "normal" could it? It seemed like the train stood still for an eternity... but eventually... it started moving again, but very, very slowly. Zara was sure she was going to be late. At this stage the other passengers were starting to get agitated. Zara's mind was racing ahead...

'I'm going to have to run up to St Martin's Lane, I really hope it's not far... I haven't really figured out how to tell yet by looking

at the A *to* Z. *Oh my god! We have stopped again, what the hell is going on? I have to be in by 9 am, and it's 8.45 am now! I wanted to be in early today to make a good impression. Ok, we are moving again, I think I'm going to have to run when I get to Charing Cross. That guy is totally staring at me, what should I do? I'll just ignore it. It's really making me feel uncomfortable…'* Zara reached for her book and started to look engrossed so as not to catch the eye of the dodgy guy who was staring at her. In reality she could not even see the lines of text in the paragraphs in front of her. It was all a blur.

'Finally we have arrived.' Zara was getting really nervous, when finally… the train arrived at Charing Cross. There was a total stampede for the doors, it was the last stop, so everyone was getting off. Zara got pushed to one side, costing her another three minutes. When she finally got out on to Charing Cross Road, it was 8.52 am. Eight minutes to get to work! The only thing to do was run!

Zara arrived at her new office, pink and flustered.

'Finally 8.59 am! I can't believe I made it. It looks good, quite trendy. I hope I'm not underdressed. I have to start taking my career seriously now that I work in London! No more slacking off in front of daytime tv, dodging lectures and handing in projects five seconds before the deadline… god I miss Uni already!'

Zara made her way through to reception, trying to compose herself.

'Hi, I'm Zara Stephens, I'm here to see Victoria.' Zara tried to look confident when she approached the receptionist. She was in reality bright red from running all the way from Charing Cross. Zara was feeling a bit overwhelmed by the whole experience.

'Oh hello Zara, Victoria is waiting for you, take the lift to the second floor.'

The receptionist seemed kind, but also a bit bemused by the sight of Zara all pink and flustered. Zara made her way up to the second floor, and there was just enough time to comb her hair in the lift.

'Hello Zara, come on in, I'm Victoria, it's very nice to meet you, take a seat. I'll just go through your role and responsibilities with you again, and then I'll take you out to meet the rest of the team'. Victoria was so glamorous and very formal, Zara was getting a bit tired of everyone, except her, being so gorgeous in London! This was her first official visit to the London office, although she had been there once before for her final interview. It seemed so different now from the inside. She had a nice desk, next to a window beside a girl called Sophie. Victoria introduced Zara to everyone, and instructed Sophie to answer any of Zara's questions.

At the end of her first day in Organicom, Zara was beginning to think that time passed very, very slowly in London indeed, this Monday had been the second longest day of her life. Zara had a lot to think about on her journey home, luckily this time there were no delays. First of all, she was finding it really hard to remember everyone's name in work, there were just so many people. There were people from all over the world working in Organicom, and many of them had names that Zara had never even dreamt of. Where Zara came from, well... everyone was from where Zara came from. They did not get much in the way of international visitors in her home town...

'That was the longest day of my entire life, I am never going to remember all of their names. There is such a variety of characters at work from what I can see. They all seem to be really friendly. It's weird being the new girl. For some reason I was expecting them all to be Londoners, but I don't think there is anyone who is originally from London working there, they are from all over the world. Loads of Australians and South Africans I wasn't expecting that,' Zara thought to herself on the train on the way to Clapham Junction.

Zara arrived home eventually absolutely exhausted, she felt like she could get into bed, and it was only 7.30 pm! She didn't think that was a good idea so she decided to stay up for a bit longer. She hung around in the kitchen for a while. She was wondering where her housemates were, surely they would be home from work by now. By 8.30 pm there was still no sign of anyone. She decided to head up to her room but when she heard the front door opening, she decided to hang around to see who it was.

'Oh hi Zara, how was your first day at your new job?' Penelope arrived into the kitchen looking immaculate, and she seemed genuinely interested.

'Oh hi Pen, it was ok, but I'm sooooooo tired now.' Zara looked exhausted. 'And the train stopped just outside Charing Cross for ages, I was nearly late, it was so stressful... I can't believe how many people cram themselves onto the trains in London. ' Zara mustered up enough energy to make it seem like she was a Londoner through and through, she had got to work and back in one piece and survived her first day, she was very proud of her small triumph. This feeling was not to last for too long.

'I suppose it does take some getting used to when you first arrive. I was lucky my parents live in London so I've been used to the Tube and the crowds and everything, but I suppose when you come from a smaller city, it must be a huge shock to the system?!' Penelope was very understanding.

'It is a bit of a shock actually, there just seems to be so much to learn, and everyone else seems to know it all, I feel so lost! I can't believe how fast people storm around the place, they would knock you over if you don't keep an eye on where you are going!' Zara could feel the tears welling up again..

'I know what you mean, London definitely has its own pace, there are a few essentials you should know about that might make things a bit easier for you... let me think now...' Penelope made a mental list of essentials in her mind that might help Zara. She tried desperately to put herself in Zara's shoes, so that she could give her some useful guidance.

'Ok, what are they?' The tears seemed to stop for a while with this glimmer of hope...

'Well, first, and the most obvious thing... always carry your *A to Z*, and an umbrella... no matter how sunny it looks first thing in the morning!

Zara clutched her *A to Z* dramatically as Pen said this, holding it like a lifeline in a stormy sea.

'And a bottle of water, you never know when you might get stuck underground... always carry some cash with you... you never know when you might need to grab a taxi if the Tube is suspended or delayed. Then always, always bring a book with you if you are going on the Tube, it will stop you making eye contact with the odd weirdo that you might find on there.' Zara was practically on the edge of her seat she was listening so intently, this was good advice from Penelope.

'I don't get the Tube, I'm scared of it!' Zara sighed, she was more scared now than before she had heard about the potential weirdos.

'Well, you may feel that way now... but it is the fastest way to get around London, so it's hard to not use it if you live in Clapham... we have three Tube stations here! Clapham North, Clapham Common and Clapham South. You will probably end up using it soon, and on that by the way... never get into a carriage if there is only one person in it... make sure there are a good few people, and definitely a few girls in there! That only applies if you are on the Tube or train and it's really quiet... which is practically never anyway.' Penelope was thinking hard about this now, the more she spoke, the more handy tips came to mind.

Zara felt like she should be taking notes... but she didn't want to look too much like a complete idiot! She hoped she would remember all of this.

'About going to work... there are a few things that you should carry with you, always bring deodorant and makeup, in case you need to run for the last bit of the journey like you did today, and I usually bring a clean top with me. It gets so hot on the Tube sometimes, you can get really sweaty!' Penelope continued in a very knowledgeable way, it seemed like she was running through a mental list.

The more Zara heard the less she liked the idea of using the Tube, but she hid this, and looked as grateful as possible with each new tip that Penelope provided!

'It's not a bad idea to eat on the go, or get your breakfast in work... you need to get onto the Tube before 8 in Clapham, if you want to… well… actually get onto the Tube.' Penelope was trying to spell it out to Zara, she couldn't understand how anyone could live in Clapham and avoid using the Tube. It just didn't bear thinking about! Penelope could not imagine anyone going to the trouble of walking to the bus stop on Clapham Park Road, going all the way to Clapham Junction and then milling around in one of the busiest train stations in the entire country. Clapham Junction is great for those who live in… well… Clapham Junction, but there were three Tube stations around Clapham Common for a good reason!

'Penelope… erm, I mean… Pen, what do you mean if I want to get onto the Tube I need to get onto it before 8?' Zara looked complete confused.

'It gets so packed that you won't be able to squeeze onto it, that applies for Clapham Common and Clapham North, the platform is really tiny and you might feel like you are walking the plank or something! I would stick to Clapham South if I were you!' Penelope was trying to be helpful, in reality she was scaring the bejesus out of Zara. Zara was now posed with a dilemma… should she brave the Tube and get into work faster each morning, or should she stick to what she knew. There was just too much to think about.

'Thanks Penelope, that was really useful.' Zara was genuinely grateful, she felt very lucky to be living with someone who seemed to know it all about London.

'That's quite alright Zara, let me know if you have any other questions, or aren't sure about anything, it's no problem at all.' Penelope made her way up to her room, she was exhausted too… Mondays were always intense at work.

Zara flopped onto the couch in the Wiccan living room, well and truly mentally, emotionally and physically exhausted. She had literally never taken in so much information in one day in her entire life. She only hoped that it would be downhill from here.

***

The very next day Zara considered getting the Tube, for all of about three seconds, and then chickened out and got the bus and the train again instead. At 11 am her mobile rang, and she snatched it up quickly, very grateful for the distraction in work.

'Zara, hi it's Simon.' Zara was at a bit of a low ebb the next day when Simon called. She was struggling with people's names in work, she chickened out of getting the Tube in the morning, it was not going well...

'Hello there, how are you?' Zara was really pleased to hear from Simon, if he would take the spare room that would be great, they could both figure the Tube out together. It would be a relief to have at least one friend in London.

'Crap, if you must know! I didn't get the job in London.' Simon sighed glumly.

Simon sounded terrible, he was really dying to move to London and this job was a major excuse to move down south.

'Oh no! I'm so sorry to hear that. So you won't be taking the spare room?' Zara's faced dropped, but she tried not to sound too devastated.

''fraid not, oh well, I think I'm going to go off and drown my sorrows now. By the way, I bumped into the girls in The Roxy on Saturday night, they were lost without you!' Simon was trying to be nice, but it was having the opposite effect on Zara, she had completely put the weekend to the back of her mind, but it all came flooding back...

'Oh no, oh no, the tears again!' Zara thought to herself.

'Oh no, I have a work call coming in, I better go. I'll speak to you soon, and sorry again about the job.' Zara got him off the phone as soon as possible, she didn't want him to hear her blubbing into the phone. *'Oh god, tissues, I need tissues, look at the state of me.'* Zara thought to herself. She thought it was the right thing to do to get the call over and done with so she composed herself to call Penelope.

'Penelope Chesterfield, Capital Markets.' Penelope answered the phone reluctantly, she hated when the number didn't show up on her mobile.

'Hi Pen, it's Zara, Zara from the house, sorry for ringing you during work but…' Zara was shocked to hear Penelope's 'professional voice', she sounded like a different person

'Just a moment…' Penelope headed out to the coffee area, so that she could have a bit of privacy.

'Em, Ok, well…' Zara stuttered, she was really shocked by Penelope's abrupt manner, she was actually quite nice at home.

'Sorry about that Zara, I never like to let them know that I'm taking private calls in work, I had to pretend you were a client.' Penelope sounded like herself again, Zara was relieved.

'Oh I see, I thought I had caught you at a bad time or something. The thing is that Simon, my friend from home, didn't get the London job, so he won't be taking the room.' Zara could feel the tears welling up again, thank god nobody was around her desk to see her.

'That's such a shame, I will have to place an ad, and god, the only time I can interview is at the weekend, we really have cut it a bit fine. We should all be there though, because we all have to live with the person. Right!? Can you be there next Saturday? I will cancel my appointments and I'll make sure Charlie will be there. I'll put the ad in right away, to get things going.' Penelope was about ten steps ahead of Zara – Zara had thought that the landlady would get the other housemate for them, this all sounded a bit like too much hard work.

'Shit! I was going to go home that weekend, I can't go now… it would look really bad… especially considering she's cancelling things, oh no! I was living for my trip home.' Zara thought to herself

'That's fine Pen, I will keep that Saturday free.' Zara tried to hide her disappointment.

'Great stuff, I better go, they can see me through the window, and I look far too happy to be speaking to a client, thanks for ringing, see you later.' Penelope was keen to get back to her desk to draft the housemate ad, the sooner they got things going the better.

'Bye.' Zara couldn't believe all of this was happening.

'Oh no! I had picked out what I was going to wear on Saturday night and everything, I can't believe this. Why is this happening to me? Interviewing bloody housemates. What a joke, I have never interviewed anyone in my life. Chocolate, I need chocolate!'

Zara headed out to get some much-needed chocolate, and it was only Tuesday!

***

To: Zara.stephens@organicom.co.uk,
          charlieboyrockstar@hotmail.com,
Subject: New housemate ad!

Hi Everyone,

Here is what I'm going to say for our ad, it's going into *Loot* tonight, so it will appear in the Wednesday edition. If I have left out anything let me know. Charlie I'm going to give your mobile number because Zara and I are in work all day, I hope this is ok, and we need you to be home next Saturday because we are going to see people then.

Single Room for Rent in a houseshare, SW4. Preferably young professional, non-smoker. £450 pcm ex bills. Please call Charlie at the number below or email pchesterfield@ jlminternationalbank.com.

Cheers
Pen

Chapter 7

Inaugural Weekend

In EC4 Penelope was getting agitated, she hated all the bravado that went on with the guys she worked with. Being one of only a few women in work really had its drawbacks sometimes. She just knew that these guys would make a mountain out of a molehill, and she was not wrong.

'I have to keep moving around in this meeting just to stay awake, I'm so bored. It must be annoying them that I am fidgeting so much. Could these idiots just make a bloody decision! I bet they will decide to go with the first proposal after all these discussions. They are so full of hot air, all prancing around in front of the partner.' She was dying of boredom in a meeting that had gone on for hours longer than it really should have. The "right" answer had been obvious to her from the beginning, and everyone's opinion was of course valid, but her intuition was screaming at her that the first proposal was the one!

'Looks like it's going to be an all-nighter again tonight Jeff.' Christopher feigned regret as he said this, but they were all really delighted to be showing the partner how "dedicated" they were by working such long hours, especially with promotion time looming.

'I'm afraid so, did everyone hear that, cancel your plans... it's going to be a late one tonight.' Jeff came back into the meeting room and announced the bad news to the group.

'Oh my god! Not another one! I hate all of these delays! When I bet they will just go with the first proposal. This kind of thing always happens on a Thursday, never a Monday or a Tuesday, they leave everything until the last minute and then we are in all night on a Thursday, and still recovering from it by Saturday. Penelope was getting so frustrated with all of the late nights, she had no life outside work these days, and more to the point no chance of meeting a nice new boyfriend, she had been single for ages! She also had to regularly let her friend George down, and this was becoming all too common these days.

'Absolutely, we need to review these five proposals and the figures, to make sure it's perfect, in time for the meeting in New York on Friday.' Christopher was delighted with himself, and he couldn't wait for the trip to New York.

'They have gone through them all a few times each already. There is NOTHING else that can be done to the figures, I hate this "face time"... Penelope gave them a big fake smile, there was no way that she was going to show that she was not one of the team.

'Let's order in food, any preferences anyone?' Jeff had the phone in his hand, already, he knew their orders practically off by heart at this stage... but it was polite to ask!

Time marched on..

10 pm...

... ... 11 pm...

... ... 12 am...

... ... 1 am...

... ... .2 am...

'Is that the final decision Jeff, we'll go with the first proposal?' Christopher announced this as if it was some kind of revelation.

'What a surprise! I'm absolutely exhausted, and then I need to be back in here for 7 am tomorrow.' Penelope was sick of having

to work so late all the time, when the decisions could be made so much faster, if it wasn't for all of the male politics that she was constantly surrounded by.

'The first proposal is the final decision, there wasn't much we could do with the figures...' The whole team was in agreement, a few hours too late for Penelope's liking.

'There are too many egos in this room... they will all be fighting over the phone now to call the partner to let him know which one we are going with. I knew Jeff would grab it first.' Penelope was mentally in the taxi on the way home already, her bed was beckoning to her from SW4.

'Hank... Hi, Jeff here, we have made a decision, yes, we are going to go with the first proposal, we have tweaked it and it's perfect now. I have left a copy on your desk, you can review it first thing and then we'll get them to print it out in the New York Office.' Jeff was positively bursting with pride.

'Jeff looks like he is going to explode he is so proud of himself, he did none of the actual work, what a joke. You would swear he did the whole thing single-handedly the way he is going on. I'm surprised he didn't offer to run a copy over to the Partner's house personally.' Penelope was getting a bit grumpy now, the proposal was done... it was time to go!

'Great work guys, time to call it a night. See you all in a few hours. The taxis are waiting downstairs to take you all home.' Within seconds the fourth floor was cleared, and everyone was down in the lobby.

'3 am... finally home... I wonder if there is any point in going to sleep at all... two and a half hours is hardly going to do me much good. I think I'll cancel my date with Peter tomorrow... or I mean tonight... I'm going to be exhausted. I don't want to fall asleep in my soup... after all... he could be the one...' Penelope drifted off to sleep, even though her mind was still buzzing with facts and figures, her exhausted body won the battle... and she fell fast asleep.

***

The next morning Zara was up bright and early, she had been in work for nearly a whole week now, and every day things were getting a little easier, she was still struggling with the commute though, and had not plucked up the courage to get the dreaded Tube…

'Morning Charlie, what are you doing up so early?' Zara was surprised to see Charlie, he was never up at this time of day.

'Hey Zara, I have booked the studio today, so I had to be up early, it costs a fortune per hour, and I don't want to waste time. Did you see Pen last night… I haven't seen her in days?' Charlie rummaged in the cupboard for the cereal.

'No, I was going to ask you the same thing.' Zara was delighted to actually have something to talk to him about, they really had run out of small talk at this stage.

'I'll give her a ring later, are you in tonight?' Charlie mumbled.

'I think I'm out with work for drinks.' Zara sighed nonchalantly, she was relieved that she did actually have plans, she felt like such a loser with no friends in London yet, especially considering how Charlie and Penelope led such glamorous lives.

'Cool, I'll be out with the lads, maybe see you later…' Charlie mumbled, he didn't really understand Zara and he never knew what to talk to her about, she was nothing like the girls that he knew.

'Bye,' Zara shouted up the stairs as she headed out the front door. The walk down to the bus stop always gave her some time to think…

I wonder if Penelope is staying over at her Saturday night date guy's house or something, could he have turned into a boyfriend that quickly I wonder? I have barely seen her at all this week. Her life is so glamorous, I would love to go out on dates. I'm pretty sure now that there is nothing going on with her and Charlie, I can't believe I ever thought that! She's absolutely gorgeous, I would be very surprised if she is still single. I wonder what the rest of Charlie's band are like, he's pretty good looking, but he is not really my type, a bit too wild for me. There are no eligible men at work, it's all girls or gay guys… probably a good thing actually, no sense in mixing business with pleasure. Rob in work is really good looking and he dresses really well, his boyfriend is amazing looking, I think he is a model. He dropped into work the other day and the two of them were so funny fussing over each other. Having Rob around in work really makes the day go faster, he is always chatting and joking with all of us, he's great. More delays on the trains… Typical!… now where's my book'. Zara settled into her seat on the train, the delays did not phase her so much these days.

'Good afternoon Zara… so you decided to join us!' Rob was delighted that Zara was a few minutes late, any excuse to start the day off with a joke.

'Shut up Rob! I was delayed on the train, what a nightmare.' Zara loved the fun that Rob brought to work.

'Ooooh that's a likely story, I bet you stayed in bed late with your new beau…' Rob was so dramatic.

'The chance would be a fine thing! I haven't met any nice men down here yet, and anyway, I have told you a thousand times… all the best looking ones are gay!' Zara was loving this, in fact most of the gorgeous men she had seen around Clapham, did seem to be gay.

'Flattery will get you everywhere! Cuppa?' Rob was delighted with himself, Zara was definitely on form today, and their morning tea or coffee was turning into a daily ritual. Rob had moved back to her department, the day after Zara started, and she was very lucky that he had lost his old desk and was now seated very near her. Rob was certainly not new to London, this made a huge difference to Zara. He had spent a few years at HQ in Manchester when it first opened, before moving to Organicom in London. He was as full of good advice as Penelope was.

'Lovely, thanks. So, how is Michael?' Zara was fascinated about Rob's boyfriend, he was the most beautiful human being she had ever seen, all the women, and even the straight men seemed to fancy him.

'Still gorgeous, but we had a bit of a tiff this morning, over something silly of course... so I'm officially not speaking to him! That should last until about midday or until he texts me a few times...whichever comes first, and I'll get back to you after that!' Rob huffed grumpily about this.

'How did you two meet?' Zara decided to try to take his mind off the tiff.

'Oh, it's such a romantic story... we were both living in Manchester, and our eyes met across a crowded bar, on Canal Street, and the rest is history. He was straight at the time, but I soon saw to that!' It seemed that Zara's plan was working, Rob went from extremely grumpy to all gooey and dreamy within seconds.

'Oh my god... you turned him gay?!' Zara nearly fell off her seat, she couldn't believe this, she thought having all of the gorgeous girls in London to compete with was bad enough, but throw gorgeous guys *turning* gay into the equation, and she thought it would be impossible for her to find a boyfriend in London!

'Don't be silly... he was always gay, he just didn't REALISE it.' Rob winked at Zara as he said this, she didn't know whether to believe him or not, but she really, really wanted to.

'I see... I must remember not to introduce you to any of my boyfriends... just in case... you have the same effect on them!' Zara struggled to regain composure.

'Yes, that might be wise, men find me irresistible.' Rob was delighted with himself now.

'Of course they do, who wouldn't!' Zara was happy and smiling again, she was sure that the story was not true.

'It's such a burden!' Rob sighed with a cheeky grin.

'Do you ever get women coming on to you?' Zara was really interested in this, she was sure it must be the case, she assumed that not everyone has gaydar. She certainly didn't.

'Oh yes, all the time, but I explain to them that I am absolutely unavailable, and then I show them a picture of Mikey, and they completely understand. One woman started crying, although she was quite drunk at the time, saying it was such a waste, such a waste! What on earth does that mean?! It is certainly not a waste as far as we are concerned!' Rob started strutting up and down as he said this.

'I see what you mean, but you see there is a great shortage of straight guys who are sensitive and dress well etc. etc. etc. so we do tend to get a bit upset when we see yet another complete hottie who is gay, for us it seems like the quota of attractive guys just reduced as we can put another one on the gay side, it can be quite upsetting.' Zara was trying to explain this clearly, trying not to upset Rob.

'I do see what you mean now Zara, I know how blessed I am with Mikey, he's an angel, and I have seen the selection of straight guys, I wouldn't be tempted from what I have seen around. All "rugby" this and "beer belly" that, they bring the male form into disrepute as far as I'm concerned!' Rob shrieked.

'I don't mainly go for looks, but it's nice to be with someone who at least dresses well, I mean, it's good if we kind of match! There's no point in being all dolled up if your man of the moment is dressed like he's going for a run.' Zara was on the fence on this one, looks weren't that important to her, and anyway… real men play rugby where she came from.

'Absoloooootely! You definitely need to match! There's just no point otherwise!' Rob laughed

'What have we got on today?' Zara was trying to keep her mind off rugby guys, there was work to do and she couldn't afford to be distracted, she still had so much to learn in her new job.

'European conference call at 11 am, you should listen in on that one, and then the weekly team meeting at 4 pm.' Rob always knew the right answer, Zara didn't know what she would do without him.

'OK, I have loads of emails to get through today, that ad needs to go in by lunchtime. It's going to be a long day.' Zara was feeling more and more in control as each day passed, she hoped that it would get easier and easier as each week passed.

'Indeed it is. We need you to do a bit of mystery shopping in the health food shops that stock our line. I have a huge list here of all of them, and you need to get it done by the end of the month, so you can divide it up whatever way you want. I would suggest taking a few days a week and put a few hours aside to do them. I know you have only moved to London recently so I will help you to figure out which ones are near each other.' Zara hadn't a clue what Rob was talking about!

'Oh my god! What the hell is mystery shopping? It can't be that bad, I mean, shopping is never bad!' Zara tried to reassure herself.

'Have you done mystery shopping before?' Rob picked up on the fact that when Zara didn't really know what he was talking about, she got a bit flustered.

'No.' Zara thought there was no point in hiding it.

'Well, it's really easy... all you have to do, is visit the shop and check that they have our line displayed properly, and that the sales assistants know what they are talking about when you ask for our products.' This was the easiest way to explain this to Zara.

'Oh, I see... so do I get a list of questions to ask them?' Relief flooded Zara's expression, this was indeed something she could handle.

'In a way, yes, look here is the score sheet, this will make it clearer... but the main thing is to not let them know that you are doing it, you have to pretend to be a customer,' Rob added.

'A bit like spying?' Zara sounded so excited, this sounded like so much fun.

'Exactly! Then you give them a score at the end of it, and you will need to feed all the scores into excel and then we can see which shops and restaurants do it best. The top 10% get our esteemed 'preferred vendor' status... it's the *Palm d'Or* of the organic food industry!' Rob had adopted his jokey tone again, even though he was actually being serious.

'Really? Sounds very glamorous,' Zara added.

'Oh it is, it's the highest honour...' Rob stood up dramatically as he said this.

'You are soooo funny... now seriously, do the top 10% really get anything to show for their efforts?' Zara thought it was a joke.

'Yes, of course! They get a beautiful gold plate… for the wall.' Rob had a more serious tone now, he stared at her intently.

'Oh my god… let's see, it's soooooooo tacky,' Zara giggled.

'I know darling, but they are literally stabbing each other in the back to get their hands on one, you wouldn't believe the things that go on…' Rob whispered conspiratorially.

'Really!? Like what?' Zara whispered loudly.

'Well… last year, a very well-known organic juice bar, which will remain nameless of course, *stole* a plate.' Rob stole Zara away to the corner where the water cooler was so that they could have a bit of privacy. He looked over each shoulder conspiratorially before he spoke.

'No!' Zara shrieked.

'Yes!' Rob shrieked back.

'How did they manage that?' Zara began to whisper again, as a few people had looked up when she shrieked a minute ago.

'The manager got me… I mean… *'a member of staff'* drunk, and decided that heading back to the office here was a great idea, and while under the influence, he took advantage and stole one! He has it bloody well framed in their main juice bar, the bloody cheek of him!' Rob was speaking really fast.

'Was he cute?' Zara raised one eyebrow.

'Bloody gorgeous!… Oh I mean… so I hear…' Rob dropped his guard by mistake and then covered his tracks rapidly.

'I never realised the organic food business was going to be so cut-throat! I thought it would be dominated by peace loving hippie types with names like "June" and "Mona".' Zara couldn't believe this, it seemed like she would have to have her wits about her in this industry, it sounded more like working at a fashion house than an organic food company.

'Oh not at all! There are a few people like that, they were the ones who started the whole thing off, but once word got out that there was a lot of money to be made it got very competitive, it's because there are only a few key players, the industry is still relatively new.' Rob was a constant source of useful information, he seemed to know everything about the job and this industry.

'I see what you mean.' It was starting to make sense to Zara, this was London after all a big, *scary*, city.

'Believe me... you've seen nothing yet! But you'll like mystery shopping, it gets you out of the office for a while, I would do it myself but this phone is practically attached to my ear, so I can't afford to be away from my desk for too long.'

'It sounds like fun, and it'll help me get to know London a bit better!' Zara was really pleased about this, she really had to get out there and start finding her way around London.

'And Victoria will pay all your travel expenses when you are doing it, so you can charge your weekly travel card if you do a lot of mystery shopping in a week.' Rob added this extra benefit of mystery shopping to the conversation.

'Great, that'll save me a bit, if I get that covered for the next few weeks... more money for shoes.' Zara was delighted, she was counting the days until her first pay day and she was dying to brush up her image, she felt so "country" compared to everyone she met.

'That's the spirit!'

Things were looking up for Zara in St Martins Lane WC2.

In EC1 things were slightly less bright and breezy. *I can barely stay awake in here today. I think I'll nip out and buy those shoes I saw in the shop around the corner... no matter how bad things get, shoes seem to solve it all. I am not happy that I got barely any sleep last night, we barely even got a thank you, and that takeaway food last night has really made me bloated today. I'm so glad that I decided to postpone my date with Peter. I feel like crap. I wonder if anyone is going to be in tonight, I fancy just going home and vegging in front of the TV, but if Charlie has the lads over that will not be an option. At least my room is far away from the living room. This day is dragging on and on. I am so bored, now that we have submitted the proposal we have to just wait. At least I can shop at my desk now without anyone knowing it... whipping out my credit card is a bit of a tell-tale sign, but window shopping is fine. I'd love to be able to do a bit of sketching… but that would be too obvious! I might invent a fake meeting and head down to get my nails done… god! I hate my job! But the money is too good to give it up!'* Penelope was getting really restless in her office. She was overtired and it was starting to get to her. There were only so many double decaf skinny lattes a girl could take in a day. There was only one thing to do… shoe shopping. Penelope made her way down to her favourite local designer shoe shop.

'Ah… new shoes! Excellent, I feel a hundred times better. I wonder if Zara is going to be in tonight. I have barely seen her since we all moved in, I have been so busy in work. I don't even know that much about her, it would be nice to actually get to know the person I'm living with! I'll give George a call and see if she wants to come over for a DVD.' Penelope was still exhausted, but she was pleased with her new purchase. She was just about to dial George's number when one of the partners dropped into her office.

'Ah Penelope… I was looking for you earlier…' Thomas, sounded serious.

'Thomas! What can I do for you?' *'Partner alert, partner alert, I hope he wasn't looking for me for long.'* Penelope perked up immediately, she didn't want to give away how tired she was when the partner was there.

'Come on in to my office, I'd like a quick word…' Thomas headed out the door and Penelope followed him.

'Shiiiit!' Penelope thought to herself as she followed him dutifully.

'Have a seat,' Thomas gestured to the seat in front of his desk as he shut the door.

'Thanks,' Penelope sighed sheepishly, she did not want to be there.

'We have been monitoring your progress, and we think that with the right mentor, you could be on track for partner.' Thomas' tone was still serious, but he finally managed a smile as he said this to her.

'Partner, is this guy high or something?!… I don't even like my job, why the hell would I want to stay here for years to make

partner!' Relief, disbelief and then gradually exhilaration flooded Penelope. It was such a surprise, and such a compliment at the same time, in her exhausted state she didn't know how to feel about it.

'Well that's very flattering Thomas, but…' Penelope was completely lost for words.

'No buts Penelope, we have been very, very impressed with your standard of work over the past two years, and we have high hopes for you here…' Thomas was not taking no for an answer.

'I can't believe I'm hearing this!' Penelope sat back into the seat.

'… so we have decided to appoint you a Senior Partner Mentor, of course you will have a say in this, but we really feel that Jeremy Eubank would be the very best candidate… he is managing less accounts these days, and he would have more time to give you guidance, would you be agreeable to that?' This was done and dusted as far as Thomas was concerned.

'Of course, that's very kind of you, and I don't really know Jeremy that well, but I'm sure he is a great candidate for a mentor.' Penelope knew that she had no choice but to agree.

'Excellent! I will have him set up an initial meeting with you next week to set the ball rolling.' Thomas beamed at Penelope.

'Many thanks.' Penelope got up to leave, and she felt like she floated back to her office in a state of pleasant shock and disbelief.

'I need a drink after that! Partner, partner! I thought he was going to give me a serious talking to for being away from my desk for more than five minutes! It's certainly very flattering, Mum would explode with pride if she got wind of this… probably best not to mention it for a while. There are practically no women partners at JLM, it would be such an honour. It means pretty much devoting the rest of my life to this place, I will have to give it some serious consideration. It's all a bit too good to be true.' Penelope sat in quiet contemplation until she was in a fit state to ring George.

'George! Hi, it's me.' Penelope struggled to get the words out.

'Penny, how *are* you?! Any men?' George was delighted to hear from her best friend.

'Is that *all* you ever think about?' Penelope laughed down the phone.

'Of course!' George retorted, as she twirled one of her long brown curls around her finger as she spoke.

'Well... I haven't met "the one" yet, if that's what you mean? I was supposed to be going on a date tonight, but I had to do an all-nighter last night in work, so I cancelled it. I look like hell,' Penelope sighed.

'But he could be *the one*!' George was so full of energy.

'I know! But he wouldn't think I was the *one* for him in this state!' Penelope rationalised as usual.

'Good point, no pretty points with zero sleep!' George agreed.

'Do you fancy coming over for a DVD, a girlie night in? I have this new housemate, and I literally haven't seen her since we all moved in together, I'll see if she wants to join us. She is completely new to London and I think it's all a bit much for her. ' Penelope was praying that George was up for a night in.

'I have a quick drinks thing after work, but I'll pop over afterwards... at about eight, maybe a bit tipsy... is that ok?' George was well up for a catch up.

'Of course, I will have the takeaway menus ready. And I've loads to tell you.' Penelope was relieved.

'Fab... see you later.' George hung up, and turned back to her Mac to finish off the design that she had been working on.

Penelope had a few more things to cover off in order to organise her night in. Their place could be full of musicians and tipsy blondes if she didn't plan this carefully.

'Hey Charlie, it's me.' Penelope was so glad that he picked up.

'Hi there, I haven't seen you all week... are you back at mum's for some tlc?' Charlie sounded concerned.

'I wish... I have been working late nights all week, and in at the crack of dawn as usual... Listen are you in tonight? I was going to have the girls over and...' Penelope began..

'I was planning on being out, but if you girls are planning on having pillow fights in your underwear then I think I could change my plans!' Charlie interrupted, he was always keen to attend any girly gatherings, so that he could be the centre of attention.

'That doesn't happen in real life! I mean really Charlie, for heaven's sake, we are just having a takeaway and a bottle of wine, but there will be chick flicks involved...' Penelope began again.

'Ok, well count me out...!' and Charlie didn't give her a chance to finish, the mere mention of a chick flick had him changing his plans back.

'Right! Do you know if Zara is going to be in? It would be good if she came for the...'

'Pillow fight!' Charlie cut in, he thought he would give it one more try.

... DVD too!' Penelope sighed.

'Can't remember whether she said she would be in or out, just give her a ring... do you have her number?' Charlie calmed down.

'No. Do you?' Penelope asked.

'No.' Charlie added.

'Ok, well I'll just have to ask her if she is home later, see ya!' Penelope was so tired at this stage. She had to hang up.

'Bye babes.' Charlie was gone.

Penelope sat in her office, in deep thought. She had a pressing issue to resolve.

This day is seriously the longest day of my entire life... it's too obvious if I nip home at five... I'll have to wait here and twiddle my thumbs until the others leave at 6.30 pm... actually, maybe... just maybe, I could get away with leaving at 6 pm. I'll chance it.' Penelope had decided now, it was worth the risk, SW4 was calling to her, and she was hoping there was a bottle of white wine in the fridge.

In Covent Garden, things were not so serious, and "face time" was not an issue. Organicom always left the office before five on a Friday, and after work drinks were well under way.

'Rob! I am not doing *anuyer* shot!' Zara slurred.

'What was that Zara? I didn't quite catch what you said there… here knock this back.' Rob couldn't hear her over the music, and handed her a B52.

'No! I'll be sick, I can barely see in front of me!' Zara was not lying, the room was moving!

'Well, there's no sense in wasting it!' Rob knocked it back.

'I had better head home now, I'm getting a bit too drunk.' Zara was having a great time but she was trying to be sensible, she dreaded the trip home sober, let alone hammered!

'Nonsense! We are only just warming up.' Rob was really getting into party mode now.

'No seriously, I have to get back, and I really can't drink another shot.' Zara had to put her foot down, she could not believe how drunk she was and it was so early.

'Alright, alright… give up then, but we will remember this on Monday!' Rob agreed with her, he knew she was right.

'Ok, see you then.' Zara was gone before anyone could change her mind. Covent Garden was a bit of a blur, there were thousands of people out drinking and on their way out. For once she was going completely against the crowd.

'I seriously thought I would never get out of there. I'm getting so hammered. I had better sober up a bit before I get home, in case any of the others are in. I would hate to stagger in like a booze hag Mmm! Chips! That will definitely help.'

Zara decided that a bit of soakage food was definitely required for the journey. Even though it took her over an hour, she was finally home. She rooted around in her bag for five minutes and finally found the key. She was expecting to go in, and collapse into bed… how wrong she was. Penelope was standing at the top of the stairs.

'Hello Zara, I'm sorry I haven't been around so much this week, I have been working crazy hours…' Penelope said enthusiastically.

'Shit! I didn't bank on Princess Penelope being in, I thought she was away, I probably stink of drink!' Zara panicked, this was not

what she had been expecting.

'… anyway, my friend George, I mean *Georgina* is coming over for a girlie night in, we are getting a takeaway, and I have three chick flicks for us to choose from…'

'Oh my god, oh my god, somebody stop her talking… I feel sick…' Zara could not believe this was happening. Penelope was talking so fast, very out of character.

'Would you like to join in…? You look like you are in for the night now anyway!' Penelope prattled on and on, she really didn't want Zara to say no, it would be a bit awkward if she just went upstairs to her room as they would be taking over the living room.

'Shit… has she noticed I'm hammered.' Zara could barely get a word in edgeways.

'That sounds great, I haven't had a girlie night in in weeks.' Zara mustered up enough sobriety to say this in an enthusiastic, but not too keen, way.

'George might be a bit tipsy, she's out after work tonight, but don't mind that!' Penelope didn't seem to have noticed that Zara was drunk, she was more concerned about warning her about George.

'Oh, that doesn't bother me at all.' *'I had better go and brush my teeth, Water!… I need water.'* Zara was delighted, if this girl George turned up drunk it would totally take the heat off her.

'Fantastic! Do you have anyone that you would like to invite over?' Penelope totally relaxed now. The evening was sorted. The wine was in the fridge. George was on her way, and it would be a lovely night in.

'I wish!' 'No thanks, everyone is out tonight… Friday night… you know the way it is.' Zara hid the truth, the fact that she didn't have any friends in London … yet.

'Of course.' Penelope was glad that she had asked, but was relieved, it would be so much nicer with just the three of them.

Zara made her way upstairs to brush her teeth and wash her face. *'That was really nice of Penelope. I don't get the feeling that she was just inviting me because I was there, I get the feeling she was actually waiting for me to come home. That's kind of sweet.*

I thought she would be out with her boyfriend, on second thought maybe she is single, why else would she be in on a Friday night.' Zara reflected as she thoroughly brushed her teeth, keen to remove any traces of the shots in Covent Garden.

When Zara went back downstairs Penelope was standing there, again, phone in hand. 'I was going to call you earlier to see what you were up to, but neither of us had your number, can I have it now?' Penelope was ready to put the number in.

'Of course, can I get yours too?' Zara hadn't realised that she didn't have Penelope's personal mobile number until this moment.

'No problem.' Penelope gave Zara her number. 'George should be here any minute... you can choose the film, I'll decide which takeaway menu we are going to rely on tonight, and George is bringing the wine.' Penelope was distracted by the takeaway menus.

'Perfect'. Zara was relieved that the most she had to do was to choose the film.

'For someone I thought I had nothing in common with, this isn't so bad! Maybe I misjudged Penelope a bit,' Zara thought to herself.

'Thank god Zara said yes, It would have been a little awkward if she didn't want to join in. I hope George isn't too pissed when she arrives, that's all we need,' Penelope thought to herself.

'Ladeeeez! You will be glad to hear that I have been saving myself for our chick flick session, I brought one bottle of red and one white,' George shrieked as she swung in through the living room door, one bottle in each hand.

'Thank god! She's not too drunk!' 'Hi there hun, this is Zara, our new housemate... Zara... George.' Penelope did the introductions.

'Lovely to meet you.' Zara said, she was relieved that George seemed to be as drunk as she was, if not slightly more so. *'Another gorgeous Londoner,'* she thought, as she discreetly looked George up and down. *'She is impossibly pretty, and her hair is gorgeous. Her skin is café au lait colour, and she has freckles!*

She's a bit Spanish looking, I wonder if she is half Spanish, I'll ask Pen later.' Zara was taking it all in.

'Ditto,' George enthused. 'So... any boys?' George shrieked. This was George's standard question. She always had a boyfriend and she wanted the same happiness for all of her friends.

'No the usual random dates, investment bankers usually... cardboard cut-outs!' Penelope was in no mood for talking about the bankers now.

'Oh dear... well myself and Frank are so in love still, this one is lasting way longer than any of the other ones, do you think he might be... the... dare I say it...?' George was slurring her words a bit.

'No! Don't say it, you'll curse it...! Let's just say, he is lovely and leave it at that!' Penelope shrieked.

'What about you Zara? Are you seeing anyone at the moment?' Penelope turned to Zara, and the two girls stared at her waiting for an answer.

'No. I had a boyfriend up until recently. We had only been seeing each other for a few months and then this job came up so I moved to London, and with the distance and everything it wasn't really worth continuing... and anyway I knew he wasn't the... oh actually I won't say it, but you know what I mean...' Zara seemed to sober up immediately as she was talking about her ex-boyfriend, and the prospect of him being "the one".

'Got it! Sounds good... two single ladies living on Abbeville Road, that's a recipe for some fun if ever there was one. Are any of Charlie's friends good looking? I remember when we were in Uni they were all posh, unwashed, rocker types, but that look is quite trendy now.' George was really enthusiastic.

'I haven't met any of them yet,' Zara added, but she was keen to learn more.

'Neither have I actually,' Penelope added.

'In that case, let's drink to ... Music... and may they all be better looking than they were in Uni.' George was always fantastic at suggesting things to drink to.

'Cheers!' they all said at once as they clinked glasses.

After more wine than was sensible on empty stomachs, apart from Zara's chips, the girls started to get a little impatient about the food. They had ordered it ages ago.

'What is taking the food so long?' Penelope paced up and down debating whether to ring up the takeaway place.

'I swear they do that on purpose' Penelope added.

'Who, the Chinese people?' George added with a mischievous grin, any excuse to turn it into a joke.

'George, now... you know they are not actually Chinese don't you?' Penelope scolded her as if she was a school teacher.

'You know what I mean, the Chinese takeaway people then!' George roared with laughter.

'I know what you mean, they say half an hour to forty-five minutes, and then they wait until you are passing out with hunger, to arrive with the food. It makes you order more in future.' Zara wasn't making any sense at all, she was completely hammered... again!

'I think I'll cancel it.' Penelope had the phone in her hand ready to dial.

'NO! We're starving' The two girls jumped up from the sofa.

'Ok, I'll give them five more minutes and then...' Penelope sighed, she had no intention of ringing to cancel, but it was so funny watching them both overreact.

'Yay! Saved by the bell!' Zara clapped her hands as the doorbell went.

'I'll get it.' Penelope headed down to collect the food.

'I'll get the plates ready.' Zara decided to try to make herself useful.

As they were all so starving, the delivery guy, who was not Chinese, only got a five-minute telling off, instead of the usual ten minutes. He was very used to dealing with people like Penelope, and he offered to not charge for delivery to cut her off mid-rant.

'Right, here we are then. Ok, so what did you order? We've got... Oh no...' Penelope began unpacking the two bags, she was not happy with what she saw.

'What!?' Zara asked.

'They have given us the wrong bloody food!' Penelope sighed, after all that, they hadn't even got their order.

'Well what is it?' George thought this was hilarious.

'If it's nice, let's just eat it anyway..' Zara thought this was the best plan.

'There is one extra bag, excellent, this looks like it could have been worth the wait. I'm not too sure what it is that we are eating, so let's just all have a bit of each one… ok?' Penelope cheered up at the realisation that the delay had actually paid off, there was indeed a silver lining to this little cloud.

'Good idea, but hurry up, I'm starving!' George was busy filling the wine glasses again.

The next thing, the front door opened. The three girls stood looking at each other in the living room and then as if he had smelled the food Charlie waltzed in sporting a cheeky grin.

'Hello ladies.' Charlie beamed at the three of them.

'Bloody typical! I bet he smelled the food. Hi Charlie, we are in the living room…' Penelope shouted out to him.

'Hi Pen, Zara… and who is this?' *'She's cute,'* Charlie thought to himself.

'Charlie, you remember George from Uni don't you?' Penelope was not in the mood for this, she would have to get the message across to Charlie that George was not single before he cosied up beside her on the couch!

'Of course, I didn't recognise you with your hair up, sorry about that George…' George had scraped her hair back to dive into the Chinese takeaway. Charlie regained composure, George was well and truly in the friend zone, no chance of any action!

'No problem, would you like some food… you are just on time,' George offered.

'Well if you have extra…' Charlie had already helped himself to a glass of wine when he said this.

'Of course we do, here grab a plate.' Zara offered him a plate.

'What is it?' Charlie peered into the bags.

'Some kind of Chinese food.' Penelope sighed, she didn't have the energy to tell the story again.

'What do you mean? Have you forgotten what you ordered already?' Charlie sounded confused.

'No! We got the wrong food, and it took so bloody long to get here, that we decided not to send it back... so it's miscellaneous Chinese food.' Zara offered an explanation.

'Sounds good to me.' Charlie couldn't' care less as long as it was food.

'Have you had much response for the room?' Penelope asked Charlie.

'My phone literally hasn't stopped ringing... are we still all on for next Saturday to see people?' Charlie answered between mouthfuls of food.

'Yep, otherwise we will have to start paying for the room with next month's rent.' Penelope was keen to get the new housemate situation sorted asap.

'I have made arrangements with any of them who sound half normal, for different times in the morning. Are we narrowing it down to a guy or a girl now, or should we wait and see what they are like? Because there was one girl who sounded lovely...' Charlie looked all dreamy as he said this.

'What do you mean by "lovely"?' Penelope sounded suspicious.

'Well you know, nice voice, interesting *hobbies*...' Charlie grinned.

'Oh really, what kind of hobbies?' Zara thought he was serious.

'Well, I don't know if you would classify pole dancing as a *hobby* or a *career path*, what do you think Zara?' Charlie roared laughing,

'Oh I don't know...' Zara winked back at him. George nearly choked on a forkful of food that she was trying to swallow before laughing.

Once they had all stopped laughing, and George had

stopped choking, Penelope decided to set a few ground rules. 'OK, let's get this clear from the start, no pole dancers, I don't care if she's a bloody nun during the day, no girls with poles, got that?' Penelope wagged her finger at him as she said this.

'But…' Charlie cut in.

'No buts, no poles, no baby oil!' Penelope shrieked and they all burst out laughing again.

'Ok,' Charlie sighed sheepishly, utterly defeated.

'Other than that I don't think we should narrow it down yet, let's just see what they are like.' Charlie added, he could be surprisingly sensible sometimes.

'Ok, do you know anyone looking for somewhere George?' Penelope asked.

'Not at the moment Pen, but I'll let you know if I do, I'll send an email out at work and let you know if anyone replies,' George said enthusiastically.

'I'll draft an email in work on Monday with the rent and a description of the room and all that stuff, and I'll send it to you George and you can forward it on,' Penelope said.

'Penelope, could you send it to me too, there's no harm in me sending out an email in work too,' Zara added.

'That would be great if you could,' Penelope smiled at Zara. This night in had been so much fun, she knew that they would all get on like a house on fire. Fingers crossed they would find a new housemate to fit in perfectly.

Chapter 8

Monday, Monday

Zara flounced into work at ten to nine, she had cut her journey time down by fifteen minutes by getting a different train, practice makes perfect in London. That was one thing that she had learned so far.

'Well hello there... fader!' Rob was delighted to see Zara, the two of them had really hit it off, and their banter made the day go so much faster, Zara felt exactly the same.

'Hi Rob, don't you start... I haven't had my first daily cappuccino yet!' Zara had had a great weekend, and was glad of it now that a whole week of worked loomed ahead.

'Oh alright, I will give you some grace for the cappuccino, but then... no holds barred!' Rob was raring to go.

'Ok, how did the rest of Friday go?' Zara was dying for any office gossip, rumour had it that one of the girls in accounts was having an affair with the IT guy.

'Oh don't ask me! I can't remember a *thing*, I was blotto after that fatal B52 that you so cleverly avoided! The rest of the evening is all a blur, I do have the feeling that it was a great night though,' Rob chuckled.

'Did Michael come out?' Zara hoped that she hadn't missed the beautiful Michael.

'Well… he's already out dear, ha ha… no seriously, I never mix business and pleasure! I like to keep him all to myself!' Rob laughed mischievously.

'Fair enough, is he really *that* good looking?' Zara knew the answer, but she loved getting Rob going.

'Absolutely!' Rob beamed at her.

'Well, can I at least meet him? I promise I won't tempt him.' Zara had seen him once, but was dying to actually meet him properly.

'I think you can be trusted!' Rob smiled at her.

'Of course you can trust me. I'm single, I'm not pathetic… running after gay men, I mean really, even if he is *that* good looking,' Zara sighed nonchalantly.

'Yes he is *that* good looking, and even if you haven't done it before, you might start fancying gay men when you meet him. But as long as I have your word of honour, then you can still meet him.' Rob sighed dramatically.

'You have my word. How was the rest of your weekend?' Zara added.

'Good, I was in bits after Friday night, so Saturday was a day of recuperation, and then Sunday I went down the King's Road shopping. What did you get up to?' Rob enquired.

'You are not going to believe this, but I spent the rest of Friday night in with my housemate…'

'The Princess?!' Rob was shocked!

'Well yes, although I feel a bit bad about judging her so quickly now, she actually seems really nice. She had her friend over and we watched a chick flick and got a takeaway. I was so drunk when I arrived home, and all I wanted to do was go to bed, but I couldn't say no, and I actually had a really good night with them. Her friend was a bit drunk too, so it took the heat off me!' Zara added sheepishly.

'Hilarious! Was the dishy rock star in?' Rob couldn't believe this, he had such a negative picture of the Princess, it seemed that Zara had judged her too quickly.

'I haven't really seen much of him either since we all moved in, but he popped in for some takeaway, and then headed back out to the pub on Friday. It's been a bit manic, we are never all in at the same time. He seems to work in the evenings, gigs, rehearsals and all that kind of stuff, and Penelope seems to work night and day, so I don't really see that much of them. And we have to get a new housemate in too… we have another room that we need to fill,' Zara filled him in.

'I see, if I hear of anyone looking for a place, I'll let you know. When do you need to get someone in?' Rob asked

'Asap – the landlady has been really good, she has given us two weeks to find someone, I mean, I don't think that is long enough, but the others told me that things move really fast in London. She gave us some grace because there was a mix up when we moved in and Penelope and Charlie thought they had the house, when I had been told that I could move in, so we agreed to move in together. It was kind of weird the way the whole thing happened.' Zara remembered that fateful day when the two of them scared the life out of her.

'That is a lot of time to find someone, you are lucky,' Rob reassured her.

'So they were saying… so we put an ad on some internet sites, and gave Charlie's number, and then we put it in *Looter* or something too.' Zara was trying to remember the process.

'*Loot*, you mean?' Rob enquired, one eyebrow raised.

'Em, yep, that sounds about right. We've had a good few calls already. I think we are going to see loads on the same day and hopefully pick someone.' Zara was dreading it.

'That's the best way to do it, try to all be there when the people arrive, so that you can suss them out.'

'Any tips?' Zara asked.

'Unfortunately there is no way of telling really, until someone moves in, they bloody well lie when you interview them, so just rely on your instincts and you should be ok. There are no rules really, I mean they'll all tell you they are clean and all that kind of thing, but you only find out the truth when it's too late.' Clearly Rob had had some bad experiences in this respect.

'Ok, thanks, I'll keep that in mind. What have we got on today? If we are not too busy I might do a bit of mystery shopping.' Zara sighed as she opened her Outlook calendar for that day.

'I wouldn't today darling, Victoria is in terrible form, she has had her door closed all morning, that's not a good sign. I'd stick around today… make sure you are seen working away furiously.' Rob warned Zara, something was not quite right in Organicom that day.

'Ok, thanks.' Zara didn't like the sound of this.

'Even if you are not busy, make sure you look busy.' This was, as always, sage advice from Rob.

'I don't think I'll have any problems looking busy, I've loads to do.' Zara was already reading her first few emails of the day.

'Good girl!' Rob smiled at her.

Hmm scary stuff. I don't like the sound of that. It's only my second week, and the boss is in a bad mood. I must try to stay out of her way. It's a good thing I have Rob to point me in the right direction, I never would have realised that having her door closed was something to look for, I suppose that's the kind of thing you pick up after being here for a while. Come to think of it, she does usually have her door open. There's so much in between the lines stuff to learn too.' Zara realised that it was not just the facts and figures that she needed to pick up quickly.

'I'm going to head down to get the coffees, the usual?' Zara was dying to get out for a few minutes, she felt a bit tense, a bit of fresh air would help.

'Yes, lovely, I'll get them tomorrow then.' Rob smiled at her again.

Life in London was never without its daily challenges, both large and small, and it constantly seemed to Zara, that the minute she mastered one of these… another one cropped up. While English is the predominant language in the capital, 'coffee' is a secondary language that needs to be mastered immediately for survival in the big smoke. While Zara was of course fluent in English, she was really struggling with her new second language. To make things even more complicated, there wasn't a universal coffee language, there were many regional dialects, for example the Costa dialect, the Nero dialect, the Starbucks American dialect, and then there were all the independent coffee houses where anything goes… This was something else that Zara had learned very quickly.

'There are so many coffee places to choose from, and they all have their own language.. I don't think I'm really fluent in coffee speak yet. I'm trying a different coffee place each day, so that I can decide which one I like best. I like the ones where they give you free stuff, like little portions of muffin… exactly what a girl needs first thing in the morning… Now, what do I want, let's see… Rob's is easy enough, a mocha, no whip, to go… ok… I can do this…' Zara marched into the next coffee place that she saw, with her fingers crossed for free muffin portions.

'Hi there, can I help you?' the barista said enthusiastically.

'Can I have a small cappuccino, and…' Zara began.

'Wet?' the barista interrupted as he began scribbling on the takeaway cup.

'Erm' *'What the hell does that mean, oh my god, oh my god, I'm going red, and there is a huge queue behind me… help!'* Zara squirmed in her size fives, she wished that she could just disappear… A large queue of impatient Londoners had formed behind Zara within seconds.

'Wet?' the barista looked at her as if she was mad, and raised his eyes to heaven.

'Yeah, wet,' Zara muttered. *'I'll agree with him, what's the worst that can happen?'* Zara thought to herself.

'Sorry was that Short, Tall or Grande?' the barista enquired about the sizes.

'Is he speaking English? What is Grawnday?' Zara began to panic now.

'Erm, short, yes short and wet.' *'Jesus, sounds like I'm ordering porn!'* Zara struggled to get the words out, she was crimson now… almost turning purple.

'With wings?' He looked up from his cup scribbling as he said this, the marker pen perched for more details.

'*Oh my god! What is "with wins"? Or did he say "wings"? Hmm… that must mean takeaway! Fingers crossed.*' 'Yes please.' Zara managed a weak smile.

'Can I get you anything else?' The barista shoved the cup in the long queue and stared at Zara. It seemed like everyone was staring at her.

'Oh yes a mocha, to go,' Zara stated. '*And a coffee dictionary!*' she thought to herself, again time seemed like it was standing still.

'A what? Sorry, I didn't catch that…?' Even the barista started to get a bit impatient with Zara now.

'A mow-kka-cheeno, to go?' Zara over-pronounced the word.

'Oh, I'm sorry… a mochaccino, what size?' Finally the message was getting through.

'*Oh no, here we go again, what did he say they were?*' 'A big one please,' Zara sighed.

'So that's one short wet cap to go, and one grande mochaccino to go… whip?' He looked up from his cup scribbling again..

'*More porn!*' Zara thought to herself. 'No whip,' she muttered, '*or not,*' 'Thanks'. Zara felt relieved that she had finally given her order and that she could move to the end of the counter to wait for her drinks.

'You can collect your drinks at the end of the counter, have a nice day.' The barista perked up now that he could move onto the next customers.

'Thanks,' Zara said over her shoulder.

'*Now… that wasn't too difficult after all. I think I'm finally getting the hang of coffee speak.*'

'One tall skinny mocha, with whip!' The next customer gave her order

'Two grande americanos,' followed by the next customer.

'*More porn!!*' Zara thought to herself.

'One short soy latte and one, tall, chai tea, latte.' The barista shouted down as he plopped the freshly made coffees onto the counter for collection.

'One short wet cappuccino and one grande mocha, no whip.' The drinks kept coming... like a caffeine and steam conveyer belt.

'Yay, that's mine... Oh no! Rob's is huge! And mine is tiny! That wasn't what I thought I was getting! Better luck next time Zara!' Zara's bubble burst the minute she saw the size of the drinks, clearly she had not ordered the right thing at all. One thing is for sure she would never go back into that coffee place again. She trundled back to the office, and managed to muster a big smile for Rob by the time she got to her floor.

'Thanks love, I take it you thought I was thirsty! It'll take me all day to drink that... and look at your teeny little one!' Rob was gasping for coffee, but he wasn't quite sure that he could get through that huge one.

'I know, I think they got the sizes wrong, but they were really busy and it would have taken ages to change them...' Zara shrugged, she started to go a little red again as she remembered the whole ordeal.

'I know what you mean, tempers can get a bit frayed when you have a big queue of people waiting for their first coffee.' Rob was dying to get stuck into his.

'Exactly!' Zara was glad that the conversation ended there.

'While you were out Victoria called a staff meeting, for 11 am,' Rob whispered dramatically.

'Oh, does she normally do that? Did she say what it was about?' Zara sounded a bit shocked, she did not like the sound of this.

'No, but it's not a great sign, she usually gives us at least a day's notice, and sends an email out, but she just came out and announced it.' Rob was still whispering, bashing away on his keyboard, pretending to be emailing.

'Hmm, I wonder what it's about?' Zara tried to sound calm.

'We'll soon see...' Rob added.

'Damn! It's half ten already. No time for emailing, I really look forward to my Monday, weekend post-mortem emails with the girls, I really, really miss them... better not think about that

now... I have to get some of these things out of my inbox before the meeting, I don't want it to look like all I do is go out and get the coffee.' Rob's comments had made Zara feel really on edge, she was dreading the staff meeting.

At 11 am Victoria stood at the top of the fourth floor, next to the window. All of the staff gathered around in front of her, standing a good two metres away from her.

'Good morning everyone, first of all, apologies for the short notice for this meeting, I'm afraid I have a bit of urgent news that I need to share with you all. All of the general managers were called into a meeting yesterday after the trade show in Birmingham, it seems that our sales forecasts were a little... optimistic... and we are not reaching our targets at all...' Victoria's speech went on.

'Oh no, what does that mean. Why is she telling us this?' Zara felt really panicked.

'Now you are probably all wondering what this means for you personally, well... I'm afraid to say that we are going to have to cut back on some of our expenditure, and seeing as how our London office is the most expensive, the main cutbacks are going to come from London. I just wanted to let you know as soon as I found out, we have not made a final decision yet, but we have a few options on the table, such as relocating our HQ to Manchester or Birmingham. There also may be some redundancies in certain departments, and all non-essential expenditure will be stopped effective immediately...' Victoria went on and on.

'Now I know that's not good, oh no, does this mean that I am going to lose my job? I have just moved into the house, and paid the huge deposit and everything, oh no, oh no, oh no!' Zara could not hear the words anymore, her head was spinning with worry.

'... I will pass on any information to you as soon as I possibly can, but at the moment I'm afraid that is all I can tell you. I'm very sorry to be the bearer of bad news, but I thought it was best that you all should know, sooner rather than later.' Victoria looked very serious as she said this, and she looked resigned to the fact that she would indeed have to speak to everyone individually in the most unpleasant of circumstances.

'Rob! What do you make of all that?' Zara was dying to find out what Rob thought.

'Nothing I haven't heard before dear, this is *London* after all, this kind of thing happens all the time… offices opening and closing.' Rob was not worried, Zara could not understand this at all!

'I thought everyone was taking it a bit too well, I nearly died when she mentioned moving the office… does that mean we would have to move too, or would they just get rid of us altogether?' Zara was speaking very quickly.

'Only time will tell, although she did mention redundancies, so that is definitely on the cards… get your CV out there darling, just in case.' Rob was busy on email to his friends, this was hot gossip and he definitely needed to get the feelers out to see what jobs were out there.

'Bloody hell, it took me long enough to get this job, I can hardly believe that I could get made redundant after such a short time working here. Look on the bright side, it might not happen, it's only a maybe… I'll get my CV together just in case.' Zara was absolutely miserable, it seemed that every little mountain she climbed there was something else big waiting at the top to knock her back down. It constantly felt like one step forward, two steps back.

'What are you going to do?' Zara sidled over to Rob's desk, she was determined not to cry.

'I'm not sure, I think we'll be ok, but I'll get my CV ready anyway. I won't worry about anything until something actually happens. I'm always registered with a few temping agencies anyway, if the worst happens then at least you will be placed straight away and the money is pretty good… I can give you the names of a few marketing ones if you like?' Rob was super busy, it seemed that this potential threat had really pushed him into gear to get his act together.

'Thanks that would be great.' Again, Zara was not sure about this, but every little helped.

'I can't tell Mum and Dad about this, they were so proud of me getting a job in London, and they lent me the money for the deposit on the flat. I'm convinced they think I'm some big city executive. I don't really know Pen and Charlie enough to talk to them about it, god… I really miss my mates! They are all expecting grand tales from the City, and I can't really go back and tell them all I have lost my job. Maybe it won't happen to me, fingers crossed anyway. I have my CV up to date at least, I just used it a few months ago to get this job, I'll start sending it out tomorrow… just in case.' Zara fought back the tears, and did her best to keep herself busy with her emails. That was the one good thing about email she thought to herself, you could hide your sadness behind the words…

In the City things were very different. Penelope started the week to a rather more upbeat mood.

'Good morning team, good weekend? Did you catch the rugby?' Jeremy bounded in, all ruddy faced and full of rugby commentary.

'Erm… no! Dull, dull, dull, they'll be talking about golf next… yawn.' Penelope was not impressed, she hated all this rugby talk… if only they could talk about culture, current affairs… something interesting!

'No, I missed it, got a great round of golf in though… ' Tony chimed in, keen to get in on the conversation.

'Aw! You missed a great game… a deciding try in extra time… ' Jamie bounded in, tossing a mini rugby ball.

'It was unbelievable!' Jeff arrived into the room.

Penelope yawned. *'Every bloody Monday it's the same old thing, golf, rugby waffle waffle waffle… do none of these people have lives!? How can they find that fun, grown men rolling around in the mud and getting injured for an hour and a half and walking around for hours hitting a tiny ball with a stupid stick.'* Sometimes being in an all-male environment was unbearable for Penelope, especially when they were talking about manly things like rugby, how on earth could she relate to that?!

'How about you Penelope, did you have a good weekend?' Jeff caught sight of Penelope yawning.

'Yes thanks Jeff, just took it easy, settling into my new house.' Penelope tried to sound enthusiastic in order to hide her boredom.

'Didn't catch the rugby then?' Jeff added.

'No, I missed out on that one.' Penelope feigned regret. *'On purpose!'* she thought to herself.

'What a shame, I managed to watch it at Twickers myself!' Jeff looked nostalgic.

'Right, back to business, I got a call from Hank first thing this morning, and he was delighted with the proposal that we sent to New York. He said the clients loved it and we won the business, which is potentially worth £3 million to begin with... you should all be very proud of your efforts, and to celebrate Hank is taking us all out for dinner on Wednesday... so mark that off in your diaries...' Rugby talk was over now, it was time to talk shop.

'Oh no, I hate these work things, but I suppose it has to be done... at least it will be somewhere nice, I hope so anyway. I spend enough time with these people during the day without spending the evening with them as well. What have I got in my diary today, let's see, morning shout, east coast conference call at 11 am, oh great... manicure booked in for lunchtime, I had forgotten about that voucher I got, I booked this ages ago... good plan booking it for a Monday... worst day of the week. Now a few calls to make...' Penelope went through her diary.

'Peter, hi it's Penelope..' Penelope dialled Peter's number.

'Hello Penelope, how are you?' Peter sounded surprised, but pleased to hear from her.

'Very well thank you, look I'm sorry I had to cancel our date on Friday, you know the way it is with all-nighters, and I probably wouldn't have stayed awake through dinner.' Penelope was genuinely apologetic. Peter was a really nice guy and she didn't like to mess people around.

'No need to explain, I have had a few of those myself, are you available this Friday?' Peter didn't like to spend time chatting on the phone, he got to the point straight away.

'Oh, let me just check'… *'Pause for effect, make him think I am actually checking my diary'*… 'Friday is looking good,' Penelope said smiling.

'Let's say, we go for the same restaurant this Friday, and let's see if we make it.' Peter sounded confident and relaxed.

'Good, looking forward to it.' Penelope had a good feeling about this one.

'I'll call you during the week to make arrangements,' Peter added.

'Great, talk to you then.' Penelope smiled as she spoke.

'Cheerio.' Peter was gone.

'Now he's not the best looking in the world, but he certainly seems very sweet, and not as completely dull as the rest of them. Definitely worth giving him a chance.' As with many people who work in the City, the hours are very very long, and it doesn't leave much time for socialising. Penelope used to mostly date guys from work, but she found that that wasn't ideal as she didn't seem to have that much in common with them! But, these days, if someone nice asked her out, it was definitely worth giving him a chance. It was either that, or complete singledom forever! Penelope had been single since she started working in her current job. She spent so much time in work, there was little or no time to meet anyone outside work.

'George, hi it's me.' Penelope began her daily calls by calling her best friend George.

'Penny! How are you?' George was always delighted to hear from Penelope.

'Fab, I've rescheduled with Friday night guy, the one from last week, remember?'

'Great stuff, where is he taking you?' George lived vicariously through Penelope's dating career, she was happy and settled with her lovely boyfriend and she wanted nothing more than for Penelope to find a nice boyfriend.

'The Ivy.'

'Nice… how did he get a reservation…?' George was

surprised, that was quite a nice place for a first date, and really difficult to get a weekend reservation at the last minute.

'I don't know, he knows someone, who knows someone's sister who is in PR or works in TV, something like that.' Penelope sounded a bit bored by this as she explained Peter's "network" to George!

'Lovely, what have you got on this week?' George enquired, hoping that there was a chance for the two of them to get together to catch up in person, Penelope worked such long hours these days and often had to cancel plans at the last minute.

'Nothing much, work dinner on Wednesday, date on Friday, otherwise nothing, do you fancy meeting up for drinks… say Thursday?' Penelope was hoping that nothing would crop up on Thursday afternoon to spoil her plans.

'Yippee, can we go somewhere trendy?' George was delighted, she couldn't wait to get dressed up and head out in Soho.

'Of course.' Penelope was already mentally picking out what she was going to wear… 'I'm in!'… and so was George!

Thank god! Something to look forward to… I'll have to get a nice new top. I get so sick of going on dates these days, they can be so dull and the only people I meet are in banking because I work such long hours. I'm going to have to start trying to make some more time for myself. I wonder if any of Charlie's friends are cute? I have been single now for ages, it's really making me wonder if this job is worth it, I don't want to be still single when I'm forty and say, oh yeah well, that's because I earned loads of money!

Chapter 9

Bus Stop

Why is it that when you desperately need one, like when it's lashing rain and you are late for a meeting, the bus stop is a barren wasteland, and every red object in the distance promises to be a bus, not even any bus, but the one with your number on it, and then as it approaches it shrinks and turns into some silly lorry delivering bread? But the minute your phone rings or you spot a cute guy heading in your direction, or you are in no hurry at all... three buses, all arrive at the same time... and yes, all with your number on them. This theory is tried and tested for public transport, it also seems to be true for men...

Zara arrived home from work exhausted and flopped down on the couch. She felt completely shell-shocked after the announcement that day in work and she was hoping that Penelope could reassure her... she noticed that the other two were not home yet. *'Good, I have the place to myself, I wonder if Charlie and Penelope are going to be in tonight. I might ring the girls. My phone bill is bloody huge, I ring them any chance I get. I can't tell them about my job, they just wouldn't understand, they would think I was stupid or something. I don't know what to do... I don't know what to do... I don't know what to do... oh no, here come the tears again. Oh god, I can't ring them now... I think I'll have an early one, all this stress is making me exhausted.*

I don't want the other two to see me like this. This is the first time in my life that I have had a problem and I have nobody to talk about it to.'

Zara stomped up the stairs to her room, keen to be out of sight if either of her new housemates arrived home.

Penelope arrived home an hour later..

'Good it looks like Zara is out, I might have a nice bath, it's nice to have the place to myself. Charlie won't be in until later, he's never here when we are, and is always here when we're not. I wonder what it would be like to live like that, sleeping in until midday everyday... lovely... I'm actually kind of tempted to chuck it all in and become a musician.' Penelope smiled at the thought of this. *'I hope we find someone good on Saturday, it's kind of a shame we have to get anyone in, we are all getting on fine, and when you add another person, it can all go terribly wrong if they are not nice.'* Penelope was in a great mood, she already had a lot on socially this week, so at least she would feel like her life was a little bit more her own, and a little less JLM's.

At 1 am Charlie came home from work, and he had been known to take his work home with him even at that time of the morning...

'Sshhh!' Charlie hissed at his latest "muse" as he ushered her through the door without turning the light on.

'What? Why? I don't want to shhh... what's the big deal anyway?' Melissa was quite tipsy, and seemingly completely under Charlie's spell already...

'I have two housemates, and they are asleep, and I'd like to keep it that way...' Charlie was not in the mood for any drama from this girl.

'Ok, ok, no big deal... I'll keep it down. Charlie where are you taking me?' Melissa whispered very loudly.

'My room, is that ok?' Charlie softened his tone a bit, he did not want to spoil the mood.

'Suppose so. So... do you live with the rest of the band then, and how long have you been together?' Melissa could not believe that she had kissed a musician, and she could not believe that she was in his house now – imagine if they all lived here, she could not wait to tell her friends all about it.

'Shh, come here Melanie… plenty of time for talking… in the morning.' Charlie put his arms around her and pulled her gently towards him.

'It's Melissa!' Melissa shrieked, and pulled away from him.

'That's what I said…!' Melissa was so drunk that she believed him.

'Whatever!' Melissa didn't actually care, she was having the best night of her life.

***

In EC1 Penelope sat at her desk and opened up her to do list for the day.

'*Wednesday already, the weekend is in sight. This week hasn't been too bad actually, no late nights or anything like that, nice for a change. Let's see what have I got on today, oh no! The bloody team dinner.*' Penelope had forgotten about the team dinner because she had been so busy looking forward to seeing George on Thursday.

'Good morning Penelope.' Thomas, Penelope's manager, breezed in to her office.

'Good morning Thomas.' Penelope was a little startled, he did not have a meeting scheduled with her, and he wouldn't usually just drop in. In fact it was challenging to get any time to speak with him at all, as he was usually so busy.

'I have set up a meeting with Jeremy for you,' Thomas announced to Penelope with one eyebrow raised, waiting for her reaction.

'Jeremy?' Penelope was a little shocked, this all happening very fast, it was very real, very immediate.

'Yes, Jeremy Eubank, your new mentor.' Thomas was beaming at her now, he was delighted that Jeremy had agreed to mentor Penelope.

'Oh yes, yes of course, how silly of me, I'm really looking forward to it,' Penelope gushed.

'Oh dear, I had totally forgotten about the 'Partner' conversation. I didn't think it was all going to kick off now… I was thinking, way, way into the future… oh no, I'm not sure I really want this. I can't say no though, that would be a serious career limiting move.' Penelope mused with an unwavering smile until Thomas had left her office.

Later that evening the Capital Markets team assembled in the lobby, Penelope had a change of work clothes with her for occasions such as these, but decided against using them, after all none of the guys would alter their appearance for a work dinner, then again… most of them were married, and not single and on the lookout like her!

'Ok, let's head off, two of the partners brought their drivers and we can all fit. We are meeting in the lobby in ten, everyone ok with that?' Chris announced.

'Yes, ok,' they all mumbled.

'I can't even remember where they said we were going, one of the Conran's no doubt, great, hopefully there'll be champagne, that will ease the pain of it all. I look ok I think, well, I'm not trying to impress any of them, but I suppose you never know who you might bump into…' Penelope decided that maybe it would not be so bad after all.

In no time they were seated and chatting about work, and only work. Penelope was savouring her first glass of champagne.

'Thank god for champagne, these guys are so boring… I had better make sure that I don't get drunk though… I had a tiny lunch because I knew I would be eating out, probably not the best idea to be shooting champers on an empty stomach. Oh my god, is that Richard? No, it couldn't be! I'll try to have a good look without being too obvious about it, I don't want to look like I'm checking guys out here.' Penelope leaned back on her chair and glanced sideways in Richard's direction. His profile was unmistakable, Richard was 6ft2, and terribly slim, he tended to layer clothing to bulk his wiry frame out. He had

naturally tanned skin (from all the foreign holidays growing up) and white blond hair. He had a nose that unmistakingly resembled the Royal Family set. He had ice blue eyes that complemented his blond features and tanned skin. He was an old University friend of Penelope's, she had very much fallen out of touch with him once she had started working in London. He used to tower over Penelope in University, and he had a slightly gauche quality, he was never quite comfortable in his own skin. Richard always wore expensive, conservative clothes, keen to demonstrate which "set" he was a member of. George had always been convinced that Richard fancied Penelope, but as far as Penelope was concerned he was firmly in the friend zone! He was a welcome sight on this boring Wednesday evening however. *'It's definitely him, what should I do...? Wait for him to see me and come over, or go over there? I'll have another drink and think about it. I wonder what he is doing in London? I thought he was off living in a castle in Scotland. Maybe it's not him... no, no, it's definitely him. Right I'm going over... here goes...'* Penelope slipped out of her seat gracefully, and headed towards Richard.

'Richard, I thought it was you, how are you? It's so lovely to see you.' Penelope beamed at Richard as she approached him.

'Oh my god, Penelope, how lovely to see you. That's right you work in the City don't you?' Richard seemed genuinely surprised to see her.

'Yes, yes I do, but what are you doing here... just on a visit?' Penelope enquired, the rest of Richard's party simply stared, it wasn't really the right moment for introductions, she couldn't stay away from her table for too long.

'I work in the City now too, I couldn't keep myself busy in that draughty castle, it's beautiful, but it will be more suitable for me when I retire.' Richard looked pensive as he said this.

'I know what you mean, I think I'd feel very out of the action if I lived rurally.' It was Penelope's idea of a complete nightmare! "Country pile" was synonymous with "torture chamber" as far as she was concerned. Functional wellies... yuk!

'Exactly, I certainly didn't want to become old before my time,' Richard grinned at her.

'Hmm... a bit late for that!' Penelope thought to herself.

'So when did you move here?' Penelope enquired.

'About a month or so ago, it's going well so far, living in the parents pied à terre in South Ken... how about you?' Richard shot back, keen for details.

'Oh no, the others are beckoning, I'm out for a work dinner, I think the MD is going to give a speech, I had better head back, look here is my card, please give me a call and we can catch up properly, that's my personal mobile number.' Penelope got a little flustered as she saw the MD standing up, glass in hand, she handed Richard her card, having scribbled her personal mobile number on it, and was back in her seat within seconds.

'Will do, lovely to see you again Pen,' Richard beamed at her.

'Likewise, see you soon,' Penelope sighed as she walked away.

Once Penelope was well out of earshot, Richard's brother Tarquin leant over to whisper to him.

'Richard, so was that her?' Tarquin said.

'Certainly was, and she's even better looking than I remembered...' Richard sat back in his seat with a mischievous and truly satisfied grin on his face.

'She certainly is a looker, lovely legs...' Tarquin added.

'Harry, I think I will be taking that apartment in Chelsea now, can you make the arrangements... and let me know when I can move in?' Richard wasted no time arranging a place to stay. His friend Harry had a lovely apartment going to waste!

'Should be all sorted in a week or so, I think it's actually empty..' Harry hadn't really been paying attention, he couldn't understand why on earth Richard would want to move out of a castle and back to London. He thought he was positively barking!

'Good, I'll arrange for my things to be moved down from Scotland,' Richard announced. The deal was done!

'Which hotel are you staying in down here? There is no pied à terre is there?' Harry asked, he hadn't really been listening, but he was the one who knew one of the guys on Penelope's desk in the bank, and he was the one who had told Richard that she would be here tonight.

'There is actually, but there is someone living in it. I'm at Claridge's... always Claridge's Harry, it's a family tradition.' Richard smirked, he couldn't believe his luck, the plan was going swimmingly.

'I see, well I'll sort out that apartment for you as soon as possible.' Harry was bored of this now, the deal was done, it was time to move on to other topics of conversation.

'Wow! That was great. I feel all warm and fuzzy inside. He was so pleased to see me. I'm really glad that I went over, imagine if I hadn't bothered. I hope he calls...' Penelope was delighted with her brief encounter with Richard, anything to take her mind off work. For the first time in ages she felt properly connected to her past, her pre-City days. First Charlie, and now Richard.

A couple of hours later it was bedtime for Penelope...

'Oh no, I'm so pissed... way too much champagne, and I could barely eat after speaking to Richard. Better not make too much noise...' Penelope tried her best not to make too much noise as she went up to her room.

'Oh, hello...!' She walked straight into Charlie and a girl on the stairs.

'Charlie! You gave me a fright, I wasn't expecting you to be in and... oh' Penelope shrieked, and then she realised that he was not alone...

'Em, this is, erm...' Charlie struggled to introduce the girl he was with, Penelope realised what was going on and jumped in to introduce herself first to save him the embarrassment of struggling with the girl's name.

'Oh, I see, hello I'm Penelope...' Penelope interjected.

'Hi I'm Felicity...' Felicity sounded a bit suspicious of Penelope.

'That's it! Felicity! This is Felicity.' Charlie stated a little bit too enthusiastically.

'I know she just told me!' Penelope glared at him affectionately. 'Well, nice to meet you Felicity, I think I'll stumble on up to bed, literally… sorry… Good Night.' Penelope tripped on the stairs as she was dying to get away from the two of them. It was so awkward.

'Oh my god, he couldn't even remember the poor girl's name. I don't know what they see in him. It's got to be the band thing, girls seem to be really into that in a big way. I wonder if I would fancy him if I didn't know him… hmmm, now there's food for thought. I never really thought of him that way before.' Penelope made her way on up the stairs.

Zara was still awake in bed upstairs. She had just got warm and comfortable and was ready to nod off, when the inevitable happened…

'I won't go, I can't bear getting out of my nice warm bed, no I have to pee, ok. Here goes'. Zara reluctantly headed down to the toilet. *'Oh, what's that noise? It sounds like someone is having sex in the living room! Wonder who it is? Well I'm definitely not going down to find out, oh, but it could be burglars! I'll just have another listen… nope, definitely not burglars, definitely people shagging! Must be Charlie, bloody musicians, they're all the bloody same.'* Zara was getting acquainted with life in the house very quickly indeed, she definitely didn't expect to overhear anything like that on her way to the toilet.

***

The next morning Penelope rang George first thing, she couldn't wait to tell her all of her news from the night before.

'Hi it's me,' Penelope said as George picked up the phone.

'Hi Pen, what time do you want to meet up?' George beamed as she spoke.

'Do you want to just drop into my office at about half six, and we can head down together?' Penelope couldn't wait to catch up in person.

'Good plan, have you decided where yet? I was thinking Floridita would be good, we could get something to eat too.' George was so excited too.

'Sounds lovely, let's do that then, I haven't been there in ages.' Penelope enthused.

'Ok, see you later.'

Zara bumped into Charlie on her way out the door.

'Hi Charlie, were you in the living room late last night? I got up to go to the loo and I thought I heard some gymnastics going on down there, I thought we were being burgled.' Zara decided to make light of it as she felt so uncomfortable about the whole thing.

'Yep, sorry about that Zara, it was me... you know the way it goes...' Charlie looked very sheepish as he said this.

'Indeed, oh well as long as you were having fun, that's the main thing,' Zara smiled at him.

'Oh yes, lots of fun, three times,' Charlie winked at Zara.

'Bloody hell! I didn't even know you had a girlfriend,' Zara blushed.

'Oh, no, no I don't.' Charlie realised that Zara seemed really uncomfortable.

'Oh, I see, bloody hell.' She regained composure.

'I know... that's Rock & Roll for you Zara,' Charlie grinned at her as he said this.

'Bloody hell!' It was at moments like these that Zara couldn't believe that this was her new life in London, this would never happen in her mum's kitchen back home!

'We're looking for a new singer for our band, we think it would enhance the music to have girl on board, and I've met quite a few hotties at the auditions.' Charlie was explaining the process to Zara.

'You're terrible!' Zara thought this was quite funny actually.

'No, no, I would never sleep with someone if I thought that she was going to get into the band, mind you I don't tell them that though.' Charlie winked at Zara again.

'You're hilarious!' Zara giggled.

'I like to think so. Actually we have loads of people to see on Saturday for the room.' Charlie thought this was great, it was probably one of the first actual conversations that they had had that wasn't small talk.

'No pole dancers I hope?' Zara teased him.

'None that I know of anyway,' he shot back at her.

'Hopefully we'll find someone nice.' She sounded a bit more serious now.

'I'm sure we will.' Charlie was reassuring.

Zara made her way on out the door.

That could have been so embarrassing if he wasn't so chilled about it. I hope I didn't come across as too much of a prude, sometimes I'm so bloody naïve, maybe it's because I have no brothers... I just don't get it. Looks like living here will be an education. Fingers crossed I don't lose my job and have to leave London really soon, hmm am I actually admitting to myself that I want to be here now? One minute I'm dying to go home and the next I actually want to stay here... make your mind up Zara!'

***

Later on that evening George and Penelope had just arrived at 100 Wardour Street in W1. Floridita was absolutely buzzing, even this early on a Thursday night. The mojitos and cuba libres were already flowing.

'This is great fun George, well done for deciding to come here. I haven't been out drinking midweek in ages, I've been so busy in work... you know the way it goes.' Penelope was really enjoying the champagne cocktails that they were knocking back like water.

'I know what you mean, and going out midweek really makes the week go much faster don't you think?' George was a big fan of making the weekend come around a bit faster.

'I couldn't agree more. It's so nice to be in the land of the living, and not in a suit. I usually just go home and go straight to bed, but it's nice to be in jeans. So it's usually just suits, gym gear and jammies all week for me until the weekend.' Penelope was loving the disconnect from work.

'Do you not have *dress-down Fridays*?' At George's office they were allowed to wear what they liked any day, but especially on Fridays.

'No, they really don't know how to do casual at our place, there'd be no point. They did try to introduce it, but they all kept coming in in suits. So they dropped the whole idea. Casual would not be a good idea in an investment bank.'

'That's a shame. We only have to be suited and booted if we have client meetings, if not it's smart casual, and then dress-down Fridays. I love those, you can go out straight after work in your own clothes and not in your work "uniform"… it makes Fridays more fun somehow, working in jeans,' George smiled.

'God, George, there are some really yummy guys here…' Penelope could not believe the amount of well dressed, interesting looking guys around her, it was such a contrast to the suited and booted crowd at dinner the night before.

'Well, I haven't really been looking, but now that you mention it… yum…' George had a good look around.

'Look at that bloke over there with the black hair, he looks like a young Antonio Banderas with longer hair… I love that "growing the hair" look, you know it's so supposed to look like that on purpose. Nice clothes too, hmmm, a bit too nice actually, do you reckon he might be gay?' Penelope was checking out one guy in particular, in a non-obvious way of course! He really stood out.

'No, not by the way he's looking at you anyway.' George had a totally different perspective, she could see over Penelope's shoulder.

'Is he looking, I didn't notice at all…?' Penelope whispered to George.

'Ah, yes, but only when he's sure that you are not looking, but I see everything… eyes in the back of my head you know, give him a smile if you catch his eye… and he might come over…' George was always very wise about men.

'Yes, mum!' Penelope agreed.

'He is bloody gorgeous actually.' George had a better view now that Penelope had got off her stool.

'I just need to pop to the loo,' Penelope whispered as she brushed past George.

'Ok, don't be long, I don't want to look like a pickup at the bar.' George sounded serious.

'Don't worry, I'll be quick.' And with that Penelope was gone.

George stared into her cocktail and played with the napkin, she was miles away until she was rudely awakened…

'Hi, I'm Alyx, Alyx Stuart-Bruges, I was just wondering… is your friend seeing anyone at the moment? I didn't want to strike up a conversation and offend… if her boyfriend is here somewhere.' The guy who had been checking Penelope out headed straight over to George when he saw that her gorgeous blonde friend had left her alone.

'Well, Alex…' George was a bit taken aback by this. He certainly was direct!

'*Alyx!*' Alyx repeated. '*Why on earth do English people always get it wrong!*' he thought to himself.

'Sorry, Ah-leeks.' George made an effort to pronounce his name properly, which was no mean feat after a couple of Bellinis. 'Very wise of you to ask in advance… and the answer is no, she is not seeing anyone at the moment, as far as I know. If you stick around for a minute, she should be back and I'll introduce you…' George was being very organised about this, and sobered up momentarily.

'Thanks, that would be great, and your name is?' Alyx remembered his manners.

'George.' She shook his hand.

'Pleasure to meet you. Your name is a little unusual, is it Welsh?' George didn't know what else to talk to him about.

'French actually, mother's side of the family, nobody can ever pronounce it properly.' Alyx gave her a winning smile.

'And what do you do for a living then?' George wanted to get as much information out of him as possible to see if he was a "suitable candidate" for her best friend. Alyx was doing pretty well so far.

'I'm a lawyer, not as dull as it sounds though, I specialise in entertainment, the music industry mainly…'Alyx was quick to mention that he wasn't some boring lawyer.

'I see, sounds fabulous, brainy and glamorous, oh here she comes…' George beamed back at Alyx. He certainly had her seal of approval, so far so good.

'Pen, you were gone for so long… I have made a new friend, and he is just dying to meet you… Pen, meet Ah-leeks.' George was loving this flurry of excitement on their midweek girly night out. She grinned as she introduced them.

'Hello Alyx, I'm Penelope.' Penelope gave him a big smile, but managed to remain composed.

'The pleasure is all mine…' Alyx was a worthy opponent, also remaining calm.

'Not Alex then? Ah-leeks is it?' Penelope was really interested in his name. She loved slightly unusual names. She was surrounded by too many Williams, Johns and Roberts… at work. Dull, dull, dull!

'Well technically yes, it's French actually, but you can call me Alex if it makes you more comfortable. The story goes that granny couldn't spell Alex properly so every generation is stuck with the name Alyx…' Alyx wanted to make Penelope more comfortable.

'No, no, Alyx is fine. And what do you do?' Penelope enquired.

'I'm a lawyer…' Alyx began…

'Oh no! Boring, boring, boring!' The smile literally fell off Penelope's face as he said this.

'Oh, your face dropped there… it's not as boring as it sounds. I specialise in the music industry… lots of perks,' Alyx added.

'Now, that's better…' Penelope's smile slowly etched its way

back onto her face.

'That sounds really interesting. Do you get to meet the stars? Are they difficult?' Penelope was really interested now.

'Yes I do, I work closely with a few big stars. I can't name names of course, and no they are not difficult, we wouldn't work with anyone who was difficult. What about you Penelope, what do you do?' Alyx wanted to leave the rest of this conversation for next time, hopefully if they got to meet up again.

'I'm in banking, Capital Markets mainly, not Rock & Roll, but it pays the bills.' Penelope began with a sigh…

'Em, hello… remember me…?' George interrupted, she was getting seriously bored. Penelope and the gorgeous Alyx were rapidly becoming engrossed in their conversation and had forgotten she was even there.

'Oh sorry George, I nearly forgot about you there…' Penelope literally had forgotten about George, she was so locked into the conversation with Alyx.

'Would you two ladies like a drink?' Alyx decided to lighten the mood.

'That would be lovely.' Penelope smiled at him again.

'I can see you are both drinking Bellinis? Same again?' Alyx was on top form now.

'Yes, yes please.' George smiled at him, as she was finishing the dregs of hers.

'Here you are,' Alyx turned to them and placed the drinks in front of them. 'I'm afraid I'm going to have to go back over to my friends. They have been waving frantically there for a few minutes. Penelope, I was just wondering if I could get your number, maybe you would like to come out for dinner or a drink sometime…?' Alyx was not leaving without her number.

'Well, I'm not in the habit of giving my number out to people in bars, but I think I'll make an exception for you, you seem like a nice fellow…' Penelope handed him her card.

'Great, thanks, lovely to meet you both.' Alyx made eye contact with both of them, and then he was gone.

'Likewise,' Penelope smiled at him.

'Bye *Ah- Leeks*... ... ...' George called after him, over-pronouncing his name and slightly swaying on her bar stool. She was a bit tipsy now, and loving all of this drama.

The minute Alyx had gone, Penelope broke into a warm smile, she was practically dizzy she fancied him so much.

'My god you're cool Pen, if I had been in your shoes, I would have been weak at the knees. He is absolutely gorgeous, I've never seen a guy with a face that beautiful, he is stunning! He's almost more beautiful than you!' George winked at Penelope as she said this. Penelope nearly choked on her Bellini.

'Oh my god, do you think?!' Penelope grimaced. 'Thank god for makeup' she shuddered at the thought of Alyx being more beautiful than a woman.

'He's very manly though. That jaw, and the jet black hair... and I know we couldn't see them, but did you see those *arms* lurking under the jacket.'

'I did indeed!' George announced triumphantly. The girls had had their farcical checklist since they were teenagers, which no man was actually meant to live up to. '... and I think he looked about 5ft11... don't you think?' The girls had decided years ago that this was the ideal height for the ideal man, not too tall, not too small. Particularly as Penelope was 5ft9, she needed a bit of wiggle room so that she could wear heels without towering over him.

'I think he probably was, but it's only when you get really up close to someone that you can actually tell...' Penelope winked at her as she said this.

'I don't think we have ever met anyone who ticks all of the boxes!' George mused. 'I mean we set the bar impossibly high, and the checklist was always a bit of a *joke*. I never thought you would actually meet the perfect man.'

'Now George, he's not the perfect man... you can't judge a man on looks alone,' Penelope chimed. 'Although the clothes do maketh the man,' Penelope giggled, slightly drunk from the alcohol and the excitement.

'Funny name, what's that all about?'

'Like he said, it's French. One of my cousins is called Alyx. My aunt is French… George, I think I'm in love.' Penelope felt like she was floating.

'Me too…! I mean, I would be if I were you. He does look kind of foreign, but not really. He has definitely got something. Wow! Well done! A good team effort there if I may say so myself.' George was delighted with herself. She could not have planned the whole thing better if she had tried.

'Yes, well done George, I couldn't believe it when I came back and he was here chatting to you, how on earth did you manage that?' Penelope needed details.

'I did nothing, he just came over when you went to the loo, and asked if you were seeing anyone, didn't want to step on anyone's toes apparently, afraid there might be a big hulk of a boyfriend lurking, ready to beat him up,' George explained.

'Wow, nice work though, I presume you told him I was single.' Penelope was very impressed.

'Afraid I had to, I didn't want him to run off before you got back,' George reassured.

'Yes, very wise, very wise indeed.' Penelope was very grateful. 'My heart sank when he said he was a lawyer.'

'I knew you'd react like that, but…' George added.

'I know, but… in the music industry, fabulous, brainy and glamorous…' Penelope interjected.

'That's exactly what I said!' George giggled.

'I hope he calls…' Penelope stared off into the distance as she said this.

'Only time will tell…'

'Let's go after these drinks, I think I've had enough excitement for one night, and it's not even the weekend… fabulous!' Penelope was thrilled with how this week was going. So much had happened and it was only Thursday night.

She found it hard to get to sleep that night when she was in bed, she was still buzzing from the champagne and the excitement.

I'm still on a high from meeting that guy tonight. It has really jolted me awake. It has just made me realise how dull the guys I normally date are. He was really smooth too. I hope he calls. I can barely sleep, I'm buzzing after all of that.'

***

The next morning Zara was up nice and early.

'Yay! It's Friday… now I hate mornings, the trek to work is bad enough, but Fridays are always good. There has to be an easier way to get to work. I might ask Rob when I get in, he's great, he has lived here for three years now, and knows it all. It's taking me over an hour to get there each day, but it's not that far on the map. A nice long shower will wake me up properly…'

Zara padded down to the bathroom, but was surprised to meet Penelope on the way.

'Good morning Zara!' Penelope was glowing.

'Penelope! You gave me a fright there, I wasn't expecting anyone to be in the bathroom, have you got the day off?' Zara was wide awake now.

'No, no, just decided to take it easy today, being Friday and all that…' Penelope breezed past Zara.

'Ok, well let me know when you are finished.' Zara didn't know what to do with herself now, she had never had to wait for the bathroom before. Penelope was usually long gone by the time Zara got up.

'Will do,' Penelope grinned at her.

'What's with her, she's like on another planet… totally glowing. Must be a man, that's the only explanation. I hope she's not too long; I need to leave here by quarter to eight. The queue to buy tickets is really long any later than that.' Zara thought to herself.

'Fi-i-nished Zara, all yours…' Penelope called up to Zara.

'Thanks.'

'Now, what to wear, let's have a look at the weather… it could rain, a bit cold, hmm, shirt and sleeveless jumper… Right time to go.' This was a daily dilemma for Zara, there wasn't really a dress code in work, and that made it actually more difficult to make the decision.

'I'm leaving now too, do you want to walk down to the Tube together?' Penelope was happy to have some company on the way down to the Tube.

'Oh, well em, I get the bus and train instead but I think I go the same way…' Zara stuttered. She still hadn't braved the Tube.

'But I thought you worked by Embankment?…' Penelope raised one eyebrow.

'Yes, I do, so…' Zara felt a bit uncomfortable, she didn't want to look like an idiot. There was only one thing to do.

'The Northern line goes right to Embankment and Charing Cross, but they are next door to each other, it only takes about twenty minutes, the bus and train must take you ages…' Penelope was trying to encourage Zara to get the Tube, she couldn't believe that she still hadn't used it.

'Well it does take quite a while actually, I'm only finding my feet in London, so I was going to try a few new ways to get into work…' Zara realised that this was a great opportunity to get the Tube with someone who knew the way.

'Well, look no further, come down to the Tube with me and you'll see.' Penelope smiled at Zara.

'Ok, thanks.' *'Oh my god, she must think I am such an idiot, I'm really scared of the Tube, I can't let her know that though.'* Zara tried to hide her panic as they both headed down Abbeville Road towards Clapham South.

'Pen, I just need to buy a ticket…' Once they got to the station, Penelope swiped her oyster card and marched straight through the barriers.

'Do you not have a travel card?' Penelope called over the barrier to Zara.

'What do you mean?' Zara sounded confused.

'You can get them weekly, monthly or annually, and you just swipe it every time you travel, it works out much cheaper that way.' Penelope waved her card at Zara.

'I didn't know about that, what should I ask for?' Zara was pleased at this development, this would save her ages each day.

'Weekly, zone one and two.' Penelope called back to her.

'Right, thanks.' *I remember Rob talking about travel cards when he was talking about mystery shopping, now I finally know what he meant. Penelope must think I'm such an idiot! Oh no! escalators, I feel like I'm going to be sick, it's so high up… ah!'* Zara was faced with the highest escalators that she had ever seen, her tummy did a little flip as she looked down.

'Looks like we are going to have to squeeze in here…' What Penelope was suggesting sounded ludicrous to Zara, the Tube was so full, there was no way they could squeeze into that space.

'What! Is she mad! I would never fit in there … too late, she's grabbed me… I swear to god I have never been this close to a bunch of strangers, and I hope that's someone's umbrella digging into my back.' Zara plastered a fake smile onto her face, she was horrified at this new experience. This was actually worse than she had imagined it.

'Right so, I need to go to Blackfriars, so I'll be getting out at Embankment too, but I go on another line then, will you find your way from Embankment?' Penelope was completely calm, this was having a calming effect on Zara.

'I have my *A to Z* with me…' Zara still looked a little worried.

'Where do you usually get off?' Penelope asked.

'Charing Cross.'

'Well Charing Cross is beside embankment, you just head straight out of the Tube and then you come to Charing Cross.'

'Oh, I had no idea, they look so far away on the Tube map.' Zara was surprised to hear this.

'That's not representative of where things really are!' Penelope chuckled.

'Oh, ok.' *'God my nerves are in tatters down here, and I'm so hot, it seems to be going about a hundred miles an hour!'* Zara was still not thrilled with the idea of being on the Tube. She felt like the journey would never end, but in no time they were at Embankment.

'Right here we are… finally.' Penelope grabbed Zara gently by the arm to make sure she got out ok.

'*What a relief, I couldn't have stuck it much longer*' 'Cool, thanks for showing me the way.' Zara was relieved to be out of there.

'No problem, see you later. Don't forget we have all the potential housemates coming tomorrow.'

'How could I! Thanks again Pen.' Zara felt like running towards the exit, she felt so claustrophobic.

'*Shiiiiiiiiiiiit, how the hell do you get out of here? Ok follow the crowd, yes! A "Way Out" sign. I must look like such a tourist! Finally, fresh air!* Zara gasped as she reached street level. *My bag nearly got caught in the ticket barrier, what a nightmare... now what time is it?... oh, it's only twenty-five past eight... I am soooooo early, this is hilarious. I may as well go on in anyway.*' Zara felt completely lost when she got outside of Embankment station, but she consulted her *A to Z* and in no time at all she was on her way to work.

'Hello Zara, you're in early,' Victoria greeted Zara as she came in.

'Hello Victoria, loads to do, you know the way it is.' Zara was delighted with herself.

'Indeed, indeed I do.' Victoria beamed at her.

'*Excellent, already impressing the boss, that's made my day. I'll go and email the girls, pay day today too, yippeeeeee!*' Zara just knew that today was going to be a great day.

'Morning Rob!'

'Hello fluffy bunny, how are you on this lovely pay-... I mean Fri-day...?' Rob flounced in.

'Fabulous! You?' Zara replied

'Glowing! You?' Rob grinned back at her.

'Ecstatic! You?' Zara shot back.

'Oh here, this could go on all day, let's just say we are both fabulous and yippee it's Friday and woo hoo it's pay day, drinkies tonight after work?' Rob announced this dramatically.

'Definitely, it's even better for me, it's my first official pay day.' Zara beamed at him.

'Excellent, let's see if the whole gang are coming out.' Rob did the rounds to rally the troops for after work.

'This day is flying by, everyone is in great form. It seems like they've all forgotten about the potential redundancies, I suppose there is nothing we can do about it until they make another announcement. Oh hello, what's this, an email from Matt, I had almost totally forgotten about him. I always wonder whether we would have stayed together if I hadn't had to move to London, I wonder if he's seeing anyone… hmm.' Zara was having the best day in work so far, in no time at all it was approaching 5 pm.

'Come on Zara! It's your first pay day, you have to have a B52, it would be *rude* not to, it's Happy Hour!' Rob was tempting Zara with a B52.

' Go on then, just the one! Yum! Tastes like chocolate… heaven.' Zara knocked back the sickly sweet shot in one go, she felt like she was in heaven.

'Now, do you see what you have been missing?…' Rob grinned at her

'Totally. Another round?' Zara was gone to the bar in a flash.

'Yay!' Rob clapped his hands.

'How many have we had now?' A few more rounds later and Zara was starting to feel the effect of all of the alcohol.

'No idea, loads, lost count, I feel so drunk.' Rob slurred.

'Me too, nearly time to go home.' Zara struggled to speak.

'Definitely. Are you heading back to Charing Cross?' Rob asked.

'Yes, well Embankment actually…' Zara was trying to convince herself as she said this.

'So you have lost your fear, finally took the plunge… underground?' Rob enquired.

'Well, not so much jumped but was pushed… marched down to the Tube station by my housemate…' Zara explained.

'The Princess?' Rob was on the edge of his seat, he loved a bit of bitching!

'The very one, and it is so much quicker on the Tube, I'm sure I'll get used to it eventually.' Zara was seriously regretting labelling Penelope so quickly. Sure… she was very different to anyone Zara had ever met, but that didn't make her a bad person. The label "Princess" was sticking a bit too much.

'Oh you don't have to tell me love, I know, it zips around London in no time, it's the only way to get away from the traffic.' Rob smiled at Zara.

'Right, let's go, before we pass out.' Zara was glad to be a bit tipsy, it helped her nerves about getting the Tube.

'Hmm, the Tube is not so bad when you're drunk, it's not as packed now either. Oh, oh, am I at my station already? That was quick. I hope I can remember my way back home...

'... Ah finally bed... lovely... I love London...' Zara dozed off with a warm fuzzy feeling about London, finally... she was very happy with her new life.

Chapter 10

Quest for the Fourth Quarter

'Oh my head, what was I thinking?!… ah, it's too bright, water, I need water… uh, I think I'm going to be sick. That is the last time I have five B52s in a row, I had nothing to eat either, no wonder I feel so rotten. I have to be human again by eleven, all the potential housemates are starting to come then.' Zara struggled out of bed and made her way down to the kitchen.

'Morning Zara, bloody hell, what happened to you?' Charlie barely recognised her.

'Oh, hi Charlie… a combination of high spirits, lack of sense and multiple B52s…'

'Nasty!'

'I know, I'll be ok in a while, I don't want to be in bits when the housemates start coming.' Zara was bracing herself for the impending toast.

'Oh great, you're both up… I have made a list of the kind of questions that we should ask the people to suss them out, you know, make sure we get the same info from everyone… I printed these out in work, so cross off any of the questions you think are ridiculous…' Penelope had a list in her hand, ready for the potential housemates.

'She is so organised, it's unbelievable…' Zara thought to herself.

'Thanks Pen, this will be a great help.'

'More of an *aide-memoire*, we are going to see so many of them, we'll need some way of remembering who's who.' Penelope handed them a list.

'God, she's brilliant, how does she even think of these things, I probably would have just picked the first one that looked ok… I want to be like her when I grow up… but for now, I just want to feel human again.' Zara stared down at her toast, trying to muster the courage to lift it up and to put it into her mouth.

'Charlie, this is the plan… if you wouldn't mind giving the first few the quick tour, and then bring them back to the living room for… well… question time really. I will do the next few tours, and by the look of poor Zara, the couch is the only place for her.' Penelope smiled over at Zara.

'Ok that's cool' Zara was relieved as she sat staring at her untouched toast.

Eleven o'clock came around really quickly and Zara had managed to look, but not feel, human again.

'Eleven o'clock, everyone ready?' Penelope was armed with her questions and ready to go.

'Yep,' Zara sighed.

'Yep, pen loaded and ready for battle,' Charlie laughed gripping his pen.

'Here's the first one now, let's see, should be Angelica, and says here Swedish?' Penelope looked over at Charlie.

'Yep, she's first.' He nodded back at her.

'She better not be that pole dancer!' Penelope looked very stern.

'Relax, no pole dancers… Pen, Jesus, take a chill pill.' Charlie was secretly hoping that she wasn't the pole dancer, otherwise he would be in trouble!

'Hello, I'm Penelope, this is Charlie, he'll just give you a quick tour… is that alright?' Penelope let the first girl in.

'Oh, yes thanks, nice to meet you…' Angelica, a tall blonde Swedish girl, gave Penelope a firm handshake and a warm smile.

'Ok, Zara, the first one is here, a girl, Swedish, she looks nice... get your questions ready.' Penelope joined Zara in the living room as Charlie showed Angelica around.

After a quick tour Charlie brought Angelica into the living room.

'Angelica, this is Zara... now we just have a few questions to ask you... Do you smoke?' Penelope gazed over at Angelica as she asked the first question.

'No,' Angelica answered enthusiastically.

'Have any pets, or strange hobbies we should know about?' Penelope continued.

'No pets, and no odd hobbies, I quite like socialising and I do yoga and go to the gym a lot, I work for a women's magazine...' Angelica went on for about twenty minutes trying to sell herself to the housemates.

'Well, what do we think of her?' Once Angelica had left, Penelope turned to the other two.

'Bloody gorgeous!, I mean, she seemed ... nice...' Charlie tried, and failed, to hide his enthusiasm.

'I'll bet you do, but seriously, looks aside, I liked her, I'd say she'd fit in well.' Penelope agreed that she was a good candidate.

'Me too, but anyway we have loads more to see, I'm just trying to stay awake here.' Zara added, the pale green colour had completely faded from her face, and she was starting to look a bit more alive.

'Three girls in one house might be a bit much though, do you not think we should go for another guy Charlie?' Penelope was trying to be sensible about it.

'Nah, the more girls the better...' Charlie grinned at the two of them.

'Oh my god! Is that all you ever think about?' Penelope gasped.

'I'm a bloke, it's what we *do*!' Charlie assured her.

'Ok, calm down, the next one is here... this should be Gerard?' Penelope headed down to open the front door. 'Oh no, it's a girl, she must be... Louise?' Penelope got a little flustered as she realised the list was now out of order if this person was early, and the guy who was supposed to be next was a little late.

'Yep, looks like we'll have to do these two together... we'll wait for Gerard to arrive and Charlie you take her on the tour, if he gets here while she's still here, we'll do the questions with him first, ok?' It was getting a bit complicated with different people arriving at the wrong times.

'Good idea. God Penelope, you are so efficient, were you always like that?' Zara was genuinely impressed.

'More or less, the job that I do at the moment demands that I'm super organised all the time.' Penelope shuddered internally at the thought of work. 'I've done this searching for housemates thing a few times before, and it really pays to have notes after they are gone, and a plan before they arrive.' Penelope was chatting away as she crossed the names off her list.

'That's him now, what was his name again...? Gerard?' Penelope checked her list of names and ticked him off.

'So... tell us a bit about yourself...' Zara began...

'Well, I'm the lead singer in this new band and...' Gerard began to tell the girls all about himself and his band.

'Oh no! Not another one! I couldn't cope with living with two Charlies... between the two of them they'd turn this place into a groupie den. I remember what it was like when we were all in Uni.' Penelope thought it would be a bad idea to have two musicians in the house.

'He's gorgeous, even in my weakened state I can see that... actually no! Maybe I'm still a bit drunk from last night... beer goggles...' Zara had other ideas.

'... and I'm a semi-professional snow boarder, so for a month or two in the winter...'

'Ok, I changed my mind back now, drunk or not, that body is probably amazing if he's a snow boarder...' Zara had perked up.

'No, I don't have any pets at all...' Gerard continued.

'Ok, Gerard, we'll give you a call later if we shortlist you... if you don't hear from us by 6 pm, then you probably haven't made the list, ok?' Penelope was trying to be rational, but he was absolutely gorgeous, she was really struggling.

'OK, great, I have about five places to see today, I'll call you if I choose one of them.' Gerard gave them a winning smile and then left them to it.

'Hi Louise this is Zara, and we all just moved in here a few weeks ago... tell us a bit about yourself...'

... The interviews went on and on and on, for the rest of the morning.

'Thank god he thought of giving us a break for lunch, how are you feeling there Zara... still alive?' Penelope was getting irritable. She felt like she had had the same conversation nine times already today, and she was sick of trying to suss people out.

'Just about... how many more are there? This is like the longest day of my life, and it's really tiring... trying to suss people out, and smile all the time... and to be quite honest I'm trying my best to keep my breakfast down.' Zara smiled weakly.

'Red Hula Hoops and Coke is my foolproof hangover cure... here we'll get Charlie to pick some up when he goes to the shop...'

'Does that really work?' Zara asked.

'Totally... it's a miracle cure, I discovered it by accident once in Uni... never looked back since.' Penelope was convinced that it worked.

'Ok, I'll give it a go, one thing is for sure, I can't feel any worse than I do now... how many more are there to see today?' Zara enquired.

'I'm afraid to ask him! And I bet he is flirting like mad with all the girls when he shows them around... they'll run a mile!' Penelope sighed.

'I know, although that guy Gerard was gorgeous...' Zara whispered to Penelope so that Charlie wouldn't overhear her, they had been so hard on him for judging the girls for their looks... they didn't want to be seen as hypocrites.

'I know... I was undecided until he mentioned the snowboarding... I mean, can you imagine the body!' Penelope looked dreamily into space as she said this.

'Me too.' Zara joined her in space.

'But imagine what it would be like living with two bloody musicians… they could turn this place into a groupie den…' Penelope snapped out of it pretty quickly, as her rational mind butted in.

'I never really thought about that, but I think that you know Charlie well enough to stop that from happening… if we were all randomers that would probably happen, but because you two are such good friends he won't want to piss you off…' Zara assured Penelope.

'That's a good point. Did you like any of the others…?' Penelope glanced down at the list again, ready to prompt Zara with it.

'I thought the Swedish girl was lovely, she would fit right in.' Zara offered.

'Totally, I agree… but then three girls in one house, that's kind of asking for trouble… I think we should try for a guy if possible, to balance things out. It's very difficult to say in advance isn't it? They can all seem really nice when you only meet them for a few minutes. The only one I didn't like was the fourth guy, Paul, I think?' He gave Penelope the creeps.

'Yeah, I know the one you mean, it almost seemed like he was casing the joint.' Zara had a bad feeling about him too, but she wasn't too sure why.

'Exactly, I didn't want to say it, but that's totally what it felt like. He had more of an eye on the furniture than on us, creepy!' Penelope shuddered.

'Let's cross him off the list then.' Zara added.

'Other than that let's not make any judgments until we see them all, oh and we'll have to see what Charlie thinks too, I almost forgot about him, although I'm sure he'll want Angelica to move in.' Penelope smirked at Zara.

'Hmm, I wonder why…' Zara smirked back.

'I think that's him back now… ok, here Zara, one Hula Hoop at a time, and then tiny sips of Coke… slowly does it, you'll be fine in no time.' Penelope reassured Zara that she would feel human again in no time at all.

'This is such a *struggle*, how long before I feel normal again?' Zara did what she was told.

'Once you have finished the whole pack and that can, you will feel a hundred times better.'

'I hope you're right.' Zara considered the Hula Hoops and the can of Coke, she was not looking forward to consuming either of them…

'Charlie, so what do you think so far? Angelica right?' Penelope spun around to ask Charlie.

'No actually…' Charlie put on a tone of mock miffery…

'No?!' The two girls cried in unison.

'I've already got her phone number don't I, I don't have to *live* with her!' Charlie grinned at them both.

'You are unbelievable! So anyone you think might fit in really well?' Penelope looked up to heaven as she said this.

'Definitely Gerry, he seems like a blast!' Charlie gave Gerry the thumbs up.

'Which one was he again…?' Penelope checked her list.

'You know the snow boarder, band guy.' Charlie actually believed that Penelope didn't remember Gerry.

'Ah, yes I *think* I remember him, Zara do you remember which one was the snow boarder band guy?' Penelope asked Zara in a mock serious tone, pretending that she didn't know exactly who he was talking about.

'No, nope doesn't ring any bells.' '*I nearly choked on my Coke there…uh oh I think it's going to come down my nose… eugh!*' Penelope made Zara laugh the way she said this.

'What are you two laughing at?' Charlie couldn't follow at all.

'The Coke nearly came down her nose, didn't you see…?' Penelope tried to distract him.

'Yeah but it nearly came down her nose *because* she was laughing! What's so funny?' Charlie still didn't get it.

'We were just laughing at this mascara emergency one of the girls had in work the other day, you see, she came in and it was all over her…' Penelope knew that this would shut Charlie up, he hated girly talk.

'Enough! I've heard enough already!' He put his hand up to stop them as he said this. 'We have twelve more coming after 2 pm, so if you two can stop laughing I'm going to make myself a toastie and recover from walking up and down those three flights of stairs every ten minutes…' Charlie headed into the kitchen.

'That was so funny!' Zara had regained composure, but was still clutching a bunch of Coke-stained tissues.

'I know! I couldn't believe he chose him, I was sure he was going to go for the Swedish girl…' Penelope sounded incredulous…

'Me too! Looks like Gerard, I mean *Gerry* might be *the one*!' Zara hoped he was.

'Shhh! Don't' say that, you'll *curse* it.' Penelope hissed at her.

'Oh no, the doorbell, damn it, this one's early. Zara… you are not going to believe this, it's a set of twins!' Penelope looked out the window and saw identical twin girls outside.

'No way! Let's have a look.' Zara was beginning to feel human again and left the couch for the first time that morning, and peered over the window box.

'Hi, we are, I mean I'm here about the room… I just brought my sister with me, I hope you don't mind, I didn't fancy calling into houses on my own.' The two girls stood there staring at Penelope.

'Of course that's fine. I'm Penelope.' Penelope plastered a big fake smile on her face, she didn't fancy a twin living in the house, she just knew that it would be double trouble.

'I'm Pamela and this is my sister Lucy.' Pamela introduced them.

'Lovely to meet you both. I'll just get Charlie to show you the room.' The fake smile was still stuck to Penelope's face.

'Zara! He'll have a heart attack when he sees those two.' Penelope whispered to Zara.

'I know! This is all too much for a girl with a hangover, all this laughing is making my tummy hurt even more… actually I'm feeling much better now after the Hula Hoops and Coke… what a relief!' The colour started to creep back to Zara's ashen face.

'Sorry, Pamela, now we just have a few questions…' Penelope began as the first girl came into the living room.

'No, I'm Lucy, Pam is in the loo!' Lucy answered.

'Oh right, ok, I'll hold on until she comes back then…' Penelope sighed, it was happening already! They were causing chaos.

'Oh god how embarrassing!' Penelope thought to herself.

'Pamela, now we just have a few questions… you know there are no pets allowed here, and you need the deposit and a month's rent in advance… … and we would need you to move in almost immediately, is that going to be a problem?…' Penelope was on automatic pilot, she had made this speech so many times already today.

'Well, I work in a design studio, I go out socialising a lot, and I like to go away at weekends a bit…' Pamela began her monologue.

'… lovely to meet you… both, Pamela, if we shortlist you we'll call you by six today…' Penelope ushered the twins out as soon as they had rushed through the questions.

And the interviews went on and on and on…

'… Peter… work as a lawyer in the city… ' Peter began.

'Oh, do you work in the music business, my friend works in that industry, his name is Ah-Leeks… do you know him?' The mere mention of lawyers had Penelope on the edge of her seat. Imagine if this guy knew Alyx!

'No, I…?' Peter barely had time to finish his sentence.

'Are you sure you don't know him!?' Penelope shot back.

'No I think I'd remember a name like that, I work in tax mainly… and I like to rock climb…' Peter ignored Penelope's fishing and went on with his monologue.

'Dull, dull, dull, oh well it was worth a try, he might have known him… I'm not listening to a word this guys is saying… I'm distracted now, I wonder if he'll call, I hope he does…' Penelope's mind was on other things.

'… I'm Mandy, … I'm a beautician… I'm twenty-three…' Mandy had implants! She was crossed off the list.

'... I'm Louise... sorry I'm late, I got completely lost, I hope you don't mind me coming at another time...' Louise was a vegan, hippy, nudist, she was swiftly crossed off the list.

'... My name is Richard, nice house, room is a bit small though... no I couldn't move in straight away, I need to give at least a month's notice...' Richard was off the list.

'... Christian, ... Model, travel a lot to Milan, Paris mainly... couture shows... I do smoke, will that be a problem...?' Despite the smoking, Christian was still on the list, the girls absolutely loved him.

'... Justin, accountant... staying in and watching TV, nature walks, reading... I have a pet budgie...' Justin was too dull. Off the list!

'... So excited about living around here! All my girls have moved in on this road! It'll be exactly like Uni!... Soooo into parties every weekend... hope that's cool, so when can I move in? I love London!... Sorry, forgot to say my name is Charlotte... but my friends call me Charlie! Oh hilarious! Two Charlies in one house!...' Charlotte was a little too enthusiastic for the three of them. She was off the list.

'Please tell me that was the last one? She was like a bloody cheerleader and she didn't stop talking! I couldn't get a word in edgeways and I'm not even listening to what they are saying at this stage... I'm so wrecked...' Penelope looked shattered.

'Me too! Charlie is getting off lightly not asking the questions... I bet we'll end up picking one of the first ones we saw...' Zara was exhausted too.

'I know, but you just never know... that's the thing really, it's a numbers game... we had five no shows, one extra ...' Penelope surveyed the list.

'The twin?' Zara knew exactly where Penelope was coming from.

'Yep, and then about six of them couldn't move in straight away, so they are off the list immediately... That leaves about eight relatively normal people out of the rest of them, five ok girls and three ok guys... here's the shortlist... what do you think?' Penelope showed Zara the list.

'I think I've made my feelings about Gerard, perfectly clear, I liked Angelica, and Christian... he was the model wasn't he?' Zara was going through the shortlist.

'Yeah, he probably won't actually be here that much, which would be ok wouldn't it?' Pen added.

'Yeah, and the twin was quite nice, as long as it's not her and her sister moving in. Pen, I agree with all of these as a first stab at the shortlist... let's see what Charlie thinks. He might knock a few more off.' Zara handed the list back to Penelope after cross-referencing it with her own.

'Ok, ok, yeah, ok, fine, not sure about the model guy... Christian, bit of a wuss, he was going on to me about how I should use *moisturiser*! I'll thank him when I'm fifty he said, what a muppet!' Charlie was going through the list of names one by one.

'You know that you should actually, it's not just girls that...' Penelope began extolling the benefits of using moisturiser.

'Don't you start, for fuck's sake!' Charlie was indignant.

'Right, sorry... go on...' Penelope admitted defeat.

'The twin has to go?' Charlie was emphatic.

'Why did you not like her?' Zara was surprised to hear this.

'No, no I do... but not in a *housemate* kind of way, if you know what I mean.' Charlie grinned at them both.

'Oh, for heaven's sake, ok...' Penelope sighed.

'And Angelica will have to go, for the same reason, oh and the beautician ... sorry!' Charlie looked sheepish, it seemed like he had gone through the list for himself, not thinking of the housemate situation as his first priority.

'Oh well, it's better that you are being honest... did you actually ask them out or what?' Penelope enquired.

'No, just shameless flirting... keeping my options open of course. Oh and they will all be auditioning for the band...' Charlie smirked at her.

'What?! That's ridiculous?! How did you manage that?...' Penelope was incredulous.

'I told them they had the right *look* for the band, that one never fails!' Charlie had such a way with women, especially when it came to combining them with his first love... music!

'Charlie! You're terrible!' Zara shrieked with laughter.

'So that just leaves, two of the girls who we weren't too sure about anyway... and then the two remaining guys...' Charlie looked at the even shorter list.

'I had a feeling that it should be a guy because three girls in a house might be a bit much...' Penelope added.

'I agree,' Zara agreed,

'Me too, I couldn't cope with three of you nagging me!' Charlie ducked as Penelope aimed a cushion at him.

'Right... so between the two guys...?' Zara asked.

'Gerry!' Charlie said.

'I say, Gerard, or Gerry or whatever you want to call him,' Penelope agreed with him.

'Ok, let's call him and see if he can move in, and if not we can ring the other guy. I've forgotten his name already... Charlie will you do the honours?' Penelope handed him the phone.

'Cool, give me his number... I'll sort it.' Charlie was delighted with himself, he couldn't wait to live with another guy.

'Fingers crossed he'll take it. How are you feeling now Zara?' Penelope was glad to see Zara looking a bit better.

'A million times better, that was a complete miracle cure. I could still do with a little nap... do you think he'll take the room.' Zara curled up on the couch, hugging a cushion.

'I'd say so, Charlie seems to think that they got on like a house on fire... and we were quite taken with his... erm... *finer qualities*...' Penelope smirked at Zara.

'I know, I hope he moves in. We're terrible, we slag Charlie off for going for looks and the two of us are no better,' Zara whispered to Penelope.

Charlie came back into the room beaming.

'Well, Charlie... what did he say?' Penelope asked him.

'Moving in tomorrow!' Charlie gave them a huge smile.

'Cool!' Penelope nodded.

'Yay!' Zara said.

That's a relief, good to get the whole thing sorted in a day… it means we can split all the bills from now on. I really hope this guy works out, it's very hard to tell after only meeting him for twenty minutes… oh hello… text message!' Penelope was deep in thought when she was rudely interrupted by a text message.

Hi Penelope,

A S B here,

hope u r well.

R u free for dinner,

wed. night?

'What a weird text. What the hell is ASB who is that? Hmm, oh another one!' Penelope stared in disbelief as another text message buzzed into her phone and it vibrated as she read the first one.

P.S. we met in Floridita

on Thursday, in case

you have forgotten…

'Oh my god, oh my god, oh my god… it's him! It's Alyx! How could I have forgotten, oh yes! Right I'll text him back but… not … just … yet. Butterflies in my tummy… I haven't been this excited about a date in ages! Things are definitely looking up… I can't wait to tell George!' Penelope's heart rate shot right up and her stomach started doing cartwheels.

Meanwhile Zara sat on the couch… miles away. Every second day in London something completely out of the ordinary happened to her. She was used to a relatively quiet, and relatively unglamorous life, and in the past few hours, she had met models, musicians and all sorts of people… who were trying to impress *her*. It was a lot to take in. None of her friends back home would even believe all of this!

'I can't wait for Gerry to move in. He's gorgeous… and I know of course he is strictly off-limits because he is my housemate, but still. Penelope was great to organise the lists and all of that. I suppose there

will be a backup if things with Gerry don't work out. I still feel pretty rough, although the miracle cure did bring me back from the brink… I swear I'll never be able to drink B52s again. Charlie is delighted with himself, bless him. I think he thinks he's got a new friend to play with. Penelope looks very happy, I hope it's not just about Gerry, must be a man involved, she's got that walking on air thing about her all of a sudden again… hmm… good for her, hopefully it's contagious.' Zara was delighted to be feeling human, and happy, again.

'Excellent that Gerry is moving in, too many women around here definitely. We are looking for a new bass player in the band, he might just fit in to that. Shiiiit I'm late for rehearsal…' Charlie was delighted to be getting a guy to move in.

'Ok, I'll text him back… oh my god, oh my god, oh my god… what will I say… I am freaking out! Only one thing to do…' She dialled George's number immediately.

'Hi it's me,' Penelope sounded so excited.

'Penny, how *are* you?' George was delighted to hear from her.

'Fine, fine, but George… he texted me!' Penelope gushed, she could barely get the words out she was speaking so fast.

'Calm down, calm down, *who texted you*?' George sat up so that she could try to figure out what Penelope was talking about.

'You know… *Alyx*… he texted me and asked me out!' Penelope's words were tripping over each other.

'Oh! Great! That's fantastic… oh no! Have you texted him back yet?' George sounded serious.

'No… no, that's why I'm calling, I'm freaking out about it!' Penelope gushed.

'Wise Penny… wise… you did the right thing… now exactly when did the text arrive and what did it say?' George needed details.

'That's the thing… he sent me two texts,' Penelope stammered.

'What? Now hold on a minute… two in a row?' George couldn't believe this.

'Yes, but let me explain you see, the first one was… well

I didn't get it, I didn't know who it was from… and then…' Penelope inhaled to continue… but George sensed the impending torrent of words, so she interrupted her.

'Ok, calm down, I can't keep up… take a deep breath and tell me slowly, really Pen, you're like a giddy teenager… I haven't seen you like this in *ages, this is so much fun!*' George clapped her hands like a seal, and of course dropped the phone in the process.

'I know, I don't really know what's come over me… anyway he sent me a text, here let me open it up… and it says… "Hi Penelope, A S B here, hope u r well. R u free for dinner, wed. night?"' Penelope read the text out loud to George.

'"*ASB*?"' Oh dear…' George was not impressed with the unnecessary use of his initials.

'I know, I had no idea what that meant… and then about two minutes later I got another one… and it said… hold on…' Penelope opened up the text and read it out to George. "P.S. we met in Floridita on Thursday, in case you have forgotten… "'

'Nice…' George was suitably impressed, despite the "ASB" bit.

'I know, I nearly had a heart attack when I realised who it was from…' Penelope started gushing again.

'OK, and when did these arrive?' George sounded matter-of-fact.

'About ten minutes ago… of course I would never text back straight away, but sometimes if you leave it too long you just don't know what to say…' Penelope's tone was pleading, she was dying to text him back.

'I know exactly what you mean… well I'm presuming you do want to go out with him…?' George laughed as she said this.

'Absolutely…' Penelope laughed back at her.

'Right, well then wait until about half eight or nine…' George advised.

'But that's nearly *three hours* away,' Penelope gasped.

'I know, but he's not going to vanish into thin air if you don't text him straight back… and that way you'll catch him just before he goes out tonight.' George was always a font of knowledge when it came to men.

'God, you're brilliant!' Penelope wanted to hug her.

'I know, I know... you can thank me at the wedding... anyway... next: what to say...?'

'Well I think I should say that I think Wednesday is ok,' Penelope suggested.

'Erm, well hmmm, ok I'll let you away with that one, I was going to suggest that you say you are busy, but he travels a lot doesn't he...? So you don't want to get into a text debate about when you are both free... the whole thing won't happen if you start playing text tennis.' George was being very sensible.

'Ok, so I say, something like, Hi, yes dinner would be lovely and am free on Wednesday...' Penelope was dying to text him back.

'Hmmm, I'm not over the moon about using the word love in any of its forms in the first text!' George sounded stern.

'Right, right, very sensible... so should it be more like, Hi, dinner on Wednesday would be nice, let me know where and when...' Penelope's rational mind started to enter the conversation, finally...

'Now that's more like it... neutral enough and then he should call to make arrangements... ok write it now, and then save it and send it at about half eight.' George was adamant that this was the right thing to do.

'Will do, thanks George, what would I do without you?' Penelope sighed with relief.

'I know I know, you'll give me a big head! Listen... what are you up to tonight? I was thinking of going to that new restaurant in the village... do you fancy it? I'm dying to hear about all the potential housemate horror stories... I'd say the whole thing was like a pantomime.' George chuckled.

'Oh my god it was, I'm exhausted from it all. We picked one though, a guy, he seems nice enough and he's gorgeous! Dinner sounds like a great idea.' Penelope agreed.

'I'll give you a ring back once I've made the reservation...' George added.

'Ok.'

'Cool.' George hung up.

'I'm so happy he texted me, yum! He's exactly my type…'
Penelope was on cloud nine, she was so happy about the text.
She picked up the phone without looking at the number, she
assumed it was George ringing back about the restaurant.

'Hi George… that was quick…' Penelope didn't even say hello.

'Hello Penelope, sorry to disappoint, but it's not George…'
It definitely was not George, it was a man's voice on the phone.

'Who is this?!' Penelope was a bit taken aback, she perched
on the end of the sofa.

'Penelope, it's Richard, Richard Lord.' Richard sounded a
little sarcastic.

'Oh, Richard, hi, so sorry about that, it's just I was waiting
for George, you know…Georgina, to call me back and I really
wasn't expecting your call…' Penelope stammered, she couldn't
believe that she had been so rude.

'Well then, I can hang up if you like…' Richard tried to
make light of it all.

'No! No, I didn't mean that, it's just that you caught
me off guard… how, erm… how are you?' Penelope was
completely flustered.

'Fine thanks, great actually, anyway… I won't keep you, I
was just wondering if you fancy meeting up during the week
for a drink, for a catch up?' Richard got straight to the point.

'Oh yes that would be nice.' Penelope absolutely couldn't
say no after all that.

'How is Wednesday for you?' Richard suggested.

'Bloody typical… feast or famine…' 'Sorry Richard I have
plans on Wednesday, the weekend is probably a bit clearer, how
about Friday?' Penelope offered an alternative.

'I can't Friday, I'm needed back in Scotland this weekend…
could we compromise and say Thursday?' Richard was adamant
that they would meet this week… strike while the iron is hot.

'Ok, Thursday sounds good…' Penelope agreed.

'Great, I'll call you during the week to make arrangements…

I was thinking maybe Floridita…' Richard suggested this, as he had heard that Penelope liked going there.

'No!' Penelope shrieked a little too emphatically. She didn't want to return to where she had met Alyx, what if she bumped into him with Richard, that was unthinkable.

'What? You don't like Floridita? I thought you loved places like that!' Richard was taken aback, he had asked around about the type of places that she would like to go and he was trying to impress her with his taste in bars.

'Oh, no, nothing like that… it's just that we go there *all* the time… it might be nice to go somewhere else for a change…' Penelope regained composure.

'Oh right, I see, well then you pick somewhere that you fancy, and I'll call you and you can tell me where we're going?' Richard put the ball back into her court.

'Good plan.' Penelope started to relax now.

'Enjoy the rest of your weekend… Bye.' Richard sounded delighted.

'Bye Richard, and thanks for the call.' Penelope hung up.

The minute she did so, the phone rang again. She tentatively answered.

'Hi… George?' Penelope enquired?

'Yes… why were you expecting someone else… *ASB* maybe?!' George said wittily.

'No, it's just that, well you are not going to believe who just called to ask me out on Wednesday…' Penelope sighed.

'Someone else?… not the famous Ah-Leeks?!' George couldn't believe all of this.

'Richard bloody Lord!' Penelope exclaimed!

'Good god, how on earth did he get your number? There's a blast from the past!' George couldn't believe this.

'I know, well I bumped into him at the work dinner thing on Wednesday, I thought I told you, but then again my brain sort of went to mush when Alyx swept into my life…' Penelope started to sound all dreamy again.

'And he wanted to go out on Wednesday too? Bloody hell

Pen, it's obviously your night!' George sounded astounded.

'I know, they are like bloody buses aren't they?' Penelope agreed.

'I know what you mean, and you can tell me all about it at dinner… say eight-thirty, drop in here first? And don't text him before you see me… ok?' George warned Penelope.

'Yes, mum!' Penelope agreed cheekily.

'No need to be cheeky!' George chided her.

'Ok, see you later.' Penelope's tone was back to normal now as she hung up.

'Wow, I can't believe it, out on Wednesday and Thursday night this week… I usually don't go out at all during the week, except for work things or calling into George the odd time. What will I wear?… I must go and get something new. And then meeting Richard too… no… concentrate on getting through Wednesday first! One thing at a time!' Penelope thought to herself as she made her way upstairs to rifle through her wardrobe for some inspiration.

Later on that evening Zara was settling down in front of the TV for the night.

'Oh… my poor little head. For the first time since I moved down I'm actually glad to be staying in on a Saturday night. I wonder if Penelope is going out, Charlie has gone off to rehearsals or gigs or something like that… oh no I hope Gerry isn't moving in tonight! I just feel like vegging in front of the TV in my pyjamas… I'm not doing that if he's around. It's awful the way you lose the whole weekend if you have a hangover from Friday night… I'm never drinking again… well at least for the rest of this week anyway. I wonder what it'll be like having another guy in the house? I'll probably have to dress up even to veg out, oh no! No more face packs in the near future.' Zara considered the situation in the house when Gerry moved in as she tucked into a Chinese takeaway.

Over in Battersea, Penelope arrived at George's flat, right on time.

'Well?' George opened the door to Penelope.

'I waited just like you said.' Penelope gushed and waltzed into the flat, walking on air.

135

'Good girl, you… may… text him now…' George announced dramatically.

'Ok… there it's gone.' The text flew out of Penelope's phone and winged its way to Alyx.

'Hungry?' George was starving.

'Not at all, with all the excitement I can't eat a thing.' Penelope couldn't bear the thought of food, but she knew she had to eat something!

'Well, I'm starving! Let's get going. So tell me all about Richard, what happened there? Does he still look the same… Is he married? I would have expected his parents to have married him off to some princess from a small country by now! George had also known Richard through Penelope at University.

'He still looks pretty much the same, suited and booted though, and I didn't ask him if he was married… that would be a major no-no!' Penelope sighed.

'Quite right, quite right… but did you see a ring?' George was great at scanning men, and sussing them out.

'For heaven's sake George, I wasn't looking, I don't care if he's married! You sound like my mother, that's the first thing she would check.' Penelope sounded exasperated.

'Is he living in London now? What happened to the castle?' George was dying to learn more.

'The castle is still standing, but he said something like he didn't want to be middle-aged before he was middle-aged, plenty of time to live in a draughty old castle in Scotland.' Penelope didn't want to talk about Richard at all.

'That's very sensible of him, he was always a planner wasn't he? Seemed to have his whole life mapped out years in advance,' George mused.

'Yeah, I had forgotten he was like that… I always thought that that was more his parents' plan than his,' Penelope sighed.

'His mother was a real battle-axe wasn't she, remember she'd come to collect him in the Rolls Royce, with the tartan blankets in the back, with the family crest I think?' George roared with laughter.

'Oh god yeah, I had totally forgotten about her... she was stern, pretty scary actually, she always had her hair in a bun, with these hair pins sticking out of it! Like a headmistress, and the family tartan was like a uniform. Guess where he wanted to go and when?' Penelope asked George, who was on the edge of her seat at this point.

'Where?' George demanded.

'Floridita on Wednesday!' Penelope screeched.

'Brilliant! What did you say?' George couldn't believe this!

'I freaked out and said no really quickly. And then I had to say that I go there all the time, and that's why I think we should go somewhere else *for a change*.' Penelope looked wide-eyed as she said this to George, still not quite believing that she had gotten away with it.

'He probably just thinks you're barking!' George offered.

'I know, and I had to tell him I'm busy on Wednesday and put him off until Thursday,' Penelope added.

'I see what you mean, they are like bloody buses aren't they?' George sighed.

'I know, nobody nice for ages, and then one and a half in one week...' Penelope sighed.

'One and a half?' George didn't understand.

'Well I'm just meeting Richard to catch up... so it's not strictly a date, even though it's just the two of us.' Penelope was reassuring herself as much as anyone else.

'Do you think he still fancies you?' George was keen to find out.

'What? He never did... did he?' Penelope was in denial about this.

'Totally! I think he wanted to make you his Scottish Princess.' George giggled.

'No way! Seriously?' Penelope shot George a stern look.

'Totally, how did you not notice?' George had visions of Penelope in a tartan wedding dress.

'I was always going out with someone when I was in University, so I didn't really pay attention to things like that.' Penelope was starting to get a little concerned, she hated it when things got uncomfortable with guy friends, she definitely didn't fancy Richard as far as she knew.

'Well, we all reckoned he fancied you like mad…' George added matter-of-factly.

'Really, I had no idea.' Penelope wasn't sure whether she was joking or not.

'Just watch yourself on Thursday then!' George warned her.

'I'm sure he probably is married by now anyway,' Penelope reassured herself.

'We'll see.' George said in a sing song voice. 'Only time will tell…'

Back on Abbeville Road, Zara was feeling a little bored and a little lonely, so she decided to phone Katie.

'Zara!' Katie squealed as she answered the phone.

'Hi Katie, how are you?' Zara's tone was a little tense.

'You sound awful, are you alright?' Katie sounded concerned.

'No… hangover… feel like I'm going to die…' Zara admitted, now knowing it was too late to take the words back and more questions were likely to follow…

'Oooh, were you at some celebrity bash on Friday? I bet it's so glamorous down there! Or some trendy bar, did you see anyone famous?' Katie interrogated Zara.

'No, no just drinks with friends from work, it was my first pay day, so I had to go and celebrate… a new pair of shoes would have been the more sensible option, but never mind. What are you up to?' Zara tried to get off the subject, it was too hard to describe her new life to Katie.

'Oh my god, it all sounds soooooo glamorous, I would love to be able to go shopping any time I wanted to. I'm not doing anything tonight, babysitting, I need money for the twenty-first next week, are you still coming home for it?'

'Of course, I would have come home this weekend but we had to *interview* housemates.' Again, the words came out before Zara had a chance to stop them.

'Interview them?' Katie sounded shocked.

'Yep, basically we needed a new housemate, and you put

this ad in this paper and half of London ring up and make appointments, then they all get fifteen minutes, have a quick look around the house and we have to try to suss them out.' Zara was not in the mood to go through the process again.

'Wow! Any weirdos?' Katie was generally shocked and excited by everything that she heard about London.

'No total freaks, but a few nerds, difficult to say in a fifteen-minute time slot. Definitely a few potential weirdos though.' Zara admitted.

'And all of this going on today and you with a hangover?' Katie couldn't believe this.

'Yep, but Penelope...' Zara began.

'The Princess?' Katie enquired.

'*God I feel so bad about my first impressions of her, why did I tell everyone!*' Zara felt so guilty.

'Yes, well, she's not as bad as I thought at first, just because she's a bit posh, doesn't mean she is not nice. Anyway, Penelope has done this kind of thing a few times before apparently, and had all these sheets printed out with questions.' Zara filled Katie in.

'How organised!' Katie shrieked.

'I know, so then after they had left we had notes to remember them by...'

'Like what they were wearing and stuff like that?' Katie completely saw the logic of this.

'Sometimes, yeah, or descriptions like tall blonde girl, blue jumper... It really helped when we were going through them later that night, there were so many of them, I was exhausted afterwards,' Zara sighed.

'So did you pick one then?' Katie demanded to know.

'Yeah, we picked this guy... because he is gorgeous!' Zara beamed down the phone.

'I don't believe you, you are worse than blokes! And did the guy you live with agree?' Katie couldn't believe this.

'He loved him, the guy I live with, Charlie, is in a band...' Zara began.

'Oh my god is he famous!?' Katie shrieked.

'Not yet, but…' Zara continued.

'Almost famous?!' she shrieked again.

'I don't know actually, I don't think so though.' Zara realised that she didn't actually know, but it was a bloody good question. There is no way they could cope with the paparazzi permanently camped out on Abbeville Road.

'Oh, anyway… go on, so he liked him too…' Katie was dying to hear the rest of the story.

'Yeah this bloke, *Gerry,* is in a band too and …'

'Oh my god, you are soooo lucky, I have never even met someone who is in a band in *London* and you are living with two of them! Some people have all the luck.' Katie sounded a bit miffed.

'If you think that's good, wait 'til you hear this… he's a semi-professional snow boarder, and Katie, you'd want to see *the body…*' Zara knew she had said too much now, how could Katie share her joy about this, when she was stuck back at home.

'What! Did you get him to strip or something?' Katie couldn't believe this.

'Noooooo! But sometimes you can just tell, and Penelope thought exactly the same, so I know it wasn't just me,' Zara sighed dreamily.

'I see! I wish I was you Zara, some people have all the luck… I'm stuck here in boring Bangor, where nothing ever changes.' Katie sounded a bit put out.

'Well you can come down for a visit any time you like. We can plan it when I'm back next weekend.' Zara offered an immediate solution.

'Right, I'll start saving. I better go, I'll email you when I get back into college on Monday, ok.' Katie was already running late for her babysitting job that night.

'Ok, bye.' Zara was sorry that she had to go. The line went dead, and suddenly Zara was alone again.

It was really nice speaking to Katie. I know I'm not missing out on anything at home if she's just babysitting. Next weekend is the big one, with Jeannie's party. With all the stuff that's been going on here, I'd completely forgotten about it. I don't feel as miserable this weekend, thank god. I think I'll have a nice bath and go to bed early.' Zara felt a little better, now that she knew she would see them all next weekend.

The next morning Zara was up nice and early, to her surprise so was Penelope.

'Morning Penelope… off for a run?' Zara asked.

'Yep, going for a quick run around the common.' Penelope was all ready to go in her trainers, with her iPod on full blast.

'You are so good, I barely do any exercise, I'll have to join a gym or something. Thanks for the hangover cure yesterday, I think you just might have saved my life, I'm totally back to normal now.' Zara felt like hugging Penelope.

'No problem, by the way I bumped into Charlie last night when I came in and Gerry is moving in today, lunch time-ish apparently.' Penelope shouted back over her shoulder.

'Oh my god, look at the state of me, I'll have to go and tidy myself up a bit, no lounging around in my jammies.' Zara jumped up.

'I thought I should warn you! It's going to be weird having another guy in the house, just when we had all gotten used to living here, just the three of us.' Penelope stopped at the top of the stairs as she considered this.

'I know what you mean, I really hope it works out with him,' Zara agreed.

'I'm sure it will, you know what guys are like, I'm sure we'll probably barely ever see him,' Penelope said reassuringly.

'Yeah, I see what you mean, I barely even know Charlie, and any time I see him he's got some blonde clinging onto him,' Zara chuckled.

'He's terrible isn't he? And he doesn't even know half of their names.' Penelope laughed.

'I know, it's hysterical. He is a nice guy though isn't he?' Zara wanted some reassurance from Penelope.

'Oh yeah, I was really good friends with him in Uni, he is really nice as long as you are not 5ft4, with blonde hair and big boobs.' Penelope tittered.

'That's great, I'm safe then.' Zara was relieved.

Later that day Charlie got a call from Gerry.

'Hi mate, yeah, that's cool, I'll be here to let you in, just out of bed myself too. No worries.' Charlie was still in bed.

'Wicked, do you have a spare set of keys?'

'Yep, extra keys all ready for you. Do you have much stuff?' Charlie struggled out of bed.

'Nah, I travel light, got my guitar and amp and stuff, but usually keep that stuff in my mate's house… it's where we rehearse. What are the two birds like to live with?' Gerry wanted to scope out the scene before he moved in.

'No problem, barely ever see them, they work during the day, friends with Penelope since Uni, and Zara, didn't know her before, but seems pretty cool, keeps herself to herself and doesn't hog the bathroom.' Charlie yawned as he filled Gerry in.

'Cool, didn't want to be moving in with a pair of drama queens or whatever.' Gerry sounded relieved.

'Nah, nuthin' like that, they're sound. See you at about three?' Charlie asked.

'Yeah, that's cool.' Gerry agreed.

'I'm in anyway, so whenever is cool, just give me a call when you are on your way.'

'Right mate, later. Cheers.' And Gerry was gone.

'Charlie, was that him?' Zara had caught the tail end of the conversation.

'Who? *Gerry?*' Charlie wasn't expecting to see her as he headed into the kitchen.

'Yeah.' Zara tried not to look too keen.

'Yep, should be here at about three, don't worry though, I'm going to let him in and all that.' Charlie was rooting around in the cupboard for the cereal.

'Ok, cool.' Zara had mastered a nonchalant tone of voice.

'Yay! I can't wait for this guy to move in. He's yum. It's a bit of excitement having a new housemate.' Zara was so pleased about the new housemate.

'Is he here yet?' Later that day Penelope was pacing up and down in the kitchen as Zara sat at the kitchen table.

'No, Charlie said about three-ish, no sign of him yet… oh hello, this might be…' Zara suggested as the doorbell rang.

'Oh my god, he is gorgeous… oh no! he's got a girl with him…' Penelope sighed as she peeped out the living room window.

'Maybe it's his sister…' Zara offered.

'I don't think so… look!' The two girls peeped out through the living room curtains.

'Oh, I see what you mean, oh well, the best ones are always taken…' Zara sighed.

'Not always… come on, let's make ourselves scarce, want to go for coffee?'

'Good idea, can you show me where the video shop is too? I've been meaning to join.' Zara was keen to get out and about.

'No problem.'

'Where are you two off to?' Charlie arrived down just as the two girls were leaving and Gerry was arriving in.

'Hi Gerry, sorry Charlie we had arranged to meet friends for coffee… going to be late. We'll be back later.' The two girls gave him and his girlfriend a big smile.

'Right so, I'll help Gerry move in and this is?' Charlie noticed the blonde girl with him.

'Sorry, everyone this is my girlfriend, Sarah.' Gerry introduced his girlfriend.

'Nice to meet you all.' The girl smiled suspiciously at Penelope and Zara.

As soon as they were out of earshot the two girls started to analyse the situation.

'It was probably better to make ourselves scarce while he moves in,' Penelope said.

'You are right, it'd probably be a bit awkward,' Zara hissed back at her.

'Completely, what with our jaws hitting the floor every time he strides up the stairs,' Penelope chuckled.

'He looks like a model doesn't he?' Zara had a faraway dreamy look in her eyes as she said this.

'I bet he does a bit on the side, but didn't want to say...' Penelope sounded like she had the inside track.

'Come on let's go, before his girlfriend comes back down and gives us the third degree.' The girls moved on down Abbeville Road to try to find a seat outside BonBon. They were lucky, there was one in the sun, and the two girls settled down for a good old chat over a couple of cappuccinos.

Later that evening Penelope had no distractions and her mind was on one thing, she tossed and turned in bed, struggling to get to sleep.

'Oh, I can't sleep. He hasn't texted me back yet. Maybe he didn't get it, no, no, I'm sure I got a receipt. What if he has changed his mind... and then I can't stop thinking about what George said about Richard. Maybe he does fancy me, I don't know how I feel about that... Oh, it's too late to ring George now, it's nearly midnight, and it's a school night. I have to be up at 6 am. I am now going to try to not think about him, it's really hard, he keeps coming into my head, stop it, stop it, stop it... this is not working. Ok, reading... nothing good to read, this is a disaster'. Penelope got up and rummaged around on her bookshelf '... *Aha...yoga, that never fails'* Penelope caught sight of her yoga mat out of the corner of her eye, and she knew exactly what to do '... *ohhhhmmm.'*

Within half an hour Penelope was fast asleep.

Chapter 11

Home?

This Monday morning wasn't quite as much of a struggle for Zara as previous ones had been. She lay in bed trying to muster the energy to haul herself out of it.

'What a nice weekend, I actually feel at home here now… I was dying to go home, but with all the activity with the housemate interviews and the hangover from Friday, I wouldn't have been able to go. I hope I don't bump into the new guy looking like this. I had a really nice chat with Penelope when we went for coffee. We had a right laugh about the two boys. She is nothing like any of my other friends, and I'm probably not the type of person she normally makes friends with. She is so posh, and even her name is posh. I was so intimidated when I first met her. I bet all her other friends are called Tizzy, Poppy and Harriet. George is really nice and she is really posh, meeting the two of them has really opened my mind. I would normally just avoid people like that. I just can't get out of bed today, it's a lovely morning… I think I'll just stay in here for a few more minutes…ahh… cuddly bed.'

Penelope had the same feeling, but for an entirely different reason… Alyx was playing on her mind.

'No, no sign of a text… ok, well it was unlikely that he'd text in the middle of the night… I slept like a baby after a tiny bit of yoga, I must remember that if I ever can't sleep again. I didn't get as much sleep as I normally do, but I don't feel tired… I do not want to get out of this bed…'

Penelope reluctantly slipped out of bed and sauntered into her en suite bathroom.

Zara arrived into work nice and early, she was becoming very good at getting the Tube. She managed it on her own this morning, all on her own, she was *very* proud of herself.

'Morning sleepy-head.' Rob said as soon as he saw her.

'Morning Rob, is it that obvious?' Zara gave him a big yawn as she said this.

'You look like you are still *in bed*!' Rob sounded so dramatic.

'I just couldn't get out of the bed this morning... I was so relaxed.' Zara yawned again.

'I know the feeling. Anyway... how are you?' Rob started the ball rolling.

'Luscious... you?' Zara woke up and rose to the occasion.

'Lovely... you?' Rob swept out from behind his desk.

'Fabulous... you?' Zara slid over towards him.

'Fantastic... you?' Rob placed the back of his hand on his forehead in a dramatic gesture.

'Smitten... you?' Zara clasped her hands together next to her right cheek.

'... Actually... lucky to be alive... How many drinks did we have on Friday? I was in *recovery* all of Saturday, and we had half of London in for the interviews.' Zara decided to stop their morning dance as she could see Victoria out of the corner of her eye.

'Oh that's right, did you find one in the end?' Rob was dying to hear about all of the weirdos that they may have seen. Finding a housemate in London was such a lottery.

'Yes, you would be so proud, he is *gorgeous*. We practically chose him on looks alone, semi-professional snow boarder, can you imagine... the body!' Zara started staring into space again.

'Good girl! How did you convince the others?' Rob was bursting with pride.

'No need, Charlie loved him... for different reasons of course, and Penelope agreed with me.' Zara glowed with pride.

'So I presume he is gay?' Rob was very sure of himself.

'No, worse… he's got a, a… *girlfriend*!' Zara sighed.

'NO!' Rob shrieked.

'I know, the cheek of him, bursting into our lives like that, giving us hope… and then having a girlfriend! She arrived with him when he moved in, she actually seems really nice though. She is gorgeous too.' Zara started up her computer.

'Oh well, not to worry… there's plenty more fish etc. etc. etc.' Rob went back to his seat, and started to boot up his PC.

'Where! Where are these mythical fish Rob!?' Zara needed answers!

'Oh don't ask me, I met my Mikey in Manchester remember, but look there are loads of young people living near where you live, you'll have a nice man in no time… no time at all…' Rob assured Zara.

'I hope you are right.' She really did.

'I'm *always* right! Now, down to business… I don't want to alarm you but, look… she's got the door shut again…' Rob had his finger on the pulse as far as Organicom was concerned. He knew all the signs.

'Oh no, do you think… maybe… more announcements?' Zara was startled by this.

'More than likely, don't worry about things until they happen though… that's my motto. Let's wait until she comes out to go and get coffee… wouldn't want to miss anything exciting…' Rob sounded like a sage.

'Totally, we can go at about eleven instead… she can't stay in there like that for hours, and she's bound to know that we know something is up because the door is closed… it's code for "serious news from HQ" isn't it?' Zara was beginning to pick up how things really worked at Organicom very quickly.

'Exactly. I better go and log in, I'm so glad I'm in early today, we're the only two in now, apart from the boss.' Rob tried to reassure Zara.

'Shiiiiiiiit! I had just forgotten about the work thing… I was so distracted by the whole new housemate carry on, and being hungover. I wonder what's going to happen. I'll read a few emails

from the girls, that'll take my mind off it. Don't worry about things until they happen, that's what Rob said… he seems to know what he's talking about when it comes to things like this. …' Zara was getting really worried now, having such an active weekend had totally taken her mind off the potential redundancies at work.

In EC1 Penelope was already steeped in work

'Penelope, good weekend?' Jack popped his head into her office.

'Yes, thanks, actually we had to find a new housemate and…' Penelope began…

'A new what? Housemate? What on earth for? Oh I keep forgetting you are not *married*…' Jack retorted.

'No, I'm far too young to be married… I live with friends and we had a spare bedroom… so we are renting it out.' Penelope explained, sick of the box that she was supposed to already be in.

'Ah, I see… didn't catch the rugby then?' Jack wasn't listening to a word she was saying.

'No, no, missed it again!' Penelope feigned regret.

'Beautiful game, you missed a corker, deciding try in extra time, beautiful, beautiful.' Jack made a rugby ball passing gesture.

'Oh, I think I can hear my phone vibrating… better dash…' Penelope lunged for her handbag.

'Oh, yes, right, quite right…' And Jack was gone.

'I am so sick of small talk, bloody rugby… who cares, well it could have been worse, could have been golf talk! I just don't have anything in common with these people. Emails, emails, emails. Oh no, I have to meet my new mentor this week. Luckily no sales pitches this week, just lots of entertaining… that's not so bad… I won't be in too late. I wish Alyx would text or something, maybe he's forgotten about it. I can't stop thinking about him. Right focus Penelope, a whole day of work to get through… oh my god!' The thought of a whole day of work without reassurance from Alyx!

Over in WC2, Zara was silently freaking out.

'She still hasn't opened the door yet, she must at least need to pee or something by now, it's gone ten! Everyone is looking really serious, and the usual jokes aren't flying around… which is very strange after our work drinks on Friday night… oh, oh, here she comes… help!' Zara's foot was tapping furiously under her desk, she was so nervous but was trying her best to hide it.

Victoria stood just outside her office at the front of the room. All the employees stood around in front of her, looking solemn.

'Good morning everyone… I'm afraid I have a bit of bad news. I have been on the phone to the Manchester office all morning, and the time has come for me to announce the changes that will be taking place, effective immediately… I'm sure you are all aware that our sales targets were very optimistic… and things are not looking good for the London office. As we are so centrally located, the cost of keeping this office active far outweighs the potential benefits, in terms of increasing sales. We need to focus our attention on increasing sales around the country, as there is quite a high demand for our product lines here, although admittedly, not as high as we had forecast. Manchester don't see the need to have a presence in London, as long as we continue to put money into advertising… I am sure you all must be thinking "How does this affect me?" Well, we have set up individual meetings with HR, they are arriving this afternoon, and they will go through your options with you…'

The speech went on for another ten minutes, but Zara didn't hear a thing.

'Rob! Oh my god!' Zara whispered, as they all made their way back to their desks in silence.

'I know love, but we all saw it coming,' Rob whispered back.

'I know, but still!' Zara was totally freaked out.

'I don't believe this! I have barely been here to settle in, and now I'm going to be turfed out! I wish there was someone I could speak to about this. I suppose I'll just have to wait and see what the HR person has to say to me. You could hear a pin drop in here, the atmosphere is terrible. Time to get out of here!' Zara thought to herself.

'Coffee?' Zara asked.

'In or out?' Rob hissed back at her.

'Out!' Zara exclaimed.

'Right, grab your coat and let's go.' Rob already had his jacket on.

As soon as they were within the safety of the second nearest Starbucks, Zara had so many questions for Rob.

'So what do you think, what will they offer us?' Zara was on the edge of her seat.

'I'd say they'll get rid of most of us, but they might offer a transfer position, in one of the other offices. So you would have the same job, but you would have to leave London, that might suit you though Zara, I know London hasn't been your favourite place.' Rob sipped his mochaccino in its oversized mug as he said this.

'I know, it's a real dilemma. I will have to cross that bridge when I come to it. Of course my first instinct is to rush back home, but I have spent so much money on rent and deposits and all that, it's seems a bit of a shame not to give it a go.' Zara couldn't believe her own words as they slipped out of her mouth, after all wasn't this exactly what she had been needing, an escape out of London?

'I see, that's a bit of a change of heart, it wouldn't have anything to do with that new guy moving in, you minx!' Rob knew how to make light of it, as dipped his biscotti into his coffee.

'No...! I told you he has a girlfriend. I don't know, I just think it would seem a bit ridiculous if I went home now, like I couldn't *cope* with London or something. I'm not sure if I could face that.' Zara was really considering it now, as she munched on her biscotti. It was days like these that they treated themselves to biscotti as well as coffee.

'When you put it that way, I see your point. Redundancy is a normal part of big city life, it doesn't mean there is anything wrong with you, but people in smaller cities mightn't see it that way.' Rob was trying to see it from Zara's point of view. 'We are still in a sort of recession after the dotcom implosion, so redundancy is becoming the norm unfortunately.'

'Exactly! My family are so proud and they think I am some big city executive, and I don't think we were particularly hit by the recession where I come from, but I guess in London the effects are more immediate, more visible.' Zara had no way of stopping her parents jumping to the wrong conclusions, or blaming a redundancy on the dotcom implosion.

'Indeed! They probably think you are running the show down here!' Rob looked aghast.

'I know, if only they knew! And the girls are all so envious of my London life! They would kill me if I moved back before they had a chance to visit.' Zara felt obliged to stick it out so that the girls could have a taste of her new life, they thought it was so glamorous.

'I see what you mean, we really do take London for granted, I mean so many people travel here and pay a fortune for hotels and things like that…' Rob considered how lucky he really was.

'Totally, the girls can't believe I can go to that huge TopShop at Oxford Circus any time I want, not to mention Bond Street.' Zara was slowly deciding, even though it was really scary, she didn't want to leave London. She could barely believe this herself.

'It really makes you think doesn't it, how much we take all of these things for granted.' Rob dipped the last bit of his biscotti into his coffee.

'Do you think we should go back now?' Zara looked worried as she drank the last of her skinny latte.

'No way! I bet everyone else has gone out for a coffee too, she said the HR people were coming after lunch, so we should be ok for a while. No use sitting around in that atmosphere!' Rob was glad that they had brought their notebooks with them, it made it look like they were working!

'Ok, in that case… it's my round, tall, skinny, wet mocha?' Zara said this without hesitating.

'Zara! You got it right! Well done, that would be lovely thank you.' Rob beamed at her, she really was finally mastering coffee speak.

***

'Oh my god ring! It's Monday, and we are supposed to be going out on Wednesday. It's nearly lunch time, oh no!' Penelope stared at her phone.

'Hi, it's me…' Penelope decided to take action.

'Pen, what's up?' George sounded concerned.

'I'm freaking out…' Penelope hissed.

'Don't ring him!' George instinctively knew what she was thinking.

'How did you know that's what I was going to say?!' Penelope was stunned, George had completely read her mind.

'Oh, I just knew… now look, it's Monday morning, he is not going to contact you during work hours, you of all people should know that, it's just too busy. He will ring or text you soon, and don't worry he hasn't forgotten about it. And he knows *exactly* what he is doing if you ask me.' George had a good feeling about Alyx.

'Do you think?' Penelope sounded a little calmer.

'Totally. Listen, I find it helps to just not think about it. So just try to put it out of your mind for the moment,' George advised.

'How?' Penelope quizzed.

'Do you not have work to do?!' George was pragmatic as always. Working in a Soho ad agency was nonstop, there were no peaks and lulls like in banking.

'Not busy at all this week, bloody typical,' Penelope sighed, 'and it's not like I can just work on a few designs… you are so lucky to be *paid* to be creative all day!'

'I know, I know… I'm living the dream here… Well, there's only one other thing… online shopping!' George grinned, she knew this would work.

'George, you're right! What would I do without you?' Penelope smiled down the phone.

'I don't know,… I don't know…, you can thank me in Kir Royales. Anyway Pen, what is it about this guy? I have never seen you like this before!' George sounded very supportive.

'I have no idea, I think maybe because I wasn't expecting to meet anyone interesting, that my guard was down and he swept into my life so unexpectedly. I'd kind of given up on meeting anyone interesting after a string of really boring dates. He was just so gorgeous George, and he just seemed quite down to earth as well. I know I only had a brief chat with him, but I have a good feeling about him. It's hard to explain really.' Penelope sounded pensive as she said this. She hadn't felt like this in years, and she barely knew the guy. I guess some people just have a certain charisma.

'I would tend to agree with you, and it's not often that I say this, but I *do* think he is good enough for you.' This was a first for George, she was usually very protective of her friend. She'd been there through all of the bad breakups and she was very keen for Penelope to meet a nice guy and be as loved up as she was.

'Really? George... I don't think I have ever heard you say that before.' Penelope sounded pleasantly surprised.

'Ok, well you get on with keeping your mind off him, chatting about him on the phone... really isn't helping! Oh by the way, before I go, has Richard been in touch?' George asked.

'Richard?... oh, Richard Lord? No, not since the weekend. I think we said we'd go out on Thursday.' Penelope sounded bored, she didn't want to talk about "bloody Richard".

'Right, well try thinking about him instead then... and start planning your weekend,' George advised.

'But's it's only Monday!' Penelope exclaimed.

'Ahem, have you forgotten where we are?... This is London, if you don't plan ahead, you get left behind.' George chuckled.

'Yes, mum!' Penelope sounded like a twelve-year-old.

'Right, oh dear, don't call me that... it makes me feel... like a grownup!' George exclaimed.

'Sorry George, anyway, speak to you later.' Penelope felt so much better now that she had spoken to George, a great sense of calm descended upon her.

'Bye.' George was gone, back to her Mac and pantone.

'She's right, now that I think of it, she's always right. I need to stop thinking about him, it's driving me mad. Online shopping here I come!' Penelope discreetly took her credit card out of her wallet and stood it up on her keyboard.

Back in SW4 the atmosphere was less frenetic.

'Hey Charlie, how's it going?' Gerry waltzed into the living room where Charlie was playing guitar.

'Cool, I have just mastered the Staunton lick.' Charlie didn't even look up as he said this.

'Ni-ice.' Can I take a look at your guitars?' Gerry motioned towards the six guitars lined up majestically against the wall.

'Yeah, sure, the rest of them are up in my room. How are you settling in?' Charlie asked.

'Great, no problem, girlfriend likes it too. She thought the two girls were nice, thank god! I couldn't put up with any *issues*, If you know what I mean.' Gerry rolled his eyes as he said this.

'Totally! That's why I keep myself nice and single.' Charlie grinned at him.

'I caved last year, I think I just fell in love or something, I was clinging to the single life too, but she is just gorgeous. We've been going out for nearly a year now,' Gerry explained.

'A year, wow, that's amazing.' Charlie was impressed.

'I know, longest ever.' Gerry sounded surprised himself.

'Pretty impressive. Here, have a look at this Strat, it was a limited edition. I got it on Denmark Street, here… hook it up.' Charlie picked up the guitar.

'It's beautiful, perfect sound… *pink* though?' Gerry wasn't too sure about the colour.

'The chicks love it, girls love pink… don't you know anything?' Charlie laughed.

'Good point, do people not think you are a poof though? Baby pink guitar screams G.A.Y, no?' Gerry wasn't convinced.

'No way!' Charlie roared back.

'Ok, just checking.' Gerry backed down immediately, the subject would never be mentioned again.

Chapter 12

Crossroads

Later that night Zara tossed and turned in bed, she was finding it impossible to sleep.

'I can't sleep, I can't sleep, I can't sleep, I can't sleep. I keep needing to go to the loo too! I just can't relax. The meeting with the HR dragon really freaked me out today. I didn't get a chance to speak to Rob, because his meeting went on really late, and I just had to get out of there. I can't stop thinking about what she said. Either redundancy, or potentially interview for a job in the Manchester office. Manchester! I can't believe this has happened to me. I was holding out hope that they wouldn't make me redundant, but when she actually said it, it hit me like a tonne of bricks. Redundancy! And Manchester! I don't know anyone in Manchester. Imagine having to move again, to the other end of the country. I wouldn't even be guaranteed a job there, I would have to interview for it, and I probably wouldn't stand a chance, the others have all been here for ages, and I'm still only finding my feet.' Periodically Zara stared at the time blinking at her in red on her radio alarm clock, it was making her feel worse.

4 am
... ... 4.59 am
... ... 5.17 am
... ... 5.48 am

… … … … … … … … .6.05 am
… … … … … … … … … … … 6.32 am
… … … … … … … … … … … … … 6.47 am
'Ok, well I suppose I may as well get up then. It's nearly 7 am after all. I am so tired, I just want to sleep.' Zara reluctantly made her way down to the bathroom.

***

'Morning sweetie.' Rob beamed at Zara as she walked in just before nine.

'Morning Rob, how did the meeting go?' Zara yawned.

'Fabulous, I negotiated myself a fat redundancy package! They were wittering on about moving me to the Manchester office, Manchester! The cheek of them, that's where I came from, and I'm not moving back there, now that me and Mikey have settled in London.' Rob shrieked as he threw his wrists up in the air.

'They mentioned Manchester to me too, not sure that I fancy that though. It's been hard enough for me just settling in here.' Zara didn't see the point of moving again so soon.

'You don't have to tell me that! Remember how scared you used to be of the Tube? And the experimental coffee outings?' Rob smiled at Zara.

'I know, and that was only a couple of weeks ago.' Zara could barely believe how much she had grown in a few short weeks in London.

'They'll be giving a pretty good redundancy package, I think I'll take the money and run.' Rob was really pleased with himself.

'They didn't mention money to me at all yesterday, how much do you think we'll get?' Zara still wasn't convinced, they hadn't mentioned money to her at all, worryingly.

'Should be three months basic, and then a month for every year you have been with the company. The whole thing is tax free too.' Rob rubbed his hands together gleefully.

'No way? Tax free!?' This made Zara perk up.

'Yep, because it's a one-off payment, and it will hopefully tide you over until you get a new job. I always temp in between jobs to keep the money coming in, that's actually how I got this job, I came here initially as a temp you know. Have a look at what your contract says, and then work out how much you'll get. You should get three months tax free... giving you three months to get yourself a new job.' Rob gave Zara some guidance.

'I had no idea there would be any silver lining,' Zara said slightly relieved.

'Always a silver lining darling! Always a silver lining!' Rob smiled at her.

'Now, that's not so bad! I really don't want to relocate to Manchester now!' Zara thought to herself.

***

'Hi,' Pen said.

'Hi Pen,' George answered, she knew what was coming next.

'He still hasn't contacted me yet!' Penelope was getting really nervous now.

'That's probably because you don't stop thinking about it!! You know what they say about a watched... erm... kettle or something... well, it never... boils, no pot, I think it was pot, well anyway, you know what I mean.' Pen knew what George was getting at, even if the words weren't exactly right.

'Oh my god! This is driving me mad!' Penelope sounded tense.

'Are you not busy this week?' George was trying to be practical.

'No, the partners are all over at some quarterly in New York until Thursday, so we are all having a bit of a break, the one time I could do with being busy.' Penelope sighed.

'Did Richard call you yet?' George tried to distract Penelope.

'Who? Oh, Richard Lord, no, no, not yet. Listen, I've got to go, something's going on outside my office, speak to you later.' Penelope saw there was some commotion outside her office.

'Bye.' George hung up.

'Simon, Roger, what's going on?' Penelope peered out of her office.

'The shit has just hit the fan, Mortimer announced his resignation in New York, at the bloody quarterly meeting, without any warning at all, no rumours, nothing! He's going and that's it.' Simon put the phone on mute and hissed this at Penelope.

'Oh my god, have our guys been on the phone?' Penelope went pale, this was not good.

'No they are stuck in the meeting but, John Bartlett managed to sneak out to make a quick call under the guise of "insulin injection", I mean they just couldn't say no, and they are holding it in the hotel our guys are staying in, so he used the phone in his room.' Roger butted in with the details as he steered Penelope away from Simon and the phone.

'Genius!' Penelope whispered to him.

'I know! Look we are calling an emergency meeting in half an hour, Scott and James are about half an hour away, so we'll wait for them to come back. We are very, very lucky to get wind of this now, even the guys in the States won't know until the end of the day, if even. I doubt it'll be common knowledge yet, I mean he probably just wanted to tell them in person?!' Roger whispered to Penelope, Simon was still on a call trying to get as much detail as possible, he couldn't put it on speaker because it was incredibly confidential and he was struggling to write and hold the phone.

'Hmm, maybe. The implications are huge, is he taking his equity stake with him?' That was the first thing that occurred to Penelope.

'I presume so, hence the call, details are very sketchy at the mo though. Jamie is our man, he has done a lot of work with the partners on internal stuff, firm strategy, that kind of thing, so he can advise. I don't know whether Jamie is going to tell the others that he told us, but better to be prepared all the same.' Roger sounded grave.

'I completely agree,' Penelope replied gravely.

'Guys, the other two are half an hour away, so… meeting in the boardroom when they get back, ok with you?' Simon asked.

'Fine.' They all said, they were counting the minutes!

'Never a dull moment in here… ok, quick google search on Mortimer, went to Yale, industry contacts… hmmm… maybe he's heading back into the retail industry? He's got a lot of previous experience. I wonder if he is going to take early retirement?' Penelope got onto the intranet immediately, she was speed-reading all of the copy on Mortimer.

'Oh, text message! I bet it's George!' Penelope nearly jumped out of her skin as her mobile vibrated loudly on her desk.

Hi, ASB here,
are we still ok for Wednesday?
I'm in the City for meetings all day,
shall I collect you from work,
at about 7pm?

Penelope re-read the text message in utter disbelief, she could not believe his timing.

'Oh… .my… god! I'm soooooo happy!' She sat back in her seat and grinned at her phone.

'Hi, it's me.' Pen had to let George know immediately.

'Hi there, is everything ok?' George was concerned.

'Yes, well, in work, no… but … he texted me!' Penelope sighed.

'Who, Richard?' George said.

'Noooooo! Alyx!' Penelope sighed.

'Oh, Ah-leeeeks! What did he say?' George was delighted for Penelope.

'Arrangements for dinner, he's going to collect me from work tomorrow, I don't know where we are going, he said he is in the City for meetings…' Penelope was speaking really fast.

'Ok, ok, calm down… bloody hell Pen, I've never seen you like this, right, have you decided what you are going to wear?' George was always so practical.

'What? Oh my god! No! I wonder should I get something new… oh no… the shops will be closed, oh no!' Penelope started stressing out.

'Ok, ok, now listen… you have plenty of nice clothes, and you don't want to look like you have gone to too much *effort* do you?' George reeled Penelope back in from imaginary shopping in Reiss.

'No, no, of course, you are right. Now I don't know whether to bring jeans with me, or to just go in my suit… if he's coming straight from work he might be in a suit.' Penelope had so many concerns.

'Just ask him, when you text him back,' George suggested.

'Ok, good idea… listen George, they are hovering outside the office here, I better go!' Penelope whispered to George, she could see that Scott and James had arrived and this was not the right time to be chatting on her mobile.

'Ok, and Pen… Don't text him without speaking to me first,' George warned her.

'Ok…' Penelope reluctantly agreed.

'Promise!' George was serious.

'I promise.' Penelope agreed meekly.

The bankers all congregated outside Room 5, the boardroom.

'Hi, Scott, James… did you hear the news?' Simon approached the two of them as he ushered them into the boardroom.

'Well not really, we thought it was a ransom situation. Harry called and said he couldn't talk about it on the phone, but we had to come straight back! How dramatic, surely it's not that bad, you all look ok…' Scott and James had been out with a client and the plan was to a have a "long liquid lunch", they were not happy at being summoned back.

'Oh it is that bad, and believe me appearances can be deceiving.' Penelope retorted.

'Are the others dialling in?' Scott said, he couldn't get what was going on at all.

'No, that's the main thing… they don't know that we know,' Roger advised.

'Know what!? This is ridiculous, will someone please fill me in!' James was starting to get impatient.

'Scott, James, into my office… everyone else… boardroom in fifteen, let me just brief these two first.' Simon took Scott and

James into his office, leaving the other two in the boardroom to start brainstorming. The lunchtime cabernet glow slowly faded from their faces as the news sank in.

Three hours later the Capital Markets team emerged, not the better of the experience, but they all felt clearer about the way forward. Each of them had a long action list to prepare for when the news broke and the media got wind of it.

Penelope was exhausted, but still, she floated back to her desk...

'I am walking on air. I can't wait to see him again. I hope he is as good looking as I remember. I love black hair, and he definitely had black hair, and just chin length, one of those impossibly expensive haircuts that doesn't look expensive at all... kind of like a musician, but in a suit , and those lovely tanned hands, I bet he has a gorgeous washboard stomach... and he isn't too tall, I hate it when they are too tall... He had the most gorgeous dark brown eyes, and really nice skin. Ooops, better not think about that now... more important things to do, the news today could have huge ramifications for our office.' Penelope was on cloud nine.

'Hi, it's me...again! I've been in a meeting since earlier...' Pen rang George as soon as she could.

'But that was hours ago!' George's meetings usually lasted an hour... max!

'I know! I'm exhausted. So, can I text him now...' she was dying to text him back.

'Well, yes, but keep it short.' George gave Penelope permission.

'Ok, and ask what to wear?' Penelope asked.

'Oh, yes, what to wear of course. He'll probably give you a ring anyway, so don't worry about saying too much in the text.' George could see how the whole thing was going to play out.

'Good point.' Penelope was relieved to have George's support for this.

'Right, I better go,' George added.

'Alright, be good!' Penelope advised her...

'Always!'

Chapter 13

Scottish Castles

George was right, Alyx did phone Penelope…

'Tonight's the night! I can't wait. He sounded lovely on the phone last night. He was phoning me from Paris. I feel like I am in a film, I was walking on air after being on the phone to him. He said jeans were fine for tonight, which is great, I don't want to feel like I'm in a meeting or something, first dates can be nerve-wracking enough without being constrained in a suit. I'll feel much more comfortable in jeans. I will have to pick a lovely top, the black and white silk one would go well with my jeans, and nice high shoes, but not too high so that I'm not towering over him… I'll get my hair done at lunchtime.' Penelope considered what to wear as she got out of bed.

Zara was deep in thought as she brushed her teeth just before leaving the house, she could barely concentrate on that simple task.

'I don't know what Penelope was doing to herself in the bathroom last night, she was in there for ages, and there were lovely smells of lavender and ylang ylang wafting around the hallway for hours afterwards. She must have been having a bath, because she doesn't have a bath in her en suite. I was hoping to run into her in the kitchen to have a chat about the redundancy thing at work. She is a real city girl, she might know what to do. I'm not sure whether

I know her well enough to ask her yet, but I'm sure she wouldn't mind. I might try to see if she is around later. Being a poor student is still fresh in my mind, so getting a tax free lump sum would be like winning the lottery. I wonder if Rob is right about getting temping work. Still though... being made redundant, I don't know if I could cope with that. I could never tell my parents, they would never understand.'

Later on, in the City, Penelope was in a meeting.

'So, I think in conclusion that with the current business model we could see a vast...'

'Oh my god, will this guy ever stop droning on! I have a bloody hair appointment in fifteen minutes...' Penelope was getting restless.

'... now, does anyone have any questions?' the speaker announced.

'Oh, here we go, they'll all be dying to be seen to be asking questions... right, I think I'll pretend to be getting a call and sneak out... . Yes! Works every time! Oh damn it! Now my bloody phone is ringing! I hope it's not someone from work...' Penelope stood up as she went to answer her phone.

'Penelope Chesterfield speaking!' Penelope barked into her phone.

'Hello, that's sounds very official!' the male voice replied.

'Excuse me! Who is this?' Penelope was baffled, this was a bit odd.

'It's Richard, have you forgotten already?' Richard sounded trite.

'Oh, Richard, erm well, it's not a great time, can I call you back later?' Penelope began to blush slightly, she hadn't been expecting his call at all.

'Of course, but before you go, are we still ok for tomorrow?' Richard pressed her for commitment.

'Tomorrow?' Penelope had completely forgotten that they had arranged to meet up.

'Yes, we said we'd meet up.' Richard started to sound a little concerned.

'Oh, yes, yes of course, I hadn't forgotten, I am really looking forward to catching up with you... can we sort out the arrangements tomorrow, I must dash.' Penelope sounded rushed.

'No problem, I'll give you a call.' Richard sounded relieved. 'Ok, thanks Richard…'

'Bloody hell… am I ever going to get to the hairdressers! I hope it's the Italian guy, he won't mind if I'm a tiny bit late…' Penelope dashed out the front entrance.

'Hi, I'm Penelope, I have an appointment…' Penelope arrived into the hairdressers with seconds to spare.

'*Buongiorno*, Penelope!' Mwah, Mwah! Penelope was greeted continental style by the receptionist.

'Ok, I can see Gianni… can I go on through?' Penelope already had her coat off and was making her way down the back.

'Well, I can't see why not, he seems like he is waiting for you…' Marco announced, as Gianni stood there, his hands on his hips waiting for her.

'Thank god! This guy is brilliant. I'm so lucky to get an appointment with him.' Penelope gave him a warm smile as she sat down.

'Espresso?' Marco reappeared as if by magic.

'*Grazie*.' Penelope consented gladly.

'*Prego*.' Marco went off to get her a coffee.

In no time at all, Penelope was back in the office, looking wonderful, and being unable to think of anything but her date with Alyx that night. Her blonde bob sat perfectly around her pretty face.

'This day is flying by, I hope nothing kicks off in work this afternoon… it can be really hard to plan things. Fingers crossed. I can always leave and come back after the date if there is lots to do. He's coming to collect me, I wonder what that means, surely he's not driving? Oh well, I'll just have to wait.' Penelope was so nervous waiting in work for Alyx to arrive. She had phoned George six times today already so she didn't phone her again, anyway she needed to keep her line free so that reception could phone her when he arrived.

'Miss Chesterfield, this is reception, I have a Mr Stuart-Bruges here to see you, shall I send him up?' The head receptionist said.

'NO!, I mean, erm no, could you please tell him that I will come down to reception in a few moments, thank you very much.' Penelope smiled as she spoke.

'Oh my god, he's early! Right, well I'll have to make him wait a while.'

Penelope paced up and down near her desk. She went down to reception ten minutes later.

'Alyx, sorry to keep you waiting,' Penelope beamed at him.

'No problem, you look lovely Penelope,'... and Alyx beamed right back at her as he kissed her on both cheeks.

'Thanks.' *'Oh my god I'm blushing, stop it, stop it, stop it, think of snow, icebergs, cool things... not red! Oh no!'* Penelope got a little flustered.

'Right, I thought we would go to Nobu, if that's ok with you... are you hungry?' Alyx gestured to her, with his hand barely touching the small of her back, to walk ahead of him out through the main door.

'A little bit.' *'That is such a lie, I am not one bit hungry and I haven't eaten anything since breakfast!'* Penelope thought to herself.

'Ok, do you want the good news or the bad news?' Alyx asked Penelope.

'Bad first, then good...' Penelope always answered that way.

'Well it's just starting to rain...' Alyx pointed out.

'Oh no! My hair!' Penelope grimaced, this was not a good sign, one drop of rain and her hair would be a complete ball of frizz!

'... but, I have a car waiting outside... I have been rushing all over London all day so the record company just send me a car it's just easier that way, I have it until midnight, and then rumour has it it turns into a pumpkin!' Alyx smiled at her, he was great at lightening the mood.

'Oh, I see, that sounds like such fun.' Penelope was smiling again.

'They are used to running around after the stars, so I guess that rubs off on the lawyers too, it can be very handy some times. Right, let's go... after you.' Alyx ushered Penelope into the car.

'Pierre, could you please take us to Nobu?' Alyx leant forward and spoke to the driver.

'Of course Alyx.' Pierre smiled back at him.

'Somebody pinch me!' Penelope couldn't believe this, it was like being in a film.

'Alyx, there was an accident up ahead, it might take us a little longer to get there than we thought...' Pierre called back to Alyx.

'Thanks Pierre... in that case would you like a drink Penelope? There's no point in seeing it go to waste...' Alyx opened a little cabinet that had some small bottles of champagne and plastic champagne flutes.

'Indeed.' Penelope beamed at him.

'Please god don't let me get pissed before I get to the bloody restaurant, that's all I need!' Penelope hid her concerns behind her beaming smile.

'Good evening, Mr Stuart-Bruges, let me just show you to your table...' Alyx was greeted by name at the door.

'They know you here?' Penelope was impressed.

'Oh yes, sorry, I know it must seem really pretentious, but we always have to take clients out when we are in London, and I like it here, so they know us, we are usually the rowdy ones in the corner with guitars everywhere,' Alyx confessed sheepishly.

'I see what you mean, I was a bit concerned that you were going all James Bond on me there for a minute.' Penelope was getting on like a house on fire with Alyx. She felt so comfortable, she could hardly believe that she had only met him briefly once before, she felt like she had known him her entire life.

'No, no, not at all.' Alyx winked at her.

'So... let's talk... rock stars!' Penelope was dying to talk about the musicians that he represented.

'I knew you were going to say that... what kind of music are you into?' Alyx sat back in his seat and focused his gaze on Penelope.

'Oh I've got pretty eclectic taste, I like some of the old stuff and a lot of the new, I'm really enjoying the recent rock renaissance, real music again… finally!' Things were getting off to a great start.

'That's exactly how I feel about it. So you said you like some older stuff, are you a Beatles or a Stones girl?' Alyx waited in silence for her to answer the definitive question.

'Well, both actually…' Penelope said, worried how he would react. 'I could never choose between them.'

'Me too.' *'Perfect,'* Alyx thought to himself , *'this is definitely my kind of girl.'*

The pair chatted for the entire time that they were in Nobu. There were no awkward silences, no disagreements… and… Penelope did manage to stay moderately sober and even managed to eat some of the delicious food.

'Thanks for dinner Alyx, I had a really nice time…' Penelope didn't want this night to end… preferably… ever!

'Do you want me to drop you home now, or do you fancy a drink?… I know this place near here, well it's a club actually, and a few of the guys from the band are playing a private gig…' Alyx didn't want to put her under any pressure.

'I'd love that.' Penelope could not believe that this was happening. Alyx actually represented one of her favourite bands, maybe they would be at the club!

'I thought you might,… let me get your coat, and we'll get Pierre to take us.' Alyx went off to get Penelope's coat.

'Ok, I'll wait here.' Penelope's head was spinning, this was all so exciting!

'Good Night Alyx, call back and see us the next time you are in town.' The maître d' led Alyx and Penelope out the door.

'I will of course.' Alyx replied.

'Oh no! What does that mean? The next time he's in town? I hope he is not leaving already…' Penelope's mind was running away on her, she needed to know what that comment meant, but she didn't want to seem too nosey.

In no time at all they were outside a black door, with no light and no sign outside, down a narrow street off Long Acre. It was a good thing that Penelope was walking on air, otherwise she would have been terrified. The door opened slightly and Alyx said his name, the next thing the door swung open and they were in the most gorgeous little purple velvet box of a club.

'Here we are, what do you think?' Alyx turned to Penelope to gauge her reaction.

'Very cool, you would barely even notice it from the street… I like to think I know London, but I never knew this was here.' Penelope was a bit disoriented, she couldn't believe this place was hidden just off Long Acre.

'Well it's new, and I think it's supposed to be a secret, here let me introduce you to the band … it's one of those places, you know, once it's opened to the public that's it, it's not "safe" for the celebs anymore… Guys, let me introduce you to Penelope…' Alyx led her over to the table where her favourite band were sitting.

'Hey, nice to meet you…' the band all jumped up to say hi to her.

'Hey, Penelope, I'm Christie,' the lead singer said.

'Hey.' Penelope shook his hand in disbelief, she felt as if she was going to wake up any second and the whole thing will have been a dream. It felt surreal.

'Hi, I'm Chad, can I call you Penny?' Chad was so cheeky!

'Hi, yes of course you can. I really liked your last album, what was your influence when you wrote …' Penelope was dying to know…

'Jesus, Alyx, she's not a bloody journalist is she?!' Chad exploded, laughing at Alyx, his eyes raised to heaven.

'Oh god no, sorry, it's just I listened to it constantly last summer, and I was dying to ask you .' *'How embarrassing, he is smiling though, so he must have been joking. I love this band, I can't believe I'm here.'* Penelope was mortified and went bright red, she struggled to recompose herself, she had not been expecting his outburst at all.

'Well, in that case… I presume you are talking about the title track?' Chad winked at her. He was constantly getting the same question. Everyone wanted to know who *that* song was about!

'Yep.' Penelope couldn't wait to find out.

'Well, I will tell you ... now that I know you are not a *journalist*, but you have to promise not to laugh...' Chad looked very serious.

'Of course I won't laugh.' Penelope put on her most angelic face. Alyx was watching this exchange, highly amused.

'It is actually about my cat...' Chad waited for her to try not to laugh, it was funny seeing her trying to hold it in.

'Oh god, now of all times, don't let me laugh... say something quick!' Penelope struggled not to laugh. The muscles around her mouth started twitching and her lips wobbled, trying to break into a smile.

'Your cat, oh, I mean... your cat died?' Penelope managed to get the words out without exploding with laughter.

'To me, yes... and you see the cat is a symbol...' Chad began...

'Erm hello, tell her who *gave* you the cat... it isn't about the bloody cat at all... Penelope don't listen to him, it's about a girl of course... his ex, they bought a cat together, and then they broke up... she got to keep the cat... he's still bitter about it...' Christie butted in, he was nearly in hysterics at this stage. Christie was standing next to Alyx watching Penelope and Chad, Alyx was really impressed with how Penelope was holding her own against an international rock god, there weren't many women who could keep it together in that situation.

'Now that explains a lot, I see, well whoever it is about, it's a really beautiful song, and by virtue of the fact that the album went platinum, I'm not the only one who thinks that...' Penelope added.

'Thank you! I'm feeling a bit better about kitty already.' Chad pretended to sniff back some tears.

'I'm glad.' Penelope smiled at him, and gave his arm a compassionate pat.

'Are you ok?' Alyx leant into Penelope and whispered to her.

'Having a great time, just talking about cats and stuff.' Penelope whispered back to him.

'So… he told you about the song?' Alyx asked her.

'You could say that.' Penelope replied still in hushed tones so that Chad couldn't hear them.

'Never shuts up about the bloody thing, if people *knew* that song was about a cat, seriously, his image would be ruined… Rock & Roll my arse!' Alyx laughed.

'What was that Alyx?!' Chad interrupted.

'Chad, em, I was just saying how great it was that we get the *cars*, you know to go around London…' Alyx changed the subject very quickly.

'Oh yeah, well it's not like we can get *the bus*… can't even go to the bloody toilet without getting mobbed!' Chad was so dramatic, he threw his hands up as he said this.

'Indeed, well I'll leave you to it… Penelope, I have a table for us over here.' Alyx led Penelope over to a table by the small stage.

'Ok, bye, lovely to meet you all.' She really couldn't believe that this was happening to her.

'They are really nice aren't they, but so dramatic! It's hilarious, mobbed in the loo! I just like going around in the cars, and we kind of know the drivers now, so that's quite nice.' Alyx was laughing about the band, they were so manly, but such drama queens at the same time.

'It must be, much better than getting random taxis…' Penelope could definitely appreciate the benefits of having a driver!

'Here, have a seat, look Chad has decided to take to the stage, I don't think they were meant to be on tonight…?' Alyx had some champagne on ice waiting for them at the table. They arrived at the table just as Chad grabbed the microphone.

'Hello, well… I would like to dedicate a song to a lovely lady I met this evening… Penny, this first song is dedicated to Penny Lane there in the black and white top… and of course to my darling Kitty, who can't be here tonight…' Chad announced looking directly at Penelope.

'I thought I went red earlier, but this is beyond red! Thank god it's dark in here.' For the first time in her entire life, Penelope

was, momentarily, completely and utterly speechless. Chad started singing, and held her gaze until the song was finished.

'Well, it seems like you made quite an impression.' Alyx was very impressed, the band had never done that for one of his friends before.

'Alyx, I actually don't know what to say... ' Penelope couldn't take her eyes off the stage until the song was officially over. It was only then that she managed to have a bit of a look around to see some of the very famous faces enjoying the impromptu performance alongside her. As soon as Chad had finished he hopped off the stage to make way for the band who were actually due to be playing that night...

As soon as the music was finished, Alyx and Penelope could chat to each other, now that they could finally hear each other properly! Penelope filled Alyx in on her job, and her life and generally how she came to live in Clapham South. Alyx loved the story about how Charlie and Penelope had met Zara. Alyx filled Penelope in on his life and how he travels a lot with work. He grew up in the UK and France, his mother was French and his father was Scottish... hence the unusual name. His grandparents had a castle in Scotland, which he inherited with his sister. He didn't mention to her whether he lived in London or not, and frankly Penelope was reluctant to ask. She was afraid that he was going to say that he lived abroad, as it would spoil the fantastic mood. Alyx filled Penelope in on his job, and all of the bands that he had met and represented. The couple chatted as if they had known each other forever for the next couple of hours... it was getting late.

'That was a great gig, I much prefer small venues.' Alyx was chatting away easily, he had a very strong quiet air of confidence about him.

'Me too totally, I love that band too... it must be different for you because it's kind of work... do you ever get sick of it?' Penelope thought this was possible, it was an occupational hazard of working at what you loved... surely?

'No way, I still love it!… Look it's nearly midnight, we better go if I'm going to get you home before the car turns into a pumpkin.' Alyx was so emphatic as he realised the time.

'Oh, that's ok, you don't have to drop me home…' Penelope was trying to be polite, she was actually *dying* for him to drop her home, she never wanted this night to end.

'Of course, I must!, after all the champagne that we have had… I have to make sure you get home ok.' Alyx was such a gentleman. 'Let's go and say goodbye to the guys, and we can head off.' He gestured to Penelope to head over to the band's table.

'Ok, thanks Alyx.' She turned around and grinned at him.

'My pleasure.' He place his hand gently at the small of her back. As they approached the exit, Alyx motioned for Penelope to go first. The door was opened for Penelope and as she was about to step out into the street she was greeted by a lady with a flat cap and a small but scary entourage who had just arrived at the little black door. It was one of the most famous residents in London, Penelope actually couldn't believe her eyes. She stood there in complete shock as their eyes met. All Penelope could think to do was to stand aside to let her and her entourage in… The lady in the flat cap gave Penelope a nod as a thank you for standing aside and letting her pass by. Penelope turned to Alyx…

'Oh my god, was that…?' Alyx cut her off.

'Shh… yeah it was, I've seen her in here a few times, I can't believe we literally walked into her on our way out. I've never been *that* close to her before, wow…' Alyx whispered to Penelope. It was simply not cool to be naming names in a club like that, so her cut her off before she said one of the most famous names in the world. That was one thing that made it 'safe' for celebs, no hysterics!…

As soon as they were safely outside, and the little black door was closed firmly behind them, Penelope turned to Alyx.

'Is it safe to talk now?' She asked.

'Yeah, pretty much, let's just move away from the cameras over the door.' Alyx motioned to Penelope.

'I can't believe that just happened, I nearly stepped on her, thank god I stopped to let her go past, I felt like such a moron standing there gaping at her!' Penelope gushed.

'I know, it definitely was a once in a lifetime situation, it was a good move to let her go past, she definitely deserves that level of respect.' Alyx winked at Penelope as he said this. 'Look it's probably best if you don't mention what happened, if word gets out at all about this club, and especially about "you know who" – I could get into serious hot water!' Alyx pleaded with Penelope.

'Yes, yes of course, I completely understand. Don't worry I will not mention a word. I know how quickly things can spread around London. Who can forget "ketchupgate". An email can get around the entire City in a matter of hours.' Penelope assured him.

'Ok, thanks, I'm so glad that you understand…' Alyx breathed a sigh of relief. He hadn't heard about "ketchupgate" but he knew she understood the sentiment. As if out of nowhere, Pierre appeared with the car.

'Pierre, can you take us to Clapham, SW4. I would just like to drop this young lady home.' Pierre opened the door for Penelope.

'No problem Alyx.' Pierre replied. There was no traffic at all at that time of night, and Pierre put his foot down. In no time at all they were heading over Chelsea Bridge, Clapham was minutes away.

'Oh no, we are getting there really quickly… I don't really want this to end, slow down Pierre! No good, there is no traffic on the roads, I'll be home in no time!' Penelope was still coming down from the adrenaline rush of the door encounter, she couldn't believe she was nearly home. In no time at all they were on Abbeville Road, and reluctantly… outside number 72.

'Ok, well this is where I live, thank you for a lovely night Alyx.' Penelope didn't know what was going to happen next, she braced herself.

'My pleasure, I'll just see you to the front door.' Alyx hopped out and opened the door for her. Penelope headed up to her front door and turned to say goodbye to him.

Alyx leant in and gave her a peck on the cheek, '… ok, I will give you a ring during the week, Good Night,' he said.

'Good Night.' Penelope replied. She stood there unable to move, he smelled incredible. Just as he was about to get into the car he turned to her and gave her a big smile… and within seconds the car was gone.

Penelope turned and opened the communal front door. As soon as she closed it behind her, she went no further. She stood there in the mundane dusty surroundings of the rented hallway, bills piled high, and random mail for people who no longer lived there shoved into a recycling bag, just staring into space. A dusty plastic potted sunflower plant from Ikea stared back up at her and brought her back to reality. Penelope was literally suspended in disbelief as the images of what had happened and who she had met ran through her mind like a film, and the hallway was such a stark contrast to all that had happened to her earlier that evening. Eventually she rooted around for her keys again in her handbag and opened the front door. She drifted up the stairs.

'Wow, what a night… I feel like I'm floating… it's too late to ring George now, it'll have to wait until the morning…' Penelope floated up the next set of stairs to her bedroom, and she sat on the end of her bed for a good half an hour trying to take it all in, before she could even attempt to take her makeup off and get ready for bed. She could still smell his cologne, it was as if he was still with her. Alyx certainly had made quite an impression on her.

***

'George! Hi it's me, oh my god George, he is perfect, you are not going to believe…' Penelope prattled into her mobile as soon as it wasn't *too early* to ring George.

'Oh my god Pen, calm down, I can't take in that many words at this time in the morning!' George rubbed her eyes and sat up in bed. She slipped out of bed as Penelope spoke so as not to wake up her boyfriend who was still fast asleep beside her.

'Oh, ok, sorry... well the date, the date last night, remember with Alyx?' Penelope gushed.

'Oh my god yes, do tell...' George started to put the kettle on in the kitchen.

'Well, he had a *car* to drive us around for the night, a chauffeur type situation...' Penelope began detailing events...

'No!' George exclaimed, this really woke her up.

'Yes! And then...' Penelope began...

'Was it a limousine?' George interrupted.

'No, but a gorgeous huge car, I was too busy looking at him to be honest...' Penelope sounded dreamy as she said this.

'Quite right, quite right... so go on... where did he take you?' George was sorry to have asked such a silly and insignificant question, the type of car was the least important detail.

'To Nobu...' Penelope announced.

'Nice!' George approved, she smiled warmly down the phone.

'Yeah, I know...and after the meal, we went to this secret club where my favourite band in the world were playing a private gig!' Penelope gushed.

'No, not...' George knew exactly who Penelope was talking about, they went to see them live last year and Penelope was practically *still* talking about it.

'Yep, and I got to meet Chad and Christie and the others, I asked him about the song, and you are not going to believe who it's about!' Penelope gushed!

'Who?!' George demanded, the mere mention of the band had George as excited as Penelope was.

'A cat!' Penelope roared laughing.

'What?!' George exclaimed, she simply couldn't believe this.

'I know! And then they dedicated the song to me, it was both embarrassing and amazing.' Penelope blushed as she remembered being singled out.

'Ok, but what about *Ah-Leeks* what was he like?' George reigned the conversation in, Alyx was the important bit, not all of the *stuff*.

'Oh, a perfect gentleman, and gorgeous, and charming and lovely,' Penelope gushed.

'Good kisser?' George was straight to the point, as always…

'Well, that's the thing… I… well, I don't know exactly.' Penelope stammered, momentarily slightly deflated.

'What do you mean, didn't he kiss you when you were leaving?' George was astounded.

'Just on the cheek, but that doesn't count for kissing really.' Penelope considered the definition of a first kiss, did the peck count?

'Indeed, hmmm, interesting. That is a lot of information for me this early in the morning, I better go and hop into the shower or I'm going to be late for work…' Time was marching on and if they weren't careful George would definitely be late for work, they could quite happily have talked about the first date all morning.

'Ok, I better go too, got a meeting in five, speak to you later though…' Penelope was already in work and opening her Outlook calendar.

'Definitely.' George dunked the green teabag into her cup of hot water, and put the kettle on again to make some tea for her boyfriend.

'How on earth can I concentrate on work now, this is ridiculous. I'm so happy.' Penelope beamed at her PC, she couldn't stop thinking about him…

Five minutes later the smile had to be temporarily removed, there was a serious meeting in progress in the boardroom at JLM.

'Gentlemen, and ahem, Penelope, sorry I didn't see you there Penelope, now this news has come as quite a shock. We have had no official statements from New York yet, we don't even know if our guys over there know yet. Our partners are on the red-eye, and they will be coming straight to work to brief us. James has done some contingency planning, for damage limitation… but at the moment there is not an awful lot that we can do, until we hear from our guys…' Simon sounded grave. He was not much wiser than yesterday, but he needed to get the team together, to ensure that they were all on the same page, and most importantly that they remembered that they were bound to the bank by a confidentiality agreement, which would see them fired… and sued… if they broke it.

'He could actually be talking about Armageddon and I don't think that would even keep the smile off my face. Oh god! He just caught me smiling, I hope he doesn't think I was smiling at him…' Penelope was on cloud nine, and a smile broke through for a minute, she wiped it off her face quickly, this was a serious meeting, very serious indeed.

'… so I propose we meet back here after lunch, and we can get the official version from our guys, ok, back to work everyone…' the meeting was over, Penelope hadn't heard one word that was said, she was miles away.

'Hi, it's me, sorry about that… I've been in a meeting for *ages*!' Penelope rang George as soon as she could.

'Pen, I'm on the edge of my seat here, I couldn't wait to hear from you…' George was so excited, she had been half asleep when she spoke to Pen earlier and couldn't take it all in. A double shot skinny latte and a blueberry muffin had got her brain in gear, and she was now dying for more details.

'George, I can't stop smiling. He is just so… I can't even *describe* it, he's just… goooorgeous!' Penelope trailed off as she drawled 'Gorgeous'.

'Certainly sounds like it,' George answered her animatedly.

'I'm glowing. He's like my ideal man, but he is real. Did you ever have a picture in your mind of your ideal man and what he was like, well Alyx actually is that guy. I never thought it was actually possible.' Penelope was delirious.

'I can tell you are glowing, I'm so happy for you!' George smiled down the phone.

'I've got more poxy bloody meetings all day, so let's meet up after work for a drink, for all the gory details…' Penelope looked down at her calendar again, the Mortimer resignation was totally dominating what would have been a quietish week. As she looked down the list another Outlook invite popped up for a meeting in five minutes, so it looked like she couldn't get out to even grab lunch.

'Yeah, I'd love to … but aren't you meeting Richard tonight?' George reminded Penelope about Richard.

'Oh my god, I totally forgot, shiiiiiiiit, I didn't even bring a change of clothes, oh no! I'm so not in the mood to meet him, I remember now… he rang yesterday to see if I was still up for it. I definitely can't cancel, that would be so rude… oh no George!' Penelope sounded totally devastated.

'Well, it'll just have to wait until tomorrow then…' George was not happy about this either, she had assumed that when Penelope had suggested meeting up tonight, that she had already cancelled with Richard.

'But that's *ages* away!' Penelope whined.

'I know! Believe me, I can't wait to hear about it too, but you should meet up with him. It's not every day that you bump into an old friend, and if you cancel he'll probably take it the wrong way. ' George advised her.

'I know, oh, well… tomorrow then… but I'll speak to you later anyway…I'll try to not have a late one with Richard…' Penelope was resigned to the fact that, that was the way it had to be.

'Ok, bye.' George sounded empathetic.

'Bloody Richard! I'm so annoyed, all I want to do is talk about Alyx, and now I can't bloody do that with Richard…' Penelope's mood was dented, but only for a minute.

Later that day, the phone rang.

'Penelope Chesterfield.' She answered curtly.

'Hi Penelope, it's me…Richard, is it a good time?' Richard was terribly courteous.

'Oh yes, it's fine, are you ringing about this evening?' Penelope mustered some cheeriness, after all, it wasn't his fault that the timing of their get together that night was so bad.

'Yes, I thought I'd drop by your office at about seven, is that ok with you?' Richard was already planning the logistics.

'That's fine, listen Richard, I hope you don't mind, but I didn't bring a change of clothes with me…' Penelope sounded apologetic.

'Oh no don't worry about that at all… neither did I.' Richard had never even considered bringing a change of clothes, he thought he looked his best in his suits anyway. He *hated* jeans, they were so *common*.

'Ok, see you later then.' Penelope was keen to get him off the line.

'Looking forward to it.' Richard replied curtly, and then hung up.

'Oh no! It'll be like a bloody meeting, the two of us sitting there in our suits. It's lunchtime, but I can't eat a thing! I don't think I'll ever eat again.' Penelope was momentarily miffed by the thought of meeting Richard, but then the memory of Alyx floated back into her head, and it was all better again…

After a full day of intense meetings, 7 pm came around rather quickly.

'Miss Chesterfield, I have a Mr. Lord down here to see you…' Richard had arrived a few minutes early.

'Damn it… he's early…' 'Ok, tell him I'll be right down.' *'Well, no point in keeping him waiting.'* Penelope went straight downstairs. .

'Richard, hi, lovely to see you again…' Penelope gave him a kiss on his cheek.

'Penelope, you look stunning.' Richard kissed her back, and gave her a broad smile.

'What, oh … erm, I mean thank you. Where are we off to sorry I forgot to pick somewhere, I've been really busy in work…?' Penelope was a bit taken aback, she wasn't even dressed up or anything, what was he going on about?

'I thought we'd have supper at the Ritz.' Richard announced.

'That sounds lovely.' *'That's weird… I thought he wanted me to pick somewhere, he must have had to book that!'* Penelope was slightly surprised at this, this had not been the plan at all.

'So, tell me all about yourself… you haven't gone and got yourself married have you Penelope?' Richard went straight in with the killer question.

'Well, no… I…' Penelope began to get flustered, she was convinced he could see how crazy she was about Alyx just by looking at her glowing.

'Boyfriend?' Richard snapped, barely giving Penelope time to finish her sentence.

'Erm, not really, you see…' Penelope struggled to finish her sentence, it felt a bit like the Spanish Inquisition, and nobody expects that… when they are meeting up with an old friend.

'Fabulous… I'm single too, great fun isn't it?!' Richard sat back in his seat and began to relax a bit and beamed at her.

'Well, not exactly, it's just that…' Penelope began… but Richard cut her off again…

'More champagne!' He was filling her glass before she had time to protest.

'Oh, alright then…' *Well seeing as I can't get a word in edgeways I may as well…*'

'… mainly looking after my investment portfolio, and then of course there's the castle, and the yacht in the south of France… I try to get down there at least four times a year… did you know that my parents play golf with …' Richard rambled on about himself, name-dropping whenever possible.

Does he actually think I'm interesting in all of this crap!' Penelope was feeling drained as Richard went on and on, name-dropping and over-emphasising how much money his family has.

'I don't actually play golf myself, you see…' Penelope struggled to get her point across, but failed miserably.

'Great game! Great game… you *should* play, did you know that most of the business deals are made on the golf course and not in the boardroom…' Richard stated matter-of-factly, as if this was a revelation that only he was privy to.

'Well, I don't feel like I've ever missed out because I don't play…' Penelope began to assert herself, the fact that she could not get a word in edgeways was ridiculous.

'Nonsense! That's settled… I'm arranging a golfing weekend for the two of us, how is May for you…?' Richard jumped in with this as she paused to draw breath.

Hold your horses there, weekend away… help! The only thing worse than a "weekend away"… was a "golf weekend away"!'

Penelope could not believe this, one minute she was having a quick catch up drink with him and the next thing they were going away on a golf weekend together. What was up with the universe!?

'So... no men on the scene then? I'm surprised at that, a stunning young lady like yourself...' Richard went on and on.

'... well actually, there is...' Penelope tried to interrupt him to put him back in his place, but failed again. She admitted defeat to herself and knocked back another glass of champagne, to help her endure all of this machine gun fire conversation.

'... I thought you'd be snapped up, can't quite believe my luck!...' Richard said with glee. He kept droning on and on, and Penelope kept sipping champagne, she was bored of this now and there was nothing else to do. She had a glazed look in her eyes.

I think this champagne is going to my head, I suppose I haven't eaten all day, and every time I look up my glass has been refilled... how is he managing to do it without me noticing it.' Penelope was starting to feel a little ill... drinking on an empty stomach was never a good idea. Richard was actually facilitating the process, but that was beside the point...

'Richard! Are you *shrying* to get me *dhhrunk*?' Penelope struggled to get the words out.

'Would I?' Richard smiled brightly at her, he seemed alarmingly sober all of a sudden, in stark contrast to Penelope.

'Well I don't know... that's why I'm asking...' Penelope was struggling to take the situation in, why on earth would Richard want to get her drunk, it was supposed to be a catch up with an old friend, not a date gone disastrously wrong!

'No, no, of course not, don't be silly.' Richard regained composure now, he was seeing the concern flicker across Penelope's gaze.

'Do you know a guy called Alyx Stuart-Bruges?' Penelope decided to try to change the subject, she was completely bored of this now, and all of the champagne had loosened her tongue.

'... no... should I? The surname rings a bell...' Richard started filing through all of the "need to know" people in his mind.

'Well, he's a ... *friend* of mine, and he was telling me he has a castle in Scotland too... and I mean there can't be that many castles in Scotland... so I thought that you might know him... maybe you are in a *club* or something, of people ... you know, who *own castles*!' Penelope babbled on, making no sense at all, drunk fuzzy logic!

'What a club!? Now you are talking complete nonsense! Although the name does ring a bell, yes, yes, there was a girl... oh a terrible tragedy, her parents died in a plane crash when she was very young, oh and she did have a baby brother, that must be your pal.' Richard knew he recognised the surname, and he recalled the tragic tale.

'Indeed...' Penelope glowed, she was really glad that she had asked now. *'I knew it! I knew it! I knew he'd know him!'* A small feeling of triumph enveloped her, maybe this night hadn't been a total waste of time after all. *'That's so sad about his parents though, the poor guy... oh my god I am soooooo drunk, I need to go to the loo, but I'm afraid to get up in case I fall over.'* Penelope squirmed in her seat, she wasn't sure of herself enough to totter down to the loo, and she couldn't make a spectacle of herself in the Ritz, she just couldn't.

'No, thanks, no more champagne for me...' She put her hand over her glass as Richard went to pour again.

'Don't be ridiculous!' Richard snapped.

'No, no really Richard I have a very early meeting, I really should go home now.' Penelope sounded as firm as she could.

'Oh, I see,' Richard sighed, 'let me get you a taxi'. He jumped out of his seat, terrified that she would disappear into the night, never to return.

Richard insisted on dropping Penelope to Clapham in a taxi even though it was a quite out of his way. By the time they got to Clapham Penelope was relieved that the evening was over.

'Thank you Richard, for a lovely night... we must... hiccup... do it... oh excuse me... hiccup, again sometime... soon...' She had given up trying to hide the hiccups by the time she saw Battersea Bridge, there just didn't seem to be any point.

'Indeed we will... now let me say goodbye properly...' Richard jumped out to open the door for her, and then without any warning...

'What...oh...!' *'There is a Richard in my mouth... eugh! This cannot be happening.'* Penelope struggled to maintain composure. A brief moment of denial was followed swiftly by the stark realisation that Richard had rammed his tongue into her mouth.

'I'll call you tomorrow, Good Night Princess.' Richard strutted off delighted with himself, he couldn't believe how easy it had been, he had won the prize.

Penelope gave him a weak wave goodbye and stood there motionless, absolutely stunned. She struggled to get the key into the lock because she was so drunk.

'I can't believe that just happened! What the hell is going on? Ok, concentrate... key in the lock... key in the lock... turn key, oops, not that way, yes! The door is open... oh no...' Penelope struggled to get the communal front door open, she was very drunk, and she was completely in shock about what had just happened. Once her front door was finally open, she lost her balance and fell in the door. She tripped, and knocked some boxes that were stacked on the stairs, making a loud crash.

'Oh my god Penelope! Are you ok there?' Charlie nearly had a heart attack, he had just arrived in himself, and wasn't expecting Penelope to fall in the door behind him, making such a loud crash.

'Oh, I'm fine, I think the door took a bit of a battering though... are you ok little red door...' Penelope bent down and started talking to the door in soothing tones, as if it were a little child who had fallen over.

'Jesus!, what the hell happened to you? You're hammered!' Charlie had never seen Penelope in this state before, he was really, really shocked.

'Not only that... my *friend* just *kissed* me!' Penelope stood up, wobbled a bit, and said this in a very matter of fact way, pretty much the way a five-year-old would say it.

'Who, George?' Charlie shrieked!

'Nooooooooooooo, Ric-a-r-d, no Ri-sh-a-rd… no, no, you know Rich-ard, Loord.' Penelope stuttered, she was feeling really hot, and she was not enjoying all the questions, but was happy to have finally got the word "Richard" out. Charlie was worse than her mother!

'Not that ponce from Uni with the castle, and the water polo and all that shit?!' Charlie was disgusted.

'Well yes, and then he, well, I think he kissed me, and then he said I was a princess, imagine… I'm a princess, and it must be *true* because he has a *castle* , and we all know the type of people that live in *castles*… and then, my key wouldn't work, and I tried and tried and tried, and then the door fell open, and I fell in, and here we are…' Penelope was really speaking like a five-year-old now, and she was very proud of the fact that she managed to recount the whole story without even one hiccup. Her vision was becoming slightly blurred and Charlie looked so cross.

'Right, come on… I'm going to put you to bed…' Charlie was fuming, but his anger was not directed at Penelope.

'What?! I don't want to go to bed!' Penelope put her hands on her hips, and stood there defiantly. One thick strand of her blonde bob hung down over her face and refused to be tucked behind her ear. She tried again and again to blow it away, she huffed and puffed and started getting really annoyed that it wouldn't move.

'Now, you know you have to go to bed Pen, you have to work tomorrow…' Charlie decided that as she was acting like a child… he should speak to her as if she were one, so he said this in soothing tones. There was no sense in getting angry with her. It wasn't her fault that she'd arrived home in that state.

'Oh, no… work… I hate work…!' Penelope took off her shoes, sat down on the stairs and folded her arms across her chest defiantly, in a huff.

'Right come on.' Charlie hauled her up and slung her gently over his shoulder.

'Put me down!' She started pounding lightly on Charlie's back. Her world had literally been turned upside down.

'No! How else are you going to get up those stairs...?' Charlie laughed.

'I think you may... just may... have a point there... will you bring my shoes up for me... please...' Penelope started to sober up a bit, the shock of being lifted up and turned upside down, had this effect. Now her shoes were the emphasis of her childlike thought process.

'You have lots of other shoes in your room, you don't need those ones!' Charlie said soothingly.

'No! It's *the only* pair that I have...' Penelope was emphatic. 'They are my faaay-vorites.'

'Oh really!' Charlie feigned surprise, and played along.

'I swear, and I'll die without them...' Penelope sighed dramatically.

'Ok, I'll bring them up after...' Charlie reassured her.

'Thanks... I love you Charlie... you're the best friend in the world,' Penelope sighed, and in that moment she really meant it.

'I know, I know... now come on ... in to bed...' Charlie carried her into her bedroom.

'My shoes!' Penelope shrieked as he placed her gently on the bed.

'They are on their way up...' Charlie stated matter-of-factly.

'They are walking up the stairs on their own...? I always knew they were magic shoes!' Penelope hissed conspiratorially.

'No... Zara is bringing them up...' Zara had heard what was going on and retrieved the shoes quietly. She arrived into the room and presented the shoes to Penelope.

'Oh hi *Shaaaaaara*, you are an angel. Thank you for saving my shoooooooes...' Penelope loved Zara now too, her magic shoes were safe and sound in her bedroom.

'That's ok.' Zara smiled weakly at her.

'I've left some water by the bed there Pen, if you feel thirsty...' Charlie came back into the room with a pint of water.

'Ok, I'm fine… nighty night…' Penelope had managed to take off most of her clothes with a little help from Zara, and she was snuggled up in bed ready to go fast asleep. She scrunched the duvet up to her chin, and passed out.

Charlie and Zara left her to it, and shut the door quietly behind them.

'Bloody hell, thanks for bringing the shoes up…' Charlie whispered to Zara.

'What the hell happened to her?' Zara asked completely astonished.

'I think she was out for dinner with some idiot and he must have got her drunk. She literally fell in the door, did you hear the noise?' Charlie fumed as he said this.

'Yeah, I just thought it was one of your guitars falling over or something… do you know who she was out with?' Zara was pretty concerned now, she had only ever seen Penelope completely composed and immaculate, even when she was drinking.

'I think so, some idiot we went to college with,' Charlie hissed.

'A friend! Some bloody friend!' Zara cried.

'Exactly.' Charlie agreed, and he stomped off to bed.

Chapter 14

The Morning After

Penelope woke up with a thumping headache and her mouth was so dry she could barely feel her tongue. She was completely confused, disoriented and probably still… a little drunk.

'Oh my poor head, how on earth did I get into bed? I remember the restaurant, and then it's all a blur after that… how on earth did I get home… I remember Charlie, was he out too? Oh my god, Richard… Richard brought me home… oh no, and I think something happened… I think he kissed me. Only one thing to do…' Penelope woke up with a splitting headache and struggled to piece the fragments of her memories of the night before together.

'Hi,' Penelope croaked.

'What's wrong with you, you sound terrible?' George was shocked, she barely recognised Penelope's voice.

'I have the worst hangover.' Penelope admitted.

'Oh no, from last night… with Richard?' George was feeling a bit guilty now, she had been the one encouraging her to go out with Richard.

'Yep, and that's not the worst part?' Penelope started to feel sick at the memory she was about to relay to George.

'No?' George sounded astonished.

'I think, although I'm not sure… but I think he kissed me.'

Penelope felt like she was going to be sick as she said this.

'Oh my god, did you kiss him back?' George gasped.

'I don't really know, I was very drunk, and my reactions were really slow, and maybe he took that as... I don't know... a positive response,' Penelope sighed.

'Well, do you fancy him?' George was being pragmatic.

'What?! No, well not after meeting Alyx, I mean if this had happened before Alyx, then maybe, but not now.' Penelope poured her heart out to George. In reality she was probably still a little drunk and the words came tumbling out a bit more than they normally would have.

'Oh yes, how could I forget. How on earth are you coping with work...?' George asked.

'I slept in, I'm not in work.' Penelope lay her head back down as she said this.

'That's not like you!' George sounded shocked.

'I know, I phoned in and said I had a migraine, and that I'd go in once the tablets started working,' Penelope whimpered. They both knew that it was highly unlikely that she'd make it into work that day.

'Oh, ok, poor you... lets meet up later and have a chat... I know we were going to go out for a drink, but I think a takeaway at home might be a bit better?' George suggested a less alcoholic alternative for this evening.

'You are an angel, that would be perfect.' Penelope lay back down and stared at the ceiling, trying to take it all in. Then there was a knock on her bedroom door.

'Penelope, hi, I'm just on my way to the Tube, I just thought I'd bring you in some tea, and a few painkillers.' Zara pushed the door open very gently.

'Oh, hi Zara, you are so good, thank you... I feel like I'm dying,' Penelope whimpered, she was as pale as a ghost.

'I thought after last night, ...well I just wanted to see that you were ok?' Zara sounded genuinely concerned.

'Were you out with me last night too? It's all a bit fuzzy... I have no idea how I got home, or into bed, and I'm still dressed

– ish.' Penelope grimaced, as she looked down and saw she was still wearing her work shirt and tights.

'You kind of fell in the front door, and Charlie carried you up the stairs… and I had the very important job of carrying up your shoes… your only pair you said, very important that they weren't left downstairs!' Zara smiled weakly as she said this.

'Oh god, I can sort of remember bits and pieces now… I can't believe he carried me up, he's such a good friend. Sorry about the shoes thing, obviously crazy drunk talk…' Penelope was mortified, it was bad enough being hammered, but involving the whole household in getting her to bed was quite another story.

'Don't worry about it, listen I better go, let me know if you want me to bring you home anything…' Zara didn't want to be late.

'Oh, thank you… you are so kind.' Penelope smiled weakly at her.

'That was so sweet of her, I must have been in such a state last night for Charlie to carry me up the stairs… I'm so embarrassed!' Penelope tried to sip the tea and knocked back two of the painkillers, it was helping, but only a tiny bit.

Zara closed the front door behind her and sauntered down towards Clapham South Tube station.

'Poor Penelope, it reminds me of the day we were interviewing housemates… I know exactly how she feels. That friend she was out with sounds a bit dodgy. I have my all-important HR meeting today… I can't wait to see how much money I'll get!' Zara was practically spending her redundancy package before she got it!

***

'Hello Zara, have a seat there.' The HR manager offered Zara a seat in front of the desk.

'Thanks.' Zara smiled brightly at her.

'Have you come to a decision about Manchester?' The HR manager was unemotional.

'Well, actually that's what I wanted to talk to you about… I was thinking of taking redundancy, depending on the package…' Zara felt a little uneasy as she said this.

'What do you mean?' The HR manager stared blankly at her.

'You know the money, the redundancy payment…' Zara began to get flustered.

'Oh no, you see, there is no money…' she explained.

'But Rob…' Zara began.

'Oh, I see now… where you got that idea from, yes, you see Zara, you are still on your three-month probation period, so it's only after your first three months that you would be entitled to any kind of redundancy payment. I'm very sorry if you got the wrong end of the stick… but the situation is different for those who have worked here for a while… obviously the longer they have worked here… well their options will be different… I'm very sorry. So, as I outlined in our last meeting, we have the option for you to relocate to our Manchester office, Manchester is a lovely city… full of footballers! We love it up there, hate the big smoke…' The HR lady began trying to "sell" the idea of Manchester to Zara.

And then, the floodgates opened… tears started streaming down Zara's face.

'Oh, no, don't cry, it'll be ok…' The HR manager tried to sound soothing, she offered Zara a tissue from a box that she had beside her… just in case.

'I can't believe I'm being made *redundant*! What will I tell my parents, sniff, sniff.' Zara struggled with the words.

'Do you not want to take the Manchester option?' The HR manager sighed.

'No! I'm only bloody well getting used to London, and they are all so *proud* of me at home, and I can't tell them that I've been fired… and…' Zara spluttered.

'Alright, alright, but I'm afraid there will be no London office in the near future… so it's either Manchester or nothing… everyone is in the same boat… And of course you are not being fired, it is simply the case that your position here does not exist anymore. It is nothing personal at all, apologies if I did not make that clear from the outset.' The HR manager explained. But Zara didn't stick around long enough to hear about it.

'Hello darling... so, millionaires?!' Rob winked at her as she eventually came back to her desk.

'No, Rob, going for broke!' Zara sniffed and blew her nose loudly. She was bright pink from all the blubbing.

'What!? Are you taking the Manchester option then?' Rob sounded confused.

'No, there is no redundancy payment for me... I'm still on *probation*... you know, for three months... *to prove myself*... and that's why I get nothing...' Zara welled up again.

'Oh no, I'm so sorry, well did you get your CV out to agencies yet?' Rob put his arm around Zara's shoulders.

'No, I was just about to when I thought I was going to get the redundancy windfall... so I was in no hurry at all then...' Zara sniffed.

'Right, well... no time like the present... come on, let's get emailing, and you can set up appointments with them.' Rob started acting busy and motivated.

'Can we go for coffee first, my eyes are all red, and I think I need to calm down before all of the others come in... I don't want them to know...' All Zara wanted to do was to get the hell out of there.

'Ok, quite right... come on let's go then.' Rob already had his jacket on.

After a very long day in St Martin's Lane, Zara eventually made it home to leafy SW4.

'Thank god it's Friday, what a day! I can't believe I started crying, in front of the HR lady, they must think I'm such an idiot. The atmosphere in the office was terrible, I don't think anyone really wants to go up to Manchester... well at least they'll all get the money... oh no, I'm welling up again... stop it, stop it... I hope the others are out tonight, I don't really want anyone to see me in this state! Maybe if I'm really quiet when I go in... I can sneak upstairs and have another cry.' Zara opened the door very

quietly and snuck up the stairs, she was sure that nobody was in as it was only 6 pm. How wrong she was, she had forgotten that Penelope did not go into work that day…

'Zara! Hi, George is coming over… DVD and takeaway… do you fancy it… oh… dear… what's wrong, are you ok?' Penelope was in the middle of her speech about the evenings' activities, when she realised how red and puffy Zara looked.

'Well, I was ok… until…' *'Here come the tears again'*… 'I got fired!' Zara gasped.

'Fired!' Penelope sounded astounded.

'Yep, they are closing the London office… and the others…' Zara began.

'No, redundant… not fired!' Penelope cut in, there was major difference after all.

'What does it matter what it's called… the thing is…' Zara sniffed.

'There's a huge difference, redundant is the position and not the person… *the job* is gone, when you get fired, it means they don't want you anymore, because you did something wrong…' Penelope reassured Zara.

'Well, my mum won't see it that way, and I started crying in front of the HR lady… and I feel awful… and… oh no, are the boys in?' Zara panicked as she heard some movement upstairs.

'Yep, afraid so… but don't worry they've already seen me in this state, so I don't think they will even notice your red eyes… I think they are still in shock after seeing me… I think Gerry thought he was seeing a ghost!' Penelope sighed reassuringly.

'All the same… I better just run up and tidy myself up a bit…' Zara headed for the stairs.

'Well if it'll make you feel better, and anyway George is coming over, she always makes me feel better…' Penelope sighed.

'Ok.' Zara smiled weakly.

'And a takeaway… it doesn't get better than that!' Penelope laughed weakly.

'True… ok, I'll be back in a minute.' This perked Zara up a bit, having George around would definitely take her mind off things, George was always so bubbly and full of life.

Within the hour, George had arrived armed with junk food and a selection of DVDs. She bounced in with her glowing café au lait coloured skin, and her vivacious curly hair, which was in stark contrast to Penelope's ashen face, and Zara's red blotches. She was a breath of fresh air and lightened the mood immediately.

'Georgie! Did you bring wine?' Penelope felt that hair of the dog was in order.

'Well, in your state I didn't think it was wise, Jesus Pen, you are so pale… and what happened to you Zara, are you ok… have I stumbled into the wrong house?' George sounded confused.

'No, well, I have the worst hangover ever, and poor Zara just heard today that they are closing her office down, so there'll be a few redundancies…' Penelope explained.

'Oh no, Zara, well at least you know it's nothing personal… and this is *London* you'll get a job in no time, people change jobs all the time here, it's part of the… well… I won't say… *fun*… but part of the *adventure*.' George tilted her head to one side as she said this and gave Zara's shoulder a little rub.

'You are right Penelope, she has made me feel much better.' Zara turned and smiled at Penelope.

'I told you she would!' Penelope smiled back at her.

'So ladies, what are we dining on this evening?' George asked dramatically.

'We were thinking… Chinese?' Penelope winked at Zara as she said this.

'No remember what happened the last time?!' George gasped.

'No, what happened? Remind me?' Penelope put on her most innocent face.

'The miscellaneous Chinese food, and the lateness… and…' George was getting exasperated, jumping up and down and pointing at her watch.

'Oh *let's* do that again… it was so much *fun*!' Penelope smirked.

'Alright, but don't start complaining when it's three hours late,' Zara sighed.

'Don't worry, I brought chocolate... as a starter!' George perked up as she pulled a huge bar of chocolate out of her bag.

'Penelope, seriously... she is the best!' Zara smiled warmly in appreciation.

'I know... I couldn't live without her, isn't that right Georgie?' Penelope affirmed.

'Well, you can thank me in vodka shots... some other time... ... so any sign of any nice men moving in next door?' George was keen to lighten the mood.

'Erm, well neither of us are really here that much, I haven't seen anyone at all, I think it's still empty, what do you think Zara?' George's strategy was working, the girls were genuinely interested in who their neighbours might be.

'Definitely no sign of nice men, I think I would sense their presence... we should ask Charlie and Gerry... they are here during the day a good bit, they might know. We are too busy looking at Gerry when we are here if you know what I mean,' Penelope giggled.

'Any other news? How's the love life Zara?' George arched one eyebrow as she asked this, staring intently at Zara.

'As good as the job situation...' Zara started to well up again, and her voice started to wobble.

'Oh dear, well in that case Pen, you'll just have to entertain us with the cartoon-like dramatics of your love life this week... let's work our way backwards, I believe Zara can help fill in the gaps...' George gave Zara a knowing glance and a little pat on the arm, hoping to take her mind off her redundancy.

'The falling in the door episode?' Zara offered, mustering a weak smile.

'The very one... did Charlie really sweep her off her feet, and whisk her upstairs?' George asked dramatically.

'George! I never said that!' Penelope shrieked!

'I know! I was just adding a bit of *colour*!' George stated knowingly as she sat back, hungry for details.

'Seriously George, he was great, he carried her up the stairs... I had the very important job of making sure her shoes got to bed ok.' Zara sat up and began filling in the details.

'Oh dear, oh dear, oh dear!' George shook her head and wagged her finger at Penelope.

'I know, between her love life and my job, we are a very sorry pair. So who was this guy you were out with? We were a bit shocked at the state he dropped you home in?' Zara asked genuinely concerned.

'I know, it's not great really is it?… and I think he tried to, or actually… did, kiss me!' Penelope spluttered as a disgusted look spread across her pale face.

'In that state?' Zara sounded shocked, she couldn't imagine anyone trying to kiss Penelope when she could barely stand.

'I know, yep, he's supposed to be a friend.' Penelope sounded hurt.

'You can't take your eye off them for a second… male friends!' George warned sagely, as the section of her curls that had been tucked behind her right ear, tumbled down in front of her face.

'Obviously not! That's definitely a lesson I needed to learn.' Penelope sat back on the couch, hugging a cushion to her.

'I always thought he fancied you Penny.' George added.

'Maybe it was just a drunken thing… it's not like I ever really have to see him again…I mean we were just having a catch up… ooh text.' Penelope jumped up and grabbed her phone, dying for a text from Alyx.

Hello Princess,
Hope head not too sore,
V. pleased about last night,
Still smiling, Richard xx

'Oh no!' Penelope went even paler as she read the text.

'What? Who is it from? Is it *ASB*?' George squealed. Over-pronouncing the initials, she thought this was hilarious.

'It's from Richard, oh no, look, he signed it off… Richard xx, oh no… it's never the one you want is it!' Penelope was heartbroken that it was not from Alyx, and sounded distraught that it was from Richard, how on earth was she going to get out of this one.

Once there had been a kiss, there was no turning back. He had catapulted himself out of the friend zone in a matter of seconds.

'Uh oh.' George looked over at Zara, who felt like she was watching a game of tennis as she followed the conversation back and forth, struggling to keep up.

'I know… and ASB hasn't phoned me yet… why is this happening to me! Oh my god another one… that's tantamount to stalking!' Penelope's heart sank as she heard that she had another text. With a heavy heart she reluctantly opened it up.

Hi, lovely time the other
night, hope you are well,
am away for work,
but will call when
back in Europe,
ASB x

'You are not going to believe this… it's from him…' The colour crept back onto Penelope's face as the largest smile unfurled across her face, her eyes glistened.

'Richard?!' Zara shrieked!

'No, Alyx!' Penelope shrieked back as she jumped up to hug George.

'No!' George gasped. George leaped up and hugged Penelope.

'Who's Ah-Leeks?' Poor Zara was on the edge of her seat now, this was all too much, first there was Richard and now some foreign guy was texting her. George pulled Zara out of her seat and grabbed her into the group hug.

'Just a sec Zara, Pen, what did he say?' George held onto Zara's arm to calm her down while they got the details. They stood there clutching each other as if some huge life changing revelation were about to be revealed.

'Says he's away for work, and that he'll call when he's back in Europe.' Penelope spoke really quickly barely catching her breath.

'Oh wow.' George flopped back in her seat, so shocked.

'Who is Ah-Leeks?' Poor Zara couldn't wait any longer, she was dying to know who he was.

'How will I put this… hmm…he's like, *the* perfect man, he's *gorgeous, charming, intelligent…* and he took me out on Wednesday.' Penelope glowed at the memory of it.

'I was wondering why you were in the bathroom for so long on Tuesday night,' Zara stated knowingly, the pieces of the puzzle were starting to come together.

'Serious pampering and preparation!' Penelope shrieked.

'Sounds like he was worth it!' Zara shrieked back.

'Oh totally…' Penelope was on the edge of her seat now.

'Look, she's got that dreamy look again…' George pointed out the obvious.

'So who is this other guy then, the one who got you drunk… this is all a bit confusing, do you have two boyfriends?' Zara was struggling to keep up.

'No! No, not at all, I went on date with Alyx on Wednesday, and then was just meeting up as old friends with Richard on Thursday, and then I got drunk and he kissed me…' Penelope's tone flattened at the memory of the unrequited kiss.

'So you kissed two guys in one week… impressive…' Zara was astounded at this.

'No, no, that's the thing… I didn't *kiss* Alyx,' Penelope explained.

'Oh, why not?' Zara sounded confused.

'Yeah Pen, about that… why not?' George added.

'Well he just didn't kiss me, I think he was being gentlemanly…' Penelope affirmed. 'Which I greatly appreciate, despite the fact that I was dying for him to kiss me.' Penelope weighed up the value of the kiss versus the manners. Manners win every time.

'Yeah, that's probably it… sounds like he could teach Richard a thing or two… and he's the one with the bloody castle…' George sighed indignantly.

'Turns out he's not the only one with a castle, Alyx has one too,' Penelope stated knowing the effect that this would have on the two girls.

'No way!?, what is it about you and guys with castles, is it in Scotland too?' George sounded incredulous.

'Of course!' Penelope stated with pride.

'Bloody hell, they are not related are they?' George sounded shocked.

'Not at all!' Penelope stated relieved.

'Thank heavens for that?' George sighed.

'Castles… bloody hell.' Zara sounded flabbergasted.

'I know, all tartan, and creepy pictures of the ancestors.' Penelope stated.

'Seriously, I don't think I've ever even been in one,' Zara sighed, she felt much younger and more inexperienced than these two all of a sudden.

'Oh, neither have we, just seen the pictures of Richard's place… on the internet,' Penelope added.

'Bloody hell! Nobody like that ever went to my university!' Zara gasped.

'We saw it all at ours, it was like a pantomime… they were all related to the Royal Family in some way… it was ridiculous,' George added.

'Sounds very exciting.' Zara sat back, eager to hear more, and she was not left waiting long. Penelope went on to regale the girls with the details of the date with Richard… bad news first… and then her perfect night with the lovely, perfect, gorgeous, Alyx… Stuart… Bruges, despite the fact that they happened in the reverse order. In no time, hangovers, redundancies and all of those *minor* irritations in life were long forgotten.

Chapter 15

New York, New York

At the very same time, which was much earlier in the day in NYC, Alyx was in a meeting with the head of Sony BMG, on Madison. His body was sitting in the meeting room, his gazed was fixed in the far distance, and his mind was most definitely in London.

'Alyx! Hello! You haven't been listening to a single word I've been saying?! This is serious!' Andrew paced up and down in the boardroom, he was finding this conversation with Alyx very difficult indeed... He felt like he had been talking to himself.

'What? Oh, erm yeah, well I think that digital piracy is still a real issue...' Alyx hadn't been listening to a single word that Andrew had been saying.

'Erm, yeah, we established that about ten minutes ago, but what are we going to *do* about it?!' Andrew shrieked. The rest of the interested parties stared blankly at Alyx waiting for his response. Alyx was miles away. Physically he was in NYC, but mentally... he was in London thinking about her...

'Oh yes, well, I have a strategy for the US and Europe, and I think I have found a way to recover lost royalties...' Alyx started shuffling some papers on the table, as if he had the right solution.

'Well thank god for that, really Alyx, it would be good if you could stay with the conversation!' Andrew fumed, he had turned bright red and had to have a gulp of water to stop himself from roaring at Alyx. He had never seen him like this before, he was normally the one leading the conversation.

'Yes, yes, of course, erm, well it must be erm, jetlag!' Alyx offered, he shrugged his shoulders and gave Andrew a winning smile.

'Never bothered you before. You looked like you were miles away…' Andrew responded.

'Erm well I've been doing a lot of traveling this month, so maybe it's all catching up on me…' Alyx offered further explanation.

'Ok, well let's crack on shall we… we need to sort this out before the band manager gets here, he's a nightmare to deal with, he's a total *prima donna*…and he's not even a musician.' Andrew gasped, the mere thought of having to deal with the manager after trying to coax the solution out of Alyx was proving too much for him. A large Scotch on the rocks was beckoning from the drinks cabinet in his office.

'Oh I know, you don't have to tell me that…' Alyx was on the same page now, neither of them liked dealing with divas!

'That was not good… I just can't stop thinking about her. I want to call her, but what do I say. Hi there, I had a great time the other night… do you want to go out again… at the end of the month! Then again if I don't call her, she'll think I'm not interested.' Alyx stared into space as he considered this. Andrew noticed the far off look again…

'Alyx!' Andrew roared!

Alyx jumped slightly in his seat, 'Sorry… listen Andy, could we just grab a couple of coffees… might help me, em, snap out of it?' Alyx was apologetic, he hadn't been listening again and he had been completely caught out.

'Fair enough, but let's be quick, ok?' Andrew conceded, he would give Alyx anything he wanted if it would help him snap out of this!

'Ok, there's a Dean & Deluca near here, and the walk will do me good.' Alyx headed for the door.

'Fine.' Andrew agreed grumpily. 'I'll have a double shot, tall, 2%.' He snapped, but Alyx was already in the elevator.

'Ok focus, work now, I'll think about her later...' Alyx tried to focus his mind on the job at hand... It felt good to be out in the fresh air, there is such a buzz of activity at any time of the day in NYC and Dean & Deluca was his absolute favourite coffee house in New York. He thought he'd pick up a nice big chocolate chip cookie for Andy too... butter him up a bit...

***

The weekend sped by in a blur of drinks, drinks and more drinks. Penelope felt elated at having Friday off for a change, and it felt like a glorious break from work. Sadly a good weekend means only one thing... that Monday comes around all too quickly.

'Ok, everybody here?' In EC1 nobody had any problems concentrating.

'Just waiting on... ah here she is... morning Penelope.' Anthony stood up to offer Penelope his seat.

'Sorry... I was just on the phone to New York... they are only leaving the office now, it's the middle of the night over there...' Penelope marched in with a tall pile of papers in her hand.

'That's fine... ok, now, are we all here? Excellent, close the door please, this stuff is highly confidential...' Anthony gestured to the guy nearest the door.

'I love it when it gets like this, we know the news before it hits the media... I wonder if we'll need to go to New York... fingers crossed.' Penelope loved all of this excitement.

'Things are really kicking off over there, Mortimer is pulling out of the business completely... we are on the verge of litigation with it. Needless to say when the media gets wind of this, it will cause ructions. I'm going to need a small team to go over there to support our east coast team during the negotiations. Does anyone have any major objections?' Anthony stood up and looked around the room, there was dead silence for what seemed like ten minutes.

'I would love to go, but my brother is getting married next weekend and I am best man…' Mike stammered, this was the last thing he wanted to say… but it needed to be said. He didn't want to look like he wasn't a team player, especially in a crisis like this.

'Ok, Mike that's fine… anyone else?' Mike heaved a sigh of relief.

'No, we are all ok I think… Penelope?' Anthony directed his gaze at Penelope.

'Fine by me…' Penelope stated earnestly.

'Actually Penelope I'm glad you said that… I know you haven't had many dealings with Mortimer, but he can get very, well… let's say… erm, loud when people don't agree with him… he used to be a military man…' Anthony added apologetically.

'Oh dear… can I change my mind?' Penelope asked in a mock serious tone.

'Not quite, the thing is he will not raise his voice if there is a lady in the room, so we absolutely need you there to keep things from reaching boiling point. We have of course got Sarah, Amy and Karyn over there, but you know what it's like they'll be popping in and out for meetings and conference calls… I need at least one lady in the room at all times… I don't want him getting overly aggressive with anyone.' Anthony sighed. 'He actually threw a printer at someone last year, we definitely don't want *that* to happen again.'

Penelope couldn't believe this, she had never heard anything like it.

'I see, ok, that's fine, when are you planning on sending us over?' She asked Anthony the one question everyone else was dying to ask as she had the floor.

'Thursday? Is that ok with everyone? Needless to say you can go overboard on expenses!' Anthony grinned at them all.

'Excellent,' Simon cheered.

'Yep, that's fine by me,' Penelope added.

Excellent, I had nothing special planned for this weekend… I can't wait to go to New York, we'll be going business class too, lovely.' Penelope was delighted at this news, a free trip to New York was exactly what she needed. Just as she was about to leave, Anthony called her back.

'Right, that's it for the moment, there's a conference call this afternoon, and they can update us then, on any developments… Penelope, hold on a sec, can I have a quick word?' Anthony pulled a chair out for her.

'Yes, of course…' Penelope was quite taken aback, she wasn't expecting this.

'Ok, now that I have you on your own, I just wanted to make sure that you didn't take offence at the remark about Mortimer and having a lady in the room at all times, of course that is not the real reason I'm sending you. You were my first choice, but I know a few of the guys' noses are out of joint since we teamed you up with Jeremy Eubank. The last person we did that to, shot up the ranks, and was our youngest partner in the London office. We are really impressed with your work, and that is why I need you in New York. All that stuff about Mortimer is true however, and Amy, Sarah and Karyn are well briefed on the topic,' Anthony sighed.

'Oh, of course I don't mind. I did think you were joking about Mortimer though. I'm glad you told me that was for real.' Penelope was relieved that he had told her it was true, she completely thought he had been joking.

'Good, I'm glad we are clear on that, I would hate to think that you would take offence…' Anthony got up to leave.

'No, not at all, and I think if I did take offence, you would know all about it…' Penelope stood up too.

'Indeed, indeed… quite right…' he agreed.

'Bless him, they are so PC in here. Little does he know I'm practically making a list of new shoes to buy… as a key priority!' Penelope flounced back to her office and began mentally packing for her trip.

***

'Monsieur Stuart-Bruges! How are we today?' the band manager bowed as he said this.

'Oh god here we go…' Alyx was not in the mood for this!

'Maureeece, lovely to see you, I'm fine… that was a very dramatic entrance… erm… as always…' Alyx held out his hand.

'Oh, I'm sure you would expect nothing less!' Maurice ignored it and planted an air kiss at the side of each of his cheeks.

'Indeed, now let's talk… digital piracy…' Alyx jumped back as soon as possible, a little flustered at Maurice's choice of greeting.

'Oh, no! I don't want to talk about Pirates! I'm only interested in the money!' Maurice flopped dramatically onto a chair, and his hand flew up to his forehead. A pink silk handkerchief appeared as if by magic, it was very complementary to his purple velvet suit.

'I know but…' Alyx began.

'No! No buts!' Maurice shrieked back.

'I'm not quite sure I can deal with this now! He just doesn't get it! He'll be ranting on about the creative concept, and the new album cover in no time… I think I'll just let him waffle on for a while. I think I'll ring her towards the end of the week anyway, and just arrange something for a few weeks' time… that's probably the best thing…' Alyx was resigned to the fact that this was going to be a long conversation with Maurice.

'Alyx! Are you even listening to a word that I have been saying?' Maurice snapped after he had rambled on for fifteen minutes.

'Of course, you were talking about the *creative concept* and…' Alyx stuttered, he had been caught red handed… Again! He hadn't been listening to a word Maurice had been saying… he had heard it all before after all…

'Well no actually, but I was just getting onto that…' Maurice gasped.

'Friday, I'll call her on Friday. Now, back to work…' Alyx knew it was time to keep his eye on the ball. Even if it was swathed in purple velvet, and bouncing off the walls.

***

Friday came around very quickly in the city that never sleeps.

'Hi, can I speak to Penelope Chesterfield please, I just tried her mobile and it's switched off, It's Alyx Stuart-Bruges here…' Alyx phoned Penelope's work switchboard number after trying her mobile a few times… he didn't want to leave a voicemail message, he hated doing that!

'Just a moment Alyx, I'll put you through…' the receptionist replied.

'Capital Markets, Jeanine speaking.' The team PA answered the phone.

'Hi, can I speak to Penelope please…?' Alyx asked.

'I'm afraid Penelope is in New York this week, you will have to ring our office on Broadway…' Jeanine began.

'What? She's in New York?' Alyx was astounded.

'Yes, would you like the number?' Jeanine offered.

'Yes, definitely…' Alyx added quickly, and he scribbled it down.

On Broadway, things were not going too well…

'Oh my god! I am dying to go to the loo… I'm going to kill Karyn, she's been gone for ages. Mortimer hasn't budged and he keeps catching me looking at the door, he's probably just waiting for me to leave… so that he can lose his temper.' Penelope was dying to leave the room, but she had to wait for one of her female tag team members to come back in before she could.

'Penelope, telephone call for you.' One of the PAs popped her head in the door and whispered this to Penelope, not wanting to disturb the others.

'I, erm, oh ok, could you just take a message, I'm in the middle of something here…' Penelope whispered back… *'Damn it, that would have been the perfect excuse to leave'…* 'Could you send Karyn in here to me, I need her to look over these figures?' Penelope asked.

'Sure.' The PA was gone without a sound.

'Hi there, yes sorry about that the conference call went on for ages.' Karyn came back into the room looking a little flustered and took her seat next to Penelope, she leant over and whispered… *'You look like you could do with a break!'*

'Shhh he'll hear you! I am dying to go to the ladies room… can you take my place for a while? Let's get some backup in here, always two ladies in the room at a time, I think would be good… a bit like a tag team.' Penelope whispered back to Karyn.

'Sure, take as long as you like, I have no more meetings this afternoon.' Karyn settled back into her seat.

Relief flooded Penelope as she closed the door quietly behind her.

'I am not going back in there for a while. What a nightmare. I wonder who called. I hope it wasn't bloody Richard… surely he wouldn't call me at work over here. He phoned just before I left, I'll call him back when I get back.' Penelope approached the bank of desks where the PAs were sitting.

'Zoe, Amy said I had a call, do you know who took the message? Did you take the call?' Penelope asked.

'No, but she wrote the name down here, let me just check, it was a Mr… em… Stuw Wart Broome, or something like that.' Amy picked up the post-it note where she had scribbled the message.

'Stuart-Brume? Did he say what it was in relation to?' Penelope had no idea who Amy was talking about.

'No, I think he said… .em… ah, yes here it is! Ok, he's staying at the W, and he's given me the number…' Amy read out the number.

'Who is staying at the W?' Penelope stared at her blankly, she was in no mood for this.

'A Mr Alex Stuart-Bruges.' Amy announced proudly, glad that she could read Zoe's writing.

'Oh my god!' *'Of course, he's away with work, I totally forgot!'* The colour drained from Penelope's face, she had not been expecting this at all. How did he know that she was in New York?

'Are you ok, you look like you've seen a ghost?' Amy got up and walked out from behind her desk.

'Yes, yes, I'm fine, it's just a little unexpected, thanks Amy… I'll give him a call.' Penelope took the little piece of yellow paper, at this moment in time it felt like all that was connecting her to Alyx.

'Sure.' Amy smiled at her and went about her business.

Penelope grabbed the nearest phone that was secluded enough for a bit of privacy.

'George, hi, it's me,' Penelope gasped.

'Penny! Are you back already?' George giggled.

'No, no, listen, I have to be quick… Alyx is in New York, and he called me in work… I didn't take it, got a message,' Penelope stuttered.

'Oh my god!' George was astounded.

'I know,' Penelope was too.

'This guy is unbelievable, are you going to call him back?' George could not believe all of this drama.

'Totally, especially since he rang me in work here, so *he knows* I'm here. I'll have to ring him to let him know how long I'm here, and all that.' Penelope sat down as she said this, she was starting to regain composure as she realised George shared her reaction.

'Yes, I will allow you to ring him so soon after he rang you… but only because you are both a million miles away… and it's all so weird, amazing, but weird. Good weird! What about Richard?' George stated.

'Oh my god! You are like my mother… what about bloody Richard?' Penelope was not happy at the mention of Richard's name.

'Has he been in touch, and have you let him know about Ah-Leeks?' George was on the edge of her seat at this stage.

'Well, no, I mean… yes, he has been in touch… he phoned just before I left, I'll ring him back when I get back… and there is nothing to tell about Alyx, yet, I don't want to jump to any conclusions… and for heaven's sake will you stop saying Alyx like that, you sound like you are sneezing!' Penelope was completely back to normal now after the initial shock of the message from Alyx, she hated talking about Richard!

'Quite right, sorry, I just still find it really funny, I can't help it... anyway good... sounds like you have everything under control there.' George was genuinely apologetic.

'I nearly passed out here, *in work*, when I got the message that he called... I *had* to tell someone,' Penelope gasped.

'I must admit, I'm quite surprised myself... it's all so dramatic!' George added.

'I know... listen I'll ring you again before I get back if anything else dramatic happens, otherwise I should be back by Tuesday.' Penelope reaffirmed.

'Ok, well... be good,' George warned her affectionately.

'Always, George... I'm always good!' Penelope smiled down the phone as she said this.

'I know, I know... but there's no harm in having a little reminder every now and again,' George chided.

Penelope took a few very deep breaths and dialled the number...

'Hi, can you put me through to Alyx Stuart-Bruges' room please.' She asked confidently, despite the fact that her heart was hammering in her chest, she hoped the receptionist couldn't hear it!

'Just one moment please.' The receptionist put her through.

'Hello?' Alyx picked up.

'Hi Alyx, it's Penelope,' she stammered.

'Oh hi, how are you? So you got my message then? You are still in New York!' Alyx smiled down the phone as he said this.

'Yes, and yes, and I'm fine thanks... how are you?' Penelope relaxed as she heard his voice, memories of their first date, and how comfortable she was with him, came flooding back to her.

'Oh, good, listen how long are you going to be here for?' Alyx didn't like long conversations on the phone, he was keen to arrange to meet up, and to speak in person.

'I should be here until Tuesday, maybe longer. How about you?' Penelope answered.

'Oh until the end of next week. Are you free on Saturday night?' Alyx got in there really quick before she could continue.

'Erm, well yes actually, I'm only here on business… and I came very last minute so didn't make arrangements with anyone over here for the weekend.' Penelope was taken aback, he was so direct!

'Good, would you like to come out for dinner?' Alyx asked confidently.

'I'd love to,' Penelope beamed.

'Where are you staying? I'll come pick you up, say 8 pm, is that ok?' Alyx asked confidently.

'That's perfect, I'm staying at The Hudson.' Penelope gave him the details.

'Ok, see you Saturday.'

'Bye Alyx, see you on Saturday.' Penelope hung up and stared at the phone trying to take it all in. She could not believe that this was happening, they were both in New York at the same time, it was almost too good to be true.

Alyx was very pleased with himself, as he picked up the phone to his PA, to rearrange his schedule.

'Hi Sarah, it's Alyx… can you change my flight back to Paris, from tomorrow… to Monday or Tuesday? Tuesday if possible?' Alyx requested.

'You are staying for the weekend now?' Sarah was surprised to hear this, he had been scheduled to fly back the next day.

'Yes, yes, something has come up over here and I need to hang around for the weekend. Can you book me a direct flight to Paris?' He knew that she shouldn't have too much trouble getting a flight.

'Ok, I'll call you with the new flight details.' Sarah sighed, she was constantly juggling his schedule for him.

'Thanks Sarah, and if there are any urgent messages for me there, can you phone me?'

'Of course.' Sarah hung up.

***

Penelope paced up and down in the break room.

'I can't wait until Saturday! I can't believe this is happening, I'm walking on air... what will I wear? Hopefully we won't have to work over the weekend, I can pop out and get something new. Oh no! Oh my god... I just realised, I have never seen him in casual clothes! That's the real test, oh no, what if I go off him. I mean anyone can do suits moderately well, although he does do suits... really well. But sometimes, oh no... sometimes... people like that haven't a clue about casual clothes, I'll die if he turns up in a pair of chinos! Only one thing to do...'

'Hi, it's me, listen, I need to be quick...' Penelope hissed.

'Pen, what's up? What happened with *Ah*... I mean... erm... Alyx?' George stopped herself from over-pronouncing his name.

'Well he's taking me out on Saturday... and...' Penelope spluttered.

'Lovely!' George squealed.

'I know, but there is just one problem...' Penelope began...

'What! What's the problem?!' George interrupted.

'Well, I've never seen him in, you know... well...' Penelope struggled to not sound too shallow.

'What, *naked*?!' George exploded!

'Oh my god no, not *naked*, Jesus George... talk about jumping ahead there... well anyway... I've never seen him in *casual clothes*, it's the ultimate test of a man's fashion sense...' Penelope sounded tense.

'Indeed it is, oh dear, I see what you mean...' George knew how easily a bubble of perfection could burst, when you build someone up that much!

'What do you think? He was wearing a suit the night I met him wasn't he?' Penelope hunted for reassurance from George.

'Yep, but a really nice one, very... trendy, yep, fashionable, I would have faith in his casual clothes...' George reassured her.

'But George, sometimes the guys that do suits well, are terrible at the casual look.' Penelope had seen this all too often as she went on dates with fellow bankers, they look lovely during the day... but casual clothes... hmmm... not great!

In a fashion capital like London, clothes definitely did maketh the man.

'True, true... yes, well there is only one thing for this...' George sounded pensive as she said this.

'What?!' Penelope gasped.

'If he turns up in chinos... you are going to have to *picture him naked*!' George roared with laughter as she said this.

'George! Really! This is serious, if you could just stop laughing for two seconds.' Penelope was trying to get George back on track, she needed some serious help here!

'I know, I'm sorry, it's just so funny! So what if he turns up in chinos?' George was still laughing as she said this.

'He is as near to my perfect man that I have ever met, and that would destroy the whole thing,' Penelope whined.

'Hmm, I see what you mean, look I have a feeling that he will look cool, he works with rock stars and stuff all the time doesn't he?' George added.

'Yeah...' Penelope was starting to sound more confident now.

'Well, they always have stylists and stuff like that floating around, and I'm sure that kind of thing can rub off on a guy.' George definitely had a good point.

'Ok, ok, you have calmed me down now, I know it sounds so shallow, but he is like... perfect, and it would really upset me if he didn't meet expectations like the last time.' Penelope sounded tense, she was so excited to see him again that she was worrying unnecessarily and over-reacting to the slightest thing. This was exacerbated by the lingering jet-lag.

'It'd be like waking up from a lovely dream wouldn't it?' George got the picture. She had seen this happen to Penelope so many times before. She built guys up only to be disappointed.

'Exactly!' Penelope was delighted that George wasn't being too judgmental.

'Ok, well I don't think you should worry about what he'll be wearing, just focus on your outfit, and then just let it happen from there, ok hun?' George was full of sound advice as always.

'Ok, thanks George, look I better go.' Penelope felt so much better, she knew that George was right about this, and her worries started to melt away.

'Ok, good luck on Saturday,' George said warmly.

'Thanks, bye.'

'She is an angel, she calms me down every time. I have no idea what I'll wear, I might have to go with jeans and a really nice top, I don't want to overdo it. I'll have to make a trip to Bloomingdales on Saturday morning and get something. I might get an appointment with a personal shopper. I really, really can't believe this is happening.' Penelope headed back to the room to give Karyn a toilet break!

***

Back in SW4 Zara paced up and down in the living room. It was Friday night and she was dreading the weekend that stretched ahead of her. Even though she barely ever saw Penelope when she *was* there, she would still bump into her every other day, and definitely at least once at the weekends. Now, somehow there was a bit of a gap in the house. Gerry was away, she didn't know where Charlie was, and she knew she wouldn't see Penelope until she was back next week. She would give anything to see her now. She really needed someone to talk to, and there was nobody else. She couldn't tell her family or friends back home what had happened, they wouldn't *understand*. She barely understood what was going on herself. The atmosphere in work this week had been unbearable, people were not dealing with the redundancies that well… all except for Rob of course, he was getting a great package and he already had a potential new job lined up for himself. Rumour had it that it was in the very company that was brandishing the pilfered golden plate. Zara had a dilemma, either she bury her head in the sand, stay in London and try to sort out the job situation, or she could head back home for the 21st that was going on… but what would she tell her family? They would definitely know that something was up. She missed her friends, she missed her family, she missed her cat... she missed her life. She felt like she was in some kind of in between place, slipping away from her old familiar life, and heading straight into the unknown. It was the scariest thing Zara had ever faced. She decided to sleep on it to see how she felt in the morning. Zara was completely emotionally exhausted after the shocking revelation of the London office shutting down. She made her way up to her room and she was sound asleep by 9 pm.

***

Zara woke up the next morning at 6 am. She couldn't believe that she had woken up that early naturally. The house was eerily quiet, and the dawn light was streaming through her curtains. It looked strange to her, probably only because she was never normally up that early. She headed down to the kitchen, and everything was awash with the morning light, she felt a great sense of calmness, and she knew exactly what she needed to do. She looked up the train timetable, and made immediate plans to head back home for Saturday night, she would surprise everyone. She was up this early, so she may as well make the most of it!

Zara ate her breakfast in the kitchen, still half asleep... mentally picking out what she would wear that night... from her own wardrobe, in her own bedroom, in her own home! By 8 am she was out of the house and on her way back to Bangor. She made her way down to Clapham South, with a big empty bag, ready to be filled up with the next load of her clothes and shoes from home. She got down to the station, swiped her oyster card, and headed down on the escalator. She had never been in the station before when it was this empty, it all looked so weird to her. There was nobody around. She remembered Penelope's advice, and strolled into the only carriage with a few girls in it. The Tube arrived at Euston in no time at all, and within half an hour Zara was on her way... home?

The train pulled into the most familiar station in the world to Zara just in time for lunch. She felt a warm feeling of familiarity and her smile stretched from one ear to the other. She couldn't wait to see her mum's face when she opened the front door. She walked up her road slowly, she felt as if she had been away for a hundred years, at the same time she felt like she had never been away at all. Mr Thomas was out washing his car, his usual Saturday morning ritual. Mrs Henderson stood just inside her front gate watching the world go by. She was so elderly now, this was her time of the day. She would come out at about eleven, struggle down to her gate, and watch the world go by for half an hour, before she went back in, and retreated to the safety of her back garden. On a Saturday morning she would come out a bit later, to watch the children go by on their bikes, and Zara was just in time to see Mrs Henderson and give her a cheery hello.

'Hello Mrs Henderson, it's a beautiful day isn't it?' Zara smiled at the elderly lady.

'Oh hello dear, yes, yes it is a lovely day, are you going on a trip?' Mrs Henderson enquired.

'Oh no Mrs Henderson, I'm actually back for a trip, I'm living in London now you see,' Zara sighed.

'Oh London! I used to love London… I haven't been there in years, I used to live there you know, many years ago…' Mrs Henderson stared off into the distance as she said this as if remembering a far-off time.

'Really Mrs Henderson? I had no idea, I thought you had lived here all your life!'

'No, dear, when I was just married I lived in London, in a place called *Clapham*, I don't suppose you know it do you Zara?' Mrs Henderson was illuminated with the memory of her life in London.

'Clapham! Mrs Henderson, that is exactly where I am living now, I can't believe you lived there, I'm sure it has changed a bit since you have been there.' Zara was astounded. She could not believe this odd coincidence, in some ways she felt like it was a sign… a little bit of Clapham close to home.

'Oh, I'm sure it has… I will root out some old photos, and

the next time you come home, I will show them to you.' Mrs Henderson smiled at Zara.

'Oh, thank you Mrs Henderson, that would be lovely.' Zara turned away and headed up to her front door, and put the key in the lock, she took a deep breath and opened the door.

'Zara! Love! Is that you? We didn't know you were coming, I would have come to collect you at the station, goodness, look at you, come here and give me a hug.' Zara's mum rushed towards her when she saw her in the hallway.

'Hi mum, I really missed you.' Zara hugged her Mum.

There was a lovely smell of familiarity in the house, she couldn't wait to go up to her room to see all of her things, her clothes, her photos… her life.

'Your Dad has gone down to get the paper, he should be back any minute, he will be thrilled to see you. The house is so *empty* without you!' Zara's mum gasped.

'I know what you mean mum,' Zara stated knowingly. For the first time in her life, she knew exactly what her mum meant.

Zara made her way slowly up to her bedroom, and inched the door open. She had the same feeling, it was like she had been gone for a hundred years, and also like she had never left. Her room was exactly as she had left it, and exactly as it had been for years, but somehow something felt *different.* Maybe it wasn't different, … maybe *she* was different. She went over to her wardrobe and was filled with joy as she opened the door and was greeted by years and years' worth of babysitting income expenditure. Her clothes, shoes, belts and handbags were bulging out of it, they barely fit in the wardrobe. Zara rushed over to her dressing table and marvelled at the amount of lotions, potions, ornaments, photos and jewellery there. It was such a contrast to her empty bedroom in London. She couldn't wait to bring some of it back to London with her. She immediately packed the clothes and shoes that she had desperately missed during the previous weeks. It was only when she didn't have them for the first time ever, that she realised how often she wore them. There was nothing worse than the feeling of going to the wardrobe to take a certain top out only to find that it was miles away in a different wardrobe. She was sick of wearing the same few pairs of shoes over and over again, she couldn't wait to bring this stuff back with her. Zara started stuffing tops into her bag until it would barely close. *'I'm going to need a bigger bag.'* She thought as she rooted around her bedroom for another case to load up, and in no time at all it was full too. Zara sat on her bed and looked around her room, she hugged her teddy who she had never appreciated as much as she did now.

***

Penelope woke up in Manhattan at 7 am on Saturday morning. She was wide awake due to the time difference and there was no point in even trying to go back to sleep. She opened the curtains and she could see the first signs of dawn bathing Midtown in a beautiful orange light. It was at moments like these that Penelope felt like she should pinch herself, her life was so amazing. No matter how many times she had been to New York, it never lost its novelty value for her. She loved looking at the skyscrapers. She could make out the gargoyles guarding some of the buildings, it really gave her a sense of how long these buildings had been around, it was magical indeed.

Penelope pulled out her guidebook and checked the pages that she had folded down. She did not want to waste one second of her free time in New York. There were a few must dos, like grabbing a few things that you couldn't get in London, including hopefully lunch in Dean & Deluca in Soho, heading to Bloomingdales, and all of the shops on 5th Avenue! She would definitely get a manicure and pedicure in the bliss spa, she had booked that in in advance thank heavens. Penelope got dressed and headed out, ready for her first adventure in Manhattan that day...

***

Back in her hotel room, Penelope checked her makeup for the fiftieth time in the mirror in the bathroom. Each time she looked in the mirror, she looked exactly the same, but still... this was helping to calm her nerves. She debated about having a quick drink from the mini bar, but decided against it, especially after her recent experience with Richard at the Ritz. She had barely eaten all day! Luckily she did not have to work that day, so she had spent practically the whole day preparing for her night out with Alyx.

'Ok... five minutes to go, I hope he's not late, I'm so nervous and the later he is the worse it will be. These jeans are so obviously new, I hope he doesn't notice. I don't want him to think I went to a major effort. The top is fantastic, I have never seen this designer in London. Oh, there's the phone.' Penelope jumped slightly as the phone gave a shrill ring.

'Hello?' Penelope mustered a smile, and struggled to hide her nervousness.

'Hi, I have Alyx down here in reception to see you,' the receptionist drawled.

'Thank you, I'll be right down.' Penelope quipped.

Penelope grabbed her bag and her jacket, and headed down the corridor towards the lift. She called the lift and waited very impatiently as it crawled up to her floor from the lobby. Finally it arrived, and on the way down it open at every second or third floor. *'C'mon, c'mon... god it would have been quicker to walk'* she thought to herself as she fidgeted impatiently, she could feel a slight nerve rash erupting on her chest.

'Hi!' Penelope approached Alyx.

'Hi, you look gorgeous.' Alyx gave her a kiss on her cheek. As he did this it felt like the most natural thing in the world, as if he had done it a thousand times before.

'Thanks, you don't look so bad yourself...' *'What a relief he looks bloody gorgeous, George was right. She is always right. No chinos thank god!'* Penelope smiled at him.

Alyx was wearing jeans and a vintage distressed t-shirt with a navy pin-striped suit jacket, he looked like he could have stepped off the pages of *GQ*, but not in an obvious way… it definitely didn't look like he had made too much effort… and he smelled incredible. Penelope could well imagine the tanned… toned body that lay beneath the amazing clothes. Alyx had a naturally tanned complexion… and beautiful jet-black chin length hair. He had amazing dark brown eyes and the most amazing long eyelashes.

'Where are we off to?' Penelope's nerves completely melted with the kiss, she felt so comfortable with him.

'Well, I was thinking we could grab some dinner in Tribeca, and then head over to the Bowery Ballroom, it's on Delancey,' Alyx offered.

'Bowery Ballroom? Is it a bar? Delancey is on the Lower East Side isn't it?' Penelope tried to sound like she knew what she was talking about.

'It's more like a venue, it's cool, I think you'll like it.' Alyx smiled in a self-assured way.

'I'm sure I will, are the band playing there tonight?' Penelope had her fingers crossed.

'No, not at all… it's just that I always make a point of going there each time I'm in New York. I've seen some major new bands there… before they were famous of course. It's pretty small. I heard that The Libertines are playing there tonight.' Alyx grinned at her, it was a long shot, but he hoped they could get in.

'Great… I love them!' Penelope was delighted.

'Do you like tapas?' Alyx turned to her as he said this.

'Yes, that would be perfect.' Penelope was relieved, she was so nervous about this date that she had no appetite at all, small morsels of tapas would be perfect.

'There is a nice little tapas restaurant in Tribeca, it's never too busy.' Alyx smiled at her.

'Great,' Penelope smiled back.

I actually can't believe this is happening. I feel so comfortable

*with him, even in New York. I feel like I live here or something...
it's quite disorienting. It feels like a dream, it's probably the jet lag.'*
Penelope was walking on air, and they talked and talked over
tapas, and really connected.

'Thank you for dinner, it's really nice down here, I've never
really been around this area.' Penelope sighed.

'You're welcome, it's not the obvious place to come if you
are only here for a few days, that's why I like it... no tourists! It
feels like a proper neighbourhood,' Alyx added.

'It does actually.' *'That's what it is about this place, no tourists!
All New Yorkers.'*

'I haven't actually got tickets for the Libs tonight, but we
should be able to get tickets on the door...' Alyx hoped that
he was right.

'Ok, great.'

As they approached the door at the Bowery Ballroom, there
was a large queue outside and apparently no tickets available.

'I'm afraid we are completely sold out. The Libertines are
headlining tonight and the place is packed.' The large bouncer
said this to Alyx who had asked whether there were any tickets.

'That's great news!' Alyx shrieked, this was quite the opposite
reaction the bouncer was expecting.

'Pardon me?' he asked gruffly.

'I am with the band, I'm legal representation... I forgot to
pick up a pass in the office, but it is absolutely essential that I
speak to them before their performance... ' Alyx whipped out
his business card as he said this, and passed the guy a twenty, it
certainly did the trick.

'Well, in that case... don't let me stop you.' The bouncer
stepped aside and ushered Alyx and Penelope inside.

'Alyx, that was hilarious! He totally bought it...' Penelope
giggled when the bouncer was out of earshot.

'Works every time,' Alyx winked at her.

'This place is lovely, Jesus... it is packed, he wasn't embellishing
there!' Penelope was thrilled, the venue was so cool, it was really
pretty, and they had a look around downstairs first.

'They are really popular here, have you ever seen them live?' Alyx was as excited about the performance as Penelope was.

'No, not yet.' Penelope couldn't wait, she had heard such good things about The Libertines live.

'They put on a great show, you never actually know what they are going to do. I went to see them at the Forum in Kentish Town, and they brought the first few rows up on to the stage with them towards the end and then continued playing at the back of the stage with all these random punters playing air guitar in front of them. It looked a bit like the *Sgt. Pepper* album cover...' Alyx explained.

'Sounds amazing.' Penelope laughed.

'It was great, totally spontaneous. The bands usually take the two little booths in the upstairs bar. Let's go up and see if they can squeeze us in...' Alyx grabbed Penelope's hand and led her upstairs.

'Ok.' '*This place is amazing. The wooden floors are lovely, it's so not like the gig venues in London, it's so pretty... and it's just the right size, to maintain intimacy with the band a opposed to being miles away from them while they are playing.*' Penelope was drinking it all in, coming to a place like this made her feel like she was a real New Yorker.

'Hi, I was just wondering if...' Alyx poked his head through the velvet curtains, into one of the booths.

'Alyx! What the hell are you doing here?!' Damien shouted over the music.

'Damien! Hi, I was just going to try to talk my way into the booth here, let me introduce you to Penelope... Penelope this is Damien. I didn't know that you were going to be over here.' Damien jumped up and gave Alyx a manly hug.

'Very nice to meet you, are you with one of the bands?' Penelope was a bit taken aback, she wasn't really expecting this. There were two small areas upstairs in the balcony bar, and they were curtained off in purple velvet. As Penelope looked in over Alyx's shoulder she saw the entourage Alyx was chatting to, they were all doing vodka shots.

'Yes, I'm afraid so... here... squeeze in, there is plenty of room, they are not here yet, they'll probably show up just before they go on... actually fingers crossed that they show up at all... they get very erm, well... *distracted* in New York,' Damien added.

'Penelope, is this ok for you?' Alyx was keen to make sure that Penelope was comfortable.

'Of course, yes, lovely, thanks.' Penelope was thrilled.

'I'll just go and get us some drinks.' Alyx headed off to the bar.

'So, Penelope, are you Alyx's girlfriend?' Damien leaned over to Penelope so that she could hear what he was saying.

'Erm well, you see, em, well we are on a date.' Penelope got a little flustered, she didn't really know what to say.

'I see, not really at that stage yet.' Damien winked at her.

'You could say that.' Penelope was relieved that he didn't probe further.

***

Penelope got in at 4 am New York time, and it didn't take her long to figure out that it was already breakfast time in the UK, so she couldn't contain herself and dialled George's number, even though it was Sunday morning!

'Oh my god George... I just couldn't wait to phone you. The date was amazing!' Penelope shrieked as soon as George answered.

'So... no chinos then?' George sounded groggy. She had just woken up.

'God no, no chinos at all... he looked so gorgeous. He was wearing really nice jeans a funky t-shirt, and a navy pin-stripe jacket. I'm telling you George he'd give David Beckham a run for his money on the fashion front.' Penelope was talking really fast, she was still really elated after her date.

'Seriously?' George had never heard Penelope talk like this before.

'Yeah, and his hair is gorgeous... it's jet-black and it's a bit longer now, sort of chin length, he looks more like he could be in the band himself.' Penelope squealed.

'Wow.' George was genuinely impressed.

'I know, and we had the most amazing time, we went for tapas, which was perfect because my body clock is a bit messed up with the time difference, and I was so nervous that I could barely eat a thing, but it wasn't too obvious. And then we went to a place called the Bowery Ballroom.' Penelope gushed.

'A ballroom? Like ballroom dancing?' George asked.

'No, nothing like that, it's a gig venue…' Penelope was still gushing.

'Ah yes, I should have guessed… and were there anymore twenty-somethings singing to you?' George laughed.

'No, no, The Libertines, and a few other bands, were playing there… they were amazing, and the venue itself was lovely, really pretty, and we ended up in this kind of booth thing behind velvet curtains in with the band people… not the actual bands, but their people.' Penelope was still talking really fast.

'And?' George sounded mischievous.

'And… he was a perfect gentleman and dropped me home,' Penelope added.

'No kissing?' George shrieked! She was beginning to think Alyx was gay!

'Well, there was a bit of kissing… but that's all I'm saying, apart from the fact that it was amazing. I can't eat, I can't sleep…' Penelope was elated.

'Now, I thought that because you were staying in a lovely hotel over there, that you might have been tempted to, well, you know… take advantage of it, the hotel that is.' George sounded concerned.

'No way, I'm blonde… not stupid!' Penelope shrieked. 'As if I would do something like that! We've only had two dates, even though I do feel like I've known him all my life.'

'So, he's a keeper is he?' George asked.

'Absolutely, I think I'm falling in love,' Penelope sighed.

'Careful now,' George warned.

'I know, I know… well I'm enjoying all of this, let me enjoy it.' Penelope pleaded.

'Ok, I'll stop being mum for a minute, when are you coming home?' George got back to basics.

'I should be back by Tuesday, but it's difficult to tell really.' Penelope replied, anything could happen while they were over there and they may have to stay on a bit longer.

'Ok, well send me an email tomorrow ok?' George slid out of bed.

'Yeah, but I can't really put stuff in it about Alyx, they have access to everything that I do online in work,' Penelope warned.

'Ok, well I'll see you when you come back, and we will have a proper catch up about it,' George reassured her.

Penelope hung up and lay down on her bed, completely unable to sleep. The sun would be up soon, and she could go out and get a coffee. This was the best trip to New York that she had ever had.

George padded down to the kitchen in her pyjamas in SW11, and put the kettle on.

***

On Tuesday Alyx skipped the queue at JFK and checked in for his upper class flight home. He wandered up to the club lounge and helped himself to a JD and Coke. He sat down at a nearby table and swerved as a bird flew down and nearly knocked his drink out of his hand.

'That gets me every time.' Alyx chuckled to himself as he considered his near miss.

'What a productive trip. A digital piracy strategy, two new bands engaged, but not signed and a second date with Penelope.'

She was nothing like the girls he usually went out with, dating a banker was definitely a first for him. But there was just something about her, he couldn't put his finger on it. She loved music as much as he did. Perhaps she had missed her calling.

Chapter 16

New Beginnings

Zara was on her way home from work, dissecting her day.

'That was the worst day ever. Some people started clearing out their desks last night. Myself and Rob were one of the last ones to leave, it's so sad... just when I was feeling settled. I just can't believe that this has happened to me. I'm glad that I didn't tell my parents, it would break their hearts, and I'd be so embarrassed if I had to go back home, after such a short time. Oh no, here come the waterworks again... not on the Tube of all places! Hold it in, hold it in...' Zara buried her head in her book, trying to hide her face.

'... Ah finally, home sweet home. The others are all out really late tonight, thank god, I could do with having a good blub. Keys, where are my... oh no, I don't believe this! I only have the key to the outside door... I must have left the full set on the table inside when I picked up the post this morning. I'll just have to wait until the others come home.' Zara slumped down in the communal hallway.

'I feel completely minging. I look a state, oh no... this is all I need, the bloody neighbours all arriving in.' Zara had slumped down on the floor outside her front door, she could not believe that she was locked out.

'Hey there, are you ok?' The neighbour that Zara hadn't met yet, walked in a few moments later.

'Oh, em, hello, well, I'm locked out actually,' Zara stuttered, struggling to hide the fact that she had been bawling her eyes out.

'You look like you could do with a drink!' he said in a soft Australian lilt.

'That's not a bad observation, my office closed down today, and now I'm locked out, I'm having one of *those* days... I'm Zara by the way, have you just moved in here?' Zara regained composure, she could see through her tears now, as they were gradually drying up, that this guy was gorgeous.

'Yeah, I'm Zack, a crew of us from Melbourne have all moved in here... Look, do you want to come in for a while, there's no point sitting on the doorstep, and I'm not an axe murderer I promise... we can leave a note on the door in case your flatmates come back...' Zack offered her his hand, and helped her up.

'Em, well, ok, if it's not too much trouble...' Zara didn't see that she had any other choice, Penelope was away and the boys would be out late.

'Nah, not at all, and I'll introduce you to the other guys.' Zack gave Zara a winning smile.

'Thanks, sniff.' Zara blew her nose.

'Tissue?' Zack offered her the box of tissues as she stepped inside their front door.

'Yes, thanks.' Zara took the box gratefully.

'Oh my god, he's bloody gorgeous, I've never met any guys from Melbourne before, I wonder if they all look like that. This house is really nice, but it's really weird, it's exactly the same layout as ours, just the other way around, it's kind of freaking me out,' Zara thought as she looked around.

'So Zara, how long have you lived in London?' Zack asked her once she had settled down on the sofa with a cup of tea and a Tim Tam.

'About a month,' Zara sighed.

'So, you are as new as me then?' Zack was glad that they had something in common.

'Yeah, you could say that.' Zara was relieved that he was new to London too, at least they definitely had that in common.

'Are you sticking around for a while, or…?' Zack asked her.

'Erm, well I'm not too sure, you see I kind of came here for work, but that kind of isn't happening now, so em, I'm not too sure what I'm going to do…' Zara simply couldn't talk about it without crying again, she was dying to change the subject.

'Oh, I see…' Zack was watching her reaction as she said this, so he was keen to change the subject to make her feel more comfortable, her day was bad enough.

'All of this has happened so fast, I'll probably take a couple of weeks to figure out what I'm going to do. I might do a bit of temping,' Zara added.

'That's a good plan.' Zack smiled at her.

I must look a total sight, mascara everywhere… what a nightmare. I think I heard someone going in next door!

'I think I heard someone going in there…' Zara gestured next door.

'Let's have a look… ' Zack got up and they headed for his front door.

'Zara! What happened, are you ok?' Penelope was struggling with her luggage and fumbling for her keys, and she was surprised to see anyone, let alone Zara, coming out of the neighbour's front door. Particularly as they thought the house was empty.

'Yeah, I got locked out and I don't know where the boys are, and you were in New York, so erm… Zack… here, well… *rescued* me.' Zara blushed a little.

'I see, well come on in, both of you, just hop over the bags there… I've just literally flown in from New York…' Penelope opened the door, glad to be home.

'How did it go?' Zara asked.

'Oh, you know, never without a bit of drama… I'll tell you later… ' Penelope winked at Zara.

'Ok, … Zack, would you like a cup of tea?' Zara led Zack into the kitchen.

'Lovely, thanks Zara.' He sat down, and they continued their getting to know each other chat over another cup of tea.

Penelope bustled around in the background unpacking and trying to do laundry.

***

An hour later, Zack headed back next door.

'Zara, talk about a silver lining!' Penelope came back downstairs from unpacking, when she heard him leave.

'I know, isn't he gorgeous?!' Zara gasped.

'Totally, you will have to drop in to borrow some sugar in the near future…' Penelope winked at her.

'Don't worry I intend to… but look at the state of me, mascara everywhere…' Zara pointed at her eyes.

'I get my eyelashes tinted, as a precaution against moments like these!' Penelope sounded sympathetic, she had been there before.

'What? Dyed?' Zara couldn't believe this, but if it solved the problem she was all ears…

'Yeah, I don't do it myself, I get it done, it lasts for about two months, it's brilliant.'

'I see, so… how did the New York trip go? What was the drama?' Zara was dying to hear all about the trip.

'You are not going to believe this but Alyx was there!' Penelope gushed.

'Which one is he? Is he the one that got you drunk that night… ?' Zara was confused.

'No!, that was Richard… no, no, Alyx is the other one, the gorgeous one… the lawyer.' Penelope was quick to correct her.

'What on earth was he doing over in New York?' Zara gasped.

'He was working there and he called me in work in London and when they told him that I was at the New York office, he called me there, in work.' Penelope was glowing at the thought of him.

'You must have nearly had a heart attack!' Zara could barely take all of this in.

'I nearly did, and I wasn't even thinking about getting calls or texts because my mobile didn't work over there, it was actually quite a nice little break from my phone… it was the last thing on my mind. We went out on Saturday night… I think I'm in love.' Penelope stared off into the distance dreamily as she said this.

'I wouldn't blame you. Are you going to see him again?' Zara was on the edge of her seat.

'I hope so… he is still over in New York, so he'll probably call or something when he's back in London.' Penelope flounced out of the kitchen once she had put on another load of washing.

Chapter 17

Vive la Résistance

At 7.30 pm Alyx waited patiently at the table in Buddha Bar, on Rue Boissy-d'Anglas, for his sister. As soon as he saw her he got up to help her into her seat.

'Alyx, I haven't seen you in ages, you look great.' Nathalie hugged him warmly.

'Thanks Nats, you look great yourself... glowing? Is that what they call it?' Alyx grinned at her.

'Em, yeah, I suppose so, only three months to go, I feel like I'm the size of a house!' Nathalie shifted in her seat to get comfortable, she was very petite and she had a rather large bump for her small frame to carry around.

'It's really weird, because from the back you look totally normal, and then from the side... well... it's more obvious,' Alyx chuckled.

'I know, it's really odd. So how are things with you, you are terrible at writing back to my emails... what's that all about?' Nathalie was so bored on her maternity leave, and she lived vicariously these days through her brother, she could barely believe some of the things that he got up to, and the people that he met.

'Yeah sorry about that, I have been traveling a lot lately, the bands I'm working with need some work done on the digital piracy issues, and anyway I love it all, going to the gigs, being backstage all of that stuff,' Alyx admitted, there was no way he was complaining about the travel, it was completely his choice to work that way.

'I wouldn't blame you! Are they playing in Paris then?' Nathalie enquired.

'Nah, I just thought I'd take a few days off here, to see my little sis… I think they might send me on the Asian leg of the tour so I could be gone for a few months, and I wanted to see how you were getting on with the pregnancy and to see if you needed anything…?' Alyx and Nathalie had always been close, ever since their parents died, they had always looked out for each other. She was in fact a year or two older, but as she was so tiny he always referred to her as his little sister.

'You are so sweet, and hopefully you will be back by the time the baby comes… So, what's all the news, are you still breaking all the hearts on your travels, really Alyx… sometimes I think you are worse than the musicians!' Nathalie laughed.

'Not really, well I haven't really had the time to be honest, I'm never in one place long enough to break anyone's heart these days,' Alyx shrugged.

'Well, Julie is absolutely dying to meet you, she saw a photo of you and she thinks you are completely gorgeous! How long are you here for?' Nathalie was dying to set him up with one of her parisienne friends, they were all dying to meet him.

'Oh god, you are not going to try to set me up with one of your mad artists friends?!' Alyx roared with laughter.

'She's not mad, she's lovely, but yes she is an artist, so very dramatic… ' Nathalie conceded.

'Hmm, might give that one a miss,' Alyx grimaced.

'Alright, alright, well I'll tell her you were not in Paris for too long then.'

'How is Jean?' Alyx asked.

'Oh, he's great, very excited about the baby, and spoiling me rotten,' Nathalie grinned.

'So he should be. I absolutely love this place, it's the first place that I come to when I am back in Paris.' Alyx looked around Buddha Bar as he said this.

'Would you believe I only ever come here with you? Jean doesn't really like it here, too many tourists he says?' Nathalie laughed at Alyx.

'What tourists?! Well I suppose it's quite famous so tourists do come here a bit, I never really notice them to be honest.' Alyx didn't want to rise to the bait.

'Well technically Alyx, you are one!' Nathalie teased him.

'Well if I'm one you're one too! I thought that half-French counted for a lot!' Alyx exclaimed.

'Ah no, it's either all or nothing.' Nathalie sighed dramatically. 'You know what the French are like, we are mere mongrels to them.' Nathalie smiled at him.

'Do you believe in this kind of … "there is only one person for everyone" business, like "the one"?' Alyx paused, and this dramatic question seemed to come out of nowhere.

'Bloody hell, where did that come from?' Nathalie was shocked, she wasn't expecting this, could Alyx actually be getting serious with someone?!

'I've just been thinking about it lately, and did you know that Jean was *the one* when you met him?' Alyx asked.

'Yeah, kind of, why have you met someone nice?' Nathalie was dying for details.

'Kind of, but I'm not sure, she's not my girlfriend or anything, it's really hard to start a relationship when you are traveling so much, but she is lovely. We met up in New York, and that was really cool…' Alyx sighed.

'She's American?' Nathalie sounded shocked, Alyx was so European, she could never imagine him with an American.

'No, no, we met up in New York… she lives in London, but she was over there at the same time as me, so I took her out over there as well,' Alyx stated proudly.

'Wow,' Nathalie was seriously impressed, transatlantic dates were pretty unusual.

'I know, pretty amazing,' Alyx agreed with her.

'And then what happened?' Nathalie was dying for more details.

'Well, she was away, and I was away and we haven't actually said we are exclusive so it is kind of hanging in the air. We've only been on two dates so it's a bit early for that. I didn't know what to say to her because I'm going to be traveling a lot, so I think I'll try to keep in touch with her on email.' Alyx considered the scenario.

'I see, and you think she might be "the one"?' Nathalie couldn't believe her ears, this was so out of character for Alyx, this girl must certainly be something special.

'Well, I don't know really, that's why I was asking you, I never really think about things like that... but the question has been playing on my mind lately, like about what if there is only one person for each person, and if there is... how do you know who is the one...?' Alyx's sentence trailed off, he wanted the answer but he was actually quite afraid of what she might say.

'Oh, you just *know*,' Nathalie stated knowingly.

'... that's not helpful, what do you mean you just *know*?' Alyx challenged her.

'It's hard to explain, it just *feels* right, and it feels like nothing else you have ever felt, it's very intense.' Nathalie struggled with the explanation... how on earth could she explain women's intuition to a man?

'And then what about people who get divorced, do they get it wrong or what happens there? It's very confusing?' Alyx wrinkled his nose.

'Well nobody really knows, because everyone has their own path to follow, but I don't think people really get it wrong, it's just that that's the one for that period of their life, and then there is another one lined up when the first one heads off!' Nathalie was considering this as she spoke. She fully intended to be with Jean for the rest of their lives, and shuddered at the thought of not being with him at any point in the future.

'Right, so then, there is more than one, *one*?' Alyx looked confused.

'Could be... like... everyone is different, it's a bit like you know the way people usually have two long term relationships, and then the third one is well… "the one", like the high school boyfriend, then the university boyfriend, and then the boyfriend when they are working, usually people are ready to get married by then so that ends up being "the one". Do you see what I mean?' Nathalie felt like she should be drawing this on a napkin for him, but she doubted that that would allowed in Buddha Bar.

'Kind of… it's a bit confusing…' Alyx looked flummoxed.

'That's because it's kind of different for everyone really, you need to just do what you feel is right. I went out with Jack for three years, and if you had asked me halfway through that relationship, I would have told you that he was "the one". Then when I went off to University that fizzled out, and then I met Andrew there, and then we broke up a year after we left University, and then I met Jean when I moved back to Paris,' Nathalie explained.

'Ok, and they were all "ones" then?' Alyx frowned.

'Kind of, in a way, the one for the time really. The girls usually call it "the one for now", because if it's really the one, you never actually *say it* in case you curse it!' Nathalie winked at him as she said this.

'What do you mean *curse* it?' Alyx asked.

'Oh my god Alyx, you just don't get it do you?' Nathalie exploded. 'It's a bit like *tempting fate*, if you start saying that someone is *the one*. It's more about a feeling.'

'Obviously not! I never thought that saying something could curse it! You see, I don't think guys give it that much thought really, but it sounds like girls think about it all the bloody time, and it sounds very complicated!' Alyx took a gulp of his beer.

'We are just programmed differently, and yes we do think about it a lot, not all the time, but a lot,' Nathalie reassured him.

'So, there isn't one *one*, there might be a few, but they are the one for that time, and then there is a one… for life, "the one", one? So why are there a few ones?' Alyx was starting to confuse himself.

One?

'A different one, for different stages of development, but this happens differently for different people. If you take me for example, I'm so different now compared to when I was with Andy, and I want totally different things from a relationship compared to back then…' Nathalie was determined that Alyx would understand the concept.

'Ok, now it's making a bit more sense…' Alyx sat back in his seat and relaxed a little bit.

'So it's all about developing yourself really, you learn what you do want from a boyfriend and most importantly what you don't want… and of course there are some people who just meet someone when they are quite young and then that's their *one*, and they develop together and that works out ok.' Nathalie waited for this to sink in with Alyx.

'Ok, I'm kind of scared of the concept of "the one", and it sounds like it doesn't scare girls at all?' Alyx was starting to feel sorry that he had asked about this now, he felt like he had opened Pandora's box. All this talk of the one was making him seriously nervous.

'Ah yes, we welcome "the one" a bit more than guys do, it's a bit of a generalisation, but if we are speaking in general terms, then you are right. The main thing is to just do what you feel is right for you, and when you are ready the one will appear. Oh, and one more thing… it's usually when you are least expecting it.' Nathalie reassured him.

'What?!' Alyx cried.

'I mean, erm well, when you feel ready, someone will come into your life and you won't know what hit you!' Nathalie patted his arm.

'Like, kind of… thinking about them all the time?' Alyx implored.

'Exactly, and it feels like the right thing to do, sort of. Sometimes it can feel like you have known them forever.' Nathalie felt that she was probably divulging too much.

'And you just know all this stuff?' Alyx scratched his head as he said this, he sounded baffled.

'Well, girls do kind of consider this kind of thing a lot… and we share our findings. We talk about it a lot,' Nathalie replied.

'I see, ok, well I'll take your word for it. I don't really know what to do next because I'm heading off with the band, it's an opportunity of a lifetime, and I can't ask her to wait or anything because we are not actually going out together.' Alyx looked perplexed.

'I don't know what to say to you Alyx, I suppose you'll just have to figure it out before you go… have you no idea how long you will be gone?' Nathalie tried to help him to come to some conclusion.

'No, it depends on how things go, the band are at a crucial stage, we think they are just about to go stellar, it'll be really exciting to be there when it all happens,' Alyx responded.

'I see what you mean,' Nathalie patted his arm again.

'And… I don't know who I might meet along the way.' Alyx was torn.

'Like supermodels and stuff like that, and it'll be hard to keep in touch, different time zones, random locations etc…' Nathalie had seen this so many times with Alyx before, he seemed to meet someone nice just before he went "on tour", it just wasn't feasible.

'Ha, yeah something like that.' Alyx chuckled.

'Well, Alyx, if you have to even ask… then… I don't think she's the one! Why don't you head off and see how you feel about it when you get back, after you have met the supermodels etc.' Nathalie was convinced now, he shouldn't be questioning it at all, he should go with the band, it was the opportunity of a lifetime.

'That sounds like a good plan.' This was exactly what Alyx wanted to hear, and Nathalie knew it. This issue was resolved just in time, as their starters were just arriving.

***

At 8 pm, Penelope stepped out of a taxi with two of her colleagues. It was a lovely evening, and even though it had been a long day, she was delighted to be in one of her favourite bars…

As soon as they walked in they were ushered to a table for four, with a good view of the whole place. She settled herself into her seat and started looking at the cocktail list. *'Yum, Kir Royale, that will be nice here,'* Penelope thought to herself.

'Un Kir Royale, s'il vous plait,' Penelope beamed at the waiter.

He took the other orders and was gone in a flash.

Penelope glanced to her left and began speaking to her colleague, there was a lot going on in the bank, but they couldn't really discuss it in a public place, so she stopped herself from saying anything about the Mortimer situation. She was just about to speak, when she stopped, mouth agape…

'Oh my god! That looks like Alyx, but no it couldn't be, what would he be doing in Paris?' Penelope's heart started pounding in her chest. She tried her best to hide this from her colleagues, she also tried not to make it too obvious that she was staring over at the back of the lookalike's head. She sat back in her chair and hid behind her menu, just at that moment the guy sat back in his chair and she just knew it was him. She started to get butterflies in her tummy. *'Oh my god! It's him, I can't believe this is happening, this is so exciting, I feel like giggling.'* Penelope sat back in her seat and hid behind her menu, straining to get a look at Alyx, unfortunately, she did not notice the young lady sitting opposite him.

'What do I do? Should I go over there?… no! I can't, hmm… I think I'll just wait here and see what happens.' Penelope couldn't think of ordering, she now couldn't eat a thing. She could not believe that this was happening. Three cities in just over three weeks! She sat behind her menu for as long as she could get away with it. Penelope's heart was still beating really fast…

'Oh my god! I can't believe this, I can't believe this!' Penelope's mind was racing, she didn't know what to do, should she go over there, what if it wasn't him? Who was he with? She couldn't see! Only one thing to do… she would go to the loo and drop by near the table to get a closer look. Penelope excused herself and tried to walk confidently to the toilets, she walked close enough… but not too close to Alyx's table, luckily the place

was packed, and he had his back to her, so he couldn't see her. As she got closer to the table, her heart nearly stopped, he was sitting there with a very pretty girl! Penelope dashed into the toilets so that he wouldn't see her. When she got into the cubicle she felt like vomiting, this was too much. Was he on a date with someone else? Was that his girlfriend? She took a good ten minutes to pull herself together, and to figure out how to get back to her table without Alyx seeing her. She still felt sick, her world felt like it was crumbling beneath her feet, and she had a whole meal to sit through with her colleagues… As soon as she felt relatively composed, she sidled back to the table.

'Penelope, are you alright you look a little pale?' Francois asked, with a concerned tone.

'Oh, well, yes, I'm not feeling very well actually, let me just get a glass of water and I will see how I'm feeling.' Penelope took her seat reluctantly, and slinked down in the chair. Just when she was starting to feel a little better, the girl that Alyx was with stood up, and Penelope got a better look at her…

Chapter 18

Surrender

Penelope cried off ill and took the Eurostar back to London late that night…

'Hi…' Penelope blubbed into the phone, sobbing.

'Pen, is that you? What on earth is the matter?!' George nearly didn't recognise her voice, she was crying so much.

'Well, em… I… sniff, sniff…' Penelope struggled with the memory, and the words.

'Oh my god, what is it? Stop crying for just a sec… are you ok?' George was trying to get some sense out of Penelope.

'No, well, you see, I was in Paris and, you know… out with work and eating in… Buddha Bar…' Each word was interspersed with sniffs, blubs and nose blowing.

'What happened?' George was getting impatient, she wasn't sure whether she should hang up and phone the police for Penelope, or keep her on the line to calm her down.

'And… we were all there and… ' Penelope was talking like a hysterical five-year-old who had been crying so much that she could barely get the words out.

'And…' George demanded.

'Alyx was there, and…' Penelope blubbed.

'And??' George's tone was getting frenzied.

'He was with a …' Penelope struggled to say it.

'Oh my god, I'm coming over, I can't bear to think of you in this state... just take a few deep breaths and I'll be there as soon as I can, ok? Shall I bring munchies?'

'No, I really ... don't think that... I could... eat anything.' Penelope sniffled.

'*Shit, this is bad, I better get over there quick,*' George thought to herself.

'Ok, I'll be right there.' George was nearly out her front door, even though it was way past bed time...

Sniff, 'Ok, thanks George.' Penelope trembled as she hung up.

Fifteen minutes later, George arrived in SW4.

'Right... what did he do to you?' George sat down in front of Penelope trying to read between the lines.

'Nothing, he didn't even see me...' Penelope could not speak properly.

'What? Well what's the matter then?' George was puzzled.

'He was on a date... with a girl... and...' The tears started rolling down her face again, and the words stopped...

'Oh my god here come the waterworks again, what girl...? Are you sure it was a date, it could have been one of the musicians?' George was searching for reasons to calm Penelope down.

'And she was... ... *pregnant*...' Penelope finally got the word out.

'Oh my god, do you think she was his...well you know... *girlfriend*?' George's tone softened.

'Yes, or maybe even worse... maybe his... his... wife.' Penelope sat back in the chair, completely deflated. Her eyes were all red and puffy.

'Oh my god, I don't know what to say.' George was nearly speechless.

'I'm so upset George, and this isn't like me, I never let guys upset me this much, it's just that I really liked him, I really, really liked him, and the time I spent with him, even doing just normal things, was amazing...' Penelope cried.

'Well, I have certainly never seen you like this, over a guy! I don't really know what to say... and what about Richard?'

'Uh oh… I just set her off again!' George seriously regretted mentioning Richard.

'He keeps asking me out, and driving me mad… he says he thinks I'm "the one", it's fucking ridiculous… no better way to scare off a potential girlfriend!' Penelope's face was like thunder, the last thing she wanted to talk about was Richard.

'Indeed… oh dear… well look, I think we need to call in an expert on this…'

'What, expert… what do you mean?' Penelope sounded concerned. Penelope only swore when she was really stressed, so her colourful language was a good barometer of her stress levels.

'Zoe, of course… she's great at this stuff, let me call her, I won't tell her it's you of course.' George picked up her phone and searched for Zoe's number.

'Of course, well if you think it would help…' Penelope sighed and blew her nose.

'I don't think we have much choice,' George stated.

'Hi Zoe, it's George, lovely thanks… look I have a bit of an emergency, yep, a friend of mine… no, no , no, it's not me, I promise, no everything is fine, you see the thing is, yeah he kind of travels a lot with work, yeah, hard to pin down, well the thing is we think he was spotted in Paris with a girl… just a sec…' George put her hand over phone.

'Pen, sorry this may hurt… but was she pretty?' George felt awful asking Penelope this, she felt like she was twisting the knife.

'Yes, very.' Penelope welled up again.

'Hi Zoe, yep, I'm afraid so, well… the thing is, it's a bit of a heartbreak situation, she seemed a bit pregnant too, I know… I know… what do you think? No, no she never met any of his friends, or family, a bit of a James Bond character… yep, gorgeous, bloody gorgeous. A bit French looking, but in a good way Yep, that's what I thought, ok well I better go, I've got a bit of a situation here, ok, thanks for your help… speak to you soon…' George hung up and took a deep breath and turned to Penelope.

'Yep, she says… forget about him, I'm really sorry Pen, I know this must hurt a lot.' George hugged Penelope.

'I have never felt pain like this in my entire life. I can't describe it, my heart feels like it hurts, I know that sounds ridiculous but I have a pain in my chest from all the crying.' Penelope started bawling again.

'I can imagine… is there anything I can do? Anything at all?' George said soothingly.

'I don't think so,' Penelope sighed.

'Do you think you should contact him to see, kind of confront him or something?' George was trying to be practical.

'No way, we were never a thing, couldn't really be, he is away all the time, couldn't really get anything off the ground, you know the way it is… he was always good about keeping in touch, but he was in the country so rarely… come to think of it, I don't actually know where he lives in London… oh my god George, maybe he doesn't live in London at all…' The truth hit Penelope like a tonne of bricks, she had these deep feelings for someone who she knew very little about. She didn't even know where he called "home".

'I'm surprised there are any tears left in there, come here and I'll give you a hug… this has really hit you hard Pen.' George hugged Pen as hard as she could.

'I can't stop crying all the time, I had to hold it in while we were in Paris, and then the minute I walked in the door here, the floodgates opened… ' Penelope welled up again.

'Is that why you didn't ring me about it from over there?' It was starting to make sense to George now.

'Yeah, I knew this would happen. I just can't believe what has happened, you know when you meet someone that you really like, and they seem to fit into the picture of the perfect guy that you have, and you really click with them *and* you really fancy them, and they seem to really like you and then they just fuck off and get married and have kids…' Penelope cried.

'Well, now we don't know that for sure…' George chided.

'I know what I saw George…!' Penelope exploded!

'Ok, ok, calm down, no need to shout at me.' George stepped back.

'Sorry George…' Penelope was sheepish.

'That's ok, I understand.' George hugged her again.

'He was the first guy I really, really, liked and I can't believe this… I had kind of *a feeling* about him, like he might have been, I don't know, he might have been…' Penelope paused momentarily '… Someone good for me… It's like, have you ever had an idea of your perfect guy in your mind… I never actually thought that he might exist, and then I met him… and it totally floored me…' Penelope nearly said the fateful word… the "one" but she stopped herself just in time.

'But…' George added.

'But what?'

'But… because you never really saw him that often, you never really got beyond the honeymoon stage…' George offered a dose of reality.

'Go, on… I'm listening…'

'He was the ultimate fantasy man, and that fantasy was never shattered because, well you never did anything normal together, think about it Pen, bands singing to you, dates in New York, it's like something from a film…' George gestured dramatically.

'But I thought that's what it is supposed to be like!' Penelope gasped.

'Well, yes, really romantic things can happen, but… it's just that they don't happen that often, and they don't keep happening the way they did with you and well Alyx…' George was trying to be realistic.

'So you think the whole thing was a bit unreal…?' Penelope was searching for answers.

'No, no, not *unreal*… just a bit erm, how can I put this… *unrealistic*.' George added. She was trying to be practical, to offer reassurance.

'As always George, you are making so much sense, it still doesn't stop me from feeling totally shit, but understanding these things always helps matters a bit…' Penelope gave her nose a definitive blow as the tears stopped flowing.

'Indeed, now what I think you should do… is take Richard up on his offer, even though I know guys are probably the last thing on your mind right now…' George knew that another man was the only thing that would help Penelope get over Alyx, even if it was *only Richard*.

'I would be happy if I never saw another man again as long as I live… why on earth do you think going out with Richard would help matters?' Penelope didn't get it at all.

'I just think that it might be good to take your mind off the dreaded Alyx, and he seems to really like you, and you know sometimes it's the ones you least expect…' George advised.

'I supremely doubt that, but maybe you are right, maybe I should give him a chance, he is certainly being persistent.' Penelope sounded exhausted.

'I reckon, you have nothing to lose there… and I would hate to see you swear off men altogether… what are you going to do … become a nun, god help us! If you pardon the pun.' George laughed lightly.

'I don't know how you managed to make me laugh in this state…' Penelope sniffled and stifled a small laugh at the thought of herself in a habit.

'Go on, text Richard back now, and arrange to meet up…' George was convinced that if Penelope arranged something with Richard, it would speed up her recovery.

'Yes mum.' Penelope picked up her phone reluctantly.

'I guarantee it'll make you feel better…'

'I hope you are right…'

'Well, only one way to find out…' George hugged Penelope as soon as the text was winging its way to Richard.

Chapter 19

Post Alyx Apocalypse

Penelope struggled through the next few weeks of work, and was actually glad that her days were so busy that she barely had time to think about him. She had finally arranged a time to meet Richard, and reluctantly mustered the enthusiasm to try to enjoy his company.

'Ah... couldn't resist could you...' Richard grinned at Penelope and kissed her on the cheek as she approached him in All Bar One on Cannon Street.

'Well no, not quite you see...' Penelope began...

'Drink?'... and promptly got interrupted by Richard.

'Em, yes thank you...' Richard poured her a glass of pinot noir from the bottle on the table.

'I haven't seen you in ages, tell me *everything*... did I tell you that I have a new pad, in Chelsea? You will have to come around for supper...' Richard was on a roll.

'Yes, I'd love to, supper would be lovely...' *'Oh my god, what am I getting myself into here?!'* The words flew out of Penelope's mouth before she had a chance to stop them. She was still completed defeated after the Alyx in Paris experience, and her defences were down.

The following evening, Penelope caught up with George.

'Well... how did it go?' George was dying to know.

'Erm, ok actually, I still couldn't get a word in edgeways but he was a perfect gentleman this time, he didn't try to ram his tongue down my throat or get me drunk! He invited me over to his *new pad* in Chelsea for dinner next week…' Penelope informed her.

'… and…?' George intoned.

'… and… nothing… look George, I have completely given up on men, and the concept of finding that one perfect guy, as far as I'm concerned I did find him and, well now he's bloody married, so don't lecture me about bloody Richard…' Penelope got testy.

'Ok, ok… so having given up on men you are still seeing Richard?' George backed off a bit.

'He's not strictly men now is he really?' Penelope bit back.

'Ah some people might disagree with you there…' George winked when she said this.

'Well are any of those people here?' Penelope challenged her, looking her directly in the eyes.

'Erm no, no of course not I mean well, some people do think he's a bit of a catch, being *loaded* and all that, great job … you know you could do worse, and your mother would *love* him…' George giggled.

'Oh, I know she would, she'd be wittering on about if she was twenty years younger etc. etc. etc…' Penelope dreaded the thought!

***

Over the coming weeks Penelope's vow of resistance towards men, and Richard in particular thawed considerably. Time was the great healer, and as the weeks passed, Alyx started to slip slowly but surely from her mind. Having put him off a few times, Penelope eventually relented and agreed to have dinner at Richard's Chelsea pad.

'Well, how was the dinner at Richard's pad?' George called Penelope for a post-mortem.

'Em, yeah, it was ok, I mean it was nothing like what it was like with Alyx, but it was nice actually, even though I've officially given up on men, it was kind of nice to have my battered ego massaged...' Penelope admitted.

'Good girl... did he try to kiss you again?' George was keen for the gory details.

'No, not this time, he was a bit more civilised this time around.'

'Good, good, glad to hear it. Do you fancy him?' George got straight to the point.

'Not sure, I'm very negative about men at the moment, but he's definitely ok, I think he could kind of grow on me, and I already like his personality, his sister is down from the dreaded castle next week, he wants me to meet her. Let's hope she's not covered in tartan from head to toe like his mother!' Penelope hissed.

'Fingers crossed. Do you reckon they have tartan family knickers too?!' George squealed with laughter.

'Probably... that wouldn't surprise me at all, big tartan granny knickers with the family crest on them... It's really hard not thinking about Alyx though...' Penelope's voice dropped to a whimper.

'Well try!' George encouraged her.

'I am trying my best, it's just not easy that's all I'm saying...' Penelope echoed.

'I know, I know... well hopefully Richard will help to keep your mind off it,' George advised.

'Yeah, that is helping a bit... and I know I'm not up for meeting any new guys at the moment, and going on dates and all of that stuff, so it's definitely better to go out with someone I kind of know and kind of trust...'

'Good,' George soothed.

I really don't know why he affected me so badly, maybe George is right, maybe it's because he was kind of a fantasy man, kind of like the perfect guy, well the perfect guy for me anyway. But she is probably right, he wasn't a realistic boyfriend, he was never in

*the country long enough to have a proper relationship with me...
what am I talking about, he's probably bloody married to that
other woman, oh no here come the waterworks again... is this ever
going to end...?'* Penelope stared into space as soon as she came
off the phone to George, and the tears started tumbling down
her cheeks.

Chapter 20

Glitter

In W1, Zara eventually found her first assignment, and clutching her *A to Z* she pressed on the buzzer, this was definitely the address she had been given… but she could clearly see a bar through the glass doors?! She approached the reception cautiously, she wasn't sure if she was in the right place.

'Good morning, Zara isn't it?' The receptionist smiled at Zara reassuringly, she did not look like a regular receptionist, she looked more like a model.

'Yes hello, the agency said that I would be meeting erm…' Zara stuttered, now that she knew she was in the right place, she was totally intimidated by it all. It had high ceilings, floor to ceiling windows, and pictures of famous ad campaigns all over the walls.

'Susan?' The receptionist smiled at her.

'Yes, sorry, it was Susan, I'm covering for somebody who is on maternity leave?' Zara stuttered, she was not too sure about this temping thing at all.

'Ah yes, follow me… I know exactly which department now, have you had much work experience in advertising?' The receptionist trotted ahead of Zara, chatting away.

'Marketing mainly, but I am also really interested in advertising.' Zara blushed.

'Great, that makes it easier! Here you go, here is your temporary desk, I will send Susan down to you.'

Zara sat down at her desk, she had a Mac with a massive screen, pink plastic stacked paper trays, furry pens and all sorts of bits and pieces. She couldn't believe her luck. Could this really be *work*? It seemed much more like *fun*.

'Thanks for your help,' Zara called after the receptionist.

'No problem.' And she was gone…

Zara looked up from her desk for the first time, there was music on in the office and there were all sorts of young people buzzing around. It was a real hive of activity. As she looked further down the office, she could see a circular space in the middle with an oval white pvc table, surrounded by transparent inflated couches, and very strange tall thin coloured plants. She felt like this is what it would be like working on Mars!

'Oh my god everyone in here is gorgeous, I'll have to dress up a bit more tomorrow. The girls are so thin!' Zara was suddenly very conscious of her small but curvy figure, and her D cups! *'I hope I can cope with this, temping in London is likely to be pretty heavy going.'* Zara stared at the Mac in dismay, she had never used a Mac before and she hadn't a clue how to even turn it on! *'Oh god! This is going to be a disaster.'* She had a sinking feeling in her stomach at the thought of looking stupid trying to turn the Mac on.

'Zara, hi, I'm Susan, thanks for coming in.' Susan arrived down to Zara's desk, she looked like a model, amazing clothes, tall, thin, gorgeous.

'Oh that's fine.' Zara was a bit taken aback, Susan was towering over her at her desk. This happened often, as she was only 5ft 2, but it made her feel about five years old, every time, without fail.

'Joanna left some instructions, we are going to have you just do the general admin on the accounts while she is out, we have an account manager covering the meetings etc., ok?' Susan continued.

'Oh yes, that's fine…' Zara was reassuring herself at the same time.

'Have a quick look through the manual, I'll head down to get us some coffees…and then I'll introduce you to the rest of the team.' Susan flounced off down to reception.

'Thanks.' Zara looked down at the "manual" it was a pink PVC folder with a big white exclamation mark on the front of it. Zara couldn't believe that this was considered "work", it was so much fun already. The pink folder helped to calm her nerves considerably.

'Ok, good start, she seems nice and these instructions look really really good. I have a good feeling about this now. It's nice to have my own desk and phone and all that. I wonder how long Joanna will be out, I'll have to check with the agency later. I'm so glad I did this now, Rob was right, temping is fun.' Zara started leafing through the manual.

Susan came back in a few minutes with two freshly made cappuccinos in beautiful cappuccino cups, she had a plate of chocolate biscuits, and a few marshmallows, that was it… Zara was in heaven!

'Here we are, let's just pop over to the coffee area so that we can have a chat…' Susan said.

Zara followed her obediently, trying not to stare at all of the gorgeous people chatting to each other and blabbering into their phones. She wasn't looking forward to sitting on the perspex sofa, she was sure her bum would look huge in it! Zara sat down on the edge of her seat, not wanting too much flesh to be magnified through the perspex in full view of all the people who sat behind the sofa. She suddenly realised how bright the office was, and that there were floor to ceiling windows looking out onto Dean Street.

'So, Zara, what do you know about Glitter?' Susan arched one eyebrow as she spoke.

'Erm, well, the recruiter told me that it was a full service advertising agency, and that it was full of young people, and that you work on some amazing accounts…' Zara trailed off, she hadn't really been paying that much attention, she was just thinking of it as a stop-gap at the time… now she had a whole new perspective.

'That's right, and it's very busy as I'm sure you can see, the creative floor is downstairs, I will take you down there after lunch, we are working on a huge pitch at the moment and the client is in. You will mainly be covering our account manager who is off on maternity leave at the moment, I think she has left you great instructions, so you should be alright with those. If you need anything just let me know… I sit three desks down from you. I will bring you around to meet everyone a bit later. Have you worked in Soho before?' Susan took a sip of her cappuccino.

'Erm, no, you see…' Zara stopped herself before she told the whole story, no negativity! She wanted to start this on a positive note… 'I have been based near Covent Garden mainly,' Zara stammered, pleased that she had managed to keep it positive.

'Great! Well if you enjoyed it around there I'm sure you will love it in Soho. We go out a lot after work, but then again, having our own bar is largely to blame for that! The people here are a friendly bunch and they are always keen to get to know new people!' Susan beamed at Zara, she was really impressed about how calm Zara was, most people were so nervous even when they were temping there. Everyone was dying to work at Glitter and they were keen to make a good impression, and it was practically impossible to get an entry-level job there. It was well known that temping was one of the routes in. Susan had no idea that this hadn't even occurred to Zara yet!

'I was going to ask you about the bar actually, is that our bar?' Zara was pleased that she had had the insight to use the word 'our' showing that she was a team player from day one.

'Yeah, we all congregate there after work. It's so handy! Then we usually head out later around the corner in Soho Square.' Susan filled Zara in.

The two of them drank their coffee and got through a biscuit each, then it was time to get back to work. Susan went off to her desk, and Zara went back to her new, temporary desk. She followed the instructions to log onto her computer. As soon as she touched the keyboard an explosion of glitter appeared on the screen as it booted up. The glitter fell to the bottom of the screen, to reveal a more normal looking desktop, much to Zara's relief. For a second she thought she might have broken it! She logged into Entourage and got through the first few emails. She couldn't believe her luck landing this job, Glitter was amazing, it was like working in MTV land. She couldn't wait to get stuck into the work and get behind the scenes of some of the ad campaigns.

She logged onto her webmail and emailed Rob…

To: Bobbyfun@yahoo.com
From: Zara.Stephens@yahoo.co.uk
Sent: 10.13am
Re: I'm back!
Hi Rob,

I miss you so much! How are you? Are you working yet? Or are you still enjoying your millions? You are not going to believe this but I have started temping already. I only registered with an agency last week. I thought nothing of it, and then next thing I know I'm working in Soho on Monday morning. I'm in this office, it's so cool… there is a bar downstairs and everyone is gorgeous! It is called 'Glitter' do you know it? I can't believe the money as well … I'm on way more money as a temp than I was on as a permanent employee, life is good…I love London!
Zara xxxxxxxx

Now that Zara had contacted Rob, she felt much better, what was work in London without him! The next thing the phone rang!

'Hi Zara, this is Tim from facilities, can you drop down to the lower ground floor to collect your security pass please?' Tim enquired.

'Sure, I'll be down in a minute.' Zara made her way downstairs in the lift. She had been in Glitter just over an hour, and already she felt right at home. By the time she got back to her desk, there was already an email from Rob…

To: Zara.Stephens@yahoo.co.uk
From: Bobbyfun@yahoo.com
Sent: 10.17am
Re: Re: I'm back!
Hello Darling!

I can't believe you are working at Glitter! Talk about good luck, how on earth did you manage that?! My friend Bubbles, real name 'Jonathan' works there. I will send him an email and get him to keep an eye out for you... you can't miss him, he is gorgeous! He is six foot two, white hair, looks Scandinavian! I know loads of people who are dying to work there. I am still making the most of the amazing weather... working on my tan here in the back garden, but I have my CV out and about there, so any day now...

Going by you, I quite fancy doing a bit of temping,... do you think they would take me on at Saatchi!? ;)

Anyway, no real news with me... when are we meeting up for drinkies!?

Love Rob xxx

PS How is the love life??

Zara beamed at her computer as she read the email, she couldn't believe her luck. This was so much better than Organicom, it was all coming together, it felt like it was meant to be... Zara couldn't wait to tell Penelope all about it.

***

At 6 pm, Zara shut down her computer and gathered her bits and pieces ready to leave, she turned around and was startled to see Susan towering over her again...

'... and where do you think you are going?' Susan said sternly...

'*Shit! Was there other stuff that I was meant to do?!*' Zara panicked; 'Well, erm, I just thought that...' Zara's sentence trailed off...

'You didn't' think you were going to escape did you?' Susan grinned at her!

'Erm, well… I…' Zara began.

'We have a rule here Zara, that on your first day, you have to be initiated into Glitter!' Susan started leading her down towards the lift. Susan pressed the G button, and Zara was having palpitations, she had no idea what was going on!

As the lift doors opened, she saw that a lot of the company were standing around the bar in the lobby, they all had one thing in common… a shot of Sambuca!

Susan handed Zara a shot from a tray and took one herself…

'Hi guys, this is Zara and she is going to be with us for the next few months, she is covering the fmcg account management admin, so drop by and say hello to her won't you… cheers!' And they all shot the Sambuca. Zara couldn't believe this… what a warm welcome! It was only her first day, but she already loved Glitter!

Zara wandered down to Tottenham Court Road Tube station, with a warm fuzzy glow, partly Sambuca induced and partly due to a great beginning at a fantastic new job. She hopped onto the Tube and was home in no time.

As she walked into the kitchen she bumped into Penelope, and she filled her in on her day. She had the feeling that something had been bugging Penelope ever since she came back from Paris, but she didn't know her well enough to ask her directly.

'That is fantastic news Zara, and to think you were so distraught about losing your other job, if only you had known at the time that something much better would come along! You seem so much happier, did going home that weekend help?' Penelope asked.

'Yeah, in a way it did, it definitely helped, now that I have more of my clothes and shoes down here, it feels more like home. I brought loads of my photos too, so my room is less bare now!' Zara considered this as she answered Penelope, the trip home definitely did help, and she loved having more of her things down in London.

'Oh, that's good, there is nothing like having all of your bits and pieces around you! Do they really have a bar in work?' Penelope was astounded.

'Yeah, it's amazing, and they have proper coffee machines and baristas, it's great, I love it already. I never knew there were jobs like that.' Zara beamed.

The girls headed upstairs to get an early night, there would be plenty of late nights ahead of them during the week, that's the way it goes in London… it was so unpredictable. It was always sensible to have an early night on Monday, and Tuesday too… if you could get away with it.

Chapter 21

Flower Power

'Morning Penelope' there is a delivery for you.' Penelope looked confused as the post room guy popped his head into her office.

'Really? I'm not expecting anything, I wonder what it is?' Penelope got up and followed him out the door, mentally filing through any recent online purchases that she might have forgotten about.

'Oh my god! Roses! Who are they from?' She was astounded when she spotted the big bouquet of roses.

'Hi, it's me, you are not going to believe this… but… Richard… has sent me a dozen red roses, a huge bouquet, they are gorgeous!' Penelope gushed as soon as George picked up.

'No way, he is unbelievable. Have you phoned him to thank him yet?' George was very impressed.

'Not yet, I just got them now.' Penelope was pleasantly flustered by it all.

'Well, go on… give him a ring then.' George advised her warmly.

***

'Richard, hi, it's Penelope. Thank you for the flowers, they are beautiful,' Penelope gushed.

'Ah, you got them, I'm glad you like them, I was wondering if you are free this weekend if you would like to come out for dinner?' Richard asked her.

'Em, yes, well I am free as a matter of fact.' Penelope smiled down the phone.

'Great, how does Friday suit you?' Richard continued.

'Em, yes, that's fine, yes Friday is fine…' Penelope looked down at her diary.

'I will let you know the arrangements once I have booked somewhere.' Richard didn't want to chat for long on the phone.

'Ok, thanks Richard… and thanks again for the flowers, they are beautiful…' Penelope replied.

'Don't mention it…' Richard sounded courteous.

As soon as Penelope had hung up, she dialled George's number again.

'What did he say??' George was dying to know.

'He asked me out for dinner on Friday.' Penelope sounded in great form for the first time since Paris.

'Nice, did you say yes?' George pressed her.

'Of course, well I couldn't not say yes after the flowers…' Penelope responded.

'Good, well it can do no harm.' George mused.

'You are quite right, and I am actually really looking forward to it, I'm so impressed with the flowers.' Penelope sounded sincere.

'I hope she is right. The last thing I need to do is to go from the frying pan into the fire. I really care about Richard, and I'm surprised that I had never thought about him in that way before, he is quite good looking in a classic kind of way. I normally prefer dark guys, but it doesn't look like I've had a great amount of success with my normal types. Better get back to work…'

'Penelope, what is your take on the proposal?' Simon popped his head around her door.

'It looks secure enough to me, let me just do a few more calculations…' Penelope glanced down at the document on her desk.

'Fine, drop into my office when you have decided, thanks for your help.' Simon was impressed with how little time it had taken her to work through it.

'Anytime, I will be there shortly.' Penelope aimed her red pen at the document.

***

'Pen, you look lovely,' Richard smirked at Penelope as he stood back to let her walk out in front of him.

'Oh, erm, thanks, eh… where are we off to?' Penelope was a bit taken aback as Richard ushered her out the front door, she constantly felt like he was *driving*.

'Well, I thought we could stay localish for you, is that ok?' Richard reassured her.

'Yes, perfect, there are lots of nice places around here.' Penelope sighed, relieved, staying local would make it easier to make a quick getaway if the night turned out anything like the first time.

'Let's get a drink first,' Richard suggested.

'Right.' Penelope smiled at him. 'Let's go to SO.UK on the high street, it's one of my favourites,' she suggested.

'Ok this is going ok so far, George was right, it's good for me to be out with someone, it definitely provides a good distraction. He has improved his manners thank god! I hope he doesn't try to get me drunk again. I couldn't cope with that at all. I'll take it easy on the wine tonight.'

As soon as they were sitting down on the brown suede couches, and their drinks had arrived, Richard launched into a name-dropping frenzy. Penelope could barely get a word in.

'I was out with Andrew Dawson the other night, do you remember him Pen? He was doing medicine… well he has gone into plastic surgery now, worth a bloody fortune, just got engaged too.' Richard droned on and on about ex classmates, and 'people to know'.

'Erm no, I don't remember him.' Penelope gazed off into the distance as Richard droned on and on, she had no interest in these people.

'You must, remember he used to be on the rowing team, constantly hammered, stripping off... ' Richard was on a roll, delighted to be so *informed* about everyone.

'That kind of rings a bell.' '*Oh god... I hope he doesn't start going on about all the guys from school and college... that's so boring! I have no interest in how much money they are earning.*' Penelope had a pit of regret sitting in her stomach, this was not a good idea, she would do anything to be with Alyx... '*Oh no, here come the tears again.*' The tears started welling up, but Penelope managed to distract herself to stop them just before they spilled out over her eyelids and onto her cheeks.

'... seems to be getting married to Bettina, do you remember her, she was doing media studies... she has turned into something of a PR guru now, they are such a power couple...' Richard smiled gleefully.

'So, Richard, are you still in touch with any of the girls, Ruth, Nancy and all of that crowd?' Penelope interjected.

'Ah... not really, well ever since myself and Ruth broke up, well things were kind of awkward, I mean they were always more *her* friends if you know what I mean.' Richard shrugged, he looked a bit sheepish. The thought of his failed relationship took the wind out of his sails a little bit.

'Yes, yes of course, I suppose they are all married off by now anyway.' Penelope mustered a bit of enthusiasm about the conversation.

'Oh yes, absolutely, but I suppose we are all at that age now, everyone is settling down.' Richard sat back as he said this, fixing his gaze on Penelope, waiting for her reaction.

'Hmm, yes, I know what you mean, I'm too busy to even think about that kind of thing to be honest.' Penelope was giving nothing away.

'Really? I thought you girls were all mad about getting married?!' Richard shot back, sitting bolt upright.

'Well, it's more about finding the right person really... ' Penelope trailed off, she did not want to get into a discussion about this with Richard.

'I see…' Richard looked a little confused, but not completely deterred.

Penelope arrived back home at 11 pm, a few glasses of wine had helped the conversation, and Richard didn't make any inappropriate lunges in her direction.

'I actually had a really nice night with Richard. He was very gentlemanly, and we had our first kiss tonight… discounting the ridiculous drunken one before. It was nice. He really is growing on me, and it is helping to keep my mind off Alyx. I'm seeing him again on Wednesday. He was talking about going up to the castle for the weekend, I don't know about that, I think it is way too soon for anything like that… hmmmmm… … I'll have to think about it…' Penelope got into bed, she wasn't sure how she was feeling, it definitely wasn't a bad feeling, and it was kind of good, but was it good enough? That was the question…

Saturday turned out to be a lovely sunny day in Clapham. On days like these all of the urbanites gathered themselves, their friends, and picnic food from Sainsburys and headed to the common to soak up the sun. The residents of 72a Abbeville Road were thinking exactly the same thing, everyone was keen to make the most of the incredible weather. Penelope woke up bright and early and she bumped into Charlie in the kitchen.

'Morning,' Charlie grumbled. He was still half asleep.

'Oh, hi Charlie,' Penelope sighed through a yawn.

'What has you so tired then?' Charlie raised one eyebrow and gave her a cheeky grin.

'Oh, nothing much, I was out with Richard last night and…'

'What?! That gobshite! What were you doing out with him?' Charlie exploded.

'Erm, well, I was kind of on sort of a well… date,' Penelope admitted sheepishly, she was quite taken aback by Charlie's reaction.

'With *him*?' Charlie's face was like thunder.

'Yeah, I guess, we are maybe kind of a thing now…' Penelope trailed off.

'Hmm, right, see you later.' And Charlie was gone. He was clever enough to not say any more in that frame of mind.

Penelope sat at the kitchen table, trying to take in what had just happened. She was already on the fence about Richard, and she was just heading to the right side, but now Charlie's reaction had brought back the whole other drunken kiss experience. Confusion and ambivalence started to cloud her thoughts again. Was she doing the right thing? Just then, Zara walked in.

'Hello there, how are you?' She said cheerily, she was already in her denim miniskirt and vest top, bikini underneath, ready to head down to the common.

'Oh, hi! Sorry… I was miles away there. ' Penelope came back down to planet earth.

'I can see that! Is everything ok?' Zara put the kettle on.

'Eh, yeah, yes… everything is… fine. Are you heading down to the common?' Penelope asked.

'Yep, can't wait to get out into the sun, do you fancy coming along?' Zara beamed at Penelope.

'Ok, good idea, give me fifteen minutes to throw my bikini on and I'll be with you then, no need for breakfast, I can grab something from Starbucks on the way down.' Penelope got up.

'I won't have brekkie here, we can both grab a muffin and a coffee and bring it down with us, good idea Pen.' Zara was so happy, she loved the sun, and couldn't believe that Clapham was a place where you could go sunbathing, it was like being on holidays for free. A few minutes later Penelope breezed into the kitchen all ready to go.

'Right, let's go, I have five magazines in here, and you have the rug… I think we are good to go!' Penelope announced, and the two of them headed down the stairs.

Just as they were double locking their front door, 72b opened up, and the lovely Australians arrived out, armed with frisbees, footballs and other common-related paraphernalia.

'Oh hi,' Zara blushed, she hadn't expected to see him again so soon.

'Oh hi Zara, are you two heading down to the common?' Zack beamed at the two of them.

'Erm, well… yes…' Zara stuttered.

'Yes, we are, would you like to join us… we just need to pop in to Starbucks to grab some breakfast first, where will you be?' Penelope saw that Zara was floundering so she decided to take control of the situation.

'Great, we will be by the pond near Firefly,' Stu added.

'Lovely, we'll be down in a bit, save us a spot,' Penelope beamed back at the three of them as she marched out the front door, Zara in tow.

As soon as they got to Starbucks, Zara felt it was safe to speak.

'God, thanks for that Pen, he really took me by surprise there, I'm so embarrassed that I got embarrassed,' Zara gushed, getting embarrassed all over again.

'Don't be silly, I know how hard it can be to chat to a knight in shining armour.' Penelope chuckled. It was so obvious that Zara and Zack fancied each other like mad.

'Yes, exactly! It's great that we are meeting them down there, it'll be such a laugh, and it'll keep any pervy men away.' Zara smiled.

'Exactly!' Penelope added.

Fifteen minutes later, with two skinny lattes, and two skinny blueberry muffins to go, the girls had joined 72b on Clapham Common. The common was completely packed, and it was as much fun taking in the sights and sounds around them, as playing frisbee with the Aussie guys. There were lots of groups of girls in bikinis, and gorgeous shirtless guys. It was early enough in the day to assume that most of these people actually lived in Clapham, come midday lots more twenty-somethings would be arriving in on the Tube from some less leafy areas, keen to soak up the rays.

'Where's Charlie today? Should we text him to see if he fancies coming down?' Zara asked Pen.

'Erm, hmm, I'm not sure, he went out in kind of a hurry this morning, so I assumed that he has the recording studio booked,' Penelope stuttered.

'In this heat!? He must be mad!' Zara laughed.

'Well, you know what he is like… music is *the* most important thing in his life.' Penelope sighed and raised her eyes to heaven.

'Yeah, I know what you mean.' Zara laughed at her. Charlie was so funny about the music. It came before everything else.

Four hours, including three games of frisbee and lots of getting to know each other later, the girls sat chatting to the three guys at a table outside Firefly. The girls had a jug of delicious Pimm's and the boys were knocking back beers like there was no tomorrow. Well, it was Sunday tomorrow so technically, there was no work tomorrow… same thing!

'What are you up to later Zara?' Zack looked directly at her as he said this.

'Erm, no plans actually, was just going to take it as it comes.' Zara was feeling a lot more confident now after half a jug of Pimm's.

'Cool, well, we are all heading out on Clapham High Street after this, if you fancy it?' Zack smiled at her.

'Yeah, that's cool, Pen are you up for that?' Zara turned to Penelope, who was having a whale of a time with Stu and the other half of the jug of Pimm's.

'Oh, yep, I'm in, that sounds like fun, if we are still standing that is!' She giggled, starting drinking at 4 pm would be pretty heavy going even for blokes on a Saturday night.

'Ok, great, we should probably just head home at six-ish, and grab showers and something to eat and head out early. Clapham will be packed tonight because it's such a sunny day, everyone will go straight out from the common…' Paul added, with a twinkle in his eye, he thought Penelope was gorgeous, and he couldn't believe his luck that she lived next door!

'Good plan.' Zara smiled back at them.

'We should definitely start off at The Sun bar, we can drink outside there, it's so hot out today,' Stu added.

'Ah yes, *Costa del Clapham,* as we like to call it.' Penelope laughed at the thought of it. On sunny days Clapham turned into a huge open-air resort, and The Sun bar was the best way to keep that *Common* feeling going as the sun went down.

At 6 pm they all headed back to Abbeville Road, Penelope and Zara were pretty hammered, but they were on a roll now, no point in stopping. They grabbed a quick sandwich and were back out with the guys at eight. George and her boyfriend arrived shortly afterwards, they had been at a barbeque all day, and they were also completely hammered. As predicted all of the bars were completely packed, but The Sun bar was a good choice because there was an extra bar outside, specifically for days exactly like this. Then they went on to SO.UK on the high street, and then later on they went on to Sand bar, it was just far away enough from the high street so that all of the 'blow ins' didn't know about it. The girls were all hammered!

'Oh my god Pen, I haven't been here in ages, it's brilliant!' George slurred.

Sand bar was full of gorgeous people, drinking gorgeous drinks and dancing the night away. The music was always particularly good on a Saturday night.

'Yeah, Pen, good choice... I can't believe this is nearly on our road, it's so near the house, it's amazing!' Zara bopped away with Zack as she said this, she was having the night of her life. She had never been to a place like this in her entire life before moving to Clapham, she couldn't believe that she lived so near it. It was practically at the end of their road.

Penelope headed up to the bar, against her better judgment to get even more drinks.

'Hi Henry, three more of your best Strawberry Daiquiris!' Penelope beamed at the barman, it was well known, by those *in the know*, that he made the best Strawberry Daiquiris in London.

At 2 am they were all still dancing off the daiquiris, when the lights went brighter and the music stopped. The Abbeville roaders reluctantly dragged themselves out of Sand bar, and started the ten minute walk home. Zara hung back with Zack, and they walked hand in hand. When nobody was looking he leaned in and gave her a quick peck on the lips and procured her mobile number for further communication. Zara gave it willingly, and was so happy after a perfect day, and night, really being part of the scene in Clapham. She no longer felt intimidated by the gorgeous twenty-somethings in SW4. Now she knew that she was one of them. So much had happened in the past few weeks, she was struggling to keep up with it all. As soon as they were safely inside, Zara flopped down on the couch and told Penelope everything. Penelope was delighted for her, as she knew how hard it had been for Zara over the past few weeks. The two girls headed up to bed, still hammered, and buzzing from the music.

Chapter 22

Another Sunny Monday

Penelope was at her desk at 7 am. She felt fantastic, she had had a lovely weekend, a total disconnect from work, and her skin was glowing from the sun on Saturday. She was raring to go, and full of energy for work that week.

At 8 am Richard Lord arrived at his desk, refreshed from a weekend golfing, and satisfied that he had increased his network by golfing with the O'Donnell's. He opened up his Outlook calendar and surveyed his social engagements for the week. It was going to be a busy week…

At 8 am Alyx woke up from a disturbing dream. He dreamed that he was in an airport and he kept missing his flight. He sat up in his bed and looked around, everything seemed normal, his bag was packed ready to go, passport, tickets… yeah, everything was fine. He was meeting the band at the airport, and he had made arrangements for his flat in Paris while he would be away. He got ready quickly and headed for Charles de Gaulle.

'Hello, so you finally made it!' Alyx laughed as the band turned up, late as usual.

'Yeah, yeah, whatever,… look we are here now, stop moaning!' the lead singer laughed at him.

'I know, I know, don't worry, I was just joking, are we all ready to go?' Alyx surveyed the luggage, he hoped that all of the instruments were safely in the hold.

'Yeah, yeah, all of the guitars are in outsized baggage, they should be fine,' Chad sighed dismissively.

'Ok, let's go then.' Alyx rounded them up.

Once they were all settled and seated, Alyx's mind started wandering. The dream was playing on his mind, he didn't normally remember his dreams. He had the feeling that he had forgotten something. He daydreamed for a while, and then it hit him... Penelope! He had forgotten to tell her he was going. He had emailed her and she hadn't written back, but he should have emailed her to tell her about the trip at least... He would email her when he got there, after a few days, that's what he would do... as soon as he had made that decision, Alyx dozed off, making up for lost sleep the night before.

At 9.22 am Zara reached street level at Tottenham Court Road Tube station. She strolled down to Dean Street walking on air. As soon as she reached her desk she found a little pink box with her name on it, she tore the ribbon up and opened it, and inside was a Krispy Kreme donut with pink icing, and 'Glitter' written on it in chocolate icing. She looked around and noticed that all of the girls' desks had a little pink box, and all of the boys desks had a blue box on them. She ran downstairs to grab a cappuccino, thinking all the way... *'I love my job, I love my job, I love my job!...'*

At midday Charlie woke up, dazed from the night before. He was still fuming about Penelope meeting up with that idiot Richard. No good could come of it. That was one thing that he was sure of. He picked up his guitar, and started strumming, within minutes he was writing down some lyrics.

Chapter 23

Time Flies

The rest of the summer passed in a blur of barbecues, afternoons sunbathing and drinking on the common, nights out in Clapham, brunch in the sunshine on Abbeville Road, and the busy-ness of the working week in London. During the course of the summer the housemates settled into 72a Abbeville Road, and the life that came with that. For Charlie, that meant, the same as always, writing, recording, and hanging out with Gerry. For Penelope her time was dotted with the odd business trip, and busy busy days in work. She met up with Richard regularly, she still wasn't sure about him, but he hadn't actually done anything wrong, so she was reluctant to reject him. They were taking things very, very slowly.

Zara was halfway through her six-month contract at Glitter, and her confidence was growing daily. She was becoming really good at her job, and she was now encouraged to have a more client-facing role, as the Soho agency was so busy. Zara had fallen in love with Zack, and she couldn't believe her luck that she had managed to find a nice boyfriend living next door to her. That was one habit that she had managed to keep going from home… she always ended up with the boy next door!

As September rolled in the evenings got shorter, and even though it was still lovely and warm, there was kind of a chill in the air. Penelope was doing a stupendous job of not thinking about Alyx. She hadn't thought about him in ages, until, she logged into her computer one wet Wednesday morning.

To: pchesterfield@jlminternationalbank.com.
From: alyxstuartbruges@hotmail.com
Sent: Wednesday September 17 3:00 am
Subject: On the road
Hi Penelope,
I am sorry that I haven't been in touch in ages, the thing is, I am on tour with the band, it's a pivotal time for them and I will be away for a while. I just wanted to let you know that I think about you sometimes and it would be good to see you the next time I am in Europe. I am not sure when that will be, because things are a bit difficult with the band at the moment.
How are things with you?
Speak soon,
Alyx xx

Penelope sat back in her chair and stared at the screen, there was only one thing she could do…

'George, hi, it's me!' Penelope sounded tense

'Hi there lovely, what's up?' George answered.

'Hmm, don't go mad when I tell you this…but I just got an email from… Alyx,' Penelope sighed.

'Oh.' George's tone was of disbelief.

'I know how you feel, George, I'm so upset, I had just literally forgotten about him completely, and now this. I haven't written back yet, what do you think I should do? I really like him? He is on tour with the bloody band, not sure when he'll be back. It has brought it all back!' Penelope sighed.

'I know, but things are going so well with Richard, and you need a boyfriend who is actually here, not someone who is off on tour! And we still don't know whether he is actually available or not?' George regretted this as soon as she had said it.

'I know you are right, but I don't want to just ignore his email, I ignored the last one…' Penelope trailed off.

'Ok, well send him back a quick response, don't mention Paris, he still doesn't know that you saw him there. And remember we don't actually know that he is married, that could have been anyone. I wouldn't close the door on that one, but I would focus on Richard, who is here and now,' George added calmly.

'Ok, I'll write him a brief email back, and I'll try not to think about him after that, I'll leave the door open, but that's it…' Penelope sighed.

'Ok, good. I better go, rushing to a meeting.' George added.

'Ok, speak later.'

Penelope hung up the phone, and sat staring at her inbox. She could see his email in the reading pane and she just didn't know what to say. This was the last thing she needed right now. Things were going really well with Richard, and she was trying to put all of that stuff with Alyx behind her. This email had opened the wound right up again. She struggled with what to say.

To: Alyxstuartbruges@hotmail.com
From: pchesterfield@jlminternationalbank.com.
Subject: Re: On the road
Hi Alyx,
It was nice to hear from you. That sounds very exciting about the band, and it sounds like you will be away for a long time. All is good with me, really enjoying the end of the summer in London. Let me know when you are back it would be good to catch up.
Take care… …

Penelope sat and stared at her response, and typed, deleted, re-typed, re-deleted the x after her name. In the end she settled with…

Pen x

After all… it was rude to not respond to two xx's without even one x!

Finally the response was gone. There was no taking it back. Penelope sat and stared at her PC, she felt a great emptiness growing inside her. It came out of nowhere, when she had woken up that morning, she was happy, she had had a fantastic summer, she had a nice boyfriend, she had a great house in Clapham and lovely housemates, and then he came back. He came back out of nowhere, and now the emptiness was growing. She tried not to think about him, but she knew she missed him, and there was nothing she could do about it. Penelope trundled through the day, her heart was heavy, and it was slowing her down.

Later on that evening Penelope wandered down Abbeville Road towards home. Zara was sitting outside The Abbeville, with Zack, Stu and Paul, she plopped down in the extra chair, grateful for an alcohol distraction… anything to avoid being alone with her thoughts.

'You look like you have had a long day.' Zara said as she put a glass of rosé in front of Penelope.

'Yeah, work is pretty busy at the moment, I'm pretty wrecked.' Penelope sighed and the others believed her.

'No worries Penelope, a few more glasses of rosé and it will all feel better,' Stu added.

'I'll drink to that!' …and Penelope raised her glass.

'Cheers' they all said.

It was a lovely warm evening on Abbeville Road and the housemates stayed out drinking until closing time.

***

On Friday night Penelope met up with Richard, as usual after work…

'Hello darling, you know Poppy and Mitchel don't you? And do you remember Tiggy and Tarquin?' Richard planted a kiss on Penelope's cheek and handed her a glass of champagne, he ushered her into the fold of "people to know".

'Oh, yes of course, hello, when is the baby due?' Penelope dutifully kissed them all on both cheeks and couldn't avoid mentioning Poppy's bump.

'Oh, yah, the baby is due in four months, we are soooo excited, aren't we muffin?' Poppy enthused, turning to her husband.

'Oh, yah darling, we are positively dying for the baby to arrive!' he added.

Penelope was starting to get bored of Richards' friends, they were all nice, but pretty settled, with babies on the way. She had been fine about it all until the email from Alyx, and she now felt as if she was being pulled out of Richard's world of golf, networking and married friends, and back into the world of bands, glamour and the Bowery Ballroom... It was so hard for her. She felt so confused. She felt torn...

'I hear that Harry has finally popped the question?' Richard chuckled, one eyebrow raised.

'Oh, yes, we were positively bursting with excitement, Melissa is soooooo delighted, another wedding in the family, Mummy is thrilled.' Bunty arrived just in time to add to the conversation. She also had a six-month bump.

Penelope zoned out. It was as if she were there in body but not in spirit.

'Are you alright darling, you look a bit drawn?' Richard whispered, when he got Penelope on her own.

'Oh, yes... well... I am feeling a little under the weather, actually, I think I may go home...' Penelope trailed off.

'Yes, of course darling, if you are not feeling well, I will grab you a cab,' Richard sighed hastily.

'Thank you that would be lovely.' Penelope began to relax, she couldn't listen to any more marriage or baby talk.

The cab arrived within fifteen minutes, and Penelope kissed Richard goodbye. She waved to him, and as soon as she was far enough away, she broke down crying. When she got home she ambled up to bed, and cried herself to sleep.

Chapter 24

On the Road

Alyx sat at the side of the stage, this was his favourite time of the day, the crowd of 20,000 were making so much noise it would be a miracle if the band would even be heard. He sat nursing his Jack Daniels and Coke drinking it all in. Life was good, he was enjoying the beautiful hotels and beaches on the Asian leg of the tour, not to mention the women...

His real life in Europe seemed a million miles away. He rarely thought about it.

'Alyx, buddy, we are going on!' Chad gave Alyx a man hug, as was the ritual before each gig.

'I know, good luck, I'll be right here keeping an eye on you.' Alyx man- hugged him back.

Chad strolled onto the stage and picked up his guitar, the crowd screamed and drowned out the first few bars of the first song...

***

On Saturday night, George came around for the dutiful post-mortem of the email from Alyx, she could tell by Penelope's tone on the phone that she was not taking it well. Just as George arrived at 'a', Zara was heading into 'b'.

'Hi George, how are you?' Zara beamed

'Oh, hi Zara, I didn't recognise you there…' George was startled, Zara looked completely different. Being in love certainly had a good effect on her.

'Oh yeah, sorry…I'm just heading into 'b' here, that's where my boyfriend lives,' Zara smiled at her

'Oh that's right, oooh it must be going well then!' George winked at Zara as she passed her by and went into 'a'.

'Hi there, Zara let me in.' George peeped around the living room door.

'Oh, hi…' Penelope said glumly.

'Oh dear, that bad is it?' George sat down next to her.

'I'm afraid so, I just can't stop thinking about him, and just when things were going so well with Richard, it's really hard.' Penelope welled up.

'I know, I know, but the thing is, he's not really here, who knows if he will ever come back?' George tried to be reasonable.

'I know, but it's hard, that's all. I have never met anyone like him,' Penelope sighed.

'There's only one thing to do, why don't we head down to Sand bar, and knock back a few cocktails? That will take your mind off it, we are not going to achieve anything by sitting in on a Saturday night.' George hugged Penelope.

'I totally don't feel like it but I know you are right, I'll clean up my face and we can head down there.' Penelope got up and went up to her room.

Chapter 25

The Matriarch

It was not long before the inevitable happened…

'Darling, mummy is absolutely dying to meet you properly!' Richard announced to Penelope as soon as she was stretched out comfortably on his couch in his flat in Chelsea, reading the Sunday papers.

'What?' Penelope muttered, only half listening.

'Well, you see, Mummy is coming down next weekend, and I thought we could all have lunch on Sunday… ' Richard gave Penelope a sideways glance to catch her reaction.

Externally Penelope didn't even look up from the newspaper, internally she was sitting bolt upright, tearing her hair out! 'Hmm, yes, that sounds lovely,' Penelope muttered and completely pulled off a nonchalant tone of voice. Richard felt like the cat that got the cream as he began planning Sunday lunch in his mind. He simply couldn't wait to introduce the two most important women in his life. He was delighted that Penelope felt the same way.

A pit of dread started growing in Penelope's stomach, she was not looking forward to Sunday lunch.

They spent the afternoon sprawled out in Richard's flat reading the papers, Penelope felt tense and change her mind about staying over. She headed back to Clapham to get a good night's sleep in her own bed.

The following Friday, Lady Elizabeth Lord-McFleurie checked into Claridges as usual. She was a creature of habit, and she always stayed there when in London. She was greeted by name by the concierge on duty. She inspected her room thoroughly before agreeing to unpack and grace it with her presence for the weekend. She was so looking forward to meeting this *girl* that Richard was intending to marry. She was planning on giving her a thorough inspection altogether, not everyone was worthy of joining the Lord-McFleurie clan.

On Sunday morning Penelope woke up early, on edge. She had a bad feeling about this afternoon. While 'meeting the family' was never easy, she had a feeling that Richard's mother was going to be more of a challenge than most. Penelope tried on nearly all of her clothes before deciding on an outfit. She erred on the side of conservative, but not dowdy... she didn't own anything dowdy!

Lunchtime came around all too quickly and Penelope met Richard at the restaurant before getting the concierge to call his mother's room. Penelope's heart was hammering away in her chest, as they both waited for Lady Lord-McFleurie to descend. Penelope's palms were clammy and she was not looking forward to having to shake hands.

Richard's mother kept them waiting long enough to irritate them, without officially being rude. The lift doors opened dramatically and she swept out, a blur of brown tweed with just a hint of lilac. She had a wonderful brooch attached to her tweed jacket, with just a hint of the family tartan on it. She wore a matching A-line tweed skirt, with a single pleat down the front. Her hair was swept back into a neat bun, she looked very much like a glamorous, old school, headmistress. She carried a waft of lily of the valley with her as she walked towards Richard and Penelope. While her features were hard and she was not particularly pretty, her makeup was subtle but very effective and completely flawless. She was not a big woman and not a thin woman, but her sense of presence was large and non-negotiable. She wore sensible, old-fashioned, but elegant shoes. The type of shoes that cost a fortune and lasted forever. The heel was not too high, it was not too low, it was just right. She had a matching sensible, yet elegant brown clutch handbag. While Penelope was by far the beauty in their trio, there was no mistaking who was boss. Lady Lord-McFleurie air-kissed Penelope after giving Richard a small peck on the cheek as soon as she got near enough to do so.

'Pen-ay-lope, it is so lovely to meet you fai-nally, Richard has two-ld mey soooooo much about you,' she announced in her slight Scottish accent.

'Lovely to meet you Lady, erm Lord, erm,' Penelope stuttered, as she squirmed in her... suddenly... too high... heels as she towered over Richard's mother. Penelope had thought that her black suit would have been a sensible choice, but all of a sudden she felt like a rebellious teenager who was trying to corrupt Lady Lord-McFleurie's son! She felt like her clothes were too revealing, even though they were not... she felt overdressed, and for the first time in her life she actually wished that she owned a twin-set, a tweed skirt and *sensible* shoes!

They made their way into the dining room in complete silence, Penelope was afraid to say a word, letting Lady L-McF. drive the conversation... .and that's precisely what she did. She kept it brief, terse, and she asked all of the questions.

'So, Pen-ay-lope, tell mey, where did you grow up?' She didn't even look at Penelope as she said this. While she absolutely, without question, spoke the Queen's English, she had a wonderful hint of a Scottish accent that only seeped out through certain words and phrases.

Despite the straightforward nature of the question, Penelope stammered, all of a sudden, and for the first time in her life... the words just wouldn't come. She stammered through a brief history of her childhood, culminating in how she and Richard had met at University. Penelope made the fateful mistake of mentioning Richard's ex-girlfriend, this was something of a conversation stopper. Richard's mother's face turned to thunder at the mere mention of someone actually rejecting her beloved first born. She found the situation quite incomprehensible. Penelope excused herself to go to the Ladies. Luckily there was good phone reception in there, despite all of the marble and the thick wooden toilet doors.

'George, hi, it's me!' Penelope squeaked.

'Oh my god, I thought you were meeting the…'

'I am! I just met her, oh my god, I feel like I need a G&T and it's only 2.30 pm,' Penelope hissed.

'Oh my god, is it that bad?' George sounded concerned.

'Yes! It's terrible, I feel like a naughty school girl, she's like the Queen,… but not in a good way… she's wearing a brown tweed suit. I'm wearing, what I thought would be… a sensible black suit, and I feel like a rebellious teenager,' Penelope sniffed.

'You poor thing, is there anything that I can do?' George was always ready to phone with an emergency at the drop of a hat, she was getting quite good at inventing things these days.

'Not really, I just have to power through really, my nerves are frayed, that rash has broken out on my neck again, I'm starting to feel like I am allergic to his family!' Penelope whimpered.

'Oh no! Don't say that! That would be disastrous!' George hissed.

'Well, it's starting to feel that way. Look I've been gone for long enough now, I'd better head back, I don't want her thinking I'm bulimic or anything!'

'What!? Oh my god, don't say that, for heaven's sake. You are starting to scare me now.' George nearly dropped her phone.

'Well, you know what I mean, she's the type of person who is just dying to find fault… with anything and everything.' Penelope's voice wobbled, the pressure was getting to her.

'Alright, alright, well ring me as soon as you can when you get out of there. I'll pop over if it's not too late,' George offered.

'Ah George, you are an angel… speak to you later.'

Penelope hung up and looked at herself, rash and all, in the mirror. As she re-approached the table in the dining room, she got the distinct impression that they had been discussing her, and not in a good way. They gave no physical indications of this away, but somehow she just *knew*. There was a stony silence as she sat back down. Richard's mother turned to her as if waiting for an excuse.

'Well, we thought you had fallen down the loo...' She peered over her reading glasses and nearly broke into a smile.

'Oh, yes, well, erm, it was, well you see there was a bit of a queue.' Penelope stopped herself before the lie got bigger. Richard jumped in to save her from this particular conversational cul de sac.

'Now Mummy, what *are* we going to have for dessert.' He rustled his menu and handed Penelope hers, she had never been so grateful for a menu in her entire life. It formed a thin, but very effective barrier between her and Lady L-McF.

'Ye-yes, quite, well now, what were you thinking of going for?' She peered at Richard over her glasses and her menu. Her glasses were rimless, and therefore barely visible, but they became quite obvious in moments like this, as she was gearing up for disdain.

'Mmm, yummy, let me see... ooh, I think I will go for the same thing as always, you know me Mummy, creature of habit!' Richard snapped his menu shut and turned to order the rhubarb crumble with custard. At the same time, Penelope just caught herself before she rolled her eyes at this... there was nothing more mundane than *habit*. Penelope was secretly dying to go for the heated chocolate brownie with organic homemade vanilla ice cream, but she dutifully ordered the mango sorbet, she didn't want to give Richard's mother anything to complain about.

'Pen-ay-lope, that's exactly what I was going to go for, great minds... ' Richard's mother defrosted for the first time during the whole meal, delighted, that finally... this girl had done something right.

'Oh, yes, yes indeed.' Penelope mustered her warmest smile, delighted that things, even in the tiniest way, had taken a turn for the better... finally! Internally she breathed a huge sigh of relief.

Richard practically had his napkin tucked into his shirt, his knife and fork in his hands, by the time his rhubarb crumble arrived. He certainly was reverting to childhood behaviour in the presence of the Matriarch.

Richard's mother had really warmed to Penelope, after the dessert incident, so she announced that they should retire to the bar for some cognac. Penelope was nearly foaming at the mouth at the thought of the alcohol, she was so nervous… and she just knew that it would help matters. As soon as they were swirling cognac around their oversized glasses, the conversation continued conservatively. Penelope asking none of the questions, and Richard filling the silences. One cognac turned into two, which turned into three, and Richard decided to get himself and Penelope out of there before they all got bombed, for fear that this might loosen their tongues a bit too much. Richard's mother showed no signs that the alcohol was affecting her at all.

'Oh Mummy, we must be off, lots of work to do this evening,' Richard announced before they had a chance to get another drink.

'Oh, really, Richard, must you go?' She peered at Richard over her glasses as she spoke.

'Oh yes Mummy, you see, Penelope also works terribly hard, and she begins her day terribly early, so it's best if we are on our way now, and I have lots of work to do tonight.' Richard reassured her.

'Indeed, indeed, well if you must… ' she sighed.

'Oh, yes, Mummy, work is so important,' Richard grinned at her.

'Yes, yes of course, you are quite right,' she agreed.

Penelope was afraid to open her mouth at this stage, in case her tongue ran away with itself. They had their escape route now, she didn't want to mess it up.

The two of them thanked Richard's mother for lunch and she extended an open invitation to Penelope for a weekend at the castle, which Penelope graciously accepted.

'Absolutely charming Richard, absolutely charming,' she hissed to Richard as she kissed him goodbye, and was sure that Penelope could not hear her.

Richard flounced off, brimming with pride. Penelope was quite taken aback by his change in mood all of a sudden.

'Well, she was certainly very nice.' Penelope forced a genuine seeming smile.

'Oh, I am so glad that you got on, I think she really liked you Penelope.' Richard gave Penelope's arm a little squeeze.

'Really! How could you tell?' Penelope realised what she had just said and backtracked immediately... 'Oh, erm, I mean... of course, I don't know what she is normally like?' Penelope searched for the right words without much success.

'Oh, you know, I just *know*. I thought that you got on like a house on fire. It's not like Mummy to drink that early in the afternoon, that was a real *sign*.' Richard added.

'Oh, I see, well, that is wonderful. She seems like a very strong lady.' Penelope mustered more enthusiasm.

'Oh, she is Penelope you are quite right, quite right.' Richard was already planning the next week in his head.

'Right, I am definitely going to have to head home, I actually do have some work to do this evening.' Penelope lied. She had a slight headache coming on, and couldn't wait to speak to George.

'Yes, yes of course darling. I would say that you have had quite enough of the Lord-McFleuries for one day.' Richard winked at her.

Penelope managed to stop herself before she agreed too strongly with him.

Penelope flounced into the kitchen half an hour later, only to find Zara engrossed in the latest edition of *Heat* magazine, dipping chocolate digestives into her tea.

'Oh, hello there, gosh you're dressed up, were you in work Pen?' Zara sounded surprised to see "Work Penelope" on a Sunday afternoon.

'Hmm, kind of, I was meeting Richard's mother... it certainly felt like hard work.' Penelope gave Zara a wide-eyed knowing stare.

'Oh my goodness...' Zara dropped a few biscuit crumbs onto the magazine as she mumbled this. She swallowed and then added… 'What on earth was she like?' Zara was completely on the edge of her seat. 'Tea?' she grabbed another mug from the cupboard and began pouring from the teapot.

'Mmm, yes please…' Penelope took a seat.

'Biscuit?' Zara offered the packet.

'Of course!' Penelope paused before the descriptive torrent began. Within minutes Zara was in the hysterics at Penelope's descriptions of Lady L-McF. Half an hour later George arrived brandishing some wine, one red, one white and the girls had a great time dissecting the meeting. It was so much fun that it made Penelope forget her discomfort altogether… for now…

***

Autumn stretched into an interminable winter and Richard and Penelope began seeing each other quite regularly. As Richard's presence grew in her life, the memory of Alyx slowly faded. Forgetting about him was getting easier with time. Due to the pace of life in London, the band she had met with him were getting less airplay lately… so thankfully the reminders were fading with them.

A few weeks later, Richard made his usual trip to the castle to catch up with the clan. Sunday lunch was quite an affair in the Lord-McFleurie household. Richard's mother would make such a fuss and they would use the master dining room. After lunch they would retire to the drawing room for coffee and cognac and the conversation would turn to the status quo and plans for the future…

'Richard, how *are* you getting on down there in London, how are things progressing with Pen-ay-lope?' The matriarch enquired, she was wearing the family tartan and had her grey blonde hair pulled back into a tight bun. She was a stocky woman and she did not look out of place among the portraits of the ancestors that decked the halls.

'Oh good Mummy, actually I am glad that you brought that up, well you see… the thing is, I was wondering if I could borrow granny's ring? To get it cleaned? We are off to Paris next weekend and I have a feeling that I might need to bring it with me.' Richard winked at his mother, everyone in the room could understand the double entendre. There was only one reason that he would be getting granny's ring cleaned, and that was that he was planning to propose.

'Oh Richard that is *wonderful* news, I'm so delighted for you both!' his mother exclaimed, showing more emotion in this moment, than she had in years.

The whole family got up and started shaking Richard's hand, and clapping him on the back. Richard was thrilled to be the centre of attention.

'I will fetch it for you this evening before you leave for London,' his mother smirked.

At 5 pm the search for the family heirloom began and ended abruptly. The ring was usually locked into the safe behind the painting of the castle, but the box was empty. They all gathered around, peering into the empty box. Pandemonium erupted. This was a calamity, granny's ring had been in the family for generations, and Richard, as the first born, was entitled to use it.

Richard made the journey back to London less than satisfied. Things were not going to plan. He needed that ring for next weekend, he would now have to buy another one. He couldn't propose without a ring. That was out of the question, the ring was half the experience, she would definitely say yes if he produced a ring...

Richard arrived back in London late that evening and made his way to Chelsea. He booked the Eurostar first class for Friday night. He booked the Ritz hotel for the weekend, he knew that Penelope would simply love that. The atmosphere would be ideal for a proposal.

On Monday morning, Richard slept in ever so slightly in order to drop in to Tiffany's on Sloane Square. He knew exactly what he wanted. He marched into the diamond section at the back and barked 'An engagement ring for about ten grand,' at the sales assistant. It was quiet in Tiffany's first thing on

Monday morning, and the mere mention of ten grand had two of the sales assistant rushing to grab their boards full of engagement rings. Richard filed through them… princess cut, no… pear… no.

Twenty seven minutes later, Richard sauntered out onto Sloane Square, his credit card eleven and a half grand lighter, and his jacket pocket eleven and half grand heavier, weighed down with a small turquoise box holding the promise of a lifetime.

At exactly the same time Penelope flounced back to her desk after two early meetings with her team. She could murder a tall skinny latte and a skinny blueberry muffin. She surveyed her inbox, nothing too juicy stared back at her. Just as she was staring into space deliberating which tall skinny latte emporium to spend her fiver in… her phone rang.

'Good morning darling, I have a surprise for you…' Richard smirked as he spoke.

'Where are you? You sound like you are outside somewhere?' Richard took Penelope by surprise.

'Quite right, quite right… I am still in Chelsea, I'm going in a trifle late this morning,' Richard replied.

'Oh, well… what's the surprise then?' Penelope sounded light and cheerful.

'Well… what are your plans this weekend?' Richard asked conspiratorially.

'Erm… well, hmm, I was going to go shopping with George, nothing major really…' Penelope trailed off.

'Well pack your bags Penelope, I'm whisking you off to Paris for the weekend,' Richard replied gleefully.

'Really?! Oh my god Richard that's wonderful news, I'm so excited… when are we off?' Penelope squealed.

'Friday, after work of course… ' Richard smirked.

'Thank you Richard, I'm so thrilled, what a lovely surprise,' Penelope replied. She began mentally packing her bag in anticipation of her trip.

'I will forward you our details for the Eurostar when I get into the office, we will be going straight from work on Friday.'

'Thanks Richard, I am so excited, that's something great to look forward to this weekend. Let's chat about it later this evening...'

'Alright darling, have a lovely day,' Richard replied.

'Same to you.' Penelope hung up and a frisson of excitement enveloped her.

Paris for the weekend, what a nice surprise. Richard isn't normally spontaneous,' she thought to herself as she turned to face the day.

Chapter 26

Proposal

On Thursday evening Penelope got ready for her trip to Paris, completely oblivious to the fact that her life was about to change forever. The best things always happen when we least expect it.

She packed lightly, she knew that the weekend would probably be predictable enough. Dinner on Saturday night, after taking in the sights during the day. Penelope packed one little black dress (nothing too short or slinky!) and elegant shoes and a matching handbag. She packed elegant, casual, daywear, nice jeans and a few tops. She knew exactly where Richard would be taking her, he had his favourites in Paris and he was a creature of habit. Unfortunately Buddha Bar was not on his list. Penelope sighed as this thought occurred to her. She removed her black, low-backed Gucci top from her case, she would not be needing it after all. Penelope placed it back in her wardrobe, hanging alongside her other clothes that had been underutilised in recent months. The snow leopard print silk top (Richard hated animal print), the extra high-heeled pointy toed shoes, (Richard hated pointed toes, he said they reminded him of *Macbeth*), the three-quarter length black capri pants, Richard hated anything too glamorous. Relationships are always a compromise and it was a small price to pay.

As soon as her luggage was ready Penelope phoned George.

'George, I'm so excited, we are going to Paris for the weekend!' Penelope squealed.

'Really, since when?!' George sounded astounded.

'Richard surprised me. He called me on Monday morning to tell me that he was whisking me off to Paris, he is so sweet.'

'He certainly is, well have a brilliant weekend and give me a ring the minute you get back, I'll be expecting a full update!' George was mildly miffed as she now had to find another shopping partner for the King's Road, but she was happy for Penelope all the same.

The next morning Penelope battled her way into work on the Tube with her luggage. She had left especially early but it didn't make much difference, the Tube was still absolutely packed! Eventually she made it in to work and the day dragged on as all she could think about was her trip to Paris. Eventually it was time to go. Richard collected her in a taxi.

'Hello darling, all set?' Richard gave her a kiss on the cheek.

'Oh yes, yes of course, thank you for letting me know on Monday... it gave me time to prepare, and of course to look forward to it all week.' Penelope smiled at him. He looked different this evening, more content, less talkative, more mellow somehow.

Richard put his arm around her in the back of the cab, this was very unlike him, he did not favour public displays of affection.

They travelled first class on the Eurostar, and the champagne was helping Penelope to unwind.

'Where are we staying?' Penelope had just realised that she had no idea where they would be staying.

'Ah, that is the next surprise, I wasn't going to tell you until we got there, but now that you have asked...' Richard peered at her, pausing for effect... 'We are staying at the Ritz,' Richard smirked.

'Oh wow, Richard, that is an amazing surprise, I'm thrilled, I have never stayed there before.' Penelope had butterflies in her stomach, she was so excited about staying at the Ritz.

As soon as they arrived in their room, they changed and went down to make their dinner reservations. Richard had planned everything with such great precision. Penelope didn't even have to think, she was just going along with his plans. As soon as they sat down to dinner a bottle of champagne appeared immediately. Penelope had already had quite a bit to drink on the two hour train journey, but it was Paris after all, so she delved right in. Richard sat back and watched her every move. As soon as she took the first sip the glass clinked! Penelope moved it away from her mouth, and held it up to the light, and she saw the diamond ring glinting at the bottom. Her mouth dropped open with shock and Richard caught her surprise by saying…

'Penelope, will you marry me?' In case she thought it had been a mistake.

'Oh, well, erm.' Penelope nearly fainted with fright. The waiter hovered next to her so that he could dispense the champagne into a tumbler and fish the ring out of the glass. The waiter performed this as if he had done it many times before, and barely blinked throughout the process. Tears welled up in Penelope's eyes as she looked at her magnificent ring. It was mesmerizingly beautiful.

'Yes Richard, yes, I will of course.' Penelope started to cry as he placed the ring on her finger, and Richard ordered a bottle of Dom Perignon to celebrate.

Penelope's left hand felt so heavy under the weight of her new ring. She kept staring at it in disbelief. It was huge, and magnificent, and hers. Richard and Penelope spent the rest of the weekend bathed in the warm fuzzy glow of being a newly engaged couple, they were completely caught up in the moment.

***

As soon as the euphoria of the weekend had worn off and everyone had been informed, the dust began to settle and the reality that she had agreed to spend the rest of her life with

Richard finally dawned on Penelope.

'George I can't quite believe... I'm... I'm... engaged...' Penelope sighed incredulously.

'I know, it's so exciting! You don't sound too thrilled... are you ok?' George probed.

'Yeah, yeah I'm fine... it's just that I thought it would be different... like... I don't know, I was expecting it to *feel* different... like... ' Penelope's voice trailed off.

'Like with...' *Crap! I nearly said Alyx there!'* George bit her tongue.

'Like with what?' Penelope shot back.

'Like, you know, with fireworks and all that hearts and flowers stuff?' George was more matter of fact. Penelope was searching for reassurance.

'Kind of, like I thought I would be feeling like *'This is it! This is the one!',* but instead I'm feeling like *'Is this it?'...* like it's no big deal at all, but I thought it would feel like a big deal, but hey... maybe that's just life for you, you never know what you are going to get,' Penelope reassured herself.

'You do love him though, don't you?' There was a slight note of concern in George's voice.

'Of course, of course I do... I don't know George... maybe it's the stress of it all. It's such a big change and he wants to get married pretty soon. We have known each other for years, so it's not like we need to wait, so I agreed... but...' Penelope sounded pensive.

'But what?'

'Ah... I don't know, I think I'm just feeling a bit under pressure, and there is so much to organise for the wedding and so much is changing. Thank god my mother has taken most of it upon herself to make the arrangements, seriously George, you'd swear it was *her* wedding!' Penelope laughed.

'That is so funny, she is so sweet, she is mad about Richard, he's exactly what any mother would love, castle in Scotland and all of that stuff, it's like something from a film!' George laughed.

'She has had a subscription to two wedding magazines since I turned 25! She took out a stack of them... she had *marked* the pages with those little coloured page marker tabs! I nearly had a heart attack. I think she is freaking me out more than the prospect of getting married!' Penelope replied.

'I wouldn't blame you, that's pretty scary.' George gasped.

'There was one weird thing though. Richard had a family ring that has been passed down through the generations, and it went missing!' Penelope said conspiratorially.

'What do you mean "went missing"?' George was dying to know.

'It was handed down from his grandmother, but when he decided to propose it just sort of vanished into thin air... that's why I got the Tiffany's one!' Penelope smiled, relieved.

'Hurray!' George cheered.

'No seriously though George, do you not think that that's a bit strange? Like a *sign* or something?' Penelope sounded nervous.

'Don't be silly, I think it's bloody good luck, you ended up with an amazing ring as opposed to some ring that has been around for years, and is probably haunted... ' George raised one eyebrow as she said this.

'Hmm, yeah well I just thought it was like a bad sign... ' Penelope sounded slightly concerned.

'No way, definitely your good luck, I think,' George soothed.

'Hmm, I suppose so, you *are* always right after all George.' Penelope perked up.

'There you go, you see... nothing to worry about,' George chirped.

'Apart from the fact that it's only a few months away!' Penelope considered the imminent wedding.

'Apart from that!'

Chapter 27

Meet the Parents

Penelope surveyed her beautiful diamond ring on the train on the way up to Scotland. She sat beside the window, and it sparkled in the daylight as the trees and valleys flew past. She was still getting used to the weight of it on her left hand. Even though she had technically met Richard's mother before, this was something more of an official visit. As they pulled into the station they were greeted by Merton, the family driver, in a rather old, bronze, Rolls Royce. Richard beamed as Merton held the door open for Penelope.

'Richard, welcome home.' Merton intoned, with a warm half smile. He stood by the car, in his grey suit and cap.

'Hello old boy.' Richard shook his hand and negotiated him into a manly hug, quite against Merton's will.

Penelope slid into the back of the car, and sat on the Lord-McFleurie family tartan blanket that covered it. It was well and truly freezing up in Scotland and she was grateful for the warmth of the car as Merton loaded their luggage into the boot. In no time at all they were on their way, and within an hour they were winding their way up the narrow driveway to the Lord-McFleurie family home. Penelope stifled a gasp as they turned the corner and the castle came into full view. It was vast and grey with a narrow turret on each side. There was a maze garden to the right hand side and beautiful trees lined the stone driveway leading up to the large, ancient, oak front door. Penelope tried to hide her surprise. She had seen countless pictures of the castle, but nothing prepared her for it in all its glory. It had clearly stood the test of time, and in the harsh Scottish climate that was no mean feat. Penelope could not help but have an enormous respect for this building that had been around for centuries, and had housed her family to be.

The car screeched to a halt outside the front door, a small cloud of dust rose as Merton pulled on the brakes in the stone gravel. Penelope sat there motionless, afraid to stir. Richard held her hand and gave it a light squeeze. He leaned in and whispered:

'Mummy will be so pleased to see you again Penelope.' He gave her a peck on the cheek.

Penelope turned to him and sighed 'Indeed, I can't wait to see her myself.' She trembled as she got out of the car. She had a feeling of foreboding, which she couldn't quite place, as she crossed the threshold. Nancy and the butler, McVeigh, greeted them at the door. McVeigh looked as if he was easily a century old, but was still clinging to the tradition and the importance of his role for dear life. Lady Lord-McFleurie stood beneath the portrait of her great, great, great grandfather, on the first landing of the vast wooden staircase in the hallway. Her countenance was stony. She mustered a weak smile as she descended and slowly approached Penelope who was standing in the doorway with Richard, reluctant to move.

'Penaylope dear, I am delighted to welcome you to my home, and indeed… into my family.' Lady Lord-McFleurie gave Penelope two air kisses as she said this in her faint Scottish accent. 'You must go upstairs and change for dinner, we will be having an aperitif shortly in the library. Richard will show you around, won't you Richard?' Lady L-McF spun around slowly as she said this.

Richard jumped slightly and he said, 'Yes mummy, yes, yes of course I will,' rather hastily.

Penelope breathed a sigh of relief as Richard marched her up the vast staircase to her room. While the castle was beautiful, she had the constant feeling that she was being watched. There were so many ancient oil paintings of people from another time, with a clear family resemblance. That nose had been handed down for generations, and no doubt would survive for generations to come. Penelope grimaced at the thought of it.

As soon as she had closed the door of her room, Penelope flopped down on the four-poster bed in despair...

'What on earth am I doing here?' she thought to herself. *'I don't belong here, this is so weird. The house is amazing, but it is so ancient and dusty and the pictures are really freaking me out. I hate the feeling that I am bit lost here. I can't even remember where the nearest loo is... oh god!'* Penelope sat on the bed and stared into space. So much was changing. She felt like she was in the middle of a tornado. A few moments later Richard rapped on her door. Penelope jumped slightly as his knuckles hit the ancient wood.

'Just a moment,' Penelope quipped.

'Penelope darling, it's only me.' Richard inched into the room, and closed the door quietly behind him.

'Oh, hi,' Penelope sighed with relief. 'Richard, I have no idea where the nearest loo is!' she gasped.

'Oh dear, I'll show you to it, it's just at the end of this corridor,' Richard laughed.

'Thanks, where is your room?' Penelope arched one eyebrow.

'Ah, my quarters are in the turret at the end of the house. I bagged that years ago. Just another one of the main benefits of primogeniture.' He smirked. 'You'll notice that Mummy put you as far away as possible from me!' Richard laughed.

'Oh my god, she is worse than my mother in that case,' Penelope laughed.

'I know, believe me I know...' Richard assured her. 'Look, dinner is at six and we need to go down to the library soon for a drink, and no doubt a friendly grilling from the rest of the family.' Richard looked sheepish as he said this.

A pit of nerves began to grow in Penelope's stomach. The castle was difficult enough to deal with, factoring in the rest of the clan was not sitting well with her...

'Ok, that's fine, let's head down now.' Penelope grabbed a baby pink cashmere pashmina. She was using it for more than just a barrier against the castle draughts. Wrapping it around her person gave her an enormous sense of security. There was no way that Richard's mother or sisters could scrutinise her figure if she hid it behind the pashmina.

'Are you not going to change?' Richard arched one eyebrow.

'Why? Do you think I should?' Penelope shot back.

'No, no, no I just thought that you might like to, but it's not necessary at all,' Richard spluttered. He was keen that this should go well, his mother could be "difficult" at times, to say the least.

'Alright then, let's go.' Richard marched ahead of her down the corridor, she felt like she was being marched to the gallows.

They entered the wood panelled library, and were greeted by the whole family who were gathered around the fireplace, an assortment of whiskey tumblers and G&Ts in hand. There was an eerie silence among them.

'Welcome *Penaylope*,' Richard's mother intoned, as the rest of the family went up to shake Penelope's hand one by one. A dozen of them gathered around her, except Aunt Muriel who was quite oblivious to the whole gathering. She kept barking, 'I can't believe Grace Kelly has finally come to visit us in Scotland!' as she would motion towards Penelope.

Every time she said this Richard's mother bellowed 'Yes, Aunt Muriel, she has come especially to see you...' and gave an apologetic glance towards Penelope, raising her eyes to heaven.

Richard was the eldest of five. He had twin, platinum-haired younger brothers and two younger sisters, all in their mid-twenties. The clan were expensively dressed in casual, hunting-type clothes. The family tartan was always present, even in its subtlest of forms, such as a well-placed hanky, detail on a sweater cuff or factored into jewellery, such as cufflinks or a small pendant. Just as Penelope felt like their stares were going to bore a hole in her pashmina, Richard's father came bounding into the library, still in his hunting gear. He was still holding his shooting rifle, he had rushed back as soon as he had seen the car back in the driveway. All of the colour drained from Penelope's face when she saw the gun, she actually felt as if her heart had stopped with fright for a few seconds.

'This must be *Penaylope*, how are you lass? You are so welcome to our household.' Angus McFleurie extended a very large hairy hand to Penelope. His ruddy cheeks gave away too many games of rugby, washed down with old Grouse over the years. Angus towered over Penelope in more ways than one and she could finally see where Richard got his 6ft2 frame from. Angus was at least 6ft4, and broad with it. He was the complete opposite to Richard's mother. Penelope was overwhelmed by the contrast.

'Oh, erm, hello Mr, erm, Lord-McFleurie,' Penelope gasped. She had not been expecting this at all, he was something of a breath of fresh air after the mute blonde twins and Richard's conspiratorial whispering sisters, but the gun and his size were a lot to deal with.

'Pah! None of that now lass, call me Angus, or you can call me "*Dadday*" if you like?' Angus leaned down and winked at Penelope, arching one of his bushy red eyebrows as he said this. 'Sure you are practically part of the family now.' He stood there grinning manically at her.

'Oh, quite.' Penelope nearly fainted at the thought of calling him "Daddy", she managed to muster a weak smile, to hide her gasp. Angus was easily twice the size of her and as he bent down to speak to her she felt as if she was eight years old again.

Richard's mother saw the grimace flash momentarily across Penelope's face, so she butted in with. 'Didn't you have time to change for dinner dear?' as she considered Penelope's outfit as she peered over her glasses at her.

Penelope began to squirm in her shoes, and she was very grateful that the pashmina was covering up the blotchy red nervous rash that was crawling up her chest towards her neck. It was much more than just a piece of clothing, she had decided, it was armour!

'Erm no, not quite you see…' Penelope began.

'Leave her alone Mummy, we have barely been here twenty minutes, and Penelope was simply dying to meet you all. She didn't have time to change.' Richard snapped.

'Ah yeyes, of cooooorse, how rooooode of may,' Richard's mother became slightly flustered and momentarily lost the battle with her original accent as she fidgeted with her glasses. Richard had certainly put her back in her place.

'Drink?' Angus motioned towards the drinks' cabinet with his glass of scotch, the ice sloshed against the sides of the glass as he did this, and a little bit of whisky spilled onto the ancient rug.

Penelope jumped slightly, 'Em, yes, yes, that would be lovely thank you, gin and tonic please.' Penelope was relieved to have made the right choice as they all nodded in agreement as she gave Angus her order. He bounded over to the drinks cabinet and started preparing a rather large G&T. Penelope was very glad of his generous measures, and she tried not to knock the whole thing back as soon as he handed it to her.

Twenty minutes passed as they exchanged small talk and examined *the ring*.

'Oooh *Penaylope*, it is lovely,' Sara-Louise gasped as she tried the ring on for size, mimicking the way her mother said Penelope's name. In reality the L-McF offspring all spoke with cut-glass English accents, without a trace of their Scottish heritage. This was the result of their boarding school education.

'Let me, let me, it's *my* turn now.' Lucinda squealed.

'Now girls, no fighting please we have guests.' Lady L-McF sternly warned the two twenty-somethings as she motioned towards Penelope. They seemed to have forgotten that she was still there, the ring had taken centre stage, it was taking on a life of its own.

'Sorry Mummy' the two girls chanted in monotone unison.

Richard surveyed the situation practically bursting with pride. He had chosen that ring all by himself and his ego was in overdrive over their reaction to it. He just knew that Penelope was "the one" she was fitting in so well.

At this stage, Penelope's forehead was completely rigid, the tension had risen up her neck and moved into her head. She could feel a migraine coming on. She knocked back the dregs of her G&T as Angus hovered ready to pour her a new one. The group moved into the dining room where the table was lavishly set. White linen, no tartan! The mahogany dining table nearly ran the full length of the room. Penelope was seated beside Richard on one side, thank heavens, and next to ancient Aunt Muriel on her other side.

As soon as Penelope had taken her seat, Muriel leaned in.

'So tell me dear, what *is* the weather like in Monaco these days…?' Muriel adjusted her hearing aid and anticipated the response.

'Oh, well em…' Penelope stalled, Richard leaned in and hissed…

'Play along, play along, she's completely senile, bless her.' He patted Penelope's hand.

'Oh, right, right, will do,' Penelope whispered back.

'Well Aunt Muriel, it is very warm indeed, Scotland is something of a shock to the system.' Penelope turned to smile at Muriel.

'Yes, yes indeed, and how is Rainier?' Muriel sounded like she knew him personally.

'He's very well.' *'Who the hell is Rainier?'* Penelope thought to herself.

'What was that dear?' Aunt Muriel was very hard of hearing.

'He is v-e-r-y w-e-l-l,' Penelope bellowed at her.

Lady L-McF gave Penelope a weak smile as she raised her eyes to heaven.

Penelope gave her a weak smile in return. This was their first bonding moment, albeit fleeting.

'Are you ok?' Richard whispered to her as he dropped his napkin and picked it up as an excuse to whisper to her.

'Yes, fine,' she said beneath her breath. Her English stiff upper lip was coming in very useful in Scotland. Very useful, indeed.

A few hours later, Penelope flopped onto her ancient four-poster bed, well and truly exhausted. Watching every word she said for the entire evening had really taken it out of her. There was a tense atmosphere all evening, as it was clear that Lady L-McF had warned the family to be on their best behaviour and she kept a stern watch over all of her brood. They in turn were watching her like a hawk. Keen for some clues about their new soon to be sister-in-law. Angus was the only one who didn't abide by the rules, and he was his jolly self all evening. Penelope lay and stared at the paintings. She was convinced that they watched her every move, the whole thing was creeping her out. Richard in London was completely different to Richard at home, it shouldn't make a difference... but maybe it did. This engagement experience was totally new to her, and she was only planning on doing this once, so she didn't know what to expect. Just as she was having doubts she caught sight of her beautiful Tiffany's ring glinting on her left hand. It was terribly reassuring and the sheer beauty of it always made her feel that everything would turn out alright.

The weekend didn't get much better. It was a constant stream of family overload as more relatives arrived to inspect Penelope and *the ring*, and she had the same conversation over and over again. By Sunday Penelope was well and truly exhausted. On Sunday evening Richard dropped Penelope off outside 72 Abbeville Road, she waved him goodbye and nearly kissed the ground as she turned to go into her flat.

'Well hello there, how was the castle??' Zara gushed as soon as Penelope arrived into the kitchen. 'Cuppa?'

'Oooh, yes please, well... have I got a tale for you!' Penelope laughed.

'Oh my god, was it really creepy? What were his family like?' Zara was dying to know the details.

'Ok, first... do we have any chocolate biscuits, I think we are going to need them!' Penelope winked at Zara. Zara lunged for the cupboard and spun around and nodded at Penelope as she grabbed the packet of chocolate finger biscuits.

'Sooo… what happened. Did they freak you out, were there eyes in the portraits, secret corridors, … ghosts?!!' Zara was talking extremely fast as she fussed around with the teapot. She arranged the mugs and hurled the biscuits onto the plate, plonking down at the kitchen table opposite Penelope. Zara sat with her elbows on the table her cheeks resting on her hands, and signalled to Penelope to start.

'Well… I didn't actually see any ghosts, but I'm pretty sure that the castle definitely has some! They talked about the ancestors so much that it was as if they were still there.' Penelope said mysteriously.

'No!' Zara gasped, and her hand flew up to cover her open mouth.

'Yes!, and, it was hundreds of years old, even my four-poster bed was centuries old, it was quite an experience. Richard had his own 'turret' as far away from me as possible… and the whole family subscribes to the family tartan.' Penelope giggled. It was easier to make light of it now that she wasn't actually there.

'No!' Zara gasped between dipping, munching and sipping.

'Yes, and… it was freeeeeeeeeeeezing up there, I thought I was going to die of the cold. It was like my bones were cold and I couldn't warm up. If I have to go up there again I will definitely bring thermals with me. Probably tartan ones!' Penelope winked at Zara.

'Eugh, gross!' Zara grimaced, Penelope was the last person that she could imagine wearing thermal undies, let alone tartan ones.

'Yeah, I know, but believe me… fashion is not top of mind up there! It was hilarious their senile great aunt Muriel lives with them and she thought I was Grace Kelly, so I had to play along with her. I hadn't a clue about what she was talking about half the time.' Penelope sighed.

'The actress from the fifties?' Zara was on the edge of her seat.

'The very one.'

'And they were practically grilling me for the whole weekend, it was like the Spanish Inquisition. Thank god the ring provided a great distraction, his sisters were drawn to it like moths to a flame, and every new family member that I met hovered around it. His mother mentioned the "family ring" but Richard shut her up before she could elaborate in front of everyone.'

'What do you mean a 'family ring'?' Zara asked between sips, dips and munches.

'Well… I think… ' Penelope paused for effect…'I think… that sometimes people propose with a ring that has been passed down through the generations, they are usually ancient and worth a fortune… and you *have* to wear it. They are usually hideous!' Penelope grimaced at the thought of some old granny ring.

'Oh my god, yuk! You are definitely better off with the Tiffany's one!' Zara stated.

'Oh, I agree, believe me, I agree.' Penelope sat back and gazed at her ring again, it was mesmerising.

'So… were they nice?' Zara asked.

'Yeah… they were ok, his Dad was hilarious! The rest of them were very stiff, but his Dad was this ruddy, giant Scottish rugby gent, he was really gregarious. He was an absolute giant and he had bushy red hair, even on his fingers. His hands were huge, I felt like a small child next to him. He kept making me huge gin and tonics, to be honest it kept me going for the weekend.' Penelope tittered.

'That is hilarious, fancy that, I thought the whole family were going to be really stuck up, it's good that his Dad was a bit of a laugh.' Zara giggled.

'Oh yeah, he was hilarious! I have never quite met anyone like him. He was so larger than life, the rest of them were very, very stiff though. The first time I met him he came straight in from hunting and still had his gun with him, it was an absolute miracle that I didn't faint when I saw the gun, I thought I was a goner,' Penelope laughed.

'Gosh, that must have been a lot to deal with, and for the whole weekend without a break. Well…anyway, you are just marrying him, you are not marrying the whole family.' Zara sat back as she considered this.

'I hope you are right Zara, I hope you are right,' Penelope sighed.

The girls chatted for another hour about Zara's love life, things were going really well with her gorgeous boyfriend from next door, and her life was considerably less dramatic and less complicated than Penelope's.

Just before Penelope went to bed she gave George a quick ring for an update.

'Hi, it's me.'

'Well hello there, how was it?' George waited for the response. They had been texting all weekend, but reception in the castle was terrible, so George couldn't wait to get the full story.

'It was ok, the mother was… the same as usual, but his dad was hilarious, I'll explain all when we meet up. The castle was beautiful, but ancient and a really creepy. There were about twenty of them in the end, and their ancient senile aunt thought I was Grace Kelly and I had to play along,' Penelope sighed.

'Oh my god, you poor, poor thing. ' George giggled sympathetically. She had witnessed Richard's mother first hand at their graduation. She could completely imagine what the rest of the clan were like. That tartan was terribly oppressive.

'Look, I'm nearly falling asleep here, but let's chat about it on Wednesday, ok?'

'Ok, can't wait.'

As soon as George had hung up, Penelope drifted into an exhausted sleep.

Chapter 28

Permanent

Penelope woke up at 6 am much groggier than usual. She looked over at the alarm clocked and groaned, she reluctantly slid out of bed and into the shower. She had taken her ring off and her left hand felt naked without it.

At 6.55 am Zara woke up five minutes before Xfm was due to wake her up. She lay there staring at the ceiling thinking… *'I can't believe my life, I love being in love!'* She bounced out of bed and headed down to the bathroom.

Zara arrived into work at 9.15 am, she got a cappuccino downstairs before getting into the lift. When she arrived at her desk, there was a heart-shaped pink post-it note stuck to her Mac. 'Please call me when you get in, we need to talk urgently, on the mobile. S xx'. Zara's smile turned upside down in a second and a pit of anxiety began swirling around in her stomach. She carefully placed the cappuccino cup down on her desk, incapable of drinking another drop. She reluctantly dialled Susan's mobile number.

'Susan, hi, it's erm, me, Zara.' She waited for the response.

'Oh hi, great… , listen I am up in the blue bottle room, can you pop up for a few minutes?' Susan gave nothing away.

'Yes, yes of course, I will be right up,' Zara replied. She had a niggling worry that she was faced with a similar situation as before, as soon as everything seemed to be going right, she was faced with some bad news. It was out of character for Susan to summon her like that, and at that time of the day too.

It took the lift an absolute age to reach the third floor, Zara reluctantly walked through the doors and she could see that Susan was not alone through the glass partition wall. Her hands began to grow clammy as she knocked on the door, more as a courtesy than anything else. Susan spun around and motioned to her to enter.

'Hi Zara, have a seat, this is Helen from our HR department…' Susan introduced them. 'We have a bit of news for you, we have just heard that Joanna has decided not to come back after her maternity leave, and we have been very impressed with how you have covered her accounts, and above all… how well you fit in here.' Susan paused to let Zara speak.

'Thank you.' Zara's pulse began to race, she had no idea what was coming next, good or bad…'I really like it here and I think that really makes a person more productive when they are happy in work,' she spluttered.

'Quite right, quite right Zara.' Helen nodded and smiled.

'… and you see, now that Joanna is not coming back, there is a position open and we would love it if you would consider it… In a way we have already seen what you are capable of…' Susan added.

'Oh, I see, I see, well I would be very interested in a permanent position here.' Zara breathed a sigh of relief and her breathing returned to normal as both Susan and Helen smiled warmly at her.

'We will have to speak to the recruitment agency and work out an appropriate salary and benefits, we would like to make you permanent asap. So the sooner we can get this sorted out the better.' Helen added. Susan nodded in agreement. 'Do you have any questions at this point?'

'No, this has come as quite a surprise, can I email you questions in the next day or so as they occur to me?' Zara was still in delighted shock about this.

'Yes, of course, you can give me a call any time, and I'm sure Susan can fill you in on any of the practicalities on the second floor.'

'Yes, Zara, you can ask me anything. Look Helen, we need to head downstairs, can I leave it with you to come back to Zara about the details and next steps?' Susan was keen to get back to her desk.

'Yes, I'll take it from here. Zara, I will be in touch as soon as I get some news from the recruitment agency. It would be good if you could give your contact there a call to discuss the practicalities.'

'Oh, yes, right, will do.' Zara got up to head downstairs with Susan, her head was spinning from a combination of all of this excitement so early in the morning... and a lack of caffeine as her cappuccino was still sitting on her desk, growing cold. She had a delighted chat with Susan on the way back to their desks, she simply could not believe her luck, it was like a dream come true, new man, new job, new life...

In EC1, Penelope was struggling to get any work done. Any time she tried to type an email, her engagement ring glinted up at her and she became completely distracted. Appointments for flower consultations, dress fittings and lunch menu tastings were piling up and it looked like she would be spending far too much time with her mother over the coming months. She minimised her Outlook and stared lovingly at her engagement ring.

At lunchtime the two girls stepped out to grab a bite. Zara wandered out onto Soho Square to grab a salad and a Frappuccino. Penelope headed down towards St Paul's to meet Richard.

At the very same time, Charlie and Gerry sat chatting in the kitchen over breakfast.

'What is up with Penelope? All of a sudden she is engaged? Is she nuts? She is only 28? What's the bloke like?' Gerry looked at Charlie intently. Charlie's face dropped at the mere thought of Richard.

'Don't ask me, I think she has lost her mind, he is an absolute gobshite!' Charlie exploded.

'Jesus, settle down, is he really that bad?' Gerry asked as he took a slurp of tea.

'Yeah, he's one of those trustafarian ponces, prancing around in his polo necks and tweed jackets.' Charlie's face was like thunder. 'I swear he is just after a trophy wife, and she is so much more than that. I have never really trusted him. He always struck me as being a bit of a closet fairy,' Charlie grunted.

'Jesus! Gay? Really? But he obviously likes birds?' Gerry was sorry that he had asked now, Charlie was furious.

'Yeah, he kind of minces around, he's tall and really skinny, blond hair… poncey looking.' Charlie took a huge bite of toast and grimaced as he said this.

'Hmm, what on earth is she doing with someone like that?' Gerry was baffled.

'I can't even begin to imagine, there is nothing I can say, she looks so happy. I'd swear he is up to something though, I've never trusted him.' Charlie was embittered. Gerry decided to move the conversation back onto music.

At the same time Richard Lord sauntered down towards St Paul's, to meet Penelope for lunch.

'Hello darling.' Richard stood up to kiss Penelope as she approached the table. 'I hope you don't mind but Russell and Alexa are going to join us. Alexa is simply dying to see *the ring…*' Richard paused to gauge Penelope's reaction. Penelope grimaced inside, but managed a weak smile to cover her disdain. She felt like a show-pony sometimes, constantly being paraded in front of Richard's coupled up friends. They were all so boring!

'Yes, yes of course that's fine.' Penelope smiled at him again as she took her seat.

'Good, good, excellent, they will be arriving shortly. Chablis?' Richard was already pouring her a glass from the chilled bottle as he said this.

'Hmm,' Penelope muttered.

Russell and Alexa arrived in a flurry of name-dropping, air-kisses and rock-ogling. Penelope was getting very tired of it all. She felt sometimes as if she was marrying Richard's friends as well, and they would never have been people that she would have chosen to socialise with. It was the same conversation over and over again, and none of the girlfriends had careers once they got married. Penelope had a niggling doubt about this at the back of her mind. Surely Richard was not expecting her to give up work as soon as they got married. She would have to make this very clear to him from the outset. On her way back from lunch, aided by half a bottle of Chablis, Penelope was deep in thought…

'I am so sick of being out with Richard's friends all the time. All they talk about is babies, weddings and who they know… that is getting married and having babies. I feel like I have gone from my mid-twenties to my mid-forties in one swift movement. I can't believe the wedding is only a few months away. It's all happening so fast. A bit too fast, but I don't fancy taking the clan on, or my mother for that matter, on that one.'

As soon as she was back at her desk, her phone rang.

'Penelope, darling, it's mummy here, I know you are soooooooo busy in work, but I just need a quick decision, about the starters for the menu, would you rather…'

'Mum!' Penelope exploded, 'I am in work for god's sake, I can't think about this now!'

'Well, there is no need to be rude dear,' Grace's voice wobbled with emotion.

'Look, why don't you decide, and then we can talk about it when I come over on Saturday…'

'But…'

'No buts mum, I am at work, I don't have time to talk about canapés and napkins…' Penelope sounded stern.

'Alright dear, I will have a list for you on Saturday.' Grace Chesterfield sniffed, extremely miffed.

'Thanks Mum, I have to go now, bye.' Penelope hung up, and shuddered. Her mother was constantly ringing her for ridiculous reasons like this, she had no interest in the bloody starters, or centrepieces, or seating arrangements. Only one thing to do…

'Hi, George, it's me… my mother is driving me mad!' Penelope fumed.

'Oh my god, what has she done now?' George sighed soothingly.

'She keeps ringing me all the time, asking my opinion on ridiculous details, I hate it all! I am not even looking forward to picking out my wedding shoes! *Shoes* George, I am not looking forward to wedding *shoe* shopping!' Penelope sniffled.

'Oh my god! That is serious, it's not like you to be reluctant about shoe shopping, whatever the occasion!' George gasped.

'I know, I feel like packing the whole thing in.' Penelope blew her nose.

'Oh no!, that's terrible, really terrible! Why don't we meet up later in the week to have a chat about it? How is Friday evening for you?' George tried to distract her with the prospect of cocktails.

'Ok, yeah, that's fine. Where will we go, I fancy going somewhere trendy, nice cocktails… you know…' Penelope sniffled again.

'Leave it with me, Pen, I'll think of somewhere good.' George reassured her.

'Ok, thanks George.' Penelope blew her nose, and perked up at the thought of having a slice of her old social life this weekend. The pressure of the impending nuptials was weighing heavily on her.

Over in Soho Zara was walking on air. She could scarcely believe her luck, Glitter was practically impossible to get into, and there she was, all of a sudden a permanent employee. She didn't care what money they offered her, she loved her job. All was going well with her new boyfriend, Zack. They had fallen into an easy pattern of seeing each other regularly during the week and for most of the weekend. The fact that they practically lived in the same house made life so terribly easy. Zara could scarcely believe how her life had turned around, and in a matter of months. She sat at her desk and started writing to Rob.

To: Bobbyfun@yahoo.com
From: Zara.S@glitter.co.uk
Sent: 15.13 pm
You are soooooooooooo not going to believe this… !
Hi Rob,

You are not going to believe this but… … .they have offered me a permanent position at Glitter?! They hauled me into a meeting this morning, I thought I was a goner, and then they announced that they would like to make me permanent. I am soooooooooooooooooo happy Rob. I love London. I love London. I love London! I can't believe I was considering packing it all in when it all went t&ts up in Organicom. I thought that was good until I found this job. I love working in Soho. When are you coming in for drinks?? How are you?

Zara xxxxxxxx

Zara stared into space after sending the email, she could not believe her luck. Rob wrote back almost immediately…

To: Zara.S@glitter.co.uk
From: Bobbyfun@yahoo.com
Sent: 15.14 pm
Re: You are soooooooooooo not going to believe this… !
Well Hello There,

I never thought I would see the day that you would be saying I love London over and over again. I can't believe you have a *real* job at Glitter, you lucky minx. Life is very good with me, I may… fingers crossed… be joining the legions of trendy agency types in Soho in the not so distant future… soooooooooooooooo… that means drinkies will be a regular occurrence.

Rob xxxxxxxxxxxxxxxxxxxx

***

On Thursday night Penelope opened her wardrobe and looked at all of the lovely tops that had barely seen the light of day in recent months. She had forgotten that she even owned half of these clothes. She started taking them out and trying them on one by one. Penelope was so excited about meeting up with George the following evening that she was already picking out what she was going to wear.

The next day Penelope made sure that she could leave work at a reasonable time and she had her fingers crossed that no major incidents arose during the afternoon to prevent this from happening. Six pm came around relatively quickly and Penelope shut down and made her way to Soho, where George was already halfway through a delicious Raspberry Mojito.

'Hello,' George hugged Penelope.

'Hi, it's so nice to see you, god, I could murder one of those!' Penelope stared longingly at the glass.

'Coming up!' George motioned to the gorgeous looking barman for two more mojitos. 'Well… how's *Mummy*!?' George tittered.

'Oh my god George, don't even start me off! She is driving me completely mad. She is stressing me out so much that I think she is causing this skin rash… ' Penelope showed the little patches of red skin to George.

'Oh no, poor you, is it sore?' George rubbed Penelope's arm gently.

'No, not really, it just looks awful, and it kind of comes and goes,' Penelope sighed.

'Oh dear, oh dear, oh dear, … look, here the mojito might sort it out!' George raised one eyebrow as she said this.

'Hmmm, yes Dr George, I think you might be right.' Penelope took a large sip of her mojito. 'I'm seeing mum tomorrow, she keeps ringing me in work, so I said I would deal with all of the decisions when I meet her. I can't stand it, George. Thank god I'll hopefully only have to do this once in a lifetime, there is no way I could go through this again. ' A thick strand of Penelope's bob kept falling down in front of her eyes and she kept blowing it out of the way with no effect. It simply would not sit behind her ear! Her usual calm exterior had totally deserted her.

'Well, that's the plan, just get married once… just one wedding to contend with. Look Pen, it'll be worth it in the end, weddings are always stressful and there is so much to organise and emotions are running high.'

'I know, but, shouldn't it feel more exciting than this. I feel like I have a pit of dread growing in my stomach and it's getting bigger every day.' Penelope searched for comfort.

'Oh, you are not preggers are you!?' George nearly fell off her seat in shock.

'God, no, nothing like that, there isn't something actually growing in my belly… it's just this weird feeling, I can't quite describe it.' Penelope trailed off.

'Are you having second thoughts?' George said softly.

'I don't know George, maybe it's because it is all happening so fast, I don't know, it's just an awful lot to deal with,' Penelope sighed.

'Yes, you are right it is, I can't say that I've been through it before, maybe you should talk to someone who has recently got married to see if everyone goes through this?' George suggested.

'That's a great idea, but who…?'

'What about some of Richard's friends? Most of them seem to be married?'

'God no!' Penelope exploded, and George was quite taken aback by her reaction. 'There is no way I would talk to any of them about this, they are all a bunch of stiffs, and they would absolutely love a whiff of scandal!' Penelope began to regain composure. The strand of hair that kept falling down finally started behaving itself.

'I see, I see, hmm, let me have a think about it and I'll see if I can come up with someone.'

'Ok, thanks Georgie, that would be good.'

'So, how is the dress looking?' George tried to lighten the mood.

'It's so gorgeous, except it is backless, so if I don't get this rash sorted I'll have to get something to cover my back up.'

'Is it really that bad?' George couldn't believe it.

'It's weird, it just kind of flares up where I least need it, and then it calms down for a while. There is no way I would risk it on my wedding day in case I looked like a plague victim walking down the aisle!' Penelope laughed.

'Indeed' George replied *'This does not sound good'* she thought to herself.

The next morning Penelope woke up a little the worse for wear from too many mojitos the night before. She lay in bed staring at the ceiling dreading the prospect of meeting up with her mother. …

'Penelope, darling, you look wonderful,' Grace Chesterfield cried as Penelope approached her. 'Have you been dieting?' Grace beamed at her pride and joy.

'Hi Mum, no, I've just been really busy in work, not much time to eat properly which is terrible really,' Penelope began…

'Nonsense darling, you look wonderful, keep this up and you will be breathtaking in time for the wedding.' Grace sighed. 'Now, down to business, here… I have the catalogues and brochures with me.' Grace proffered the brochures with the pages open and tabbed in coordinating colours… chattering away about place-settings and matching napkins and menu options…

Penelope stared into the distance scarcely hearing a word. She smiled and nodded a lot, as she had the distinct feeling that most of the decisions had actually already been made without her.

Zara woke up next to Zack, and crept down to the kitchen to make some tea and toast for the two of them. The sun was streaming in through the window in the kitchen. Life was good and Zara knew it.

Chapter 29

T- Two Months

With two months to go the days sped by in a blur of dress fittings, menu tasting and place-setting juggling. Penelope, despite her better judgement, was happy to let her mother take the lead.

Spending more time with Richard's friends was helping Penelope to assimilate into their group. She was relieved that she had the wedding to talk about with them, and was surprised that she did have a bit more in common with them than she first thought after all. The rash took on a life of its own flaring up when it felt like it, and disappearing without notice. No cream or stress management technique could keep it under control.

***

In Asia, the tour was in full swing and Alyx was having the time of his life. He knew that this would be consigned to rock history and he was delighted to be an integral part of it. It was a great opportunity to actually have an excuse to see Asia, to have a *reason* to be there, and what better reason than traveling with a world famous band on tour. Alyx was well and truly living in the moment, and he was enjoying every second of it.

The final Asian tour date arrived all too soon, and all of the girlfriends were arriving to enjoy the final gigs and kick back for a well-deserved break. As soon as they all arrived, it hit Alyx, that he was very much… alone. And his mind invariably started wandering towards London, and thoughts of her.

As the band start to head back towards Europe, Alyx started thinking about the future and what his life would be like after such a life-changing experience.

'Nats, it's me.' Alyx finally had signal.

'Alyx!! I can't believe it's you. How and where are you?' Nathalie squealed.

'I know, sorry, mobile reception is a nightmare over here, and we are not really in our hotel rooms very much, as I'm sure you can imagine!' Alyx apologised.

'I miss you so much! When are you coming back?' Nathalie was dying to see him.

'About six weeks or so, we are making our way back, slowly but surely…' he laughed, reluctant for this experience to ever end.

'Ok, well, let me know when you've booked your flights and we'll sort out dinner. Are you going to come here first or go straight home?'

'I'll go straight home, you know, jetlag and all that, and then I'll see you after a day or two.' Alyx was referring to his apartment in Paris, where he called home for now, despite the fact that it was empty most of the time.

'Have you met anyone nice, how are the supermodels?' Nathalie quizzed him.

'Hmm, they are always nice.' He joked. '… .but no, I haven't met "the one" if that's what you mean. But I will be holding on to those supermodels' numbers *just in case*. As you never know…' He laughed.

***

Penelope paced up and down in her living room barking into her phone… 'I'm freaking out George. There are only two weeks to go and there is so much to do!' Penelope exclaimed.

'Ok, ok, breathe, did you speak to Cheryl?' George was trying to reassure her.

'I did, George, thanks for that. She was really helpful, and she said that the nerves, the rash, and any doubts are completely normal when getting married. After all, we all only do this once in a lifetime, so it's not like something that we experience over and over again.' Penelope's tone softened, reassurance enveloped her.

'Excellent! I knew she would help, she has something like six sisters, and they are all very experienced with the wedding stress!' George was pleased, as she couldn't really help her herself as she wasn't married.

'She was loooooooovely, and made me feel totally reassured. This good feeling fades the minute I see my mother George! She is stressing me out so much, I don't know what I'm going to do!' Penelope shrieked, the pressure mounted again.

'Ok, ok, breathe!' George soothed. 'There must be a way of cocooning yourself from your mother. Does the yoga breathing help?'

'Yes, yes, it does. You are right George. Quite right, I'll try the yoga breathing.' Penelope sighed.

'Just don't let her get to you. *Decide,* that she won't stress you out. I know that's easier said than done Pen, but give it a go.' George was always so sensible.

'Well I have to do something, I'll never make it down the aisle at this rate,' Penelope sniffed just before hanging up, and turning around to survey the myriad of packing boxes around her.

I can't believe this is it. This is my old life, in boxes, soon to be new life, as someone's wife. It sounds so weird when I say it out loud, and calling Richard my husband will take some getting used to. And having a title too, I thought my mother was going to actually explode with pride when she got her hands on that little detail. Penelope shuddered at the thought of how her mother had reacted to this extra juicy detail. *'Cheryl was so helpful, she said all of the nerves were totally normal and not to let them get the better of me.'* Penelope was pensive as she continued packing her handbags.

'I'm not sure where I'm going to put all of this stuff. It's definitely not all going to fit in, in Richard's place. Thank god George suggested finishing the packing after the honeymoon, that was genius. Move gradually was her sage advice. I'm very grateful for that suggestion now. A totally new life in one fell swoop is a bit overwhelming.' Penelope caught sight of her beautiful ring and was reminded of the promise of a lifetime.

'Hey, how's it all going?' Charlie hovered in the doorway.

'Oh, Charlie, you startled me!' Penelope jumped slightly, in the middle of all of the boxes.

'Looks like you are making good progress.' He arched one eyebrow. 'Managing to fit all of the shoes in?' He laughed, reminding her of the day that they had moved in.

'Oh yes, yes, indeed… these boxes are simply for "confidential work papers". Penelope adopted her most innocent "I'm not lying, but I really am" expression.

'I see, well let me know if you need a hand with anything,' Charlie called back as he made his way down the stairs.

'Will do…' and he was gone.

Chapter 30

Dawn

For the first night in weeks Penelope woke up feeling completely rested having had a lovely night's sleep. This was surprising considering that it was the night before her wedding.

'I feel so relaxed, I don't think I have slept that well in years. Everything looks so beautiful. Fabulous, it looks like it's going to be a sunny day for the wedding, I don't think I could have gone through with it if it had rained. I think my rash has calmed down a bit, this is the first time in the last six months that it wasn't the first thing that I thought about when I woke up. Now what time is it? Oh my god, it's only 6 am, and I'm wide awake! My rash has really gone down. I actually feel back to normal again for the first time in ages. I have this feeling that everything is going to be ok. Maybe it was just pre-wedding jitters, and now that the day has finally arrived everything will go well. I may as well get up. I feel kind of sad leaving this house, even though I don't technically live here anymore. Still, setting up a new "home" with someone is such a big change. I hope it is as nice as the life I had here as a little girl… oh my god, tears already, well I may as well get it over and done with so I don't cry during the ceremony. I have two hours to kill before I'm supposed to be woken up, I think I'll just read for a while.'

6.15

… 6.30

… … 7.00

Penelope struggled to concentrate, only one thing to do…

***

In the other wing of the house, some other people were stirring.

'Bernard! Bernard! Wake up!' Grace Chesterfield tugged at her husband's arm until he reluctantly admitted that he was awake.

'What time is it? Are we late?' Bernard sighed groggily, as he sat up he was confronted with his wife looking as white as a sheet, with her hair in rollers. He thought that she looked like something from a ghost train!

'No, no, it's just, I had that awful dream again!' Grace gasped.

'What, love… about the wedding?' Bernard's tone was soothing, now that he realised how upset his wife was.

'Yes, but this time, it was the priest that took a turn for the worse, he fell ill and…' Grace began her daily rant about her nightmares about wedding disasters.

'Now look, love, this worrying is ridiculous, you will make yourself ill, everything will go fine, we have organised every last detail, NOTHING can possibly go wrong…' he said rather over-emphatically.

Bernard stared intently at her as he said this, and then he turned over and lay back down, head beneath the pillow this time!

'"Nothing"… you say?'

'Yes, "nothing", now for heaven's sake will you go back to sleep and get some rest?'

'But…'

'No buts Grace, you'll need all of your energy for the day ahead, you are the most important person there apart from the bride…' Bernard reminded her.

'Yes, yes, of course you are right… if you say that nothing can go wrong then…'

'… Nothing can go wrong…' He repeated.

'Yes, sorry about that darling, I just want it to be perfect…' Grace finally calmed down.

'We all do, believe me… we all do.' Bernard raised his eyes to heaven beneath the pillow!

'You go back to sleep there, I might just pop my head in and check on Penelope.' Grace put on her dressing gown and slippers, and padded down to Penelope's room.

'Alright, if that'll make you feel better.' Bernard looked out from beneath his pillow… but she was gone…

'Penelope Darling… are you awake yet?' Grace peeped around the door.

'Pen, Penny?' Grace's heart started racing… there was no answer.

'It's the big day, and I just couldn't sleep so I thought I would see if you were up yet…' She continued…

'Penelope!' She raised her voice slightly.

'Penelope!' Grace screeched.

'Bernard! Bernard! Come quick, she's gone!' Grace raced down the hallway to her bedroom to get Bernard out of bed.

'What on earth is the matter woman?!' Bernard sat bolt upright in the bed knocking the pillow onto the floor as he sat up.

'She's gone, she is not in her bed!' Grace was struggling for breath.

'Of course she has not gone, she's probably in the loo, did you check the bathroom? Bernard was trying to be practical, there was no reasoning with Grace when she was like this.

'Yes… no sign of her.' Grace stood in the doorway looking terrified.

'And downstairs?' Bernard raised one eyebrow.

'No but I shouted so loud when I saw the empty bed, I think I woke the neighbours, so if she was downstairs I think we'd know by now.' Grace looked startled.

'I see, let me just get my dressing gown and I'll help you look, have you had a look in the garden?'

'The garden! The garden! What would she be doing in the garden!?' Grace was getting more panicked by the second.

'Alright, calm down, it was just a suggestion.' Bernard shrugged his dressing gown on reluctantly.

'Should we ring the police?' Grace already had the phone in her hand.

'No, we should not ring the police, you have to be missing for a certain amount of time before you can call them...' Bernard raised his voice a bit louder than he had planned to.

'But she could have been missing since last night and we didn't *realise* until this morning,' Grace shrieked.

The bedroom battle between reason and hysteria continued for at least another half an hour, until Penelope came back from her run...

'What was that?!' Grace hissed to Bernard as she heard the front door slam shut.

'Well, it sounded like the front door.' Bernard sighed soothingly as Grace perched at the top of the stairs peering down, just in time to see Penelope dump her sweatshirt at the end of the stairs before going into the kitchen to grab a pint of water.

'Penelope! Is that you?' Grace shrieked. Penelope still had her iPod on full blast so she was completely oblivious to the panic upstairs. 'Penelope!' Grace roared... still no answer.

'Let me... I'll go.' Bernard sighed, motioning to his wife to sit back down on the bed. He made his way down to the kitchen, only to find Penelope doing a few cool-down stretches in the conservatory. He motioned to her to take her earphones out.

'Hi Dad, what's up?' Penelope said, still a little breathless from her run.

'Well, love, it would seem that your mother thought that you had, well, em... flown the coop, so to speak...' He waited for her reaction.

'What!? Has she gone mad? I think I've had just about enough of this, Dad.' Penelope cried.

'I know, love, but I suppose we just have to keep the peace, she only wants the best for you and she wants today to go off without a hitch,' Bernard soothed.

'I know, Dad, but I'm nervous enough as it is, and these kind of hysterics are making me even worse, it's ridiculous! She is being ridiculous!' Penelope huffed.

'Right, here, put the kettle on, I'll bring her up some tea.' Bernard resigned himself to calming duties.

Penelope stomped upstairs, storming past her mother's room, and slammed her own bedroom door and flopped on her bed. *I'm actually going to kill her, she is driving me mad. I don't know how I am going to get through today, thank god George will be standing nearby, I don't know how I would get through it without her.'* Penelope's head was spinning. She looked over at her dress hanging on the front of her wardrobe and the rash on her chest started to flare up a little.

The rest of the early morning passed by in a haze for Penelope. Bernard kept Grace out of her hair so that no other arguments could erupt before they had to go to the church. Luckily George had suggested separate hair and makeup for her mother, so that Grace would feel as pampered as Penelope did. It was a brilliant idea, it would also give Penelope a break from her mother for an hour or two.

Richard's brother came to collect Grace and Bernard bang on eleven o'clock and she felt like The Queen heading off to the church in a Rolls Royce.

Charlie showed up for Penelope shortly after eleven. He looked stunning in his morning suit and Penelope was quite taken aback. He had borrowed his father's Rolls Royce for the occasion. He was practically speechless when he saw Penelope.

'Penelope, you look... stunning,' he stammered.

'Oh, thanks Charlie, you don't look too bad yourself.' Penelope gave him a little peck on the cheek.

He hesitated for a moment and then said. 'Well, I suppose we had better go?'

'Indeed.' Penelope beamed at him.

In EC1 the scene was not quite so dramatic... yet.

'Hi, can I speak to Penelope Chesterfield please?' Alyx had had no luck with Penelope's mobile, so he assumed that she had a new number, so he tried her work line.

'I'm afraid Penelope is going to be off work for the next two weeks.' The receptionist informed Alyx.

'Oh, is she on holidays, well in that case...' Alyx was about to leave a message, undeterred.

'Well you could say that... she will be on her honeymoon...' the receptionist stated.

'What?! Is she getting married, when, oh my god!' Alyx nearly dropped the phone.

'She is getting married today actually, in St Augustine's Church... Hello, Hello? How rude!' The receptionist fumed into the phone, she couldn't believe that he had hung up on her.

'Pierre, hi it's Alyx.' Alyx was gasping.

'Hi, did you leave something in the car?' Pierre was used to picking up after Alyx he was constantly leaving his Blackberry behind him.

'No, listen, I need you to take me somewhere, how fast can you get back here?'

'Twenty minutes?'

'Fine, see you in twenty.' Alyx paced up and down and thought to himself...

'Shiiiiiiiiiiiiiit!'

Chapter 31

One?

Charlie pulled up outside the church twenty minutes later. Fashionably half an hour late… Penelope sat in the back looking immaculate, with perfect hair and makeup, and finally she had conquered the mysterious red rash that seemed to have a mind of its own. Charlie turned to look at her, and without stopping the engine he blurted out.

'I don't want you to get married.' Despite himself.

Penelope inhaled deeply and it was as if everything was happening in slow motion.

'But I am getting married, I want to get married, the time is right for me…' Penelope stated in a shocked monotone.

'But I don't want you to marry *him*,' Charlie whimpered.

'Why not?' Penelope asked calmly.

'I… just don't' Charlie stammered.

'That's not a good enough reason,' Penelope probed further.

'I just, don't think he is the right *one*,' Charlie added.

'What do you mean?' Penelope was breathing deeply to maintain composure and to process this bombshell.

'I don't think he really loves you as much as… as much as…' Charlie trailed off.

'As much as what?' Penelope snapped.

'As much as… he should.' Charlie just couldn't say it.

'Well you took a great time to tell me! Why didn't you tell me this before.' Penelope retorted.

'I didn't think you were going to go through with it.' Charlie admitted his state of denial…

'Even with the ring, the dress, the reception, the church booked… you didn't think I would go through with it!' Penelope shrieked.

'No, I just always sort of thought that we would end up together.' Charlie looked sheepish.

'Oh…' Penelope was pleasantly speechless.

'I know I don't have a big City job, or wear a suit to work every day, but I think I could… really… love you…' Charlie's confidence was growing as he saw her reaction to his revelation.

'You know those things don't matter to me…' Penelope reassured him.

'Yes, but they matter to him!' Charlie blurted out.

'I'm listening…' Penelope leaned a little closer. It was the first time she had dared to move since he had started his speech. Time felt like it was standing still despite the engine running in the background.

'I know he is not the right guy for you, because I really know you. I can't promise that I am exactly the right guy either, but I think if we don't give it a go, we'll never know… and I don't want to see you make this mistake. Even if you don't want to be with me, please don't marry him!' Charlie pleaded.

Even though what he was saying seemed surreal, and the implications were huge, both for that day, and for the rest of her life, for the first time since her engagement Penelope felt like a great weight had been lifted off her shoulders. Up until Charlie's revelation, Penelope had no idea she had been carrying around this burden.

She sat there, like a queen in her beautiful ivory dress, flawless hair and makeup, and reviewed the situation, for what felt like an eternity to Charlie, but was in reality a moment or two… letting the information sink in. The engine ticked over. Her Dad was standing at the church door, waiting to signal to the organist. He smiled and waved at her and pointed at his watch. She looked over at her Dad and mouthed the words 'I'm sorry' to him, and with a weak smile she turned to Charlie and said…

'Let's get out of here!'

And in a cloud of Rolls Royce dust… they were gone.

With a knowing smile, Bernard Chesterfield slowly turned around. *That's my girl'* he thought, *'That's my girl'* as he walked down the aisle… alone. Row by row the congregation started to turn around and stare at him, and then the whispering started. The noise grew louder, so loud in fact that Grace Chesterfield, who was beaming at the front of the church, wants to turn to see what the commotion is…but she can't. She can't because she is afraid. This is the moment she has been waiting for since her own wedding day. She wants to turn around and see a perfect bride approaching the altar, but she can sense that something is wrong. She can see Richard, he looks a little flustered. Has Penelope's shoe got stuck, did she trip on the step, did the veil fall off? The questions rush through her mind? The noise is unbearable, they are *talking* now… not whispering… actually talking! She has to turn around, so very slowly, with a smile plastered onto her face, she slowly turns, she sees her husband walking down the aisle… ALONE! She sees the sea of faces all talking and frowning, and then it all goes blurry and she sees no more…

Pierre delivered Alyx at St Augustine's… just in time to see the Rolls Royce, and a glimpse of Penelope, leaving the church and disappearing into the distance. …

'Is this alright Alyx?' Pierre called back to him as they pulled up at the church.

'What? I mean, oh em, no… no… no it's not alright, it has all gone horribly wrong.' Alyx retorted as the reality of the events happening before his eyes began to sink in.

'Are you ok back there?' Pierre sounded concerned.

'Yes, yes, just give me a minute.' Alyx tried to pull himself together.

'No problem, I'll wait here…' Pierre knew when to keep his nose out of things.

Alyx got out of the car and paced up and down. Had he not been suffering from lingering jet-lag, and had he not been so wound up... he might have noticed the amount of cars still parked in the car park and the distinct lack of confetti and beaming onlookers.

'Grace, darling, wake up, wake up... you're rambling.' Bernard held his wife's head in his lap.

'But the dress... the beautiful dress, and the pearl necklace, and the Rolls Royce and where is she?...' Grace's croaky voice ricocheted off the marble columns and echoed throughout the church.

'Shhhh, shhh, everything is ok.' Bernard tried to soothe her.

'No! The satin shoes, especially designed...' Grace kept babbling as she slowly regained consciousness.

'The shoes are fine, just fine!' Bernard cajoled her.

'Everything is fine, where am I, what is going on?' Grace snapped as she began to regain composure.

'You are in the church, we are all here, at the wedding, except Penelope...' Bernard trailed off.

'Except Penelope what?' Grace sat bolt upright on the church floor.

'No... we are all here except for Penelope.' Bernard dreaded the torrent that was coming next.

'Well where is she?' Grace demanded.

'She has gone,' Bernard admitted reluctantly.

'No, no! She is just late, wedding jitters, maybe she had too much champagne...' Grace was in complete denial.

'No jitters love, she was fully sober when I last saw her, and she has gone...' Bernard soothed her. The whole congregation was privy to this entire exchange.

'I don't understand, why would she do this to us after all that we have done for...' Grace began her usual rant.

'Love, the whole family is here, and everyone can hear you...' Bernard reminded her.

'Where did she go?' Grace hissed to Bernard as he helped her to her feet, and she dusted herself down.

'She did the right thing love, she didn't feel that it was right, so she left, she made the right decision, if it wasn't right...' Bernard reiterated.

'But it *was* right, he was all we could ever want for her!' Grace was indignant.

'What we want is not as important as what she wants... for herself... we have to be happy with her choice....let's discuss this later... we have other things to deal with here...' Bernard motioned to the gaping congregation.

'Yes... I see... let me just sit here for a few minutes and take this in...' Grace sat back down in the pew at the front of the church and took a moment to regain composure.

'Alright, I'll speak to the guests.' Bernard turned to address the congregation.

'Ladies and Gentlemen, thank you all so much for coming, as I'm sure you have realised by now... there will be no wedding today. The good news is that the reception will go on as planned, and we would be delighted to see you all there. As I'm sure you can imagine this has been a difficult morning for all of us, and we could all do with a few drinks... .' Bernard chuckled as he said this, avoiding Richard's mother's steely glare.

Richard stood at the top of the church deflated, but not heartbroken, his reaction was more like disappointment that a business deal had gone sour, as opposed to just losing the love of his life.

The Lord-McFleuries whispered amongst themselves, and remained poker-faced, all except Angus, who thought the whole thing was hilarious and he went up to clap Bernard on the back.

'Kids these days, totally unpredictable! Good on you for carrying on with the merriment, I'll just round up the clan and we'll see you at the reception,' Angus winked at Bernard as he motioned to his family. Lady Lord-McFleurie didn't budge and inch. She had no intention of going to the reception, the humiliation in the church was bad enough. She glared at Angus until he got the message.

Meanwhile back in the Rolls Royce, Charlie and Penelope were going as fast as was legal in a car like that. They didn't know where they were headed, but as far away from the church as possible was the initial plan.

'Where are we going?' Penelope asked.

'I have no idea… any suggestions?' Charlie muttered.

'We have to think of somewhere where my mum can't find us?' Penelope sighed.

'Yeah, good idea… she will *not* be happy about this…' Charlie grimaced.

'Well she can bloody well marry him herself, then, I'm really not ready to deal with her wrath yet!' Penelope retorted.

'Well we can't drive around like this all day!' Charlie chided.

'I know! Work!' Penelope cried

'What?' Charlie looked baffled.

'Work… I always leave a change of clothes in work, I can go there and at least change into something a little less dramatic.' Penelope motioned to her outfit as she said this.

'Great idea! And then we can go somewhere and talk.' Charlie agreed.

'Ok, work first, let's go!' Penelope started giving Charlie directions.

In no time at all, they were in the City and Penelope had to explain herself to the weekend security guard, who was highly amused, as she stood in front of him like a vision in white. She managed to talk her way in and within minutes she was at her desk rooting through her drawers. Thankfully her colleagues had already left and her office was empty.

'Now what have we got here, let's see… Oh my god! I love me… for being so organised. Look jeans, and a clean top, oh a full outfit, shoes and everything. I remember now, I was supposed to go straight out after work on Wednesday last week so I brought these in, I must have forgotten to bring them home.' Penelope cried with glee.

'Could you help me out of this dress, there are about a million little satin buttons…' There was no way that Penelope could get herself out of the dress all on her own.

'Gladly!' Charlie chuckled.

'Ah…I can breathe again. Should we bring the dress with us or leave it here?' Penelope was reluctant to leave it in work.

'I think we should bring it with us, what would your bosses think if they saw it first thing on Monday morning?' Charlie suggested.

'Good point, I'll take it now… it'll be safe in your Dad's car.' Penelope agreed.

'Exactly.'

'Do you have your mobile with you? I left mine at home… it didn't really go with my outfit.' Penelope laughed.

'I have it here, what are you thinking?' Charlie got his mobile out of the car.

'I'm thinking let's go somewhere that they can't find us for the moment.' Penelope had a mischievous twinkle in her eye.

'Like where? Everyone you know was at the wedding, we can't go home, that's the first place they'll go. And we stand out like a sore thumb in this car.' Charlie challenged her.

'There is one person who wasn't at the wedding.' Penelope stated matter-of-factly.

'Zara?' Charlie suggested.

'Exactly!'

'But she is with her parents for the party.' Charlie didn't get it.

'Oh… I'm sure they wouldn't mind if we headed up there to join in on the birthday celebrations… stop here and let's give her a call.' They pulled over and gave Zara a call.

'Charlie, hi, is everything alright?' Zara said as she answered her mobile.

'Hi Zara, it's not Charlie, it's me, Penelope, I'm calling from Charlie's phone.' Penelope giggled.

'Penelope! Hi… Congratulations.' Zara sounded baffled.

'Not exactly *congratulations*… but everything is ok… I didn't go through with it…' Penelope exhaled as she said this.

'No!' Zara gasped.

'Yes!' Penelope cried.

'You left him at the altar?!' Zara couldn't believe it.

'Oh my god… that's what they'll all say isn't it! Well to put a label on it… yes… kind of… yes, well yes that's exactly what I did.' This was the first time that it had sunk in what she had actually done.

'Where are you now?' Zara was totally intrigued.

'That's the thing, we were wondering if you wouldn't mind if we joined you, at the party.' Penelope sounded sheepish.

'Of course you are more than welcome… what do you mean "we"?' Zara sounded curious.

'Well, me and, erm, Charlie.' Penelope beamed.

'Charlie who?' Zara wasn't catching on.

'You know… *Charlie!*' Penelope restated.

'Our Charlie?' Zara sounded astonished.

'Yes,' Penelope stated calmly.

'Well what's he doing with you?' Zara was dying to know more.

'He's kind of *the reason*!' Penelope confided.

'No!' Zara gasped.

'Yes!' Penelope gasped back.

'Ok, I demand that the two of you get up here as soon as possible, I can't wait to hear all about this!' Zara couldn't wait to see the two of them.

'We are on our way,' Penelope laughed.

'Are you getting the train?' Zara asked.

'That's the other thing I meant to tell you… we are in Charlie's Dad's Rolls Royce.' Penelope roared laughing at the thought of herself and Charlie arriving in a Rolls Royce to an eighty-year-old's birthday party. Penelope was wearing jeans, with immaculate hair and make-up. Charlie was still in his morning suit.

'Hilarious! Granny will *love* this!' Zara giggled.

'But Zara… please don't tell them what happened, myself and Charlie need to sort this out between the two of us before we are ready to face all of the questions… I haven't even spoken to my parents yet,' Penelope pleaded.

'No problem, I won't say a word.' Zara hugged this juicy secret to herself.

'That's sorted then... Zara can't wait to see us,' Penelope turned to Charlie as she hung up the phone.

'Great. We are nearly halfway there now,' he replied.

'I think I am still in shock actually, I don't think it has sunk in.' Penelope stared into space.

'Call your mum... that should help!' Charlie laughed.

'No thanks! I'm definitely not ready for that yet.' Penelope snapped out of her daze pretty quickly at the mention of her mother.

I can't believe this has happened. Poor Richard! I don't know how he is going to take this, and his poor mother. I hate the fact that I have hurt all of these people. I will have to face everyone in work. Oh no!' Penelope grimaced as the reality of what she had done began to sink in. *'I can't believe it! Charlie... all this time, and I had no idea. I knew I loved him, but I never thought it could be in that way. I still don't know if I love him in that way, but it's definitely worth giving it a go. I feel such a sense of relief at not marrying Richard. I must have known at the back of my mind that it wasn't right. What a huge mistake it would have been, even though everything seemed perfect. He said he would give me everything, and I have no doubt about that, but it was always with unspoken conditions... I have to look perfect all the time. I have to give up work when I get pregnant. I have to socialise with his friends and their wives. I have to learn to play golf. I have to be interested in current affairs... but not too interested. His career comes first, always, always comes first. Now that I think of it, what the hell was I thinking.'* Penelope shuddered at the thought of all that she would have had to give up to be with him.

Chapter 32

The Lord and the Ring

Although not quite as bad as the exchange with her mother after the wedding fiasco… Penelope was dreading her meeting with Richard to return the ring. They had arranged to meet briefly at the Duke of York Square off the King's Road to get it over with. Penelope took one long last look at her beautiful ring before she knew that she would never see it again.

'Richard, I am sooooooo sorry,' Penelope began as he approached her.

'No need to go on about it, what's done is done, it's a bit late for any apologies now,' Richard replied abruptly. 'Did you bring the ring?' he snapped.

'Yes, yes of course, here it is.' Penelope handed the turquoise box over, hiding her reluctance.

'Good, good, well, I must be on my way, have a nice life,' he snapped, and he turned on his heel and stormed off.

Penelope stood there gazing after him for quite some time. *'I suppose that I deserved that.'* She thought to herself, as the tears started welling up. She ran into the toilet in Patisserie Valerie to try to stop the deluge.

'George, hi… sniff, it's me.' Penelope began.

'Oh my god, what happened? Did he take it very badly?' George asked.

'Oh, he *took* it alright. He didn't even let me apologise, or say anything, he just snapped the ring off me, said "Have a nice life" and stormed off. It was horrible, really horrible. I dread the thought of ever bumping into him again George.' Tears began welling up again as soon as Penelope recalled the scene.

'Oh my god, what an asshole! I know that you did a terrible thing, but surely if he was in love with you he wouldn't act like that?' George sounded baffled.

'I know, it's very odd.' Penelope mused, as the tears dried up momentarily. 'Thank god I have Charlie, otherwise I would be completely devastated,' Penelope sniffled.

'Indeed, indeed, where are you now?' George could hear background noises.

'I'm in Patisserie Valerie at Sloane Square. I nearly started bawling in the middle of the Duke of York Square, so I had to run in here to stop the tears. I've got coffee and chocolate mousse now, I'm hoping that will help!' Penelope sounded miserable.

'Ah, good plan, listen, why don't we do something later. Let me know when you get back to Clapham and I'll head over and we can have a good chat. We can eat out or in, I don't mind,' George suggested.

'Ok, that sounds great. Thanks George, I'll text you when I'm on the 137.' Penelope hung up and stared into space. *'Judging by his reaction, all I can think is… Thank god I didn't marry him!'* Penelope finished off her coffee and a little bit of her chocolate mousse and headed home. Even the delights of the window displays in her favourite Zara couldn't tempt her into the store, as she passed by on her way to the bus stop.

***

Later that evening, Alyx Stuart-Bruges sat at the bar in St Martin's Lane hotel, feeling very sorry for himself indeed. He played with his tumbler of whisky, swirling it around in the glass, deep in thought. He wore his uniform of faded jeans, and distressed vintage t-shirt, his navy pin-stripe suit jacket was slung over the back of his bar stool. Alyx was still shell-shocked after the wedding incident. He had been so sure, so confident, he finally knew what he wanted. Alyx was not used to dealing with rejection in any form, and this was his first major taste of it.

'I can't believe that I missed the boat on this one. Bloody typical, the one I actually want is now bloody married, and I don't even know who she married... I checked the newspapers for announcements, but couldn't find anything. I couldn't face her now anyway.' Alyx's train of thought was disrupted by the waft of Coco Chanel emanating from his right hand side. A willowy stunner had perched herself next to him at the bar half a drink ago, and she was playing with her Blackberry. She caught his eye just at the right moment.

'Hi, I'm Alyx,... look, I'm just getting another drink, would you like one?' He offered as he sucked the dregs of his whisky.

'Well, that's very kind of you, I'll have a Bellini.' The woman beamed at Alyx as she stared into her empty cocktail glass. She spoke in a slight South African accent and she was clearly a model, or someone who had missed her calling if she was not.

Alyx motioned to the inconspicuous barman. 'JD and Coke, and a Bellini for the lady.' Alyx flashed her a winning smile as he said this.

'On your tab, sir?' The barman enquired.

'Yes, of course... thanks.' Alyx turned to introduce himself properly to the beauty at his side. 'I'm Alyx Stuart-Bruges, what are you doing in London?' He held out his hand.

'I'm Alexa. I'm just here for a few weeks, on a modelling contract. The others are all arriving on Monday, but I thought I would get in a few days shopping before work.' She smiled at him. Alexa was stunning! She had dark hair cut into a fashionable pob, a perfectly symmetrical face, and huge almond eyes. Her beautiful, naturally tanned skin was flawless.

'Very wise indeed.' Alyx winked at her.

'Yaw, but it's a little boring on my own in the evenings.' Alexa sighed.

'Hmm, I know what you mean. I'm in hotels a lot myself. I live between here and Paris actually. I'm thinking of buying a place here.' Alyx sympathised with her, he was glad that they had something in common.

'Paris, wow, that's amazing, it's on my list of places to visit.' Alexa looked impressed.

'It's a really beautiful city. I'm half-French you see, my sister still lives there. I've just become an uncle.' Alyx waited for her reaction.

The conversation went on late into the night, at the end of which they swapped a little more than just phone numbers...

Acknowledgments

Thank you to all of my friends and colleagues who have encouraged me to write over the years, there are simply too many to mention. A special thanks to Rishi Dastidar, a great friend and fellow writer, for leading by example by getting published before me!

Huge gratitude to Gareth, Hayley and Kate for working with me to get my first book published. I was delighted to be working with such an innovative team.

And finally, a special thank you to my family, and in particular my mum Helly, for her unwavering encouragement and belief in me from day one.

About the Author

Jennifer Cahill moved to London in 2001 shortly after graduating from business school. She has a lifelong passion for writing and communications. When she is not writing, she works with individuals and blue-chip clients to help them navigate and master transformation and change. Jennifer currently lives in London and is working on her second book.

@JLCAuthor   #one?

www.JenniferLCahill.com

Lightning Source UK Ltd.
Milton Keynes UK
UKHW02f0008120718
325591UK00001B/23/P